Weed *Line*

Another
Shagball and Tangles
Adventure
By

A. C. Brooks

Other Shagball and Tangles Adventures
Include:

Foul Hooked - 2011
Dead on the Dock - 2012

For more information go to: www.acbrooks.net

This book is a work of fiction, like a fictional book should be. Names, characters, places and events are products of the author's occasionally disturbing imagination and/or are used fictitiously. Any similarities to real events, locations, or persons, whether living, dead, or in a zombie state, are coincidental.

ISBN-10: 1480256781
EAN-13: 9781480256781

Acknowlegements

As always, I must thank my beautiful wife Penny for her patience and guidance while I toil to produce a product worthy of my reader's time and money. If not for her hard work and support, I wouldn't have the time to develop the characters and stories you have come to embrace. Like Shagball and Tangles unfailing ability to find humor in any situation, she is the rock who never fails to keep me rolling.

I must also thank owner Wayne Cordero and the rest of the wonderful staff at the Old Key Lime House in Lantana, Florida, for promoting my work. I appreciate all the help I can get. In that vein, I would also like to thank *The Coastal Star* for the nice feature articles they published on my first two novels; *Foul Hooked* and *Dead on the Dock.* Hopefully, they will find it in their hearts to do another story about *Weed Line.* If not; I take back what I said.

Lastly, I would like to thank retired US Air Force Lieutenant Colonel Paul Strama for his assistance with the aviation portion of the book. If something isn't quite right, don't blame him, blame Tangles.

WHAT THEY SAID ABOUT *FOUL HOOKED:*

"Midgets and mobsters, schemers and dreamers, corrupt politicians and hard luck fisherman. *Foul Hooked* brings them together in hilarious fashion… what's not to love?"

- *The Southern Florida Times*

"Shagball and Tangles are like the Lone Ranger and Tonto, except they fight for beer, not justice… loved it!"

- *The Albuquerque New News Journal*

"*Foul Hooked* is like a boner; one way or another it's bound to make someone happy."

- damngoodreads.com

"Shagball and Tangles are the Huck Finn and Tom Sawyer of the 21st Century...God help us!"

-*The Central Missouri Telegram Review*

WHAT THEY SAID ABOUT *DEAD ON THE DOCK*:

"Reading *Dead on the Dock* is more exciting than watching Peyton Manning direct a no-huddle offense with the game on the line…minus the interceptions."

- Terri Bradshaw

"This book is not for the weak of stomach, the faint of heart or for those easily offended…but for the rest of us it's pure magic. Thank God for A.C. Brooks!"

- *The Midwestern Collegiate Book Review Club*

"Forget Salmon Rushdie, A.C. Brooks must die."
- *The Tehran Tribune*

"A.C. Brooks is the Norm Crosby of fiction; he never met a word he couldn't destroy, how refreshable!"
- *The Delaware Dominion Informer*

WHAT THEY ARE SAYING ABOUT *WEED LINE*:

"A.C. Brooks writing a truly great book like *Weed Line* is about as likely as me admitting to doping."
- Lance Armstwong

"*Weed Line* kept me glued to my seat; of course, everything keeps me glued to my seat. Thank God for black holes."
- *Renowned Astrophysicist Stephen Haweking*

"I laughed, I cried, I questioned the existence of God...all before the first chapter."
- Game show host Pat Sayjak

"A.C. Brooks writes like Tina Fey with a dick...hang on, that didn't sound right."
- *Thorne Michaels/ TV producer*

"Reading a book by A.C. Brooks is like going down the rabbit hole with a handful of carrot's, a James Beard cookbook, and a bottle of whiskey. You'll love the dish but you may throw up at some point."
- *Southern Fried Cooking Light Magazine*

"Like *Foul Hooked* and *Dead on the Dock,* I heard *Weed Line* was funny as hell. I'm just not into fiction, I like keepin' it real."
-Maniti Te'o/ All American Notre Dame linebacker

"If heaven has a library it'll be filled with titles by A.C. Brooks…it will also have lots of porn."
- TV and Film actor Fred Wilard

"Like Homer's *The Iliad* or Steinbeck's *The Grapes of Wrath,* the Shagball and Tangles trilogy culminating with *Weed Line* is epic and thought provoking…like a beer-bong enema."
- *Higher Times Magazine*

"A.C. rips everybody; Politicians, Wall Street, Celebrities, the Pope…OK, maybe not the Pope, but give him time. He's got more skewer's in his quiver than China has Chen's."
- *Soldier of Misfortune Magazine*

Prologue

Sometimes life doesn't just throw you a curveball that leaves you off-balance and scratching your head; it throws you something from the blindside that nearly decapitates you. And just when you pick yourself up and dust off the dirt, it throws you another...and then another. That's pretty much how I would describe the crazy series of events that led me to where I am now. Where exactly is that? Trolling on my 1982, thirty-eight-foot, Viking convertible named the *Lucky Dog*, about forty miles south of Puerto Rico and headed to St. Croix.

Thanks to a tidy chunk of change from an unexpected inheritance, I pimped out the *Lucky Dog* with some high-def cameras and paid to have her taken to Puerto Rico. My new friend, Captain Ferby (from The Old Key Lime House Marina), flew down with Tangles and me to fish the final leg to St. Croix. The idea was to get some footage for my TV show, *Fishing on the Edge with Shagball and Tangles.* Once my girlfriend Holly flew down, we'd try to unravel the mystery surrounding her aunt's secret past. Of course, plenty of overdue R and R was also on the agenda. At least that was the plan.

With the threat of a Mob hit man trying to whack us at every turn no longer hanging over our heads, things were looking rosy. But we would soon find out that, like Brett Michaels of the '80s hair-band Poison sang, "Every rose has its thorn." In fact, they're usually loaded with 'em.

Chapter 1

Blip...Blip... "Whatta we got?" asked the startled submarine captain.

The navigator glanced at the radar screen. "It look like a big ship coming fast from dee south, maybe three mile."

"Maybe? Shit, take the controls while I have a look." The captain slid out of the cramped helm of the cocaine-laden sub which was skimming along the surface of the Caribbean at a comfortable ten knots. He grabbed a pair of high-powered binoculars and quickly side-stepped down the narrow aisle between the bulging sacks of contraband. The observation turret was just forward of mid-ship on the hundred-foot sub, and he took a deep breath before stepping up to the view-port. As the familiar orange and white colors of the US Coast Guard came into focus, he mumbled, "Fuck."

"*Qué pasa*?" asked the machinist, as he monitored the nearby systems controls.

"*Qué pasa* is we got a Coast Guard cutter running up our ass."

As the navigator translated to the machinist and cook, the captain slowly swiveled the binoculars around, searching for vessels the radar may have missed. A shadow moved across the crystal blue water in front of him, and he tilted the binoculars up to see a plane passing over the sub from the north. It too had the distinctive orange and white coloring of the Coast Guard.

"Shit! There's a fuckin' plane too!"

As the three-man Colombian crew conversed in rapid-fire Spanish, he noticed another large shadow on the ocean's surface maybe a half-mile to the east. *What the hell?* He swung the binoculars up again, but the sky was clear. As he focused on the strange shadow hovering on the water, he realized it wasn't a shadow at all, but a giant weed line. It stretched to the northeast as far as he could see. *Hallelujah!* He hustled back to the controls, barking out orders to his navigator and translator, Diego.

"Outta my seat, Diego! Go help Manuel with the ballast valves; it's time to see how well this fish swims." As the captain settled into the forward helm and steered the sub east, Diego balked.

"Dee valves?" The captain glanced at him and noticed that he was nervously looking at Manuel, the machinist.

"*Si, si.* Not the scuttle valve, the *ballast* valve… the *ballast. El lastre.* It's time for a little dive." He made a dipping motion with his hand, trying to gesture the sub slipping below the water and plateauing off… hopefully. Then he yelled, "*Presura!*"

The captain didn't know *much* Spanish, but he knew enough to get by. The crew wasted no time acting on the captain's order and hurried to open the valve that would flood a compartment in the hull running the length of the submarine. As water rushed in and the sub began descending, the captain and crew collectively held their breath. Although they had briefly submerged several nights prior while trailing a freighter through the Panama Canal, everybody was understandably tense. It was one thing to be tested at high tide in a mangrove-lined channel in Tumaco, Colombia, and another to be tested in the open ocean where hull failure meant certain death.

The fully-submersible sub was the latest weapon in the ever-evolving, drug-smuggling arsenal of the Colombian cartels. At no small cost, the Colombians built and began utilizing semi-submersibles at the end of the twentieth century. The first models were crudely built, but surprisingly effective. They were thirty- to forty-feet long and ran on diesel tractor engines. Although they were incapable of fully submerging, only the small turrets on top of the subs—where the pilot sat—were above water, and they were almost impossible to spot in the open sea. Most importantly, these subs couldn't be picked up by traditional radar. The only way they could really be spotted was from the air, but to the unsuspecting aviator they looked like a shadow on the water, or perhaps a sea creature. The Colombians ran semi-submersibles for more than five years before the DEA even got a whiff of their existence. They proved to be a reliable means of moving illicit cargo up the coast to Mexico and into the United States, as well as through the Panama Canal into the Caribbean, to destinations such as Jamaica, Puerto Rico, the Virgin Islands, and the Bahamas.

By the time US authorities began searching for and occasionally intercepting the semi-submersibles', the

Colombians were rolling out the next generation; fully submersible subs capable of running at a maximum depth of thirty-feet for hours at a time. The new subs were more than twice the size of the old ones and were capable of carrying seven tons of cocaine along with a captain and three crew. Although being able to submerge to thirty feet doesn't sound very impressive, it made them pretty much invisible. Unless there was a tracking device onboard, there were only two ways they could be followed. The first was by a pursuing sub using sonar, but since the DEA had no subs in its fleet, the fleeing captain had little concern for such a possibility. The second was by air, either from a plane, a dirigible, a helicopter, or an unmanned drone. This was incredibly difficult and could only be accomplished under near-perfect sea conditions and water clarity, but it was possible nonetheless.

An hour before dawn the previous day, this particular sub rendezvoused with a yacht some eighty miles due east of Kingston, Jamaica. The purpose? To off-load a thousand kilos before heading to St. Thomas. The captain had met the same yacht nearly a dozen times over the years and looked forward to it as the grateful customer always gave him a couple pounds of killer weed as a tip. *Had the Coast Guard been on them since Jamaica? How? Was somebody tipping them off?* Having already spotted a Coast Guard plane, he wasn't about to wait to see if the cutter had a helicopter or speedboat ready to take up chase. A lot was at stake—namely, the remaining two-hundred-million-dollars' worth of coke, a small crate of explosives and grenades, and a pair of Soviet-made surface-to-air missiles. The captain's take was a half-million dollars upon delivery and another half million on the subs return back to Tumaco. Consequently, he was taking no chances; he stood to make more money completing the round-trip than he could have in twenty years of service in the navy, which was where he learned about subs.

As the sub reached a depth of fifteen feet, he strained his ears for any unusual sounds that might indicate an impending hull breach. Hearing nothing, he let out his breath. The sub continued descending to twenty-five feet before he pulled back on the controls and leveled off. He steered the sub due east toward the weed line, toward cover from any probing eyes in the sky. Then he turned to face the anxious crew. "Diego! Tell the boys to check for leaks. They see any water, they better make more noise than Shakira at a gang bang. *Comprendo?*"

"*Si,* we check for leaks." Diego turned and rattled off some Spanish to the machinist and the cook, Juan. Immediately they began inspecting the hull, starting from the stern and working their way forward.

The captain turned back to the controls and looked out through the forward view-port at the clear blue water rushing by. As the sub silently slipped toward the vast weed line, he relished the feeling of adrenaline coursing through his veins. He chuckled to himself, thinking that this was more excitement than he ever had in his brief stint in the navy, which ended with him being dishonorably discharged for... you guessed it...smuggling drugs. He never actually *ran* a sub; he was just a navigator, like Diego. But for once in his life, his propensity for embellishing his naval career finally paid off when his supplier heard him boasting that he had once been a submarine commander. What started out as a routine trip to Cartagena to pick up a couple kilos turned into an expedition under heavily armed escort up a remote river channel in Tumaco. There, amid a densely-lined mangrove channel, he was shown the notorious Cordero brothers' ambitious new creation; a crudely built, forty-foot, semi-submersible designed for transporting cocaine.

After being given a tour of the sub and its rudimentary control systems, one of the Cordero's asked him if he would run a trial shipment up to Panama. He would be paid ten grand upon delivery and ten grand on return. Although he had never actually piloted a sub in the navy, he thought the controls looked a lot like an arcade game he played back in the eighties named Battleship Down, and readily agreed. *How hard can it be?* He thought at the time. Besides, he was smart enough to know that after being shown the sub, to refuse would be like saying, "Please, shoot me until your AK-47 runs out of bullets." It was the same reason that, although he wasn't keen on it, he didn't say spit when they began adding a small number of weapons and explosives to his cargo.

In seven years he had piloted nearly twenty successful runs. Now he was running the new submersible for the first time and stood to make a cool million dollars. It would be by far his biggest haul yet. It was enough (along with his considerable savings) that he could finally retire, which meant disappearing off the face of the map, and as far from the Cordero brothers as possible. As the sub neared the weed line, the light began fading from the once brightly-lit sea in front of him. Moments later they crossed under the western edge of the weed line into near darkness. A small school of dolphin darted in front of the sub as the captain began changing course toward the north-northeast, following the weed line toward the waters off St. Thomas. Only fifty feet above the fleeing sub, a Coast Guard chopper pilot cursed under his breath, and his co-pilot slapped a knee.

"They're gone, Cap. They're fucking gone. We'll never find 'em with this heavy weed everywhere. It goes on for miles."

"Radio it in, pardner. We're heading back to the ship."

Chapter 2

Snap! For a quick shot of adrenaline, nothing beats the sound of an outrigger clip releasing when a fish takes your bait. If you're not familiar with the sound, or if you're not paying attention and listening for it—*hoping, praying, willing* for it to happen—then you have no business in the cockpit of a fishing boat. None whatsoever. Take up tennis or something, or maybe bridge, or yoga, but for God's sake don't get between me and a fishing rod when the rigger-clip goes off. That's like coming between a mama bear and her cubs. Hazardous territory indeed. These are the thoughts that flashed through my mind as I spun and lunged for the rod, knocking Tangles to the cockpit floor in the process. Even though he was a gifted mate, he was caught with his guard down and paid the price. He was testing his new iPod by blaring Kid Rock into his ears and didn't hear the snap of the rigger-clip. His mistake. *Oops.* I quickly lifted the bent rod out of the rod-holder as Tangles picked up his iPod and scrambled to his feet, complaining about my knocking him over.

"Dude! Easy with the—"

Snap! A rigger clip on the port side let go, and we both turned to see another bent rod and then heard the drag of the reel sizzle as line started peeling off. Tangles ditched his iPod and snatched the second rod out of its holder, just as I yelled,

"Fish on!" I didn't really need to yell this, because I knew Captain Ferby was aware of the situation and was already pulling back on the throttles. It's just something you do on a fishing boat. You yell, 'Fish on!' when you hook a fish. Even when everybody knows there's a fish on the line, you yell it anyways. Just like in golf. When you hit a wild shot, you yell 'Fore!' even if nobody's around. You do it 'cause you're supposed to. In golf it's called etiquette; in fishing its *wet*iquette.

Wetiquette dictates you let everyone within a nautical mile know you have a fish on the line and getting that fish in the boat is the most singularly important thing in the universe until accomplished. Wetiquette also dictates that you keep your fellow anglers apprised of any developments that take the situation from manageable to potentially unsustainable, like when the flat-line rigger clips attached to the stern simultaneously snap open and two more rods bend over.

There are good problems to have, and there are bad problems to have. Having only two anglers in the cockpit when there are four fish on four separate lines is a good problem, but it is a problem nonetheless. Ferby saw what was happening and came down from the bridge to help.

So even though *I* knew, that *he* knew, that we were on the verge of a clusterfuck, I followed proper wetiquette, by yelling, "They're thick! They're THICK!"

Yelling 'Fish on!' is fine for one or two fish, but when all the lines are hit at once, that's when they're 'THICK!' When you hear somebody scream, 'They're THICK!' on a fishing boat, it's like a soldier in a trench yelling 'INCOMING!' All hell breaks loose and your adrenaline spikes accordingly. Tangles handed his rod to Ferby as soon as he reached the cockpit floor and turned to the flat lines off the stern.

"Let me get these two in the boat and then we'll bring in the big boys!"

By 'big boys' Tangles meant the large bull dolphin that was on the end of my line and the big cow that was on the line he handed to Ferby. And they were *big*, in the forty-pound class. While Tangles reeled in one of the flat lines with a nice twenty-pounder on it, I worked my way over to the electric downrigger and pressed the retrieve button. The motor whirred as the fifteen-pound downrigger weight retracted on a cable back to the surface.

Ten, semi-heart-pounding minutes later, we landed the last dolphin, a forty-five-pound bull that we slid through the tuna door amid much high-fiving and back slapping. I asked Ferby to step to the side so Tangles and I could hoist the big bull up in front of one of the new high-def cameras mounted on the bridge of the *Lucky Dog*. I held the head, Tangles held the tail, and we smiled up at the camera. Then I delivered our trademark line:

"That's Fishing on the Edge . . . with Shagball and Tangles."

We had tried it where I would say 'Shagball' and Tangles would say, 'and Tangles,' but it had come off a little too cheesy. Like those guys on *Hee-Haw* who said 'I'm a pickin" and 'I'm a grinning.' In theory it seems clever, but in reality, it's kinda douchey.

"Is that it?" asked Tangles.

"Yeah, that's a wrap, I guess...for now at least. I'm not used to talking to a camera with nobody behind it. It's kinda weird, you know, like... Doogie Howser."

"Huh? What do you mean?"

"You know, how Doogie Howser used to sit and talk to the camera at the end of the show? It's *kinda* weird."

"I wasn't a big Doogie fan, but I'm pretty sure all the shows ended with him typing diary entries into his computer with the viewer hearing his thoughts as he typed."

"Hmmm... is that *so.* But of course *you* weren't a fan of the show."

"What? Me? A fan? No, hah. You kidding? Pffft, puh-leez. I will say this though; that show was heavy man...very heavy... and way ahead of its time, I might add. "

"Wow, I never woulda guessed."

"Guessed what?"

"That you're a Doogie lover."

"I just told you I'm—"

"Hey guys!" Ferby was back up on the bridge and was pointing ahead at something. "Come take a look at this."

Tangles scrambled up the ladder in his usual gibbon-like fashion, and I followed like your average Homo sapiens. When I reached the top of the ladder,

Tangles was commenting on the sight ahead. "That is one *serious* weed line. Wow! It looks like Davy Jones drank too much rum and threw-up a salad bar."

"I never seen a weed line like this, boys, and I been doing this a loooong time," added Ferby.

I was momentarily at a loss for words as I took in the sight. There was a solid mass of green floating on top of the deep blue water as far as the eye could see. It was about a half-mile wide and forever long, just like Ferby said. The weed line was running more toward the southwest than to the southeast, which was the way to St. Croix, but there was never any question that we were gonna fish it for a while. It was way too thick and juicy to pass up.

"It's like the mother of all weed lines," I marveled. "Look at how thick it is. It's like a giant strip of algaeic sod, just lying on the surface."

Tangles and Ferby both looked at me funny.

"What?" I asked.

"Algaeic sod?" replied Ferby.

"Yeah," said Tangles. "You think you're just gonna throw algaeic sod out there, and we're gonna let it slide?"

"Just trying to be accurate...and informative...as always."

"You trying to tell me that's not just another one of your made-up words? C'mon, man, I'm not falling for that again."

"Suit yourself; guess you never heard of farm-raised catfish."

"I'm from Louisiana, bro. 'Course I've heard of farm-raised catfish...and salmon too."

"Well, then I'm surprised you haven't heard about algaeic sod. That's what the fish farmers grow to feed the fish. You don't really think they still feed 'em corn, *do you?* It's too expensive now, thanks to ethanol subsidies."

"Really?"

"Yep. Now they grow algaeic sod and lay it on the surface of the fish tanks. The fish swim up under the sod and have at it. Kinda like on a *real* weed line." I pointed at the massive weed line directly ahead of us.

"Hmmm. I'll be damned. How do they grow it?" Tangles was scratching his head, apparently giving it some serious thought.

"Uh…they uh, they use algaeic seed starter… mixed with…mixed with, uh….Miracle Gro." I shot a sideways glance at Ferby, whose grin morphed into a big belly laugh, and we bumped fists. Tangles was not amused.

"You asshole! Algaeic sod….what bullshit…it's getting so I can't believe anything that comes out of your mouth."

I thought I saw something up ahead and asked Ferby for the binoculars. After briefly raising them to my eyes, I described the situation.

"Well, believe this, my gullible little munchkin. I'm seeing a lot of bird activity ahead. It looks like they're diving on something on the edge of the weed line. Let's get some fresh bait out there and see what gives."

I lowered the binoculars and handed them back to Ferby, who took a look and let out a low whistle.

"Good eyes, Shag. Why don't we put one of those split-tail mullet on the downrigger? Maybe we can scare up a wahoo."

"Excellent call, my brother from a blacker mother. How far are we from St. Croix?"

Ferby pushed a button on the chart plotter and held his hand over the screen, trying to block out the bright sunlight.

"Forty-seven-point-two miles from the Salt River Marina."

"After we catch a few more fish, we better pack it up and motor the rest of the way. That should get us there before nightfall."

"Sounds like a plan. Let's do it."

Tangles mumbled, "munchkin my ass," and started re-deploying the fresh bait while I used the head. As I looked out the window toward a distant island, I couldn't help but smile. I was fishing on my freshly pimped-out boat in the middle of the Caribbean *and* getting some great footage for the show. By the end of the day, I'd be living on island time in St. Croix, reunited with my girlfriend, Holly. I was looking forward to some serious R and R, some serious fishing, and some not-too-serious sleuthing into the secret past of Holly's Aunt Millie. Life was good and seemed destined to get even better if the amazing weed line we were on was any kind of omen, which I believed it was. I grabbed three beers from the galley and tossed one up to Ferby on the bridge before cracking open the other two and handing one to Tangles.

"Thanks, man," he said. "A cold one is just what the doctor ordered."

"Consider your prescription filled."

I looked back at the beautiful spread of Black Bart Lures and dead bait we had trolling behind us and felt confident about our immediate prospects. Things were getting fishy, I could feel it.

I looked over at Tangles, who was sporting one of his many Kid Rock T-shirts. His camo-patterned visor was pulled down over the pair of circa-1980, Porsche-Carrera sunglasses that he had won in a pool game. He didn't look like your average mate in any sense of the word… and he wasn't. He was a freak of a freak of nature. He moved about the cockpit like a member of Cirque de Monkee—poetry in motion on the ocean. And I had a fishy feeling the curtain was about to be raised.

Chapter 3

The submarine had been quietly traveling northeast under the vast weed line for more than an hour when the captain started hearing increased chatter between the seemingly nervous Colombians.

"*Qué Pasa,* Diego?" He inquired.

"Dee men no like dee dark. Me no like either."

"Oh yeah? Well I'm not too crazy about it myself, but I'm not too crazy about spending the rest of my life in the pokey either."

It was a mild understatement, if anything. Several times the captain had to employ evasive maneuvers in order to avoid hitting or getting tangled in debris suspended under the thick weed line. Twice they came across a snarl of heavy buoy lines, and more recently a large tree trunk suddenly appeared in front of the sub. As they swerved around it, the hull made a sound like fingernails on a blackboard as a branch scraped against its side, unnerving everyone.

"How much longer?" asked Diego.

The captain glanced at the instrumentation panel and did a few quick calculations.

"Well, we're about fifty miles from St. Thomas. Call it five hours, depending on the current."

"Five hour? Ees no good, ees too long to stay under dee weed...very dangerous. Dee radar no work underwater."

"I tell you what else is dangerous, my bean loving friend. Getting blasted out of the water by a Coast Guard cutter and sent off to Sing Sing in a sling. Tell your little amigos not to sweat it. As much as I'm hoping this weed line goes all the way to—hey! What the—?"

The captain sniffed the air and swiveled around. In the dim light he saw the silhouette of the cook and the tip of a joint glow red as it was inhaled and then passed to the machinist. "God dammit! I told you ass-holes to stay out of my weed! That shit's mine; it's not part of the cargo."

Juan responded in Spanish, and Diego translated. "He say they need it to calm they nerve. I tole you nobody like being in dee dark so long."

"And I told you I don't like it either! Shit. You think I'm not nervous? We got six tons of blow and an array of missiles, weapons, and *explosivos* on board. Now, I'm no expert, but I'm *pretty fuckin' sure* we wanna keep that shit away from flames, or ashes, or anything that could make this tub go kaboom! *Comprendo*?"

"Okay, Okay, I tell them to put out dee joint." Diego started rattling off the captains order's when the captain suddenly reached over and squeezed his shoulder. "Wait, go get it and bring it up here. A few tokes will help me relax a little too."

"Are jew sure?"

"Yeah, I'm mucho fuckin' sure. *Presuro!*"

Diego hustled down the cramped aisle, and retrieved the half-smoked joint. Then he brought it back to the captain, who quickly took a couple deep drags. As he slowly exhaled the sweet smoke, he held the joint out behind him. "You wanna hit this? It makes that shit you call 'Colombian gold' taste like ragweed. I don't know what else they grow in Jamaica, but this stuff rocks."

Diego held his hand out palm first and shook his head. "*No gracias.*"

"No gracias? Really? *Por qué?* You religious or something?" The captain turned, took another deep drag, and looked out through the forward viewport, keeping an eye peeled for more debris under the weed line.

"No...ees illegal."

Diego's words triggered a coughing fit and smoke burst out of the captain's lungs as he bent over laughing. In light of their situation, he thought it was one of the funniest things he had ever heard. As he fought to catch his breath, he turned to face him. Diego was grinning from ear to ear, exposing an incomplete set of yellow teeth that would make anyone but an Englishman cringe. He took the joint out of the captain's shaking hand and shrugged. "I was jus' joking you."

Tears flowed from the captain's eyes as Diego took a couple monster hits off the rapidly disappearing joint. He was laughing so hard he could barely breathe. Somehow, he managed to wave a hand and spit out, "water...need...*agua*...bring, bring *agua.*"

Diego said something in Spanish and the cook rushed up to the red-faced captain with a bottle of water. The captain took a couple of swigs followed by deep breaths and finally regained his composure.

"Wow... that was close. Seriously, Diego... don't ever pull that shit again. I almost blacked out. Whew... I tell you what. Seein' as how everybody's a little antsy from runnin' under the weed line, I'll swing outside the edge and bring us up to fifteen feet for a while. It'll be nice and bright and we can re-check our bearings. What do you think? You think if I do that Juan might whip me up something that's not rice and beans?"

As the captain changed course and steered the sub toward the outside edge of the weed line, Diego grinned and winked. "*No problemo.* You get us out of dee dark and Juan make jew whatever jew want."

Chapter 4

As we trolled fifty yards from the edge of the massive weed line, I was struck by its consistency. It looked thick enough to walk on and had all kinds of crap caught up in it. Crap like sardine boxes, pallets, buoys, ropes, and of course, plastic....lots and lots of plastic. There were plastic soda containers of all sizes and shapes, plastic coolers, plastic bags, plastic buckets, even a plastic friggin' lawn chair.

"What are you shaking your head at?" asked Tangles.

"All that plastic, we're in the middle of the Caribbean for Christ's sake, where does all this shit *come* from?"

Tangles shrugged his little shoulders. "Some people just have no respect for the ocean... you know that."

"Well its bullshit and its getting outta hand. Did you see that lawn chair we just passed?"

"Yeah, looked like a K-Mart special. Probably blew off the deck of a cruise ship."

"Then they oughta require those floating germatariums to use bamboo furniture. That's *exactly* what they oughta do. There should be a total ban on plastic furniture on cruise ships, or plastic cups....or plastic—"

"I get it dude, no more plastic on cruise ships. I couldn't agree more."

"Seriously, what would it matter to the cruise lines? They'd just pass the extra cost on to passengers."

"I like it; they could charge it to their credit cards. It'd be *using* plastic to *eliminate* plastic."

"Amen to that. It'd be a win-win. I mean, c'mon, there's more plastic in this weed line than on Bruce Jenner's face. It's disgusting."

"What, his face?"

"Both. But yeah, have you seen him lately? He looks more feminine than any of his Kardashian step-daughters."

"Yeah, I saw him on DWTS. That guy creeps me out. Hard to believe he was once an athlete."

"Bruce Jenner? He wasn't just an athlete; he was once considered the greatest athlete *in the world.* He won the gold medal in the decathlon in the 1976 Olympics. He was on the cover of Wheaties back then. Now he's more likely to be on the cover of Redbook."

"The decathlon? No shit. I don't know if he runs marathons anymore, but based on his looks, I'd say he's still vaulting a few poles."

After we got done laughing, I swore that as soon as we got back to Florida I would start a movement to eliminate the use of plastic on cruise ships...*except* for credit cards. I know that cruise ships aren't the only ones to blame for polluting the seas, but you gotta start somewhere. I noticed we'd tracked further from the weed line and, in light of the fact that we weren't catching anything, decided to change tact. I turned and looked up at the bridge.

"Hey, Ferby!" I shouted over the sound of the engines. My big, burly, three-hundred-and-twenty-pound bear of a captain turned his massive frame my way.

"What's up?"

"Let's try swinging' it in closer to the weed line. It's so thick I think we need to be right on top of it to get noticed."

"You got it, Shag."

Ferby changed course so that the portside outrigger line was only five feet from the edge of the weed and the downrigger line was fifteen or twenty feet outside it. I could almost picture the split-tail mullet we had on the downrigger, which I figured was swimming about fifteen feet below the surface. Any predatory fish hunting near the edge of the weed line would have a hard time missing it.

***

Only a quarter mile to the south, the drug-sub slipped out from under the weed line and into the sunlit water of the Caribbean. The captain looked out the helm viewport and turned the sub north, staying just outside the edge, only fifteen feet below the surface. As soon as they left the claustrophobic darkness of the weed line, the three man Colombian crew started cackling with delight.

"Everybody happy now?" asked the captain.

"*Sí*" answered Diego. "Like *cerdo de mierda.*"

"Say what? Like Merdith Viera?"

"*No, señor. Cerdo de mierda.* Like pigs in sheet."

The captain chuckled. "I'm gonna have to remember that one. *Cerdo de mierda.* Has a nice ring to it. Speaking of pigs and shit, why don't you bring me up a plate of whatever it is Juan whipped up back there?"

"*No problemo.*"

Diego spit out some Spanish, and Juan worked his way up the narrow aisle with a plate. He handed it to Diego who tapped the captain on the shoulder. "Here jew go."

The captain took the plate without taking his eyes off the viewport and set it in his lap. Then he looked down. "Very fucking funny."

"*Qué pasa?*" asked Diego.

"Another plate of rice and beans, that's what."

"Sí, jus' like you ask for, only dees time he add some chorizo."

"No shit, only I asked for anything *but* rice and beans."

"Ohhhh, *mi mal.* I thought jew say jew *wan* rice and beans. I see if Juan can—"

"CLANG!" Something metallic slammed into the sub just above the helm viewport, scaring the shit out of everybody. A second later it clanged again, twenty feet farther down the sub. Everybody flinched and looked up as a third "CLANG!" sounded, followed by a "CRACK!"

"WHAT THE FUCK!?" shouted the captain.

The machinist quickly stepped to the mid-ship hatch and climbed two rungs up the ladder before panicking in rapid-fire Spanish. Diego rushed back to see what happened as the captain slowed the sub down and anxiously asked, "What's he saying? What the fuck happened?"

Manuel stepped down from the ladder and Diego stepped up to see for himself. "Oh, sheet."

"What? What is it?"

"Something crack dee window. She is leaking. Ees no good. Ees bad, ees *very* bad."

As the sub continued slowing, the captain shook his head in disbelief. "No *shit* it's bad, what the fuck did we—?"

Suddenly there was a terrible grating, grinding sound, and the sub lost all forward propulsion. The captain looked at his instrumentation in disbelief as Manuel started spewing out more Spanish. Diego translated. "He say dee engine still running but something no right. We no moving."

"No kidding something's not right. We're dead in the fucking water, and we're leaking. Tell him to shut the engine down, we're going up."

"Shut down dee engine?"

"Sí, Sherlock, shut it down! Something's wrong with the prop."

Moments later the sub went silent for the first time since leaving Tumaco nearly two weeks earlier. Juan looked at Manuel, who looked at Diego, who looked at the captain making his way down the aisle.

"You heard me boys, blow the ballast, *presuro*!"

The captain yanked Diego down from the hatch ladder as Manuel activated the ballast valve and the sub began rising to the surface. He stepped up to look at what had crashed into the viewport, causing water to seep in. He could see a big black ball or weight of some sort wedged into a handle gap on the small turret that rose from the center hatch. It had a thick, stranded wire attached to it. *What the hell?* As the sub broke the surface a dead fish with a big hook in its belly slapped against the cracked viewport, startling him. He flinched, and Diego asked, "*Qué pasa*?"

Not believing what he was seeing, the captain turned and looked out the opposite viewport facing the rear of the sub. The wire was draped along the entire backside of the sub, disappearing over the stern toward the propeller. Some distance away, a fishing boat was just completing a turn and heading toward them.

"You have *got* to be shitting me."

"What ees it?" asked Diego again.

"We got company. A fuckin' fishing boat snagged us."

"A feeshing boat? No sheet."

"I'm afraid so, amigo. Tell Manuel to grab his dive mask, and you and Juan grab a rifle, this is liable to get dicier than a Ginsu commercial."

Chapter 5

Out of the corner of my eye, I saw the tip of the rod that we were running the downrigger line on briefly dip. I turned to watch it closer and saw it dip again, but none of the line pulled off the reel. As I stepped toward it, wondering what could have caused the movement, the heavy wire on the electric downrigger started peeling off with alarming speed and a loud, "ZZZZZZZZZZZZ!!!" The line from the rod attached to the downrigger started peeling off the reel as well. *What the hell?*

Something was clearly wrong. The downrigger line was made of heavy stranded wire and there was a fifteen pound weight secured to the end of it. The rod next to it with hundred pound mono on the reel and a split-tail mullet for bait was clipped to the weight. The idea being that the weight and the bait are sent down together below the surface, where large predatory fish might be more likely to strike. When a fish takes the bait, the line releases from a clip attached to the downrigger wire and the fight is on. Once the weight is sent down to the preferred depth, there's a locking mechanism that keeps it from going any further. At least it's supposed to. *Had the locking mechanism broke and sent the wire and line into free-spool?*

Tangles sprung to action and tried reeling with the rod still in the holder. "I can't stop it!" He yelled. "Do something!" Ferby heard the commotion from the bridge and turned to face us.

"Stop the boat!" I shouted and then told Tangles to tighten the drag on the reel. He turned the star drag on the Penn 9/0 reel and the rod tip snapped back as the line released from the downrigger cable.

"Shit!" cried Tangles as he cranked the handle with little resistance. "It's gone. I think the leader broke!"

I had bigger worries though. The downrigger wire was vanishing at an alarming rate. Ferby took us out of gear, and the boat slowed as it coasted forward but the wire didn't. I knew there was little time because the downrigger only had about three-hundred feet on it. I had a model with an electric retrieve, so I hit it and hoped. The small electric motor hummed, then sang, then screamed bloody murder as the gears stripped. Smoke started billowing out, and I knew the end was near. I relayed my concern to Tangles who was sitting on the gunnel to the side of it, still cranking the handle on the reel.

"Get Back! It's gonna—"

"SCHWINK!" The heavy wire reached the end of the spool and broke free with a loud sound. It slashed across the rod, breaking off two guides and slicing what was left of the line. Tangles fell off the gunnel onto the cockpit floor as the wire whipsawed into the sea.

"Holy shit! You guys alright?" Ferby was looking down from the bridge with concern on his face. I knew

I was okay but wasn't so sure about Tangles. I helped him up from the deck and then killed the power on the downrigger. The motor grinded to a stop and the boat went quiet. Tangles shook his head and broke the stunned silence. "What the—what the *fuck* just happened?"

"Hell if I know, you alright?"

Tangles did a quick inventory check of his fingers and arms and nodded. "Yeah, but that was close. That wire is nasty."

I looked at the rod in front of the downrigger. Not only were two of the guides broken off but the rod-tip was gone. *Shit.*

"What the hell *was* that?" I wondered out loud. "What could take the downrigger weight and never slow down? That thing weighs fifteen pounds and was moving at seven knots."

"Moby Dick?"

"Very funny."

"I'm serious, dude. What else could it be but a whale?"

Suddenly, Ferby hit the throttles and turned the boat northeast. I looked up and he was using the binoculars to focus on something.

"What's going on?" I asked.

"I, uh, I'm not sure, but I see something, uh, something—what?" He lowered the binoculars, blinked his eyes, and then raised them up again.

"What is it?" I repeated, as I climbed up to join him on the bridge.

"I don't believe it—no way" He chuckled. Tangles scampered up to join us as Ferby handed me the binoculars. I raised them to my eyes and focused on an area maybe a half mile in front of us, the same area we had just trolled through.

"Is that a, is that a freakin'—?"

"Submarine?" answered Ferby. "Sure looks like one to me."

I handed the binoculars to Tangles so he could have a look as the distance between us and the sub narrowed. I had to laugh too.

"I can't believe it. You think we really hooked that thing? What're the odds?"

"In light of what just happened, I'd say pretty good."

I nudged Tangles in the shoulder as he trained the binoculars on the sub. "You see any markings on it?"

"Uh, well, it's uh, blue on top, almost the same color as the—wait. Some guy just popped up out of a hatch and he's waving at us. This is crazy, are the cameras rollin'?"

"You better believe it. This could be a MasterCard moment."

"How's that?'

"Priceless."

As we got closer, we could see that the top of the sub was painted almost the same color as the water. If not for the guy waving at us, it would be nearly impossible to spot. I turned to Ferby, who was staring intently at the sub as we approached.

"What kind of sub *is* that?" I asked.

"I got no idea. I've never seen one painted *that* color. Let me see if I can raise them on the radio." Ferby picked up the mic on the marine radio and dialed it to channel 68. "This is the sport-fishing vessel *Lucky Dog*;

can anyone on the submarine that just surfaced read me? Please identify yourself."

We were met with radio silence and were about four-hundred yards from the sub when Tangles gave an update. "Hey, another guy got out of the hatch, and he's walking on top of the sub. He's got a mask in his hand. Did you see that? He just jumped in the water! What's he doing?"

My eyes were good, but not *that* good. "Gimme the binoculars."

Tangles handed me the binoculars, and I watched the guy in the water take a deep breath before slipping below the surface. "Looks like he's diving on the...is that the stern?" Thirty seconds later the guy popped up and started swimming back toward the center hatch. We were only a couple hundred yards away.

"What do you want me to do?" asked Ferby.

"I guess we should pull alongside them and see what's going on...right? It's not everyday you hook a sub."

"I suppose... "

We drew up to the stern of the sub just as the swimmer climbed up some built in steps that led to the mid-ship turret and hatch. He shook his head and said something to the guy that had been waving at us, then climbed back into the sub. It was then that I saw our downrigger wire draped along the top of the sub and disappearing over the stern. It finally dawned on me the reason they surfaced. Our downrigger wire must have wrapped around their propeller. *Unbelievable.* I headed down from the bridge, and Tangles followed. As soon as I hit the cockpit floor, the guy waving at us shouted, “We’re dead in the water! There’s a wire wrapped around our prop. I take it it’s yours?” He held up our split-tail mullet by its hundred-pound leader which had wrapped around the weight that was wedged into the turret. I shook my head, laughed, and shouted back at him.

“We were hoping for something big, but this is ridiculous!”

The guy smiled, held out his hands and shrugged. “Can we tie off to you? I’m the captain and I’d like permission to board. Maybe I could stretch these old legs while my guys work on freeing up the prop.”

I was about to say ‘sure’, when Ferby said, “Ask him what he’s doing and who he’s with. I’m coming down. You got the controls.” I stepped to the lower helm station to keep us positioned properly and yelled back to the captain. “Who are you with? What are you doing out here?”

He held his hands up to his mouth for the bullhorn effect. “Research! We’re with the Cayman Islands Oceanic Institute! And I have some good rum!”

It sounded legit to me and I told Tangles to put the fenders out. The number one rule on the high seas is to always help a fellow boater in distress, and after all, we were partly to blame for their predicament. As Tangles scampered around like he always does and tossed a few lines over to the sub captain, Ferby whispered in my ear. “I’m not so sure about this.”

The tone in his voice got my attention, and I whispered back. “What do you mean?”

“They’re a long way from the Caymans and the guy who jumped in the water looked Latino, not like an islander.”

"It is quite a ways, but what are you saying? There are no Latino's in the Caymans?"

"No, but the sub doesn't have any identifying markings on it either, like you would expect on a research vessel."

Ferby smiled and waved at the sub captain as he worked with Tangles to tie the sub up to the *Lucky Dog*. After tying up to the bow and stern, the captain tied a heavy line to the sub's turret and tossed it to Tangles who wrapped it around our mid-ship cleat. I looked at my watch, slightly concerned about the impending delay, but didn't expect we'd be there any longer than it took to knock back a couple rum and tonics. The three of us looked on as the captain leaned over the turret and was handed a bottle from below. He held it up and smiled. "Permission to board?"

I thought about what Ferby said and was starting to have doubts, but we were already tied up. I waved for the captain to come aboard, and as he jumped onto our swim platform, I whispered to Ferby. "Grill him while we drink his rum."

Chapter 6

As the airplane began its descent from thirty-thousand feet, Holly gazed out the window at a few lonely white clouds set against a brilliant blue sky. Drifting by they seemed to grow transparent, as if conceding that there would be no rain on this glorious day. She leaned her head against the window and looked down at the Caribbean, wondering if one of the white flecks on its surface wasn't a cresting wave, but perhaps the *Lucky Dog*. She started to daydream about her last lovemaking session with Kit when the flight attendant startled her.

"Would you care for another glass of champagne, Miss Lutes?"

"What? Oh, uh... no thank you. Could I have a glass of water though?"

"Sparkling or flat?"

"Just, uh, just plain old regular water will be fine. Thanks."

As the flight attendant poured the water, Holly shook her head and smiled, almost embarrassed at the attention she was getting. She had never flown first class before, considering it a waste of money. Kit managed to talk her into it though, reasoning that she flew so little that she could afford to splurge once in a while, especially considering her recent inheritance. Still, she felt guilty. While Kit had the 'you can't take it with you' mentality, she thought like her late Aunt Milfred. Whenever anybody said to Milfred, 'You can't take it with you,' she always countered with, 'Especially if you don't have anything to take 'cause you blew it all.'

Holly smiled and thanked the pleasant flight attendant as she set the water down on the tray of the empty seat next to her. It was another benefit of flying first class, as only eight people filled the twelve person section. Brushing another pang of guilt aside, she lifted Millie's letter from the empty seat and began reading, searching for what was left unwritten between the lines. She picked up where she left off. Millie had decided to tell Kilroy that she and Joseph were keeping the baby.

I was five months along and showing to the point where I couldn't use the excuse of too much rice and beans. Joseph wanted to present me to his family at Thanksgiving where he planned to announce our secret marriage and my pregnancy, but first I needed to tell Kilroy that I wouldn't be giving the baby up for adoption. I knew I would have to tell my parents at some point but hoped to convince Kilroy not to spill the news just because I was going to raise the baby with Joseph instead. I was nervous, but reasonably confident he would still support me. I worked hard for him on the dock, and Joseph and I were friends with Kilroy and his fiancée, Genevieve (the girl he met on St. Maarten). She was a strikingly beautiful French girl maybe five years older than me. All the women envied her milk-chocolate skin and perfect complexion. When we went out together, Kilroy and Joseph usually went scuba diving while Genevieve and I snorkeled or tanned on the beach.

Joseph wanted to accompany me when I told Kilroy, but Kilroy still thought Joseph didn't know about my pregnancy, so I chose to do it alone. Since it was Thanksgiving week it was fairly busy. Joseph was out on a fishing charter with his dad, and Genevieve was in the marina office with Kilroy. There was a lull on the dock when I went in the office and asked to speak with Kilroy in private. Kilroy looked at me funny and said that whatever I needed to say could be said in front of his fiancée. That made me more nervous because I hadn't told Genevieve a thing about being pregnant. I started stammering and finally he said to just spit it out, which I did. I told him that Joseph and I were going to raise the baby ourselves; that I wasn't giving it up for adoption. I said I had just told Joseph, and that we were going to break the news to his family on Thanksgiving, just a few days away. Genevieve started to say something, but Kilroy quieted her and asked her to leave the office. I thought she would hug me or congratulate me or act surprised, but she just walked right past me.

Holly stopped reading and looked back out the window, thinking, *huh?* Something clearly didn't add up. Millie implied that Genevieve seemed to know she was pregnant but never let on. Why? Had Kilroy told her not to? If so, again, why?

Holly shook her head and continued reading the letter.

At first, Kilroy was very upset. He began telling me what a mistake it was, and how my parents would be destroyed, and how it would ruin my life. He kept reiterating that there were so many couples who could give the baby a good stable home right away, and that I could always have more kids in the future. I could see he was unhappy with my change of heart, and I felt a little guilty about deceiving him, so I asked him to be the baby's godfather. He seemed oddly put off and said he needed to think things through. Thankfully, a customer walked in, and I was able to excuse myself.

I didn't talk to Kilroy or Genevieve the rest of the day and didn't know what to expect the next morning when I came down to the dock. When I entered the marina office, Kilroy came out from behind the desk and gave me a big hug. He said he would be proud to be the baby's godfather but thought we should still keep my pregnancy under wraps. I told him that nobody else knew but Joseph, but he couldn't keep it from his family any longer. And besides, I was starting to look pregnant. Kilroy was agitated. I thought it was because of me, but I found out later that morning that Genevieve had cancelled her plans and gone back to St. Maarten.

Holly looked out the window again. *Genevieve left?* Why? Did it have to do with Millie announcing she was keeping the baby? *It must have.* What difference should it make to Genevieve? She was upset enough to leave her fiancé over Thanksgiving and return to St. Maarten? And why was Kilroy pressing Millie to continue keeping her pregnancy a secret? Holly wracked her brains and resumed reading the letter after skimming over the part where Joseph is found dead. She couldn't read that part without choking up and didn't want to be seen crying in first class.

I was devastated over Joseph's death, and it's no exaggeration to say that I still am. Whoever said time heals all wounds, never lost the love of their life, I can tell you that. Well, you can imagine my plight. I was eighteen and pregnant with a dead man's child. I was lost and didn't know what to do. At Kilroy's urging, I kept my pregnancy hidden by wearing baggy clothes; not that any islanders would notice or care if I put on some weight. The investigation into Joseph's death was cursory and ruled an accidental drowning. The autopsy revealed a large contusion on the back of his head, but it was attributed to being washed up against the rocks where he was found. Kilroy seemed genuinely upset. He blamed himself for losing sight of his dive partner and friend. I wanted to call Father and go home, regardless of the consequences, but Kilroy convinced me otherwise. He reminded me I was only three months from giving birth and that my pregnancy would remain secret if I gave the baby up for adoption.

With Joseph gone and my dreams crushed, I wasn't thinking clearly and agreed. When Christmas came, I told my parents that I had an island bug and was too ill to travel. They were none too happy, but I promised them I would be back by April first at the latest. When I was in my eighth month, Kilroy hired a private doctor to examine me, and I was prescribed bed rest until I gave birth. Kilroy's fiancée, Genevieve, returned and helped take care of me. She seemed almost as excited as I was and assured me I was doing the right thing by giving the baby up for adoption.

The overhead 'fasten your seat belt' sign lit up and chimed, setting off a similar reaction in Holly's brain. *Wait a second!* Joseph dies scuba diving with Kilroy, Kilroy hires a private doctor and urges Millie to keep hiding the pregnancy, and then Genevieve excitedly returns? She has some kind of fight with Kilroy and leaves the island when Millie announces she's keeping the baby, but happily returns when the adoption is back on? Why? She felt the answer was close and continued reading.

She must have sensed that I needed assurance, because I can tell you I was having second and third thoughts about my decision. Genevieve said she met the couple who were adopting my baby and that they came from a fine family who would make sure the baby never wanted for anything. I asked to meet them, and she said she would talk to Kilroy to see if it was possible.

I wasn't due for a few weeks, but the very next day my water broke and I went into labor. I expected Genevieve to rush me to the hospital, but instead she called the doctor, who showed up ten minutes later and began barking orders at her. I was giving birth in Kilroy's rented house! So began the four most painful hours of my life. When I finally thought my insides had split open, out popped the most precious little boy in the world! The doctor wanted to immediately give me a shot of pain medication, but I wouldn't let him until I held my baby. I counted his fingers and toes and was relieved to find them all there when I noticed that he had an unusual birthmark. On his lower right arm he had a dark red stain that resembled a four-leaf clover. I called him "Lucky" and was kissing his face when I felt the sting of a needle in my thigh. That was the last thing I remembered until waking up the next morning.

Kilroy and the doctor were at my bedside when I woke up. It was February 23, 1949, and I had given birth the day before on President's Day. I asked to see my baby, and Kilroy said it wasn't possible because the baby was with his new parents and that they had left the island. Kilroy had me sign some papers regarding the adoption almost immediately after Joseph's death. According to Kilroy, the adoption agreement ensured the adoptive parents would remain anonymous. I was sick to my stomach. I was so distraught after Joseph's death that I had barely looked at the agreement before signing. I felt I made a horrible mistake by giving up the baby and was desperately trying to think of a way to undo it. I thought maybe Genevieve might help me persuade Kilroy to try to fix things and asked to talk to her. I couldn't believe it when he told me she was back in St. Maarten. It finally occurred to me that Kilroy had manipulated my naiveté and trust in him as my father's friend. Within a week I was back home in Florida and shortly thereafter developed a pelvic infection which left me unable to bear any more children. I felt that God was teaching me a lesson about motherhood, and I sunk into a deep depression. I never went back to St. Croix, and I would never see my baby "Lucky" again.

Hold the phone, Margaret! Holly skipped back to the beginning of the paragraph and re-read the part about Kilroy saying the baby had left the island. Then she skipped back to the part where he said Genevieve was back in St. Maarten. *She left the island too!* Was it a coincidence or did she take little Lucky back *with* her? Was that what this was all about? Suddenly, it all made perfect sense. Kilroy was the driving force behind keeping Millie's pregnancy secret *and* giving the baby up for adoption. He even hired a doctor himself and let Millie have the baby in his house. Why? Wouldn't the adoptive parents be paying for that? And how come she never met the adoptive parents? The answer seemed obvious now, she *had* met the adoptive parents—they were Kilroy and Genevieve. It had to be. She finished reading the letter as the flight attendant checked to make sure all the trays were up and the seats in their upright position.

As she gazed out the window at the lush green foliage of the rapidly approaching island and beautiful seashore below, it seemed pretty clear that Kilroy and Genevieve conspired to trick Millie into giving up her baby for adoption. But did they want a baby so badly they were willing to *kill* for one? Or was that all Kilroy's doing? By her estimation, Genevieve would be in her late eighties and Kilroy somewhere in his mid-nineties. Was it possible either were still alive? And what about Lucky? He would be about sixty-five if Millie had him when she was eighteen. Surely *he* should still be alive. Did he have his own family too?

She was jolted back to the present when the wheels touched down and the plane taxied to the gate. The flight attendant made the requisite landing announcement and welcomed everybody to the island of St. Croix. A few minutes later, Holly was walking across the tarmac of the Henry E. Rholsen International Airport. She was anxious to see Kit and anxious to get some answers. She thought about Millie writing that she never went back to St. Croix and would never see Lucky again. *Well, I'm here Millie,* she thought. *I'm here and I'm not stopping till I find him.*

Chapter 7

Although I explicitly told Ferby to grill the sub captain *while* we drank his rum, Ferby jumped the gun and started in on him as soon as he stepped through the tuna door. Trying but failing to act nonchalant, he scratched his scruffy gray face and raised an eyebrow. "You're a long way from the Caymans. What's the name of the research organization you're with again?"

The captain seemed surprised, perhaps expecting a friendlier greeting and an introduction. "Uh… the uh…the research organization?"

"Yeah," pressed Ferby. "It sounded familiar. What's the name again?"

The captain fidgeted and answered as he handed me the bottle of rum he was holding. "It's uh, the uh, the Cayman Islands Institute of Oceanics. Sooooooo, what say we have a taste of that rum? I'm told it's the finest in the Caribbean. Names McGirt…and *you* are?" He extended his hand out, but I didn't shake it. I shot a quick glance at Ferby and Tangles before answering.

"Confused."

"What?"

"I'm a little confused. Before, you said the name was the Cayman Island's Oceanic Institute."

The captain shrugged. "Same thing. Tomato-Tomahto. Man, I can't believe you guys snagged us. It's a shame too… a real shame."

Now I really *was* confused and shot another glance at Ferby, who was frowning. You might describe accidentally hooking a sub as being a freak thing, or being unbelievable, even incredible, but definitely not a shame.

"What, uh, whadda you mean? What's a shame?" I asked.

The sub captain's easygoing demeanor suddenly evaporated as he stepped to a corner of the cockpit and pulled out a large semi-automatic handgun from behind his back.

"It's a shame I gotta swipe your boat before we sampled the rum… DIEGO! *Presura!*"

As he waved the gun back and forth between me, Ferby, and Tangles, two guys climbed out of the sub holding assault rifles and jumped on to the swim platform of the *Lucky Dog*. I looked at Ferby, who was slowly shaking his head. "I told you," he said. Then I looked down at Tangles, who had taken the bottle of rum out of my hands and unscrewed the cap. He lifted it to his lips and took a long pull before handing it to Ferby and giving his assessment of the situation. "We are so *fucked.*"

Ferby nodded and took a healthy pull. Then he handed me the bottle and added,

"He's right. I told you so."

The sub captain who called himself McGirt was talking to one of the guys holding an AK-47 as I downed a slug of the amber rum. It really *was* good. When he stopped talking to him, the guy turned to the other guy with the AK-47 and started rattling off in Spanish. I was kicking myself for not taking Ferby's initial skepticism seriously enough and allowing us to be overtaken by…by… *exactly what the hell were they?*

Tangles took the bottle out of my hand again and just as he raised it to his lips, McGirt turned and warned, "Not so fast, Tattoo. Gimme the rum."

Oh shit, I thought. *Here we go again.* Tangles lowered the bottle from his lips and cocked his head a little. "Excuse me?"

"You heard me. Gimme the goddamn rum."

"Did you just call me Tattoo? The guy from the TV show *Fantasy Island*?"

"You know *another* midget with a speech impediment named Tattoo?"

"You saying I got a speech impediment, asshole?"

I looked at Ferby who looked worried. He was probably thinking the same thing I was. *Are you trying to get us killed?* McGirt extended his gun toward Tangles, but before he could respond, I interjected. "Just give him the rum, Tangles…*now.*"

Tangles exhaled slowly and gave McGirt the evil eye as he stepped forward and handed him the rum. As soon as he was handed the bottle, McGirt smashed the butt of his gun into the side of Tangles head. Tangles managed to deflect it with his forearm, but it still had enough power to send him crashing to my feet. As I helped him up, McGirt said, "The next time you call me asshole, Diego's breaking out the machetes. You got that, you little fuck?"

A nice purple welt rose at the edge of Tangles' hairline, next to his ear. He put his hand to it and then pulled it away to check for blood before answering. "Yeah… I uh, I got it."

McGirt inspected the top of the rum bottle closely and wiped his greasy T-shirt over the rim. Then he looked straight at Ferby, all three-hundred-plus, African-American pounds of him. "Guess I don't need to ask who nigger-lipped it."

McGirt trained the gun on Ferby's massive chest and watched him out of the corner of his eye as he hefted the bottle and did a double chug-a-lug. Ferby silently fumed, and I noticed his fists were clenched.

"Easy, big guy," I whispered. Ferby unclenched his fists, and McGirt looked at me.

"*You* the captain?" he asked.

I nodded at Ferby. "*He* is, actually. But it's my boat and I—"

"Shut the engines off." He pointed the gun at me for emphasis, and added, "Now."

I did as I was told, not liking the way things were going—not liking them one bit. *Shit.* The boat went silent for a second. Until McGirt spoke again, the only sound came from the waves splashing against the submarine tethered to our port side.

"So, here's the situation. We have six tons of coke we need to transfer from the sub to the boat. How it's gonna work is this; *you* three guys are gonna get in the sub and form a human chain, sorta like passing sandbags. You lift the cargo to the top of the turret and my Colombian friends will take it from there. I'll be up on the bridge keeping an eye on things." He said something to Diego, and they switched weapons so McGirt had one of the AK-47's. I couldn't believe what I'd heard. *Six tons of coke? Are you kidding me?* Ferby's mouth hung open in disbelief and Tangles eyes were popping out of his little head. We were so deep in shit we could taste colon.

"Wait a second. Why go to all the trouble?" I reasoned. "We'll help you free the prop, and you can be on your way. I swear, we won't tell anybody....seriously. C'mon man, cut us some slack, we stopped to help."

"That was your first mistake...and no...we can't fix the prop. The wire got behind it and destroyed the seal. Even *if* we could get the wire off, the props fucked, just like you are. And don't worry, I *know* you're not gonna tell anybody. So you better do what Diego says or he'll chop you up like a pig on Cinco de Mayo."

"But—"

"But nothing, asshole." He nodded to Diego who pointed his gun at me and waved me toward the tuna door. "Jew hear de Cap-e-tan. Move it."

I stepped through the tuna door onto the swim platform with Tangles right behind me, but Ferby hadn't budged. I looked back and McGirt pointed his rifle at him.

"Hey, Rosie Grier, did you not hear me? I said move it!"

"No way I'm climbing down into that thing...no fucking way. I'm, uh, I'm...claustrophobic."

McGirt lowered his rifle a notch and smirked. "For real?"

"Yeah...for real."

"Well, don't worry, fat-ass, you won't be for long."

Chapter 8

It was Holly's first time In St. Croix and she wasn't sure what to expect, but having to drive on the wrong side of the road caught her completely off guard.

"What do you mean?" she asked the rental car girl at the airport.

"We drive on the left side of the road, no worries, you'll get used to it. Just be sure to keep the driver's side on the shoulder, by the trees."

"The trees?"

"Yes, they are beautiful this time of year, the end of rainy season. Keep them by your window and you will have no problem. Just make sure to look all around at the traffic lights; we have some five-way intersections."

"Five-way? How do—"

"No worries, Miss Lutes. Just go slow and enjoy the scenery. If you get lost or have a problem, just ask someone for help. We are a friendly island, welcome to St. Croix."

Despite the detailed map highlighting the route to her hotel, Holly got lost. Not once, but twice. Both times she had locals give her directions that didn't included a single street name. Instead it was something like,

"Turn left at Johnnie's restaurant, and go down the river road till you get to the big tree, and then take a right."

A half hour later, she finally found the Hibiscus Resort on the west side of Christiansted, right on the beach. Check-in went smoothly, and she was personally greeted by the resort's manager who thanked her for staying with them. "And if there's anything I can do to make your stay more enjoyable, don't hesitate to ask," he added.

A bellhop carried her bags and escorted her to the room. She found the room clean and accommodating. The view, however, was breathtaking.

"Oh my God!" She exclaimed upon opening her sliding door. She stepped out onto a covered patio that was right on the beach. Fifty yards away sat the sparkling blue Caribbean with nothing but palm trees and gorgeous white sand in-between. *I think I'm gonna like this place,* she thought.

Looking out at the water, she thought about Kit on the *Lucky Dog*, making his way from Puerto Rico. He said he'd call her when he got close, and she'd meet them at the Salt River Marina. That was the plan at least, but she'd learned that when it came to Shagball and Tangles, plans were always subject to change. She looked at her watch. One-thirty. Kit said he'd be at the marina around four o'clock, so she had ample time to unwind and get her bearings.

After freshening up, she changed into her bathing suit and opened up the gift-wrapped package on the bed that she assumed was some sort of welcoming gift from the resort. To her utter amazement, it was a beautifully framed photograph of her as a child, flanked by her parents and Aunt Millie. They were standing on the bow of their family owned drift boat, the *C-Love.* Ten year-old Holly held up a nice sized grouper in one hand and her fishing rod in the other as she proudly beamed at the camera. A grinning Millie had her hand on Holly's shoulder, and her mom was planting a kiss on her father's cheek. Holly shook her head in disbelief as she opened the envelope that came with the picture. The note read;

I'm not very good at this kind of stuff, but I just wanted you to know I'm here if you need someone to talk to.

Your humble servant and manwhore,

Kit

A big lump formed in Holly's throat and tears welled in the corners of her eyes. Just when she had Kit pegged as being overly insensitive and immature, he managed to shock her with a show of thoughtfulness right when she needed it. She *did* need someone to talk to, but was afraid to open up to him with her divorce still in the rearview mirror. Technically, she was still on the rebound with Kit, but they had been through so much together in such a short time, it didn't feel that way. He certainly had his flaws, but he also had a big heart and a passion for the sea, just like she did. Plus, she had to admit he was easy on the eyes, possessing a sharp wit and keen sense of humor (see manwhore). She chuckled and reminded herself how desperately she needed to break out of the doldrums her disastrous marriage had left her in and her relationship with Kit had certainly accomplished that.

There was never a dull moment with Shagball and Tangles.

Something caught her eye and she looked out the sliding glass doors to see two big horses galloping down the beach. They had on bridles and reins, but no saddles, and only one had a rider, a young man with dreadlocks. He stopped a hundred yards past the boundary that marked the resort beach and jumped off, leading both horses into the water. She watched in amazement as the horses swam out and decided to investigate. After setting the note down and wiping her eyes, she jogged across the sand, briefly stopping to test the temperature of the water. Happy to find it accommodating, she waded in and swam toward them. When she was about ten yards away, she stopped and stood in the sand in chest-high water. The young man was leading the horses back to shore, and she couldn't help but comment on them.

"Your horses are absolutely beautiful. I never knew they were such good swimmers."

The young man smiled and flashed a set of brilliant white teeth, giving the horses teeth a good run for their money. "Tank you. Dey love to swim after a nice run on de beach. So do I. It helps beat de heat and it's good for de muscles." He led the horses out of the water, and Holly followed, somewhat mesmerized by the magnificent animals as they glistened and shook their coats dry. The young man eyed Holly appreciatively, the way young men do. "You're first time in St. Croix?" he asked.

"Why…yes, how'd you know?"

"De horses. People don't realize dere is a big farm community on de island, and it always surprises dem de first time dey see horses in de ocean. It shouldn't dough, just about every western movie shows horses swimming in a river at some point. Dey good swimmers. Very powerful."

"I...uh, you're right. Now that I think of it, I can picture John Wayne riding across the Rio Grande chasing the bad guys. I just never imagined them in the ocean."

"You never heard of sea horses?" He flashed his Colgate smile and laughed, as did Holly.

"Very funny. I grew up on the water. I know all about sea horses and lions...and bears."

They shared another laugh and the young man held his hand out to introduce himself. "Dat was a good one, Miss...?"

"Holly." She shook his hand and then added, "and you are?"

"Jackson. So, Miss Holly, would you care to go for a quick ride on Brown Thunder?" He slapped the horse nearest to him on the rump, and the horse snorted, clearing some seaweed from its massive nostrils.

Holly was caught off guard again. First having to drive on the wrong side of the road and now being asked to go for a ride on a horse across a Caribbean beach.

"I, uh, geez, I'm not sure—"

"Not sure you remember how? Doan worry; he's a real sweetheart, just like me."

Jackson flashed his winning smile again, and Holly laughed.

"Really?" Realizing she sounded a little skeptical, she backtracked. "I mean, I'm sure you are, but I just got here and I—"

"No worries, Miss Holly. I should take dem back to de farm and go down to de marina anyway."

"The marina? Which one?"

"Salt River. I work part-time dere when I'm not tending horses, or doin' sometin' else."

"Are you kidding me? That's where my boyfriend is bringing his boat this afternoon. He should be calling in a little while to let me know when to pick him up."

"What's de name of de boat?"

"The *Lucky Dog.*"

"If you're de one waiting for him, he certainly is." Jackson couldn't help himself and winked at her. Holly smiled, amused by his flirtatious nature. "So, what's the something else?"

"You be staying here at de Hibiscus?"

"Yes, I just checked in."

"Well, for one ting, I run karaoke night here once a week...tonight, in fact. Maybe I can get you to sing a song?"

Holly laughed. "Not a chance. I sing worse than an American Idol reject. I'd clear out the bar in a heartbeat."

"Well den, are you sure you doan want to take a quick gallop? Not everybody can say dey rode a horse on de beach on St. Croix."

Holly laughed at the notion, but the temptation was too much. She hadn't ridden a horse since she was a little girl and was feeling adventuresome. Besides, the animals were beautiful, just like the scenery. She smiled and responded, "Aw heck, why not? So, how do I get on top of Brown Thunder?"

Jackson smiled and cupped his hands together. "Dere are many answers to dat, Miss Holly, but in dis instance, just put your foot right here and I'll hoist you up."

Holly groaned at the sexual innuendo. "At least you didn't say, 'that's what *she* said.' My boyfriend's buddy Layne wears a button that says that when he presses it, and I think he's worn it out already. Okay, here goes nothing." Holly put her foot into Jackson's cupped hands and put her hand on his shoulder as he lifted her onto the horse. Then he got the other horse to kneel and climbed on it.

"Alright, here we go. You ready, Miss Holly?"

Having some reservations at this point, she tentatively held the reins as Brown Thunder shuffled in the sand. "Woah, boy, easy now. Uh, I, uh, I guess so, but, uh, I've never ridden bareback before, is it hard?"

Jackson beamed from ear to ear. "Dat's what she said." Then he slapped his horse in the rear and yelled, "Heeeyaaaa!"

Holly held on for dear life as Brown Thunder chased Jackson down the beach, loving every minute of it.

Chapter 9

Despite Ferby's revelation that he had claustrophobia, he also had bulletphobia, just like me and Tangles, and reluctantly followed us into the sub. We were led by the guy with the handgun named Diego, who positioned himself in the bow of the sub. He sat on the other side of the ladder that led up to the open hatch we had just entered through and pointed his gun at us. "Jew carry packages to top. Give to Manuel." He pointed at the stacked rows of packages that lined the shelves on both sides of the sub, then pointed at some boxes lined along the bottom shelf. "First carry boxes up, *pronto.*"

I looked down, and there were four tubular boxes about six feet in length, next to a small crate that had the word "*explosivos*" stenciled on the side. I picked up the crate, which I estimated to weigh about fifty pounds, and handed it to Ferby who was standing at the foot of the ladder. He stepped on a rung and lifted the crate up through the hatch where it was handed off to Manuel. Tangles slid one of the long boxes out from the bottom shelf, and Ferby and I guided it up through the hatch. It didn't weigh much more than the crate, but it was awkward work in the cramped sub. Ferby and

I both had to hunch a little because the subs ceiling was only six-feet high. In just a few minutes, we had the boxes out of the sub and were looking at a shit load of neatly packaged cocaine.

"How's your claustrophobia doing?" I asked Ferby.

"I'll be alright as long as I stay under the hatch and can see out."

"Okay then, we'll hand you the packages, and you lift them up."

Tangles started tossing me the packages one at a time, which I guesstimated weighed about twenty pounds each. They were tightly wrapped in blue plastic and stamped with a white stallion reared up on its hind legs. I did the math and calculated that there were roughly six hundred packages. It was gonna take a while. After a few minutes of slinging packages, Tangles said,

"Six tons of coke. I'll bet this is what Charlie Sheen's man-cave looks like."

"Unfortunately, minus the porn stars and hookers," I added.

"Jew shut up. No talk. Work." Diego apparently didn't like the commentary and waved his gun in our direction.

As we worked our way deeper into the sub, I was amazed at its size and complexity. It was reasonably well lit and even had some type of air circulation system that was powered by an unseen generator that droned continuously in the background. Toward the rear there was an engine-control panel with two sets of valves next to it. One was marked '*Lastre/* Ballast' and the other was marked '*Hundir/* Scuttle'. It didn't take any stretch of the imagination to figure that once we off-loaded the cargo, McGirt would gun us down like fish in a barrel and send us to the bottom of the sea. We needed a plan, and we needed one quick. We had been slinging packages for nearly an hour, and as I handed another one to Ferby I gave him my best 'we gotta make a move' look. It consisted of attempting to bug my eyes out like Marty Feldman on crack and then mouthing the words, "Do something."

With his back to Diego, Ferby nodded imperceptibly and gave me a thumbs up. At least I thought that's what he was doing until he stuck a thumb with an overgrown fingernail straight through the plastic wrapping of the package I handed him. It sliced it wide open.

"You guys ready?" He asked.

Diego snapped to attention upon hearing him. "I say no talk."

"And I say I need a break," answered Ferby, as Tangles came walking up with another sack of coke. "Me too," he said, looking at Diego. "It's fucking hot in here. You got any drinking water on this tub, taco breath?"

"I say no—what jew call me?" Diego took a step forward so he was just behind Ferby's right shoulder and pointed his gun at Tangles. I looked at Ferby who exhaled and then mouthed the word, "Now." I wasn't exactly sure what he was gonna do, so I half-stepped to his left, out of the line of fire.

Tangles still had Diego's attention and responded, "I called you—"

Out of the corner of his eye, Ferby saw the barrel of the gun pointing at Tangles and made his move. Gauging where Diego's head was in relation to the gun, he threw the sliced open sack of coke over his shoulder and into Diego's face. A cloud of white exploded everywhere, and Diego staggered backward. I leapt past Ferby, grabbing Diego's gun hand by the wrist as I slammed him into the side of the sub. When we fell to the floor, the gun went off with a thunderous blast, and Ferby screamed. Sensing that the other guy on top of the sub was reaching for his AK-47, Tangles scampered up the ladder and slammed the hatch shut. Although I was six inches taller and outweighed Diego by a good fifty pounds, he fought like a banshee, perhaps aided by the uncut cocaine covering his sweaty face like a mask. We fought on the floor with the gun pressed between us and when I took my other hand off his throat to try to pry the gun loose, he bit me in the shoulder. I'm not talking about a little nip either, I'm talking werewolf style, and it was my turn to scream. With both hands on the gun now, I jerked backward and the gun went off again, but this time it was muffled by Diego's chest. He released his death grip, and his mouth went slack before his head banged on the floor. I pushed myself off him and there was a growing red splotch in the center of his chest. I stared at his lifeless body for a few moments before realizing he was seriously dead. I heard Ferby groan and turned my attention to him. He was slouched on the floor next to the ladder, grimacing.

"How bad is it?" I asked.

"Not as bad as old taco breath there, but my Dancing with the Stars fantasy is over. Smelly bastard got me in the knee... God damn, it hurts!"

From what I could see of the bloody mess that used to be his knee, I had to agree. "We need to get a tourniquet on that."

"Gimme a hand here!" yelled Tangles. He was at the top of the ladder, hanging on to the latch with all his might as the bad guys tried to yank it open from the topside. I stepped up a couple rungs and figured out how to lock it shut. Then I pointed the locking mechanism out to Tangles and grabbed the hatch cover. "Alright, I got it. Now latch it shut," I instructed.

Tangles took his hands off the hatch and locked it shut. I stepped off the ladder, and Tangles followed. "What do we do now?" He asked.

"First, we get a tourniquet on Ferby's leg so he doesn't bleed to death."

"That would be nice," commented Ferby, through gritted teeth. He had to be in incredible pain, but for the most part the big man handled it as well as could be expected. I noticed Diego the Dead had a belt on and quickly relieved him of it. No sooner had I cinched it around Ferby's upper thigh when we heard a loud "Crack!" followed by another "Crack!" as the butt end of a rifle suddenly came crashing through the viewport on the turret.

"You idiots hear me down there?" It was the voice of McGirt, the sub captain.

"Yeah" I replied. "Everybody but Diego. He's taking a power siesta."

"That's real cute, but exactly what do you think you accomplished by locking yourselves in there? The subs disabled. It's not going anywhere and neither are you, at least not until after you get the rest of the blow outta there."

I looked up toward the helm of the sub at the electronics, noting the radio. "I think we'll radio for help. Something tells me you won't be sticking around for that."

McGirt let out a derisive snort. "You think I'm stupid enough to leave a working radio onboard? *Really?*"

I looked at Tangles and nodded toward the helm. "Check it out."

Tangles hustled up to the helm and held the back of the radio up for me to see. The wires were all torn out. *Shit.* "Even without a radio, we'll take our chances in here. Another boat's bound to come by sooner or later. Besides, we both know that as soon as we unload all the coke, you'd kill us."

"That's true, but you're dead either way. I'll tell you what, open the hatch and unload the rest of the coke, and I'll make sure your bodies are found. Otherwise, I'll send you to the bottom and nobody will ever know what happened to you."

I looked at Tangles, who shrugged, and then at Ferby, who was growing pale, which is not easy to do for a black man. "How, uh, how exactly do you think you're gonna do that?"

"Remember that crate marked '*explosivos*' that you unloaded?"

Unfortunately, I did. *Shit again.* "Yeah, what about it?"

"There's two dozen hand grenades and ten pounds of plastic explosives in it. If you don't open the hatch, I'm gonna toss a couple grenades through this view-port and blow you to smithereens. Then I'll put some plastic explosive on the hatch and blow it open. Once I get the rest of the coke out, I'll scuttle the sub. So open the hatch, asshole. You got ten seconds, or I'm going for the grenades."

I didn't know what to do, but I was *pretty* sure of one thing; McGirt wasn't bluffing. I looked at Tangles who was rubbing his chin, seemingly mulling over our fucked-up situation.

"What do you think, Tangles?"

"I think he's bluffing."

"What about you Ferby? What do you think?"

Ferby opened his eyes and smiled the way a father might smile at his daughter's wedding. Happy and sad at the same time…letting go.

"You know what? I think my claustrophobia's gone."

Chapter 10

"Fine, have it your way," said McGirt as he jumped off the sub onto the gunnel of the *Lucky Dog*. "You guys wanna get blown to smithereens; I can get you there."

I turned to face Tangles. "Still think he's bluffing?"

Tangles climbed up the ladder to peek out the viewport and some shots rang out that ricocheted off the sub. Tangles slipped off the ladder and yelled, "Shit!" when he hit the floor. I quickly helped him up, wondering if he was shot. "You alright?"

He did a quick check to confirm that he was okay and then looked at me wide-eyed. "They fuckin' shot at me!"

I tried to downplay the situation. "Good bluff." My mind was racing though; once again we were in serious shit and needed to act fast, or we were gonna be mincemeat. Ferby sat oddly silent, perhaps accepting his presumed fate, but Tangles was frantic. "Dude, what are we gonna do? I think I was wrong. I don't think he's bluffing anymore."

I looked toward the rear of the sub, remembering the valves by the engine controls, and had an idea. "Tangles! Quick! Grab that roll of duct tape hanging on the wall by the engine controls." I pointed at the tape on the wall and then grabbed a sack of coke and raised it up toward the viewport, visualizing whether it would cover the hole. It looked like it would. Tangles handed me the duct tape and inquired as to what the plan was.

"I'm gonna wedge this coke in the viewport. Tear me off some tape so we can try to waterproof the seal."

Quickly, Tangles tore off four strips of tape. "Ready when you are," he announced.

"Alright, as soon as I wedge it in place, start taping off the sides. Here we go."

As soon as I shoved the shrink-wrapped coke into the viewport, I heard shouting in Spanish. Tangles taped off the edges and climbed back down the ladder.

"Okay, it's wedged in there pretty good, but now what? They can just push it in with a rifle-butt."

Concerned that's exactly what was about to happen, I hustled back to the engine controls.

"Shag! What are you doing?" pressed Tangles.

I looked at the valve marked "ballast" and closed my eyes for a second, trying to visualize what would happen. *Shit.* There was only one way to find out. I opened the valve and heard the sound of water rushing as I ran forward to join Tangles and Ferby. "I hope you taped that up good!" I shouted.

"Holy shit! We're sinking! You didn't tell me you were gonna sink us!"

"You said you didn't like surprises."

"I don't, I—"

Suddenly we heard yelling in Spanish and then automatic gunfire strafed the hull of the sub as we slipped below the surface. I stepped up on the ladder to hold the sack of coke in place, worried that the water pressure would push it in. Immediately, water started seeping in around the edges, but I managed to keep the sack in place. Ferby came to life when some dripped on his head.

"You decided to drown us? We shoulda voted. I prefer the grenade scenario."

"We're not gonna drown," I insisted. "We're still tied to the *Lucky Dog*. I figured by submerging, we might pull the *Lucky Dog* over on its side."

Ferby started laughing. "You figured *what?* This sub is damn near a hundred feet long and made of metal. The *Lucky Dog* is thirty-eight feet of fiberglass. You're gonna rip the cleats out and we'll go Titanic."

"Hey, I didn't hear any *better* plans and besides, I'm allergic to shrapnel. No worries though; we can always dump the ballast and pop back up to the surface."

"You sure about that, Captain Nemo?"

"Of course not, but that's the plan."

"We stopped," said Tangles.

"Huh?"

"We stopped. We stopped going down. The cleats must be holding."

"Not for long," replied Ferby. He wasn't helping morale, and I let him know it.

"You know, Ferby? I liked your fat-ass a lot more when you had claustrophobia. Can you cut the tube-of-gloom crap?"

The muffled sound of gunfire erupted again, and a few dings rang out as a couple bullets plowed through the water and hit the hull.

"What the hell's going on up there? What are they shooting at?" cried Tangles.

"Fish in a barrel," responded Ferby. "Fish in a *sinking* barrel."

Chapter 11

After a brief but thrilling horse ride on the beach, Holly took a quick shower and pondered her next move. It was only two-thirty, and Kit wasn't due to arrive at the marina until four or five. Her first thought was to keep soaking up the tropical ambience and maybe have an umbrella drink at the hotel bar. Then she thought about the whole purpose of the trip; namely, finding out what happened to her deceased Aunt Millie's secret son, "Lucky." On the plane ride down, she had decided a good place to start would be the local library. Where exactly that was she had no idea, but she was confident she could find out in short order.

Realizing that she was thirsty, and having been warned not to drink tap water on the island, she decided to go to the bar for a bottle of water and to ask for directions.

As she walked into the dining room/bar area, the large tiki hut reminded her of The Old Key Lime House back in Lantana. Since it was mid-November and not yet in season, most of the tables were empty. Since it was pre-happy hour, there were only a couple people at the bar. Holly took a seat facing the beach, and a friendly bartender greeted her. "Good afternoon, how can I help you?"

"Could I have a bottle of water?"

The bartender reached into a cooler and placed one on the bar. Holly thanked him and took several large gulps before setting it down nearly empty.

"Wow, you really *are* thirsty." The bartender reached down and placed another bottle on the bar. "Here, this one's on me."

"Oh, that's not necessary. Just put it on my room… number three."

"Ah, but I insist" he replied with a smile. "I like to keep my customers fully hydrated. Otherwise, they might pass out before I cash out. I'm just looking out for my best interest, and right now, that's you, Miss..?" The bartender extended his hand and she introduced herself as they shook.

"Very nice to meet you, Holly. I'm Bradshaw. Your first time here at the Hibiscus?"

"As a matter of fact, yes. It's my first time on St. Croix too."

"You just checked in?"

"A little while ago." Holly downed the rest of the water and unscrewed the cap on the second bottle. She took another gulp before setting it down.

"Well, now that you're all hydrated, would you like your complimentary glass of our famous rum punch?"

"Complimentary?"

"The first one's on the house—resort policy. As long as you're hydrated, they want you drinking as soon as possible."

"I guess if it's policy I should go with the flow… pour away."

"That's the spirit. You're on island time now, relax and enjoy."

As he poured a watermelon-colored drink into a large plastic cup, she commented, "My boyfriend and his crew are gonna love this place."

"His crew? Like he's got an entourage? We got a celebrity staying with us?"

Holly laughed, "No, no, he's not a, not like a *real* celebrity. He just has a fishing show."

"Really? Which one? Fishing's pretty big down here."

"It's called 'Fishing on the Edge… with—"

"Shagball and Tangles?"

"You've actually seen it?"

"Are you kidding me? The one with the midget? That show is *great.* Me and my friends watch it every Sunday morning at five. I think it's on ESPN7…or 8. We do have cable down here, you know…and satellite too."

"You get up at five in the morning to watch fishing?"

Bradshaw looked at her like her hair was purple and laughed. "*Get up?* No way, we watch it after we hit the clubs. It's always good for some laughs before going to bed. I can't wait to meet them; when are they coming in?"

Somewhat amazed that the bartender was familiar with the show, Holly shook her head and looked at her watch.

"They should be coming in pretty soon. Actually, I'm expecting a call any time."

"You picking them up at the airport?"

"No, the marina, they're coming by boat."

"Don't tell me they're coming in on the *Lucky Dog.*"

"You guessed it. Kit had it delivered to Puerto Rico, and he's fishing his way here with Tangles and another friend."

"Kit?"

"Of course, sorry, that's Shagball's real name. It's short for Connor."

"Good thing they went with 'Shagball' for the show—has a better ring to it. This is awesome! Wait till I tell the manager; he *loves* celebrities. If there's anything I can do to help, just ask."

Incredulous that the bartender thought of her boyfriend as a celebrity, Holly rolled her eyes as Bradshaw moved away to tend to another customer. When he returned, she took him up on his offer. "There is one thing you might be able to help me with."

"Shoot."

"Is there a library anywhere near here?"

Bradshaw gave her the same strange look as before. "A *library?* Wow, never heard that one before. If you don't mind me asking, why do you want to go to the library?"

Holly resisted the urge to say, 'to get a book,' and instead went with, "Research. I need to do a little research. The punch is very good, by the way. What's in it?"

"Rum, lots of rum. It's one of the reason's I'm still down here. The people of St. Croix, or Crucians as they're called, make great rum. It's dirt cheap down here too; a lethal combination."

Holly took another sip of punch and closed her eyes while pinching the bridge of her nose between her index finger and thumb. She had a sudden vision of Tangles dancing on the bar in his jockey shorts with a bottle of rum in his hand while Kit and Ferby drunkenly cheered him on. Involuntarily, she shuddered.

"You alright?" asked a concerned Bradshaw.

Holly snapped out of it. "Huh? No, I mean, yeah, I'm fine. It's the guys I'm concerned about. I've seen them all rummed up before, and it's not pretty. Promise me you'll do your best to not let them get completely schnockered. *Please?*"

Bradshaw put his hand over his heart. "Scout's honor. At least for tonight, 'cause I'm off at seven. But don't worry; I look after all my customers, not just the celebrities."

Tired of the celebrity reference, Holly muttered, "Super."

"What's that?"

"Great, that's great. Believe me, you'll be doing everyone a favor, not just me. Now, what about the library? If it's not too far, I might have time to get started on my research."

"Oh, yeah, the library. I have no idea about that. I mean, who needs books when you have fishing shows and rum?"

"Really?"

"Alright, you got me there. I've been known to watch an occasional episode of *Family Guy* too. That is one sick, twisted, show. Now that I think of it, you know what would be cool? If Shagball and Tangles were turned into cartoons and they took Stewie and Brian deep-sea fishing."

"*What?* I think you've been drinking too much punch."

"No, I'm serious, think about it; Stewie reels up a fish and has no idea what it is. He says, 'What the deuce? What the deuce is it?' Then, as the fish breaks the surface, it's a jack, and Brian replies in his rich baritone, 'Well, well, jack crevalle.'"

Holly was taking another sip of punch and some went up her nose when she laughed. She hated to admit it, but she was also a big fan of *Family Guy*, possibly the most politically incorrect show ever aired. As she wiped her nose with a cocktail napkin, Bradshaw continued. "That'd be a riot. That's Shagball and Tangles new catchphrase, isn't it? 'Well, well, jack crevalle.' It even rhymes. Then, maybe Stewie gets a crush on Tangles… and Brian—"

Holly laughed again and held up her hand for him to stop. "Okay, Okay, that's pretty funny. Stupid, but funny."

"'Cause it rhymes, like a good catchphrase should."

"No, I mean the Stewie-getting-a-crush-on-Tangles part, *that's* funny. 'Well, well, jack crevalle' isn't a catchphrase, because it hasn't caught on. As far as I know, you're the only person other than them to ever utter those words."

"No way."

"Way."

"Well, I say it all the time. I think it's gonna be bigger than, 'Where's the beef?' That didn't even rhyme."

"I'll tell you what, if you can point me in the direction of someone who knows where the library is, I'll be sure to bring the guys by before your shift ends."

"Awesome! Let me think...Zelda. I bet Zelda knows. She's working in the office today; you probably met her when you checked in."

"Big lady, big smile?"

"Bingo. Unlike me, she's a native, been here her whole life. If anybody knows where the library is, it's her."

"Okay then, I'm off. Bill the water to my room, please. Thanks for the punch."

Holly slid out of the bar chair, and Bradshaw waved her off.

"Don't worry about it. By the time you get back we'll have the red carpet rolled out from the parking lot to your room. It's not too often we get celebrities here at the Hibiscus. This is gonna be great!"

Chapter 12

McGirt was in the cabin of the *Lucky Dog* and had just finished prying open the box of grenades when he heard the Colombians yelling. He looked up and saw Manuel standing on top of the sub, up to his knees in water. *The sub is going down!* He threw open the cabin door just as Manuel dove toward the swim platform. He managed to grab hold and haul himself up but lost his weapon in the process. The cook, Juan, not knowing what to do, was standing in the cockpit and strafing the sub with machine-gun fire. Suddenly realizing the boat was still tethered to the sub, McGirt yelled, "Stop! *Detener*!"

Juan stopped firing and turned to face him as Manuel climbed over the transom into the cockpit.

"*Presura*! Untie the lines! Untie the lines! *Presura*!" McGirt urged them to hurry and pointed at the lines tied to the mid-ship and stern cleats before rushing forward to the bow line. Even before he reached the bow, he knew it was too late. The sub had slipped below the surface and was pulling the *Lucky Dog* over on its side. The lines were so tight there was no way they could be untied. He pulled out his buck knife and held it up for the Colombians to see. "Cut the lines! Cut the lines!" he screamed.

As he sawed on a line, he could hear the Colombians growing more frantic as the boat listed further to port. He braced himself against the bow-rail to keep from tumbling over the side and heard more gunfire just as the buck knife severed the line. It had little effect, however, because the other two lines were still pulling them over. When he looked up, he saw that Manuel had taken the machine gun from Juan and was firing at the line attached to the stern cleat. He half-crawled along the teetering boat back toward the cockpit, and a second later the stern line snapped free. The only line keeping them tethered to the sub was the one attached to the mid-ship cleat.

With one hand grasping a side rail, McGirt pointed at the mid-ship cleat. "Shoot the line! Shoot the line!"

Manuel turned and grabbed a side rail with one hand, and with the other he pointed the machine gun at the cleat and pulled the trigger. Unsurprisingly, accurate he was not. Bullets peppered the port gunnel around the cleat, and one ricocheted through the exterior wall and down through the cabin floor before he managed to zero in on the rope. Suddenly, the line snapped and the boat sprung back so sharply the men were nearly flung over the opposite side. With a few wobbles, the *Lucky Dog* finally settled upright on the sea's surface.

McGirt rose to his feet and peered into the water with his hands covering the sides of his aviator sunglasses. The current appeared to be pushing the boat away from the sub, which disappeared before his eyes. "Shit." He darted into the cabin and came out holding four hand grenades. One by one he pulled the pins and lobbed them into the water where he thought the sub might be. He watched the grenades sink below the surface, and the boat rocked as the first concussive blast surged upward. A big bubble surfaced near the boat, just as the next grenade detonated and the process repeated itself twice more.

"There's no way they can stay down, the sub's gotta be leaking like a sieve. They gotta come up... if they can." He smiled and turned to the Colombians who were talking rapidly in Spanish. "Diego's dead boys; we got no translator. You're gonna have to try and tell me what you're saying. *Qué pasa?*"

The cook elbowed the machinist, Manuel, who pointed at the ocean and then motioned his hand across his neck like a director does when he says, 'cut.' Then he shook his head. "*Patos muerto.*"

"*Patos muerto? Muerto, muerto...* that means dead, right?" McGirt sliced his hand across his own neck for confirmation that muerto meant dead, and the Colombians both smiled and nodded. "I agree, but what the fuck does 'patos' mean? *No comprendo 'patos.'*"

Manuel stepped into the cabin and returned with a pen and piece of paper as McGirt scoured the horizon for approaching vessels. Thankfully, there were none. Manuel scribbled on the paper and then held it up for him to see. It looked like a bird, but it had a flat, wide, bill. *Was it a duck?*

"Is this a, is this a duck?"

"*Sí, sí, patos.*" Manuel smiled and Juan flapped his arms like a birds wings.

McGirt laughed and smiled back at them. "For once you smelly bastards are right. You better believe they're dead ducks. No way can they keep that busted out viewport from letting in water. I don't care *what* they wedged in there, the pressure's gonna push it in and they'll be maritime history. If they haven't surfaced by now, it's 'cause they're on a one-way trip to sediment city."

Although the Colombians didn't understand a single word, they vigorously nodded and agreed. "*Sí, sí.*"

"Well, at least we got the missiles and most of the blow off. The only thing we can do now is vamoose, so let's hit the road, boys." He gave the international symbol for getting the hell out of dodge by sticking his thumb out from a closed fist and swinging it past his ear.

"*Vamos?*" asked Juan.

"*Sí, vamos.*"

McGirt climbed to the bridge and fired up the engines while the Colombians sat on opposite sides of the open cockpit area and lit up cigarettes. As he pulled a map from the console and got his bearings, unbeknownst to both he and his crew, the bilge started to slowly fill with fuel. The stray bullet that ricocheted off the cleat and through the cabin floor had nicked one of the fuel lines belowdecks, which was now spraying diesel into the engine compartment. Anxious to get going, he pushed the throttles forward and the *Lucky Dog* was soon on plane, cruising at a comfortable twenty-knot clip. Had anybody gone in the cabin, the smell of fuel would have been quickly detected and the problem fixed with a patch. But with the captain and crew on the outside, the only smell they experienced was the rush of ocean air swooshing by with an occasional whiff of the exhaust.

In the engine compartment, the increased throttle pressure in the fuel line had fuel spraying everywhere—including directly onto the turbocharger. In three minutes, the temperature of the turbo had climbed to nine-hundred degrees. In five minutes, it had reached eleven-hundred degrees. Less than a minute later, the temperature of the turbo reached twelve-hundred degrees; the temperature at which diesel fuel ignites. The fuel spraying from the fuel line ignited like a blowtorch and began melting the fiberglass underside of the cabin floor. Black smoke began filling the engine compartment and the fuel line began melting at the point where the bullet nicked the line. The size of the flame increased, and the direction of the flame began shifting toward the fuel-filled bilge as the hose disintegrated.

Up on the bridge, McGirt eyed the fuel gauge suspiciously. It showed that it was a little more than half full, but he could have sworn it had showed nearly three-quarters full when he started the engines only ten minutes earlier. He turned and looked down at the cockpit, but everything appeared normal. Then Juan turned to Manuel and yelled something, pointing at his nose. Manuel took a step toward the cabin door and disappeared from McGirt's view as he stuck his head inside. Suddenly he reappeared and started waving his hands, yelling at the top of his lungs. "*Los barcos en el fuego! Los barcos en el fuego!*"

McGirt didn't need Rosetta Stone lessons to know that "*fuego*" meant "fire," and when he pulled the throttles back, he could smell the smoke. Then he could see it. Black smoke started billowing out from a cabin window and an engine-access hatch in the cockpit floor near the cabin door. The boat was on fire. *Holy shit!*

He turned off the engines with a panicked feeling in his gut. As he hurried to the top rung of the ladder, he thought, *this is bad, this is really fucking—*

"KABOOM!"

The engine compartment exploded in a ball of fire. It blew out the windows and sent the cabin door hurtling into Manuel like a projectile, smashing his skull and killing him instantly. Juan was ablaze and lying on the deck in a corner of the cockpit. He staggered to his feet and flailed his arms around before falling over the side with a blood curdling scream. The tremendous force of the blast had blown the roof off the cabin and sent McGirt, up on the bridge, flying into the ocean. Seconds later, a dazed McGirt struggled to the surface and looked on in disbelief as a black mushroom cloud rose above what was left of the blazing boat.

Chapter 13

Suddenly, the submarine lurched and began descending again. It was impossible not to notice, but Tangles made sure everybody was aware anyways. "We're goin' down!" he cried.

I hurried over to the ballast control valve and shouted back an order. "Make sure that package stays wedged in the viewport!"

Tangles scurried up the ladder and pressed his hands against the sack of coke, trying to keep it in place. "It's leaking, Shag! I don't know how much longer it's gonna hold!"

I looked at a depth gauge next to the control valves. We were twenty feet down...and sinking. *Shit.* "Anybody have a clue how deep these things are designed to go?" I asked.

Like the lyrics to a Wet Willie song, Ferby started laughing through the pain.

"You kidding, Shagball? This thing isn't designed for depth; it's a frigging drug-running sub. I'm surprised it hasn't imploded yet. If you don't start blowing that ballast—" There was a muffled thud and the submarine shuddered from a shock-wave from some sort of explosion.

"What the hell was that?" cried Tangles.

Before anyone could answer, something struck the hull with a distinctive, "Clank."

Not good. I had an inkling of what was to come and grabbed hold of a hand rail, just as Ferby yelled, "Better brace your—"

A much louder explosion rocked the sub again, and Tangles fell from the ladder as the force of the blast knocked the ten-kilo sack of cocaine loose from the viewport. An avalanche of sea water cascaded down on top of Ferby and Tangles, who were sprawled on the floor of the sub. With panic setting in, I activated the valve to blow the ballast and get us back to the surface. The depth gauge read thirty feet as I turned and grabbed another sack of blow to try to plug the viewport. Water was rushing in so fast that I struggled to wedge it into place. After about ten or fifteen seconds, I managed to stem the flood, but I strained to hold the package against the immense water pressure. Two more muffled explosions rocked the sub, but nothing like the one that had us taking on water. I was standing on the second rung of the hatch ladder with my hands above my head and looked down at Tangles. "Please tell me we stopped going down. I don't know how long I can hold this."

Tangles scrambled around an equally drenched Ferby to the helm controls and spotted a depth gauge. "Twenty-nine feet, Shag. Hang tight; I can hear the valves working."

"I'm hangin' tighter than a hardpan lie at St. Andrews in July. Shit, my arms are getting rubbery."

"Twenty-eight feet, Shag, the valves are working! I think we're going up!"

Ten tense minutes later we broke the surface, and I was able to release the pressure I was exerting to keep the package wedged in the viewport. Exhausted, I let the coke fall to the floor and peered outside. I could only see in one direction, but there was nothing there. "I don't see anything," I commented, before collapsing on the floor next to Ferby in two inches of water.

"I'm gonna take a look around," announced Tangles. He scooched up the ladder and unlocked the hatch. With a mighty heave, he pushed it open and stuck his head out. Ferby and I looked on as he pirouetted on the ladder to get a three-hundred-and-sixty-degree view of our surroundings. "They're gone. Those fuckers took the *LD* and tried to kill—wait a second! There's smoke up ahead, lots of black smoke. Something's on fire."

I reached for a pair of binoculars that were hanging on a hook so I could take a look myself. Tangles climbed down to make room for me, and when I popped my head out of the hatch, Ferby started singing a classic Deep Purple song. "Smoke on the water…. fire in the sky. Smoke on the water…"

Then Tangles joined in, singing the guitar licks, "da, da,da…da, da,da-da… da, da, da…da-da."

I was trying to focus the binoculars on the smoke but couldn't concentrate with the karaoke duet going on below. "Can you guys shut up for a second?"

Thankfully, they obliged, albeit begrudgingly. "Just trying to keep my mind off my knee, Shag," answered Ferby. "Trust me when I say, it hurts."

"Alright," I conceded, having momentarily forgotten the severity of his injury. "Sing if you want to, but no duets. That's where I draw the line."

"Hey, I'm a professional," answered Tangles.

"You were an Elvis impersonator on a cruise ship, dude. Don't let it go to your little Pez-head."

Tangles started to protest my short joke, but I waved him off before zeroing in on the source of the smoke. "It looks like, I think it's... I think it's part of a boat. I think there's a boat on fire. Man, it's really burning. What a bummer."

"Wow, Shag, you're really sharp today," countered Ferby. "I think it's a boat. *Really?* You *think* it's a boat? Of *course* it's a damn boat. We're in the middle of the Caribbean for Christ's sake, what the hell else would it be?"

"Yeah, smartass," added Tangles. "Even my little Pez-head figured it was a boat. The question is...is it the *Lucky Dog?*"

"*What?*" I quickly trained the binoculars back on the smoke in the distance. I don't know why, maybe I was in denial, but I never considered that it might be the *Lucky Dog*. An instant later a bright flash left me blinded, and I ducked down as a monstrous explosion reverberated through the air.

"What the hell kind of explosion was *that?*" said Tangles.

"I hate to say it," answered Ferby. "But it sounded like the kind of explosion that might involve a crate of explosives and some missiles."

I popped my head back up and didn't need binoculars to see the massive black plume rising against the setting sun. Ferby had me thinking it could be the

Lucky Dog and I began to get nauseous. It was my *boat,* it was my *baby,* and I just spent a ton of dough pimping it out with all kinds of cool gear.

I took a last look around for signs of another vessel but saw none. With a sick feeling in the pit of my gut, I stepped off the ladder. "It can't… it just can't be the *Lucky Dog,* can it?"

Tangles shrugged and looked at Ferby, who drove home the horrible notion with the finesse of a serial DUI offender. "Hope you're right, Shag. Cause' if it was, it's now the *Kibbles' n' Bits.*"

Chapter 14

McGirt found a cooler floating nearby and clung to it for dear life as he watched the *Lucky Dog* burn. The stern and the entire bridge section of the boat were gone. He watched with morbid fascination as the fire worked its way through the rest of the cabin toward the bow. *Oh, shit, the bow!* The bow was where he had the Colombians stash the missiles and explosives. *Shit!* Realizing what was about to happen, he started kicking as hard as he could to get away from the boat.

After a few minutes, he grew tired and turned to look at the wreckage, maybe a quarter-mile away. Suddenly, a white-hot flash singed his face, and the explosion deafened him as his head snapped back against the cooler. He rolled with the blast and held his breath underwater for as long as he could before re-surfacing underneath the cooler. After a few deep breaths he stuck his hand up and out of the water to make sure there wasn't some sort of fire around him. Feeling nothing, he slowly lifted the cooler off his head and wiped his eyes. He blinked a few times and looked around in all directions, confused. Then it hit him. It was *gone*. There was nothing left but a giant plume of black smoke rising into the evening sky.

As he looked up, something was on fire and fluttered down into the water in front of him. He was close enough to hear it sizzle when it landed. Curious, he paddled over and lifted it up, only to discover that it was the remnants of a Kid Rock t-shirt. *Huh.*

An eerie silence replaced the sound of the burning wreckage and momentous explosion. Utterly alone, he nervously scanned the horizon. He was hoping that maybe a passing boat had seen the fireball or smoke from the wreckage and would come to his rescue. He started to convince himself that he could come up with some sort of plausible story, but then he noticed all the white stallion-stamped packages of coke floating around. It didn't matter at the moment though; there wasn't a single vessel in sight.

One of the packages floated within arm's length, and he had an idea. He grabbed the package and set it on the cooler, then pulled his buck knife out of the sheath attached to his belt and sliced it open. No way was he going to just tread water until a hungry shark came by and made a snack out of him. Not with a pile of cocaine in front of him he wasn't. He figured it was far better to overdose than to be featured on a future episode of *Shark Week*.

Deftly he dipped the end of the knife into the coke and extracted a heaping mound. Three mighty snorts later, it had disappeared up his nose, leaving him with a thick cocaine moustache that would rival any *Got Milk?* advertisement. Almost instantaneously his neurons went haywire, and his eyes bugged out. *Wait! What's that?* He squinted his eyes to focus on something in the distance. It sorta looked like...*was it land? An island, maybe?* Suddenly he felt a glimmer of hope, despite his wildly arrhythmic heartbeat. Fueled by nearly three grams of pure Colombian cocaine, he zeroed in on the spec of possible land and began kicking like a spoiled five year old on a Ho-Ho high.

Chapter 15

True to Bradshaw's word, Zelda in the front office knew exactly where the library was. After another white-knuckle drive on the wrong side of the road, Holly found herself in downtown Christiansted. Fortunately, it was only ten minutes from the resort. As she drove down the narrow streets, she was taken aback by the beautiful churches and classic architecture of the city. In between the narrow roads were lush, ivy-covered walkways where tourists ambled from one store or restaurant to the next. She finally spotted King Street and the Florence Williams Public Library and looped back around to try to find a parking spot. A van suddenly pulled out in front of her, and she quickly maneuvered the rental jeep into the spot.

Since the parking spot she found was near the waterfront, she decided to take a quick look at the harbor and was amazed at the number of sailboats moored there. She walked east along the boardwalk past several restaurants and noticed a small island in the harbor that looked like it had a hotel on it (which, as it turns out, it did). Then the unmistakable Fort Christiansvaern came into view, the one her Aunt Millie had described in her letter as looming over the harbor. By Millie's account, the fort looked nearly the same as it did in 1948, except for the fresh coat of yellow paint that adorned its massive walls. A short five minute stroll from the boardwalk, past jewelry shops and boutiques, and she was at the step of the Library. Like many government buildings on St. Croix, it too had received a recent major refurbishment and was beautiful in its own right.

Holly entered the stately building and walked up to the information desk. She was greeted by a handsome elderly woman who wore her hair back in a bow and had a pair of reader glasses perched on the tip of her dainty nose. Her name tag read "Ivy."

"How may I help you?" She asked, setting down the paper she had been reading.

"Um, this might sound a little weird, but I'm trying to find the name of a young man who died on Thanksgiving, and I only have his first name."

"On Thanksgiving? Well, that shouldn't be too hard, I can't imag—"

"I'm sorry; I forgot to mention it was Thanksgiving of 1948."

Ivy's voice went up an octave, and she cocked her head to the side. "Did you say *1948?*"

"Yes, 1948. His name was Joseph, and he died in an accident on the water… a diving accident."

"A diving accident… in 1948?"

"Yes."

"On Thanksgiving?"

"Yes, Thanksgiving morning. He was diving to get some lobster for dinner...scuba diving."

Ivy's voice went up another octave. "*Scuba diving? In 1948?* You sure you got your facts right young lady?

I may have only been eight years old at the time, but I don't remember any scuba diving. Maybe he was snorkeling; back then the lobsters were everywhere."

Holly was starting to get a little exasperated at the way Ivy repeated and questioned everything she said. Having just re-read Millie's letter on the plane ride down, she was up on the facts and stood her ground. "Yes, I'm sure about it. Scuba was invented by Jacques Cousteau a few years earlier, and Joseph's father was a charter-boat captain who managed to acquire some tanks and equipment. In fact, his boat was probably the only one at the time that offered scuba-diving trips. Maybe *that* will help figure out who Joseph was?"

"What was the name of the boat?"

"I-I don't know, but it was docked at the Salt River Marina."

"The Salt River Marina?"

Holly glanced at her watch, thinking that if Ivy kept on repeating everything she said, she would be there all night. "Yes, maybe there are some old newspaper articles or obituary notices I can look at from that time?"

"Maybe, follow me this way."

As Ivy led her up a set of stairs, she explained that some archived material was lost when hurricane Hugo ravaged the island in 1989. "We had some older stuff down on the lower level and it got flooded when part of the roof blew off. Since then we don't keep anything historical downstairs. Its hell on these old legs, but my doctor says it's good for the ticker, all this stair climbing."

Holly smiled and counted the steps to the top... a whopping eight. Ivy led her to a corner section of the library that had cabinets with roll-out drawers. Above the cabinets were bookshelves, filled to the gills, spanning all the way to the top of the twenty-foot ceiling. In place was a traditional, rolling, wooden ladder. Ivy pulled out a drawer and said, "This is as good a place as any to start, miss…"

"Oh, I'm sorry, I'm Holly," she answered, and shook her hand.

"No worries, you can see that the drawers are labeled chronologically. They contain newspaper articles and magazines, basically anything that isn't in book form. As you can see, all the books are on the shelves above. They're sorted by genre; you can use the ladder at your own risk."

Holly eyed the ladder suspiciously. A fear of heights made it unlikely she would do any climbing. "Thank you so much, Ivy. Hopefully I won't need to use the ladder."

"Well, make yourself at home. We close at five; I'll be down at the front desk if you have any other questions."

"Thanks again. I'll see you on the way out."

"Not if I see you first," she replied, with a wink and a laugh.

Holly chuckled and turned to the file in front of her as Ivy shuffled off. The front of the file was marked "1948," as were two other drawers below it. She pulled the contents out of the open drawer and placed it on a nearby table. It didn't take long to go through, because in 1948 there wasn't a daily paper on the island. There was only a monthly paper called "The Island Times" and some smaller publications put out by educational groups and US Virgin Islands institutions. The first drawer yielded nothing, as most of the contents were dated during the winter and spring. Surmising drawer two was summer and fall, she skipped to the bottom drawer. As she spread its contents out on the table, a faded yellow paper caught her eye. In a bottom corner of the front page of The Island Times, Christmas Edition, dated December 15, 1948, was a headline that read: *Tragedy Strikes Twice.* Her interest piqued, she sat on the edge of the table and began reading the article:

Tragedy has struck a Mt. Hope family for the second time in less than three weeks. Mr. & Mrs. Alfred Brodie and their daughter Elizabeth were killed December 14, when their plane crashed into the sea in shallow water near Buck Island, less than two miles from the coast of St. Croix. According to witnesses and a local fisherman who was first to arrive on the scene, the plane went down after encountering a sudden and violent thunderstorm. The pilot of the chartered plane was also killed.

The family had been visiting their oldest son, Joseph, now the only surviving family member. He remains comatose following a diving accident that occurred on Thanksgiving Day off St. Croix, near a popular snorkeling and fishing area locals have dubbed, "The Wall."

Holly stood up and clutched her heart with a gasp. Her hand started to tremble as she finished the article.

Initially believed to be dead, young Joseph was resuscitated at a local hospital but has yet to regain consciousness. The family was returning from St. Thomas where Joseph was taken for specialized treatment.

"Oh my God!" she blurted out.

An old man sitting at a table next to her said, "Excuse me?"

"I'm uh, I'm sorry," she stammered. "I have to go."

Hurriedly she put the rest of the material back in the drawer and walked quickly down the stairs clutching the old paper. Ivy started to say something as she approached the front desk, but Holly cut her off. "Please, Ivy, can you make a copy of this for me?"

"Sure, honey. You find what you were looking for?"

Holly handed her the paper but forgot to answer because her mind was reeling. *Joseph didn't die?* Suddenly, she realized Ivy was staring at her. "I'm sorry, what uh, what did you say?"

"I *said*, did you find what you were looking for?"

Holly took a deep breath before she answered, trying to steady her nerves.

"No, I sure didn't. It's... it's something else entirely."

Chapter 16

"Thanks, Ferby," I commented. "Thanks for painting that picture of my boat being blown to high heaven."

"Coulda been worse."

"How's that?"

"We coulda been on it."

"He's right, Shag," added Tangles. "We didn't get blown up, and we didn't sink either. Man, that was touch and go; I really thought we were going down. You might say we were headed down Fuck Street, but now we're on, uh, we're on...shit, what *are* we on?"

"How about, I'm-Slowly-Bleeding-to-Death Boulevard?" answered Ferby.

"Could be worse," I responded.

"How's that?"

"Coulda been me who got shot."

"Thanks, asshole."

"Don't mention it."

"Seriously, Shag," said Tangles. "What are we gonna do? We got power now, but what happens when the generator conks out?"

"It'll get hot, dark, and hard to breathe in here."

"That's what she said," cracked Ferby.

"Channeling your inner Layne again? Glad to see you didn't lose your sense of humor along with all your blood."

"I'm fuckin' serious here! What are we gonna do?" Repeated a frustrated Tangles. I put my hand out palm first, trying to calm him down. "Take a chill pill, my brother from a shorter mother. You're not the one with a bullet in his knee *or* an exploding boat on his mind. Shit, I can't believe—"

"What's that?" Tangles cut me off and put his hand up to his ear before scampering up the ladder. Then I heard it too, the distant whirring sound of a helicopter rotor.

"Gimme those binoculars!" Tangles reached down and I handed him the binoculars. "It's a helicopter! It's circling the smoke!"

I looked around for something to signal the helicopter with but didn't see anything handy. Quickly, I moved down the length of the sub to the makeshift kitchen and grabbed an apron and a large dish towel. In no time flat I was climbing up the ladder behind Tangles.

"Comin' up!" I announced. Tangles climbed out of the hatch on top of the sub where I joined him. Ahead in the distance the sun slipped below the horizon and the smoke from the explosion was disappearing into the night sky. I handed Tangles the towel, and he followed my lead as I started waving the apron over my head. "I don't see the chopper," I commented.

Tangles raised the binoculars to his eyes but kept waving the towel with his other hand. "It's, uh…there! There it is again! Shit, it's too fucking dark. We're never gonna get noticed."

"You're right. Go see if you can find a flare or something… check on Ferby too."

"You got it."

Tangles was down the ladder in a flash, and the next thing I heard was Ferby sounding none too pleased at Tangles' concern for his well-being. "How do you *think* I'm doing? I'm sittin' in a pool of blood in a stinky-ass sub with a bullet in my knee and a dead bean farmer for company. You wanna help? Find me a bottle of rum. *Shit.*"

I heard Tangles mutter something, and then a searchlight lit up the ocean in the distance. It circled a few times and then started heading in our general direction.

"Hurry up, Tangles!" I shouted. "They got a searchlight on! I think they're leaving!"

Tangles head popped out of the hatch a few moments later. "I couldn't find any flares, but I got a flashlight!"

He handed me the flashlight, and when I switched it on, the searchlight on the chopper went out. I couldn't believe how fast it got so dark. My momentary elation at Tangles finding a flashlight was squelched when I saw how dim the bulb was. It was about as bright as a Tim Burton film. No way was anybody going to spot it. Hell, I could barely see it myself and vented my frustration.

"Dammit! Nobody's gonna be able to see this piece of shit. If I only had my Surefire we'd be—wait!" I handed Tangles the lame-ass flashlight and checked the pockets of my cargo shorts. When we left Puerto Rico earlier that morning, I had been using it in the pre-dawn darkness. *Bingo!* I felt the familiar shape of my cherished Surefire flashlight and pulled it out of a side pocket by its lanyard. I slipped it over my head and clicked it on. " Now we're in business!"

Although my prized flashlight is only five-inches long and weighs less than five ounces, it puts out a stellar two-hundred lumens of light. I pointed the beam in the direction I last saw the chopper heading and held my breath as I waved it back and forth.

"I forgot how bright that thing is," commented Tangles. "They *gotta* see us!"

"C'mon," I urged. "C'mon you bastards, over here!"

Like magic, about a mile or so due east of us, the searchlight came on and the helicopter turned in our direction.

"Yes!" shouted Tangles.

I leaned over the open hatch and relayed the good news to Ferby as I shined my Surefire on him. "Hang in there, buddy. Help's on the way."

He looked up at me and waved a bottle around. "I'm good, Shag. The little guy hooked me up with some hooch. It's not half bad, really… whatever it is."

"Well, go easy on it, we're gonna have to get you up that ladder."

"I know. That's why I'm drinking."

"Shit! Where'd it go?" cried Tangles.

The sound of the rotors wasn't increasing anymore, and the searchlight was off when I turned to look. I waved the flashlight around and the searchlight came back on. Less than a minute later, the chopper hovered only fifty feet above us. The sound was so loud you couldn't hear yourself think, and the light from the searchlight was so bright it blinded us. We shielded our eyes until the searchlight swept over the length of the hull, and then I shined my little Surefire up at the chopper. *It was the Coastguard! Yes!*

Suddenly, the searchlight went off and the interior lights came on. Then a helmeted head appeared from the cargo door of the chopper. He had something in his hand and signaled he was going to toss it down. I gave him the okay sign with my thumb and index finger and let the Surefire dangle from my neck. Thankfully, I only had to take a half-step before the package dropped right into my waiting arms. Tangles yelled something as the searchlight came back on, and I held the package up to show them I had it. The chopper circled the sub once and then headed off into the darkness. As the sound of the rotors faded, Ferby yelled, "What the hell's going on up there?"

I pointed at the open hatch and said, "After you," to Tangles. I followed him down the ladder and clicked the Surefire back on, because there was little light inside the sub except for a few instrumentation panels. I spotted what appeared to be a light switch and flipped it on. The ceiling of the sub forward of the hatch lit up with the soft glow of LED lighting. It seemed the sub-builders had thought of just about everything.

"What did they drop?" asked Tangles, as I opened a waterproof bag containing a small electronic device.

"It looks like a walkie-talkie."

"I thought you said help was on the way," said Ferby. "Where the hell did they go?" I turned on the walkie-talkie and replied, "Let's find out." I climbed a couple of steps up the ladder toward the open hatch to improve reception and pressed the 'talk' button. "Hello, hello, Coastguard?"

I could still hear the sound of the rotors, and when I stuck my head out of the hatch there was the faint light of the chopper hovering in the distance.

"Yes, this is Coastguard Captain John Hill. Please identify yourself."

"My name's Kit Jansen."

"Are you the commander of the submarine?"

"Uh, no…I mean, *hell no!* This is the first time I've ever been on one and can't wait to get off. I was hoping you could help with that."

"Don't worry, a Coastguard cutter is on the way. We've been looking for you."

"Looking for— *what?* Wait a second, you don't understand, we had a…a freak, uh… run-in with this sub. It got disabled and they hijacked our boat when we tried to help. We have nothing to do with this."

My explanation was met with silence. *Shit.* "Hello? Hello, you there?"

"Yes, I'm still here. How many crew are on board?"

"Just me and two others, but one is seriously injured with a gunshot wound to the knee and needs medical attention."

"You should know it's not a good idea to discharge a firearm on a submarine, or any vessel for that matter, the results can be catastrophic."

"No shit, Sherlock. We were the ones getting shot at! They tried to sink us!"

"Listen wise-ass, save your lip service for the DEA. They have agents onboard the cutter who can't *wait* to talk to you."

"Fine, but like I said, I have a seriously injured man on board who needs help. Can you come back and airlift him off?"

"No can do, not until we secure the sub. Our go-fast boat's out of service so you'll have to wait for the cutter. We're heading back to it now. Don't lose the walkie-talkie; it has a GPS locator on it."

"How long until they get here?"

"They're about twenty-five miles to the south, so maybe an hour, unless…"

I waited a few seconds for him to finish, but when he didn't, I pressed 'talk' again.

"Unless? Unless *what?*"

"Unless they get hijacked, over and out."

I could hear somebody laughing in the background before the walkie-talkie went dead, and the sound of the helicopter faded into the night.

Chapter 17

Chanceaux "Lucky" VanderGrift settled into a leather club chair in the plush library of his estate overlooking Charlotte Amalie Harbor on the south shore of St. Thomas. With a brandy in one hand and a fine Cuban cigar in the other, the sixty-three-year-old senator relished the view and all the trappings his fortuitous rise to wealth and power provided. The fact he had done so despite growing up the son of an inter-racial couple in a time when prejudices ran particularly hot was testament to his burning ambition and greed. As darkness fell, a pair of massive cruise ships simultaneously switched on their exterior lights and lit the harbor up like it was the Fourth of July. Charlotte Amaile was the capitol of St. Thomas, and its bustling harbor and downtown area was the most frequented destination for cruise ships in all the Caribbean. The tourist industry was what made St. Thomas tick, and cruise ships full of passengers who left their money behind were its heart and soul. But for Lucky and his son Remy, the cruise ships also represented a means of efficiently and effectively distributing cocaine throughout the Caribbean.

For the senator, getting large quantities of cocaine on board a cruise ship in the harbor was easier than getting laid by a Kardashian. The reason was simple; corruption permeated all levels of government in the US Virgin Islands and the more authority you had, the more corrupt you were likely to be. Lucky was living proof of this fact, and by the beginning of his second term in office, he had all the key port officials, custom agents, and cruise-line security personnel on his payroll. They not only knew how to look the other way, they knew how to make others who weren't on the take (like pesky DEA agents) look the wrong way at the right time.

While getting coke onto cruise ships was a snap, obtaining it was a more difficult and riskier endeavor. That is until the Colombians began using submarines—the subs changed everything. Lucky blew a smoke-ring that drifted toward the open French doors leading to the veranda and smiled. He was expecting a call from Remy to tell him that their largest shipment ever was secured in the marina. It was so big that even after delivering a thousand kilos to Puerto Rico, it would still supply a year-and-a-half's worth of cruise-ship traffic. It was also large enough to necessitate a financing arrangement with the Cordero brothers. He had agreed to pay them twenty-million dollars in advance followed by monthly payments of ten million until his two-hundred-million-dollar shipment was paid in full. Although the Corderos had a perfect delivery record, it was a lot of money, and he wouldn't fully relax until the shipment was safely secured. He took a sip of brandy and stepped out to the veranda for a better view. The Tiara Bay Marina sat adjacent to the port in Charlotte Amalie

Harbor and turned out to be ideally situated for drug smuggling. It had been in his family since the early sixties, after his father purchased it with money he made from the sale of another marina on St. Croix.

His thoughts were disrupted when the cell phone in his pocket vibrated and started ringing. He looked at the display and saw it was Remy before he answered. "Remy, I was beginning to wonder why I hadn't heard from you, but then I remembered how much cargo you had to move. I take it everything's in order?"

"No, it's not. I tink someting's wrong." Despite attending the finest private schools on St. Thomas, Remy still had a tendency to revert to island-speak. He did it even more so when conversing with working class islanders. The senator cringed every time he heard Remy say 'tink' this or 'ting' that. It drove him mildly crazy, and he pointed it out to Remy for the umpteenth time. "What do you mean, you *tink* some*ting's* wrong? For once can you pronounce the 'h'? Please? Say it for me Remy, 'some-*thing's* wrong.' Got it? Some- THING...THING, THING! I spent a fortune sending you to university, the least you can do is to speak like it."

"Okay...Some*things* wrong. Feel better?"

A sinking feeling started to develop in Lucky's stomach, and he set his brandy on the balcony railing. "No, I don't. What is it?"

"I should have heard from our friends hours ago, but they failed to make contact."

"So what, they're probably just running late. You'll hear from them. They *always* come through."

"I don't know...there's chatter on the radio about some sort of explosion on the water, about forty miles southwest of here."

"An explosion?"

"Yeah, a big one. I heard a boat blew up."

Lucky looked across the harbor toward the southwest, but didn't see anything on the horizon. "What's that got to do with us? Our shipment's coming by sub. If it exploded, it'd be underwater and they'd sink—nobody would ever know."

"That's what I thought too, but a sport-fisher was headed to the scene, and before they got too close, a Coastguard chopper buzzed them and radioed to stay away."

"What are you saying?"

"Normally, if there's an accident on the water, the Coastguard encourages vessels to help look for survivors. This time they didn't— that's strange."

"Hmmm. Maybe they're trying to clean up an oil slick or something. Just because a boat blew up doesn't mean it had anything to do with us."

"Or maybe it does."

"Shit. We put twenty-million up front on this deal."

"I know, that's why I called."

"I still think you'll hear from them, but just in case, see what else you can find out about what happened and why the Coast Guard doesn't want anybody around. If you don't hear from them by morning, I'll make a call."

"Alright, let me see what I can find out."

"Good." Click.

As soon as he got off the phone, Remy spread word on the dock that he was paying for information about the explosion. Then he began calling contacts on neighboring islands.

Suddenly, esteemed Senator Chanceaux “Lucky” VanderGrift didn’t feel so lucky, despite his namesake. He looked down at the harbor lights again, only this time the view wasn’t so enchanting. Feeling out of sorts, he steadied himself against the balcony railing and downed the rest of his twenty-year-old brandy in one gulp. It usually gave him a warm, comfortable feeling, but not this night. Despite it being a balmy seventy-eight degrees, he felt cold and shivered with the fear that his luck might finally be running out.

Chapter 18

Sure enough, just like the smart-ass helicopter pilot had said, the Coast Guard cutter arrived about an hour later. From a quarter-mile away, they shined a blinding spotlight on the sub and quickly maneuvered alongside us. The deck of the cutter was lit-up like a Christmas tree, and it looked more like a battleship than anything else. What added to the war theme were all the guns pointed at us as Tangles and I scrambled on top of the sub. A bullhorn crackled to life from the deck of the looming ship. "Keep your hands in the air! Do not make any sudden movements! Do not attempt to re-enter the submarine!" Suddenly, a rope ladder dropped down within arm's reach, and the bullhorn started up again. "One at a time! Hang on to the ladder! We will pull you up! Keep your hands where we can see them!"

I pulled the ladder over and looked at Tangles. "You first."

"You don't have to tell me twice, bro. See you on deck."

As soon as he secured a good hold, the deckhands quickly hauled him up. When he was half-way to the top, I heard, "Shagball!" and turned toward the open hatch of the sub. "How you doing down there, Ferb?"

"The claustrophobia's back since it got dark! Get me outta here!"

The bullhorn came to life again and the voice behind it sounded agitated. "PAY ATTENTION! GRAB THE LADDER!"

"Don't you leave me down here, Shag! Don't leave me!" Pleaded Ferby.

I grabbed the ladder and turned to tell Ferby he was next, but before the words got out, I was yanked skyward. As soon as I hit the deck, my hands were zip-tied behind my back by a guy wearing a DEA T-shirt. There were a dozen guys in Coast Guard uniforms standing by with assault weapons. "What the hell are you doing that for?" I complained. "Where's Tangles?"

"Save it, pal. We ask the questions here, and we got plenty of 'em."

The DEA guy stood behind me with a hand on my shoulder and prodded me forward with a gun barrel in the middle of my back. Suddenly, I remembered Ferby. "Don't forget my buddy with the bullet in his knee. He's still down there."

"Don't worry, the bullet's the least of his problems."

"You're right, he's claustrophobic too."

"That's not what I meant, asshole. Just shut up till I say otherwise."

I was led inside the ship and down a corridor to a room with a table and a few chairs. The DEA guy pushed me into a chair, and said, "Stay put. I'll be back in a couple minutes." He locked the door behind him, and I sat there thinking about the situation. It occurred to me that, since we hadn't made it to St. Croix, Holly was probably concerned as to our whereabouts; at least I hoped she was. A few minutes later, the door re-opened and there was a second DEA agent accompanying the first, along with a guy from the Coastguard who had a lot of stripes on his uniform. He was about six-foot-six and bald with dark circles under his eyes, resembling that actor and senator from Tennessee, Fred Thompson. Before anybody said anything, I inquired about Ferby. "How's Ferby doing?"

Mr. Coastguard, answered, "He the big black guy with the gunshot wound to the knee?"

"Yeah."

"We'll know more when he wakes up. We had to put him under to get him off the sub. He's in the infirmary; there's a doctor taking care of him."

Before I could say anything, the door opened and a young kid stuck his head in.

"Commander?"

The Coast Guard guy with all the stripes answered, "Yes, what is it?"

"We counted a hundred and forty-five packages on the sub with the same white stallion logo as the one's we plucked out of the water where that boat blew up. They're testing it in the lab now, but if it's the same as what we found in the water, its ninety-nine-point-nine-percent pure."

The commander whistled, and asked, "How much do they weigh?"

"Ten kilos each, sir. Comes out to over thirty-two-hundred pounds total, not including what's in the water."

"Anything else?"

"Yes, sir. We also found an unidentified male on board who looks to be of South American descent, dead from a single gunshot wound to the chest. A forty-five caliber automatic missing one bullet from the magazine, and a couple pounds of high-grade marijuana were recovered as well."

"Thank you. That'll be all." The Commander nodded, and the young man shut the door. All three men stared at me, and the second DEA guy put in his two cents. "You got balls, buddy. I'll give you that."

"What the—what the hell are you talking about?" I stammered.

"Double-crossing the Cordero brothers, that's what I'm talking about. You got balls to do that. Not much brains, but balls galore."

"The *Cordero brothers?* Who the hell are *they?* I didn't double-cross anybody. I had my boat hijacked. We didn't have anything to do with this, we were just—"

"In the wrong place at the wrong time?" DEA guy number one interrupted.

"Yeah, pretty much. It was a freak thing, really. We were trolling with an electric down-rigger along this incredible weed line, when—" The Commander stuck his hand out palm first in front of my face so I would stop talking, which I did. Then he turned to the DEA agents. "I can tell this is gonna take a while so I'm going back to the bridge. I have a couple guys posted outside the door, let them know if you need anything."

As he stepped to the door, I said, "I could sure use something to drink. Wouldn't mind a bite to eat either; it's been a long day. Oh, and can I use your phone? I need to let my girlfriend know what's going on. She's probably worried sick. We were supposed to be in St. Croix by dark."

The Commander turned and gave me a look like I ran over his dog. Then he said, "He's all yours," to the DEA guys and left.

"So, guys," I continued. "Like I was saying, we were—"

"Shut up," said DEA guy number two. "You're not saying anything unless we say something first. We ask the questions, and you answer them. If we like what we hear, you might get something to eat and drink. What's your name?"

"Connor Jansen, but everybody calls me Kit, or Shagball. That's my show name. Maybe you've heard of it? It's called *Fishing on the Edge with Shagball and Tangles.*" The DEA agents looked at each other and shook their heads no in unison.

"Yeah, I know. We've got some screwy show times; they're always changing. It's a real problem for our viewership."

"It's a real problem for you too, Mr. Jansen, because we're not sure who the hell you are and everything coming out of your mouth sounds like bullshit. All we know is there's enough cocaine in that sub to raise Rick James from the dead, not to mention what was on the boat that blew up. Maybe we should start there?"

At the mention of the boat, I got a sick feeling in my stomach. I knew it had to be the *Lucky Dog* but couldn't come to face it. Evidently, the expression on my face was telling.

"So… you *do* know how much was on the boat?" DEA agent number one smiled at number two. I let out a deep breath before answering.

"Yeah, pretty much. I'm afraid it was my boat."

"Now we're getting somewhere," said agent number two. "Why don't you tell us what happened… from the beginning. You want any chance of leniency with the court, you better come clean right now. If the information you provide helps us nail the Cordero brothers, you might get out of jail by the time your Medicare kicks in."

"Jail my ass!"

"Yes, that's the idea. You want to try to limit how much time you do? Then cooperate. That's my advice." He pulled a small digital recording device out of his pocket and set it on the table.

"How do you know the sub belongs to the Cordero brothers?"

"By the white stallion emblem on the packages. It's their trademark."

"Well, if you two Dudley Do-Rights would just let me tell you what really happened, you'll realize I—we—are the victims here! They stole our boat and tried to kill us!"

"Who did?"

"The guys in the sub."

"Correct me if I'm wrong, Mr. Jansen, assuming that's your real name, but you *are* the guys in the sub. The guys in the boat weren't so lucky. Like I said, looks like a classic double-cross gone wrong."

I could only take so much and snapped. "I don't give a rat's ass *what* it looks like, Sparky! I was there and you weren't!"

Agent two didn't like my tone and started rising from the table. "You call me Sparky, smart-ass?"

"No, just Sparky."

"That's it!" The agent lunged forward like he was going to smack me, but agent number one pulled him back and tried to calm him down.

"Let it go, man. He's just playing head games. Let him talk, then we'll see who the real smart-ass is."

Agent two glared at me as agent one clicked on the recording device and nodded.

"Okay. You wanna talk? *Talk.*"

Amazingly, the agents let me talk uninterrupted for the next fifteen minutes, despite sharing numerous skeptical glances that had me wondering whether they were graduates of the Joe Biden School of Mocking Facial Expressions. I concluded with, "That's it, that's exactly what happened."

Agent one led the interrogation. "You're saying there were approximately six-hundred packages of cocaine on the sub? Are you sure?"

"Very, and don't forget about the explosives and missiles."

"What about the dead guy?"

"What about him? Like I said, he forced us at gunpoint to off-load the coke until we managed to overpower him."

"Overpower him my ass," agent two responded. "There's a hole the size of Texas in his heart."

"No shit, but I prefer that song title over 'Shagball and Company got Shot-Up and Sunkity'."

"*What?*"

"Forget it."

"Do you have a single shred of evidence to support your story?"

"No, everything I had was on the boat."

"You mentioned you fueled up in Puerto Rico before leaving, you don't have a receipt? Nothing at all?"

"Sure I have a receipt, but it's in my wallet, which was on the…wait a second! My wallet! I think my wallet's still in my pocket!" I stood up with my hands still zip-tied behind me. "Check my front left pocket; I think it's in there."

Agent one looked at agent two. "You didn't frisk him?"

"I thought *you* did."

"Shit, pat him down, quick."

Agent two turned my pockets inside out, and the only thing I was carrying was my new wallet. Holly got it for me for my birthday, and it was made from incredibly fine Italian leather. It was softer than a careless whisper, smoother than Al Jarreau, and lighter than Clay Aiken's loafers. It wouldn't be the first time I thought I wasn't carrying it, it was that unobtrusive.

Agent one opened it up on the table and spilled out my driver's license and the few credit cards I carried. He pulled out ten, crisp, hundred-dollar bills from the cash compartment along with the fuel receipt, and I cringed. The cash made me think about the eight grand I had in a Rubbermaid container on the *Lucky Dog*. From another compartment, he pulled out my Florida fishing license and a laminated card with nothing but a hologram and a telephone number printed on it. I had been given it nearly six months earlier, as a thank you present of sorts, after Tangles, Holly, and I helped a supposed FBI agent in a shootout with some mobsters. He later claimed *not* to be with the FBI but with another US agency he refused to identify. Whoever he was, he told me that if I called the number on the card and gave the password, help would be forthcoming. It was an option I had dismissed earlier, thinking my wallet was on the boat. *Not anymore.* The way things were going, it was looking like Plan A.

Agent one picked up the license. "So, we got a Florida License in the name of Connor Jansen. Where the hell is Lantana, Mr. Jansen?"

"In between Boynton Beach and West Palm, just a little ways south of Lake Worth."

"Well, guess what. You're a lot of ways south now, in more ways than one." He looked at agent two. "Go see if the midget's story matches up. Not that it means anything, what with all the time they had to get it straight. You might as well check on the guy who got shot, too."

As soon as agent two left the room, agent one turned back to me. "You really expect us to believe you hooked a submarine while you were fishing? *Really?* That's the best you could come up with?"

"No, I could probably come up with something more believable, but I thought you wanted the truth. My bad."

He slammed his fist on the table. "Cut the bullshit!"

"I'm not bullshitting! Wait...the wire!"

"What wire? What are you talking about?"

"The wire from the downrigger got wrapped around the sub's prop, that's what stopped it. You want proof? Go check for yourself."

He stood up and opened the door, then pointed at me as he pulled out a walkie-talkie. "Don't try anything stupid, Jansen." He closed the door, and I watched through the window as he talked into his walkie-talkie and nodded a few times. The Coast Guard Commander came walking up with a plastic bag in his hand, said something, then pointed at me and entered the room. Agent one nodded and disappeared from view.

"What's your girlfriend's name?" asked the commander.

"Holly, Holly Lutes, why? Did you talk to her?"

"No, I sure didn't, but our St. Croix office did. She called in to report a thirty-eight foot Viking, named the *Lucky Dog*, was due in from Puerto Rico before dark but never made it."

I looked at my watch, and it was after nine o'clock. *Shit.* "I hope they told her I'm alright."

"They didn't tell her anything, 'cause they don't know anything. The *Lucky Dog* was yours?"

"*Was?*"

"Yes, was. Unless you don't recognize *this.*"

He pulled a two-foot-long white piece of fiberglass out of the bag and handed it to me. The letters *uck* were written across it in gold with black trim. It was from the stern of the *Lucky Dog*; no doubt about it. As I turned it over in my hands, I felt sick. "I can't believe she's gone. I've never lost a boat before. Did you, did you find anything else?"

"Very little besides the cocaine; this was the biggest piece of boat we found before it got too dark."

"Shit, I just spent a small fortune on cameras and gear, too."

"*Cameras?* What for?"

"For the show."

"What show?"

"My fishing show. I told the Do-right Twins, but they don't believe me. We were filming our way to St. Croix when we foul hooked the sub on our down line. The downrigger wire stripped off and got tangled in the sub's prop. When we stopped to help, they pulled guns and—"

"Hold on a second, *what's the name of your fishing show?*"

"Fishing on the Edge...with Shagball and—"

"Tangles? Are you shittin' me? Wait a second.... Here...." He grabbed my Ray-Bans off the table and positioned them on my face, then placed my visor on my head.

"Goddamn, it *does* look like you! Say something for me."

I couldn't believe it, but I needed all the help I could get, so I took a deep breath, and muttered, "They're thick."

The Commander leaned forward, uncertain. "What's that? They're what?"

"Just remember, you asked for it."

"Asked for what?"

I leaned forward in my chair so our faces were less than two feet apart, and let go with a powerful, "THEY'RE THICK!" Followed by a vein-popping, ear-splitting, "THEY'RE THHHHHHHHHHHHHHIIIIIIIIIIIIIIIIII—"

The Commander reached over and clamped one of his large, leathery, hands over my mouth, as the guards rushed in. With his other hand, the commander signaled for them to stop. "It's okay men. I got this." Then he stared me down with a pair of pissed off eyes and quietly said, "Alright, I believe it's you. When I take my hand off your mouth, they'll be no more screaming, understood?"

I nodded and he removed his giant paw from my mouth. Instinctively, I wiped my face on the shoulder area of my shirt and did a dry spit. The Commander instructed the guards to go back to their posts, and when the door shut, I said, "Sorry about that, but there's just no other way to do it properly, and I needed to be convincing."

"Job well done, but I'll tell you what else is thick—the large pile of shit you're in. How in hell did you ever get mixed up with the Cordero brothers? The fishing shows not doing so well?"

"I'm *not* mixed up with the Cordero brothers! I told you it was just a chance encounter! They stole my boat and tried to kill us!"

"Alright, calm down now. I have to confess you're not who we expected to find on that sub, but facts are facts. Unless you're in a courtroom, and unfortunately you're not, least not yet."

I looked at the contents of my wallet spread out on the table and eyed the card with the hologram and phone number on it. "I could clear this up with one phone call…if you'd let me."

"As much as I'd like to, those DEA boys would have a fit if I let you use my phone."

I sensed a way to get through to him and gave it a shot. "*Really?* Huh. That surprises me. You don't strike me as the kind of commander who gives a shit *what* the DEA thinks. Right now they're checking out the wire wrapped around the sub's prop, the one that came from my downrigger, just like I've been saying all along. Besides, what kind of drug smuggler has his girlfriend call the Coast Guard when he's a few hours late? I'll tell you—none of 'em."

The Commander rubbed his chin and raised an eyebrow. "You're *completely* innocent here?"

"Completely. I swear, and same for Tangles and Ferby."

He reached up and pulled my sunglasses off my face, so they dangled down my chest on their straps. "I'm two years from retirement, son. You fuck it up for me, and I swear I will hunt you down and skin you like Custard. Are we clear on that?"

I tried to swallow but something got stuck and I coughed. The Commander knew how to intimidate, no doubt about it. "Yes, yes, sir. We're, uh, we're on the same page."

"The one that has me sitting on the front porch of my cabin in Montana? You know, with a scotch in one hand, a fly-rod in the other, and my beautiful wife Martha by my side? Look me in the eye and tell me."

I looked square in his menacing eyes. "That's the one, sir. Two minutes on the phone, that's all I ask. Trust me."

He took a step back and squinted at me. "There's only three things I trust: my knots, my nuts, and my guts."

"Wow, you trust your nuts?"

"Not since a five-day furlough in Hanoi back in '72, but that's beside the point."

He stood up, opened the door, and said a few words to the guards. They drew their weapons and entered the room. The Commander pulled a military-style knife out of his pocket and flicked the blade out as he stepped behind me. "Just so you know," he said. "You try anything fancy, and my guys will make you holier than Mother Theresa." He sliced off the restraints, and as I rubbed my wrists, I thanked him for the warning. He unclipped a phone from his belt, pressed a button, and handed it to me. Then he stepped in front of the guards with a wary eye and a warning. "Make it quick."

I picked the card off the table and dialed the number on it. After two rings an automated voice stated, "Identify yourself."

"Shagball."

"Password?"

"Help…with a capital H, as in hurry."

"Please remain on the line."

I looked up just as the two DEA agents barged back into the room. The one in charge was wild-eyed. "Commander! What in the *hell* is going on here!?" The agent went straight for the phone in my hand and managed to grab my wrist. The Commander yelled, "Hold on there!" as he swung a meaty arm in-between us. Unfortunately, he caught me in the elbow, and the phone flew out of my hand and clattered on the floor. Agent two quickly scooped it up and put it to his ear. "The connection's lost; it's just a dial tone," he announced.

"You're lucky that phone's not broken or somebody else might be too," warned the commander. "Now everybody relax for a second…at ease!" He pointed at me and told me to take a seat. I sat down, worried that my call for help would go unheeded because I didn't get a chance to plead my case. The lead DEA agent turned and faced the bristling Commander. "With all due respect, sir, you may have just blown our entire case."

"How's that? The way I see it, you guys are barking up the wrong tree." He pointed at me and explained why. "I watch this guy on TV every Sunday morning at o-five-hundred on ESPN 8...or maybe it's 9. In case you didn't know, he happens to have a fishing show. I'm having a hard time believing he's some kind of drug-smuggling mastermind, especially after talking to him."

"Hey, wait a sec—" They both turned and said, "Shut up," to me at the same time.

"We know about his so-called fishing show," said the DEA agent. "But that doesn't mean spit. If anything, it helps explain it. Remember John DeLorean? He owned a friggin' car company for crying out loud, but found selling coke was easier and more profitable...*much* more profitable. It's called greed; it's what keeps us so busy."

"As I recall, he was deemed entrapped by overly zealous prosecutors and acquitted in a court of law," responded the commander.

"That's...irrelevant." The agent had a cell phone clipped to his belt, and it started ringing. Without looking, he reached down and shut it off.

"The hell it is. You guys are so hot to nab the Cordero brothers, you're ignoring evidence that suggests Mr. Jansen is telling the truth."

"Such as?"

"Such as, how did we find the sub in the first place?"

"We, uh, found it when we were searching the area where the explosion occurred."

"That's right, because someone on the sub flagged down our chopper with a flashlight." He noticed my surefire flashlight on the table, picked it up, and looked at me. "I take it that was you?"

"Me and my Surefire—all two-hundred lumens of it. It kicks ass."

The Commander nodded and faced the DEA agent again. "Now, I don't know what they teach you in DEA camp, but it seems to me signaling the Coast Guard when you have a sub full of cocaine would be counterproductive to one's smuggling operation. Not to mention the fact they had plenty of time to dump what was on board by the time our cutter arrived."

"*Or* maybe they pulled a double-cross that went wrong and want us to think exactly that, when in fact they were just worried about sinking."

"What?"

The agent's phone rang a second time, and he shut it off again without looking. "You heard me. They had plenty of time to concoct a story; that's probably why the midget's version matches up so nicely…*too* nicely, if you know what I mean."

"What about his girlfriend calling to report their boat missing? You have that happen a lot during a drug deal?"

"Could be a red herring."

Agent two's phone started ringing, and he glanced at the display before stepping toward the door and answering. I saw a chance to plead my case and took it. "See what I mean, Commander? There's no reasoning with these guys. They wouldn't know a red herring from a ball bearing. I was a Good Samaritan who got hijacked and had his boat blown to kingdom come. Why is that so hard to believe?"

Agent number two clicked his phone shut and turned around with a frantic look on his face, just as the lead agent's phone started ringing again. "It's him. Its… it's the boss. He told me that if you don't answer your phone, we're being permanently re-assigned to the Amazon Basin."

Agent one frowned and said, "Shit," as he unclipped his phone and flipped it open. "Hello? Yes, yes, sir… yes, I'm sorry…I was conducting an—" The agent had his back to me but turned and gave me a funny look. "Yes, his names Jansen. How did—sorry, sir…of course…uh-huh….yes, right, one has a gunshot wound, uh-huh, uh-huh… *what?* Can you repeat that again? You want me to *what?* But we found—! But they were—! But he was—! But I haven't—! No, no, sir. I haven't had my malaria shots. That won't be necessary, sir—No, no I'm not questioning—whatever you say, sir…understood. Yes, I understand perfectly… uh-huh, uh-huh, okay…they'll be here *when?*" The agent looked at his watch and shook his head just as the Coast Guard Commander's phone started ringing. The Commander looked at it and stepped in to the hall to talk. Like the DEA agent, he turned and stared at me through the glass window while nodding his head in conversation with the other party. The DEA agent finally said, "Yes, sir, consider it done, sir…no, sir. We won't let you down…thank you, sir, thank—" He pulled the phone away from his ear, looked at it, looked at me, and flipped it shut. After he clipped it onto his belt, he sat on the table and crossed his arms with a shrug. "Mr. Jansen? That is your name, right?"

"Actually, it's Connor, but, like I said, everybody calls me Kit or Shag—"

"Cut the smart-ass routine! Who are you with?"

"What?"

"You know exactly what I mean! Why didn't you tell me you had clearance? What are you trying to prove? I mean, besides making me look like a moron and getting me shipped off to the jungle."

"*Clearance?* What the hell are you talking about *clearance?* The only clearance I have is about eighteen feet under the Boynton Inlet Bridge…at mean high tide, of course."

"Oh, please, give up the 'Oh, I'm just a guy with a fishing show routine.' It's getting' really—"

"Excuse me," bellowed the commander as he stepped back in the room. "But I was just given explicit instructions to accommodate Mr. Jansen and company in any way possible while on board, which, I understand, won't be for much longer."

"*Really?* That's great! I think… right?" I didn't know what to expect when I called the number on the card, but it wasn't this.

"Please, don't act so surprised, Mr. Jansen," said the exasperated DEA agent. "I just received direct orders to escort you're injured friend by chopper to St. Thomas, where he'll be transferred to a waiting jet and flown to Miami for medical treatment. There's another Coast Guard chopper on its way here to take you and the midget to St. Croix…assuming that's still where you want to go."

"His name's Tangles, and he's not a midget. I'd remember that unless you're practiced in the art of cage fighting rabid baboons."

The Commander chuckled, and added, "You best take that to heart. I talked to him earlier. He's got more spunk than a two-dick dog in a bitch-humping contest."

"Fine, I'll remember that. But I don't appreciate being kept in the dark when other agencies are involved...especially an operation this size. So who are you with, Jansen? Homeland Security?"

"What?"

"That's it, isn't it, Commander? Homeland Security is in charge of the Coast Guard now; it makes sense. You were in on this the whole time. So why play dumb? We're all on the same team, right?"

The Commander went chest-to-face with the DEA agent, towering over him. "Enough with the questions. If you were supposed to know any more than you do, you would. The chopper will be ready to leave in five minutes. My medical staff will help you get the patient on board, so move it."

The DEA agent back-pedaled a step and glanced over at agent number two, who was taking it all in. "You heard the commander, let's go." Both agents shook the commander's hand before leaving, and he dismissed the guards before turning to face me. "I gotta hand it to you, son. You sure had *me* fooled. So...if you don't mind me asking, who *are* you with? I'm pretty damn sure it's not Homeland Security."

I didn't know what to say, I wasn't *with* anybody. If anything, I was *without*— without a boat. But the DEA agent and Commander seemed convinced otherwise, so I played along. "I'm, uh, I'm sorry, sir, but I'm not at liberty to discuss that." I stood from my chair, feeling much better about the situation. "But I would like to discuss accommodations."

He squinted and cocked his head to the side. "*Accommodations?*"

"Yes… sir, you said you were under explicit instructions to accommodate me and my crew in any way possible, right?"

"That's, uh, that's right, what do you have in mind?"

"Well, I'd like to see Ferby before he gets sent to Miami. I'm sure Tangles would too."

"Done, follow me."

As we headed down the hall, he radioed to have someone bring Tangles up to the flight deck. "Anything else?" He asked.

"Yes, please get word to my girlfriend that we're okay and that we're on our way to St. Croix." He barked out more orders to the radio transmitter attached to his shoulder and led me up some stairs. "Is that it?" he asked, glancing back.

"It's been a long day, Commander. We could all use something to eat and drink."

"No problem. I'll have some sandwiches and sodas brought up."

"Great, I'll have my soda with Stoli and a splash of cranberry. Tangles likes his with—"

The Commander stopped in his tracks, and I bumped into him. He turned and looked down at me, none too amused. "I happen to like your show, but don't push it. Even if you *are* some kinda big-shot spook working for God-knows-who. This is the Coast Guard cutter, *Justice*, not a cruise ship."

"So?"

He looked at me and raised an eyebrow. "So, how 'bout a long-neck Bud and a sampling of tequila?"

"Commander?" I smiled. "You'd be doing your country a great service."

Chapter 19

As soon as we lifted off from the deck of the Coast Guard cutter, the pilot informed me that he was patching through a call on a secure line.

"The call is for your ears only," he warned, "so if you need something, you need to signal me…got it?"

"Yeah, sure."

I had no idea who was calling and shrugged as I glanced at Tangles in one of the rear seats. He was holding an ice-pak against the side of his head where he got pistol-whipped by McGirt. Before we got on the helicopter the commander had taken us by the infirmary where they also cleaned and bandaged the bite wound on my shoulder.

"Okay...I'm patching it through now," announced the pilot.

"Patch away, flyboy." I smiled at him and he shook his head after pressing a button on the side of his headset. I heard a click and then a strangely familiar voice that I couldn't quite pinpoint.

"Mr. Jansen? Can you hear me?"

"Yes, yes, I can, but…what's going on? You sound like somebody I know but I can't put—"

"Forget about who I sound like, Mr. Jansen. My voice has been digitally altered for security purposes, just concentrate on what I am about to tell you."

"OOO…kay, I guess…shoot."

"Somehow, for the second time in less than six months, you have managed to embroil yourself in a matter of national security. This time, besides arms trafficking, it involves international drug smuggling on a scale and manner US authorities have never encountered before."

"Me neither. There was more blow on that sub than a Pam Anderson home video, if you know what I mean."

"I…yes, I understand there was an extremely large quantity of cocaine onboard, most of which is now floating in the Caribbean…thanks to you."

"Thanks to *me?* How 'bout thanks to those assholes that blew up my boat? Like an idiot, I tried to help 'em when—"

"Please, we don't have much time, Mr. Jansen. I heard what happened—and it was a compliment. It was pure luck the Coast Guard stumbled across the sub before it submerged below the weed line. If you didn't get tangled up with them, they would have been gone."

"Like my boat."

"Yes, like your boat. Assuming you and your friends don't want to suffer the same fate, it's imperative you stay silent about what happened today. Based on your account, and the storage capacity of the sub, we believe there was upward of seven tons of pure Colombian cocaine on board, with an estimated street value of over two-hundred-and-fifty-million dollars."

I let out a low whistle in deference to the amount and gazed at the lights in the distance that were rapidly approaching.

"That's right, Mr. Jansen. That's a lot of money, even for the Cordero brothers, and you can bet they'll be doing everything in their power to find out what happened to their precious cargo. If you get implicated in any way, well, consider yourself a dead man trolling."

"That's pretty funny, but I can't do much trolling without a BOAT!" I yelled so loudly the pilot shot me a look. "In fact, my fishing show just got blown to hell too! Do you have any idea how much money I just spent on high-def cameras? Plus, I had nearly eight grand in a tupper—"

"Mr. Jansen! Listen to me! Numerous federal agencies have unsuccessfully tried to bring down the Cordero brothers for years. Now, thanks to a chance encounter with you, they have been dealt a major setback. The sub you snared today is the first fully submersible and most technologically advanced sub ever captured by US authorities. Based on the general direction it was heading, we think somewhere offshore of St. Thomas, or possibly Puerto Rico, was a likely transfer point for the shipment. It's extremely important that whoever's waiting for the delivery doesn't know what happened. When the sub fails to show up, there'll be a concerted effort to find out why, and we've got satellites and surveillance equipment monitoring every mode of communication in the region. Hopefully, somebody will make a call that leads us to the local players. So you see, it's imperative you claim no knowledge of a cocaine-laden submarine. If you can do that, it will greatly increase your odds of survival *and* of getting a new boat, courtesy of Uncle Sam."

"*That's* what I'm talking about! A new boat? Now we're getting somewhere."

"Naturally, it depends on how well you and Mr. Dupree can stick to the story and avoid any further involvement in the matter."

"What story?"

"You had an engine fire and abandoned ship just before it blew up. The Coast Guard rescued you, and if anybody asks, you don't know anything about anything else."

"We can do that, no problem. Mr. Dupree is world class at not knowing shit. What kind of, uh, what kind of replacement boat are we talking about?"

"I strongly suggest catching the next flight home, just to be safe. Without your boat, there's really no compelling reason to stay in St. Croix... *is there?*" When no reply followed, the caller asked, "Mr. Jansen?"

"Huh? Oh, sorry, I was just thinking about new boats. Um, yeah, no, there's really no reason to stay, except... I, uh, promised my girlfriend I'd help her find some relatives she might have down here. So, what kind of budget would I be working with?"

"What budget?"

"You know, for my new boat."

"Mr. Jansen? We're a long ways from—"

"Since you're buying me a new boat, please, call me Kit, or Shagball if you want. By the way, what did you say your name was? You kinda sound like Dan Tanna. Come to think of it, that's *exactly* who you sound like...Dan the man Tanna. Son-of-a-bitch."

"Congratulations, you can recall the voice of a milk-drinking, fly-by-night, detective-show star. Show me you can remember how to keep your mouth shut and maybe, *just maybe*, you'll end up with a new boat."

"Don't worry, for a new boat I'll keep my mouth shut tighter than Tom Cruise's closet door."

The caller tried to stifle a laugh but failed miserably. "Good, that's good. Try to wrap up this personal business of your girlfriend's as quickly as possible. The longer you're in the islands, the more likely it is something could happen that might put you behind the eight-ball. The Cordero's have an extensive network, and they don't take kindly to people who interfere in their business. You'd be doing yourself and your friends a big favor by remembering that." Click.

I signaled to the pilot that the conversation was over, and he punched in another button that re-connected radio contact between me and him and Tangles.

Less than a minute later, the pilot brought the chopper to a hover and slowly started setting us down. "Okay, this is it," he announced. I could see a cluster of buildings on a beach and a large tiki-style restaurant/bar with people milling about.

"You're landing right here on the beach?" I looked at him questioningly from the co-pilot's seat.

"Unless you feel like jumping in the water, yeah, this is where you get off. Let's make this quick before the gawkers get too close. Don't forget to keep your head down."

For some reason, I thought we would be landing at a nearby airport and then driven to the resort. I hadn't expected to be dropped off literally *at* the resort, but there we were. Like the pilot predicted, a group of people had left the bar and were walking our way across the beach. As soon as the chopper runners hit the sand, I said, "Thanks for the lift," and flicked my radio headset off.

I ducked as I stepped onto the sand, and Tangles instinctively did the same. The chopper immediately lifted off and headed back out to sea. As the sound of the rotors faded, I started laughing.

"What are you laughing at?" asked Tangles.

"You— ducking."

"Fuck you, man. The pilot said 'duck,' so I ducked. I never been on a helicopter before, what the hell do *I* know?"

"He was talking to me… you're four-foot-two, dude. I'm surprised you even knew how." The group of people who left the bar to watch our unusual arrival was walking toward us, silhouetted against the background light.

"Well, excuse me for obeying the pilot's instruction. He didn't say 'you only gotta duck if you're six feet tall'…asshole."

"I'm six-two."

"Yeah, six-feet-two inches of *asshole*."

"*Tangles?*" A familiar voice came from the approaching group. "*Kit?* Is that you?

Holly separated from the group and hurried across the last twenty feet of beach into my waiting arms. We kissed, and I hugged her tightly while she bombarded us with questions.

"What happened? I've been worried sick about you. Where's Ferby? Why wouldn't the Coast Guard tell me anything? Where's the boat?"

"The boats gone, baby. Ferby's gonna be alright, but the boats gone."

She pulled away and looked up at me in disbelief.

"*Gone?* What do you mean, *gone?* What happened to—"

"We have a couple rooms, right?"

"Sure, I checked us in earlier. Kit, what—"

"Let's go inside, and I'll fill you in."

Most of the group that came out of the bar was headed back, but a few people were still standing nearby. I decided it would be prudent to debrief Holly in private. Tangles and I followed her across a small stretch of moonlit beach to the nearest building.

"This is it. We have these two rooms on the end," said Holly. Both of the rooms had sliding glass doors facing the water that led onto a small covered patio. We walked around to the front, and Holly handed Tangles a keycard. "This is for the room next door." She slid another one into the lock and opened the door. The room was simple, clean, and neat, with a big, king-sized bed in the middle. It had a safe, refrigerator, TV, and a decent-sized bathroom; all the essentials. There was an open suitcase on a stand in the closet, and Holly's clothes were neatly hanging from the hangers above. There was another unopened suitcase on the floor, and I put it on the bed.

"This is the one with our extra gear, right?" I asked. I had Holly bring it with her on the plane, because I didn't want to overload the boat.

"Yes, now tell me what happened."

I unzipped the suitcase and had to laugh when I saw a DEA T-shirt sitting on top. I don't know who came up with the idea, but The Old Key Lime House in Lantana sold them by the boatload in their gift shop. DEA was printed in big, bold, letters on the back of the shirt, and below, in very tiny letters, were the words 'drink every afternoon.' Naturally, there was a small restaurant logo on the front, but all anybody noticed were the big DEA letters on the back. You literally could not visit The Old Key Lime House at any time of the day or night without encountering a customer or staff member wearing one. As their popularity grew, they were liable to be seen anywhere. Layne (the owner) had given me and Tangles one each when we relocated the *Lucky Dog* to the restaurant's docks, and I could see we had both packed one in the extra suitcase. The one on top was mine, and as I lifted it up I said, "Check it out, Tangles."

He shook his head and laughed too. "How appropriate. At least we got some clean clothes. Let me get my stuff out so I can go take a shower."

As he started going through the suitcase, Holly said, "Tangles, how'd you get that lump next to year ear?"

He gently touched it and replied, "Oh, it's nothing."

"Nothing? *Really*? Can somebody please tell me what happened? I've been worried silly."

"First of all, this can't go any farther than this room, understood?" I said.

"Of course. So, what happened?"

I looked at Tangles and said, "This goes for you too. If anybody asks, we had an engine fire and abandoned ship just before the boat blew up. You bumped your head on a rod-holder when we were scrambling to get off. The Coast Guard rescued us, and that's all there is to it."

"Got it."

"So what *really* happened?" asked Holly.

As I glossed over our near-death experience on the sub, her eyes grew wider and wider until she blurted out, "WHAT?" She semi-covered her mouth with one hand and covered her left breast with the other. She probably intended to feel her heart beat, which I'm sure she did, but there was no getting around the fact that to me it looked like the luckiest hand in the world, squeezing that beautiful breast... *Mmmmm.*

"My God! You guys could have been killed! What happened to Ferby? Kit?"

"Yeah?"

"What are you staring at?"

She caught me ogling her lovely cleavage which was nestled in an Old Key Lime House tank-top that I'm sure my buddy Layne handpicked for its overly-plunging neckline.

"Huh? Oh, sorry 'bout that. I've been at sea too long." I snapped out of my temporary trance and continued. "Ferby got shot in the knee, but he should be alright. They flew him to Miami for treatment. The *Lucky Dog*, though... she wasn't so lucky today."

"Hey, speaking of Ferby, look at these." Tangles held up a pair of Ferby's boxers and half the room disappeared from view. They were enormous. "If we'd a had these," he cracked, "we coulda sailed here."

Tangles and I started laughing, but Holly was still trying to get the story straight.

"*Who* flew Ferby to Miami? Quit joking around and tell me what happened. I'm glad you're alright, but it wasn't so funny for me."

"You do the honors, Shag," said Tangles. "I'm taking a shower and then seeing if I can scrounge up something to eat in the bar. Hope it's not too late."

"Sounds like a good plan. Those sandwiches they fed us on the cutter just didn't cut it."

Tangles groaned and looked at Holly who was shaking her head. "Mister, 'I've got a way with words,' is all yours," he said, and then headed out the door with some clothes under his arm. "See you in the bar."

As soon as the door closed, Holly said, "So, from the top, tell me everything that happened. Then maybe I'll tell you what I discovered at the library this afternoon."

"You went to the library? What for?"

I kicked off my boat shoes and stripped off my sweaty and slightly blood-stained shirt, tossing it on the closet floor.

"To find out whatever I could about Joseph's accident and what happened to his and Millie's baby. Kit?"

"What?" I walked over to the sliding glass doors and drew the curtains all the way closed.

"What's that bandage on your shoulder?"

"I got bit by a Colombian. We got any peroxide?"

"You *what?*"

"It's no biggie. At least I didn't get pistol-whipped on the noggin like Tangles."

"Will you tell me the whole story already?"

"You first. What did you find out at the library?"

She grinned and let me have both barrels. "Joseph didn't die."

"*What?* But—"

"But nothing, I'm telling you he survived."

"How—"

She put her finger up to my mouth and cut me off, still grinning. "Uh-uh, big boy—the story...I wanna hear *everything*."

Although it had only been five days since I had last seen her, it was the longest we had been apart in six months. Six highly-charged, very fulfilling months. She was smart, sexy, fun, and caring—even suddenly rich. Everything a man could want. Most of all, though, she was one-hundred-percent woman, and I wanted her, *bad*. In a move so fast it would have made Bruce Lee flinch, I grabbed her wrist and spun her around and down, back-first, on the bed. Her eyes went wide as I grabbed her other wrist and pinned her arms over her head. "Not so fast," I warned.

With our faces nearly touching, I pressed my knee between her long legs and lightly kissed her lips. She arched her back and kissed me hard…long and hard. There was more heat rising between us than Mount St. Helens in the spring of '80. I let go of a hand and deftly yanked off her shorts and panties in one motion as I rolled to the side. As she fumbled with my zipper, I rolled back over and re-pinned her free arm to the bed. I kissed my way up her neck and murmured, "I thought you wanted to hear the rest of the story?"

She nibbled on my ear, and then started licking it. "It can wait…I can't. Please…now…"

"Don't good things come to those who wait?"

When I groaned, she whispered, "You'll never know."

Per usual, she was right.

Chapter 20

Franklin Post (aka "Stargazer") leaned back in his command-center recliner and shook his head in semi-disbelief over the conversation he had just had with Kit Jansen. As director of the Department of International Criminal Knowledge (DICK) for over ten years, there was little he saw or heard that surprised him. That was until finding out that Jansen and his crew had somehow managed to survive another chance encounter with notoriously dangerous criminals. Once again, not only had they lived to tell the tale, but the bad guys got the short end of the stick. And this time, it turned out to be a stick of dynamite. Jansen's boat had been blown to smithereens, and there was almost no likelihood that any of the drug-running hijackers had survived. It was nothing short of amazing that a few happy-go-lucky guys filming a fishing show were responsible for foiling one of the largest drug shipments in US history. Neither the Coast Guard nor the DEA nor Homeland Security were even *aware* the Colombians had been utilizing fully-submersible subs. Now, thanks to Jansen and company, they had one in their possession. *Unbelievable.*

He closed his eyes for a moment and then stared up at the vast circular ceiling painted to replicate the solar system. Some people used yoga to get their body and mind in tune—he used stargazing. As he contemplated the cosmos, he grew increasingly concerned over the well-being of Jansen and company. He could tell by Jansen's cavalier attitude that he wasn't taking the threat of retaliation by the Cordero brothers too seriously. He was resourceful and seemed to be living a semi-charmed kind of life, no doubt about it, but Post knew that when it came to crossing the Cordero's, the good didn't just die young, they died horrifically. Only six months earlier, a pair of undercover DEA agents went missing in Tumaco, Colombia, while investigating reports of a sub-building project in the jungle. Less than a week later, what was left of their mutilated bodies had been dumped in the middle of the business district to send a message. The rumor circulating was that the agents had been stripped naked, tied to stakes, and had ground beef rubbed all over their genitals. Then the Cordero's sicced a pair of hungry pet Tiger's on them. It was even rumored that one of the brothers had filmed the gruesome attack on his iPhone.

Not willing to take any chances, Post pressed a button on the arm of his recliner that connected him to one of his field agents, Raphael Angel-Herrera, who went by Rafe (pronounced like chafe but with an r). Rafe was an ex-DEA agent who had a black-belt in Jujitsu and advanced degrees in both marine engineering and hydrodynamic propulsion. He was also a master of disguise and was currently doing undercover work in Maracaibo, Venezuela. Post quickly scrolled through the menu of the Oralator, the device he invented that converted his voice into the voices of any number of celebrities, both living and dead. He settled on Adam West, of Batman and Family Guy fame, just as Rafe answered the call.

"Hey, boss. What's going on?"

"The Colombians are using fully-submersible submarines just like we suspected, *that's* what's going on."

"It had to happen sooner or later; how'd you get confirmation?"

"The Coast Guard is towing one to Miami as we speak. If my calculations are correct, and they usually are, they'll be at Port Everglades by tomorrow night."

"How in the hell did the *Coast Guard* get a hold of one?"

"It's a long story, my friend, almost as long as the sub itself—a hundred feet."

"A hundred-foot submersible? Jesus, what were they carrying?"

"If you're waiting for Jesus to answer, perhaps you should get on your knees and pray. But if you're asking me, the answer is about seven tons of coke along with a few surface-to-air missiles and grenades."

"Son-of-a-bitch!"

"Actually, Jesus was the son of a virgin, but who knows? She was probably a bitch too. Maybe that's why the innkeeper made them sleep in the manger."

Rafe pulled the phone away from his ear and looked at it in disbelief. He had heard his mysterious boss on the other end of the line was a confirmed genius, but sometimes he wondered.

"Sir?"

"Rafe?"

"I understand the logic behind altering your voice. Sounding like Batman is one thing, but when you morph into Mayor West from Family Guy and take on his persona, don't you think it's going a little overboard?"

"As a master of disguise, you should know there's no such thing as being too rich or too thin, just ask the Olsen twins."

"*Who?*"

"Never mind, we've got a situation on our hands. Remember that unlikely bunch that brought down Donny Nutz and his crew almost singlehandedly?"

"*Brought down?* Hell, they all ended up dead. Sure, I remember. Wasn't it the guys with the fishing show?"

"You are correct, sir. Their names are Kit Jansen and Langostino Dupree, aka Shagball and Tangles. Tangles also happens to be a midget. Not technically, I guess, but you get the idea."

"A midget named Langostino? You're kidding me, right?"

"I never kid about midgets, especially ones named after South African shrimp, those tasty little buggers."

"So, what about 'em?"

"They've done it again."

"Done *what?*"

"They captured the sub that's now in the hands of the Coast Guard."

"WHAT? How did—"

"Like I said, Rafe, the story's longer than a quick shower with Jerry Sandusky. That's why I emailed the account of what transpired to all DICK operatives. Check your inbox."

"You know, a hundred-foot submersible would explain a lot. I've got a local informant who says a sub full of military weapons and explosives was supposed to be delivered somewhere along the Gulf of Venezuela in the next two weeks. I seriously doubted it, but now I'm not so sure. Maybe the Colombians were gonna bring back a shipment from Miami or Cuba after they delivered all the coke. If they have submersibles, who knows? It's certainly a possibility."

"And the weapons were no doubt intended for Chavez and his no-good, guerilla-terrorist counterparts."

"No question, and the Cordero brothers are gonna go ape-shit when they find out they lost their sub and seven tons of blow, not to mention the arms delivery."

"Which brings us back to the situation I was telling you about."

"I know all about the Situation."

"You do?"

"Sure, he's the star of that reality TV show, The Jersey Shore, right?"

"Ha! You got me there, you clever devil. That's the kind of sharp wit the DEA promised and that attracted me to you like Jack Black to a plate of nachos. I *knew* I called the right man!"

"So, let me guess. You called because you're concerned about Jansen and company and want me to keep an eye on them."

"Bingo! Bango! Bongo! I can't *believe* the DEA let you go!"

"Sometimes I can't believe it either. And you want me to catch the next flight to…?"

"St. Croix. My God, man, how did you know? You're a flat-out mind reader, that's what you are!"

For the second time, Rafe held the phone away from his ear and stared at it, shaking his head. He could faintly hear the voice on the other end of the line calling his name. "Rafe? Rafe, are you there?"

"Yes, sir, I'm here, but can you stop with the Mayor West thing? It's hard to take you serious."

"Sorry, Rafe, you're right. I tend to get carried away with the Oralator. Especially when impersonating the greatest character in the history of television. Here, let me switch to someone a little more, shall we say... *apropos?*"

Franklin Post quickly scrolled through his available characters list and pressed the button for Jack Webb, of Dragnet fame.

"How's this?"

"Fine."

"Okay, like you guessed, as resourceful as Mr. Jansen seems to be, I'm afraid he isn't taking the Cordero threat seriously, particularly with a girl involved."

"A girl?"

"Yes, a girl. They're like dick-less men, with soft skin and tits. In this case, it's Jansen's girlfriend, Holly. She's a real looker. I urged Mr. Jansen to go back to Florida with her, but he said he had to help her track down some relatives first. They're at a resort called The Hibiscus. Go there and keep an eye on 'em. I don't have to tell you what could happen if the Cordero's find out these guys are responsible for their missing sub."

"No, you don't."

"Good, so get moving. I'm sure the bad guys are."

"Don't worry; I'm on it like Travolta on a masseuse."

"You're a sick man, Rafe. Keep me posted."

"Nothin' but the facts, sir. Nothin' but the facts."

"Rafe?"

"Yes, sir?"

"That was my line. Since you stole it, I guess I'll have to revert back to esteemed Mayor Adam West for our next conversation."

"Please, sir, please, no more—"

"You know you love it." Click.

Chapter 21

The Department of International Criminal Knowledge (DICK) had been the brainchild of the Texas-two-steppin', forty-third president of the United States of America, created in the wake of the 9/11 terrorist attacks. Its main purpose was simple—to help find and kill terrorists. Its secondary purpose was to aid other federal agencies in thwarting international criminal activity (i.e., the war on drugs, arms trafficking, and cyber security, to name a few).

When the president was briefed that the attacks might have been prevented had there been a better sharing of intelligence information between federal agencies, he called for a meeting at Camp David. In attendance were the heads of the FBI, CIA, DEA, NSA, the Defense Department, and the newly created Department of Homeland Security. After acknowledging long-standing deficiencies in intelligence sharing, the president took them to task. At his urging, they agreed to form an autonomous agency that would have access to every shred of data, communication, and intelligence gathered. They would then analyze the information and disseminate it as seen fit.

Still stinging somewhat from the verbal lashing they received, the heads of these security organizations named the organization in the president's honor. Each agency head volunteered one of its own agents to form the initial group, and the eccentric high-tech billionaire, Franklin Post, had been selected to build and run it.

Other than Franklin Post and his agents, nobody knew about DICK but the man he reported to (the president) and those in attendance at the Camp David meeting; neither congress, nor the senate, nor the American public, nor any foreign intelligence agency even had a whiff of its existence. Its two-billion-dollar annual budget was funded equally by the slush funds of each of the attendees.

For seven years, DICK ran smoothly and successfully, despite having to filter and analyze incredible volumes of data. As a bonus, sometimes it even developed intelligence information of its own. Then, although the president and its creators were thrilled with DICK's rise *and* the fact they had been able to keep the whole thing secret, they were faced with a dilemma: How to bring the president's newly-elected successor, the young, Democratic senator from Illinois, Barack Obama, into the fold. If told of DICK's existence, would he eagerly take the baton and run with it as overseer of the most top-secret, terrorist-hunting organization in the world? *Or* would he be appalled by its very existence, looking at it as a knee-jerk reaction to the terrorist attacks by a warmongering predecessor? It was agreed by the president and the Camp David attendees that since there was no way to know, the new president would have to be kept in the dark.

Why? Because if Obama reacted negatively, everyone involved in creating DICK would face utter professional and political annihilation and possibly jail time. Even worse, they could lose their disgustingly cushy pensions, health-care benefits, and perks. So, rather than report directly to the president, once a year the agency heads secretly met with Franklin Post. He would give them an annual report, of sorts, and they would give him a wish-list of high-priority operations they wanted assistance with.

This was the reason Franklin Post found himself dialing the former president's number, instead of the current president's, to inform him that DICK had just bagged another high-level terrorist. It was a promise he had made when he accepted the job, and since he couldn't call the sitting president, he saw no harm in calling the one who gave him the job in the first place. It also didn't hurt that Post had a genuine fondness for the man and his ability to make him laugh. His sense of humor often blurred the line between intentional and innate. After several rings, the former president finally answered. "Dubya here."

"Mr. President, its Franklin Post."

"*Stargazer?* How the hell are you?"

"I'm doing well, sir. Business is booming."

"Lemme guess, you got another one?"

"Yes, sir, the number two man behind Bin Laden."

"Let me go outside so you can fill me in; the wife's got ears like Obama. You ever take a good look at those things? I bet with a little headwind he could flap 'em a few times and get airborne." Franklin heard a woman's voice in the background, and then the President added, "What'd I tell you. Hang on a second." The President fanned his hand over the mic slot on his cell, but Franklin could still hear him. "I'm just going out to the barn, honey. Gonna see if the, if the, uh, hay needs seeding." Suddenly his voice grew louder. "You still there?"

"Yes."

"We're out of earshot now. So, you said you got Bin Laden's number two?"

"Yes, earlier this week."

"Considering his diet, I bet it's chunkier than curdled camel milk and smells like rotten goat."

"Guess I stepped into that one."

"Better than stepping into number two. Man, I'm on *fire* today, Stargazer! Go on now, tell me the details."

"One of our drones took out Abu Yahy-Wah in the remote Pakistan high country last night. It hasn't even hit the news wires yet."

"You gotta be kidding me. That little Chinese fella who plays the fiddle on his lap? *He* was a terrorist? Damn, they're sneaky bastards, who'd a thunk it?

"No, not him. You're thinking of Yo-Yo-Ma...but he's Korean and plays the cello."

"Bet he's a helluva fiddle player, too. If he came to Texas and changed his name to Yippie-Yo-Ma he'd be more popular than T. Boone Pickens in an LBJ, 'kiss my ass,' contest."

Franklin Post shook his head and laughed. "That was good, sir. I needed a laugh."

"What can I say, Stargazer? Killing terrorists brings out the best in me."

"Well, chalk up another one for DICK. One of our operatives discovered his full name was actually

Abu Yahy-Wah- al-Libi, which led us to his hideout in a relative's mountain hut. Of course, now it's a valley."

"Now that's what *I'm* talking about—the Valley of Boom. But I gotta ask you, Stargazer, what's with their names? Al-Qaida? Al-Libi? What's next, Al Dente? Speaking of al dente, you're a smart guy, why do they call it al dente, when you can't make a dent in it? Doesn't make sense, does it? They oughta call it al harde. Fortunately, the wife makes it just the way I like, mushier than a Hugh Grant film."

"We're on the same page there, sir; I don't like my pasta too hard, either."

"Great minds think alike, Stargazer. I *knew* you were the perfect DICK head. Heh."

"I'll...take that as a compliment. So, are you still enjoying retirement? I'm sure it's nice being out of the public eye."

"Retirement's okay, and I can tell you unequibitably that I don't miss the press, but dang if I don't miss the action. You know, somebody pisses you off and BOOM! You start a war! It doesn't really matter if they were the insulator or not, you just start bombing the shit out of somebody. *That's* how you gain respect as a president. Everybody thought I got it wrong going after Iraq and the big mustache, but it was just a rouge. It's called, keep the bastards guessing. Once I did the Baghdad shuffle, those other goat humpin' countries fell right in line 'cause they knew if they so much as looked at me sideways they'd be facing World War Me. Yep, those were the good old days; sure do miss 'em. I tell you, it all went by so fast. Time flies, especially with cruise missiles at your disposal. Now, it's just me and the missus and fifteen-hundred acres of ranch. Things are so slow I'm thinking of turning some of it into a reserve."

"What, wild game?"

"No, Mexicans. Heh, just kidding. People will pay good money to shoot an antelope. But that reminds me, I finally came up with the perfect solution to our border-control problem. The Democrats are always talking about wanting to spend money on infrastructure and green energy, right? You know, e*specially* now that we got past that physical cliff thing. Well, I got a plan that does both. Wanna hear it?"

"More than you know, sir. I live for this stuff."

"Me too. It's so simple, it's brilliant. Too bad I didn't think of it while I was still in office; it woulda added to my legacy. My plan is to build an electric fence from San Diego to Corpus Christi."

"How is that using green energy?"

"That's the beauty of it. Get this, Stargazer; it's a *solar-powered* electric fence."

"A *what?*"

"You heard me right. I call it the Freedom Fence. Think about it. All day long it soaks up the desert sun. Night falls and it glows like Tijuana on Cinco de Mayo, but lay a hand on it and it's fireworks like the Fourth of Julyo—brilliant, right?"

"Sir, no offense, but aside from being an affront to this country's role as the humanitarian leader of the free world, I don't think the charge from a solar-powered fence would be sufficient to stop those seeking a better life."

"I went to Yale, Stargazer; don't you think I thought about that? It would actually be a solar-powered, *hydro*-electric fence. A supplemental high-voltage charge would be generated courtesy of a new hydro-electric plant built on the Rio Grande. The dems want green energy? Well, I'm talking about Jolly-Green-Giant-sized energy! So, please don't give me that humanitarian crap about denying people a better life; under my plan they'll get one. It's called the afterlife. Heh."

"I don't...quite know... what to say, sir. As usual, you make a compelling argument in support of your case."

"I was on the debate team at Yale, Stargazer. My opponent's couldn't tongue-tie *this* Eli. No, sir. Never lost once in five years. How else do you think I got to be President of the United States with a straight C average?"

"You make a good point, sir. I guess it's about conviction, too."

"That's right, and fortunately, I never been convicted. It's not just about brains, it's about guts... and instinct, and I got plenty a both to go around. You need some? Don't be afraid to ask, that's what I'm here for. So, any other news on the DICK front?"

"As far as terrorists go, no, but some...I guess you would call them... friends of DICK, just put a huge hole in the pipeline of a major Colombian drug cartel."

"Friends of Dick? What do you mean? I thought Cheney shot 'em all. What happened?"

"You remember early last summer when I told you about the fishing-show guys who inadvertently brought down the big east coast Mafioso, Donny Nutz?"

"Hell yeah, I remember. Sorta like the way the Federal Reserve brought down Lehman Brothers."

"Not exactly, but the end result was the same; here one day and gone the next."

"What were their names again?"

"Shagball and Tangles."

"*That's* right— and one of 'em's a midget. I've seen their show a few times on ESPN 9...or maybe it's 10, I forget which. I gotta tell you, Stargazer, that's one funny damn fishing show. 'Course, you give me a midget sidekick and I'd split your sides like you got run over by a combine. Enough about that, though. What happened?"

"They were fishing in the Caribbean, doing some filming, when they accidently hooked a submarine loaded with cocaine and a few surface to air missiles."

"How much cocaine?"

"An estimated seven tons."

The president let out a whistle and then lowered his voice a notch. "Reminds me of the Skull and Bones initiation back in the seventies."

"What's that, sir?"

"Huh? Oh, nothing, just reminiscing. As you were saying..."

"Yes, the sub became disabled when a wire-line from the boat got wrapped around the prop. The Colombians hijacked them when they unwittingly stopped to provide assistance. They forced Shagball and company to transfer the coke onto the boat and then tried to sink them on the sub when they overpowered one of the captors. Despite having grenades bounced of the hull, they managed to get the leaking sub back to the surface. It was there they witnessed a massive explosion, which turned out to be the hijacked boat full of cocaine. No survivors were found and the cause of the explosion is unclear, but the Coast Guard has been scooping cocaine out of the water ever since. Shagball managed to flag down a Coast Guard chopper and the submarine is being towed back to Miami as we speak. It's the first fully-submersible sub ever confiscated by US authorities. Until now, we only had rumors of their use."

"So, let me see if I got this straight. Twice in one year these guys have managed to do what highly trained-agents of the US government have been unable to do...*by accident?*"

"To be fair, sir, we did provide assistance in the Donny Nutz takedown."

"Fair schmair, there's no such thing as fair in love and—"

"War?"

"No, marriage, but that's another story. Look, when I had the idea to form the most super-top-secret, terrorist-and-international-crime-fighting organization the world has never known, I didn't follow any manuals."

"You certainly thought outside the box, sir. I'll give you that."

"No, I didn't, 'cause I wasn't in the box to begin with. That's a twentieth-century expression used by people who never had an original idea in their life—present company excluded, of course. There the same ones who use the word 'proactive', 'cause they think it makes them sound smart. I'd like to take that word, put it in the box, and stick it up Jay Carville's ass. How's that for proactive? Heh. Anyways, as I was about to say, I have my own expression for how I come up with great ideas like the Freedom Fence."

"What's that?"

"Gettin' uranium on the brainium."

"Uranium on the branium?"

"That's right, I got a little uranium on the branium, and the next thing I knew I had the border problem figured out. The Freedom Fence solves it all; immigration, deportation, immunization, sequestration, inundation, and veneration...all thanks to a little electrification."

"Veneration? What's that got to do with it?"

"Simple. They can't spread around all those Mexican STDs if they don't make it past the fence."

"I, uh, don't know what to say to that."

"Words aren't necessary, Stargazer. Brilliance speaks for itself, and right now, it can't shut up. If Shagball and Tangles managed to do what they did unintentionally, think of what they could do if they really tried."

"I have, that's what worries me."

"Worry is the road that goes from where you've been to where you're going and along the way it passes through a little town called Doubt. When you're in Doubt, you turn down a street called, 'Wherethefuckami Boulevard.' If you don't know where you're going, nobody else can either."

"What the hell does *that* mean? What are you saying?"

"Put a little uranium on your branium, Stargazer. It *means*, you should consider making Shagball and Tangles part of the DICK team."

"*What?* Are you, are you serious?"

"Damn straight I am. Think about it. You got a couple guys who've proved to be extremely resourceful in life-and-death situations. They travel around the world on a fishing boat. It's the perfect cover. You know as well as I do, no matter how good our homegrown agents are, they carry themselves in a certain way because of their specialized training, and it makes them easier for the enemy to identify. No one would ever suspect a fishing-show host and his midget sidekick would be working for the most top-secret terrorist and international crime-fighting organization in the universe. *Nobody.*"

"I…uh, I can't say that that's the, uh, *craziest* thing you ever suggested, sir, and I mean that with all due respect."

"Respect isn't due, Stargazer; it's earned. I'm merely suggesting you consider it. As always, the ultimate decision is yours."

"Thank you, sir. I'll take it under advisement."

"Take it anywhere you want, just make sure you take it to the bad guys like they've never had it taken to them before. If you wanna be proactive, drop a bomb on 'em—always worked for me. Heh."

"Understood, sir. Till the next time then."

"Till the next time, Stargazer. Keep making me proud." Click.

Chapter 22

After we shared a quick shower, I exited the bathroom so Holly could get ready. While toweling off, I noticed the open FedEx package in the trash.

"So, did you like my package?" I asked. She kicked the bathroom door open, and grinned.

"You know I did. Do you really have to ask?"

"Well, I wasn't sure when to give it to you."

"You sure fooled me. You gave it to me like you actually knew what you were doing."

"Did it cheer you up? That was the whole idea."

"Mission accomplished, stud-boy."

"*Stud-boy?* What the hell are you talking about?"

Her grin was gone now. "What am *I* talking about? What are *you* talking about?"

"The package. The package I had delivered with the framed picture of you and your parents and Millie."

Holly started laughing. "Oh...*that* package. Why didn't you say so?"

"And you accuse *me* of having my mind in the gutter?"

"You do. It must be rubbing off on me."

"Well, I—"

"Don't even say it Kit. For once, quit while you're ahead. The picture is great. I love it. Where did you find it?"

"In Millie's storage locker. I thought you might like it, so I had it framed." I put on a fresh pair of shorts and my DEA T-shirt.

"Sometimes you surprise me. I was thinking about everything that's happened on the flight down and it's a bit overwhelming. Now that Millie's gone I don't have any one to confide in."

"What am I? Mullet paté?"

She came out of the bathroom with a towel wrapped around her and kissed me on the lips. "Well, you certainly know how to swim upstream."

"You're thinking of salmon." I kissed her back.

"Salmon, mullet, whatever..." We shared a laugh and she slipped into a pair of shorts and a top before putting her hand on my chest. "Thanks for the picture and especially the note, it really means a lot. Millie told me I could trust you, but after what happened with my first husband, I'm a little gun shy."

"Your first husband had to be an asshole."

"He didn't have to be, but you're right, he was... and a secretive one at that. I don't want any secrets between us, Kit. I don't want to go through that again."

"Works for me."

"I'm serious."

"Me too."

"Promise?"

She looked up at me with her big beautiful eyes and I kissed her on the forehead. "I promise. Speaking of which, have you given any though to where you want to spread the rest of Millie's ashes?"

"A little, but I want to get to the bottom of what happened to Joseph and Lucky first. I'll know when the time's right."

It was about midnight when Holly and I strolled into the semi-crowded bar. The patrons were mostly cheering as a woman finished singing a karaoke version of Gladys Knight's classic hit, "Midnight Train to Georgia." The young man running the karaoke machine said, "Give it up for Latisha! Dere be more soulful crooning after a short break… Doan forget to take care of your servers. Be back in ten."

Tangles was never that hard to spot, but it was made even easier by the big, bold DEA letters stamped across the back of his T-shirt. It was identical to the one I had on, and I immediately wished I had something different to wear. Guys wearing matching T-shirts are only acceptable when playing on the same softball team. I believe it's rule number twenty-eight of the Bro-code. Unfortunately, our pickings were slim after losing everything on the *Lucky Dog.*

I slapped Tangles on the back as Holly slid onto a barstool next to him. "How's the grub, bub?" I caught him in mid-chew, and he held up a finger as he finished munching whatever it was he had in his mouth. Then he took a long pull from a bottle of *Presidente* and pushed his empty plate forward before belching.

"Sorry 'bout that. I ordered another burger and some nachos for you guys before the kitchen closed. It should be out any minute. What took you so long?"

"Oh, you know, I just had to fill Holly in on what happened and then, uh, take a shower. So… how was the burger?"

"The burger was good." He nodded toward Holly who was ordering a couple beers from the bartender. She had her hair pulled back in a ponytail because it was wet, like mine. "I see she took a shower too; that must have been some kinda fillin' in." He winked at me, and I elbowed him in the shoulder, nearly sending him airborne. He grabbed the bar to keep from flying off the stool and let out an, "Oww! Geez, man. What'd you do that for?"

Holly turned to hand me a beer before scolding me. "C'mon Kit, knock it off. Why are you always picking on him?"

"What do you mean, 'picking on him?" I wasn't picking on him, he was—"

"Yeah, dude," interrupted Tangles. "She's right. You're always picking on me. If you really need to pick on someone, you should pick on someone your own size. Didn't your mother ever teach you that?" I might have let it go with a shrug and apologized under normal circumstances, but then the little bastard had to smirk at me. I set my beer down after a healthy pull and looked down at his smugly little face.

"Well, why don't you stand on that barstool, and then we'll be about the same size?" I had matched the wee man's smirk and raised him a smirk. He was now smirk-less and I was rolling in the smirk…deep in the smirk. But not for long.

"Really, Kit?" Holly gave me one of her looks. "*Really?* Another short joke? I swear it's like you never left high school sometimes."

"It's alright, Holly, really," said Tangles. "I, uh, I probably brought that one on myself." She looked at him suspiciously and then gave me a steely-eyed stare.

"You guys are like best friends; you should try acting like it once in a while…especially you, Kit."

"Why especially me? Why not him?" I stuck my thumb out sideways at Tangles just as the bartender set the food in front of Holly. She turned to thank him, and Tangles nudged me in the side and gave me a wink before jumping into the fray.

"Yeah, Holly, why especially him? Why *not* me?"

Holly stuck a french fry in her mouth and quickly snarfed it down before responding. "That's not what—"

"You think just because I'm short, I shouldn't be held to a higher standard? Is that what you think?"

"No, no that's not what—"

Tangles was like a dog with a bone, and he wasn't gonna stop until it was buried in the yard. In a slightly louder voice he said, "Go ahead. Tell me how you *really* feel about short people. You think we should have our own checkout line at the supermarket?"

"*What?* No, I mean—"

Tangles got to his knees on the barstool, and I stepped back so he had a direct line-of-sight to Holly. He raised his voice another notch and people at the bar started looking our way. "You think we should have TINY little pumps at the gas station for our TINY little cars?"

"Huh? *Gas stations?* What are you—"

"Go ahead, Holly!" He was practically yelling now and swept his arm in a grand gesture to make sure everybody in the bar was paying attention. "Tell everybody here what you really think! THAT SHORT PEOPLE GOT NO REASON TO LIVE!"

The bar went eerily silent, and Holly had a horrified look on her face. The bartender leaned over the counter, and quietly said, "Is everything alright here?" Tangles and I burst out laughing, and Holly's face went beet-red a fraction of a second before she punched me in the shoulder.

"Yes, everything's fine," she tersely responded. "Except for these jokers who think they're auditioning for Dumb and Dumber II."

I noticed a bunch of people were still staring at us and announced, "It's alright, people. He was just joking…it's all good." I gave a wave of the hand, and the bar went back to its normal festive mood…except for Holly. She gave Tangles an icy stare and said, "No more Mrs. Nice Guy for you."

Tangles gave her a funny look. "*Mrs.* Nice Guy?"

"You know what I mean!" Then she pointed at me "And you…you just eat your *stupid* burger. I'm going to the restroom." Before I could say anything, she huffed out of the bar.

"That went well," said Tangles.

I was just about finished with the burger when Tangles gave me a nudge. "Looks like Holly made a new friend." He pointed to the entrance of the bar where Holly was laughing and engaged in conversation with the young black guy who was running karaoke night. I took my last bite of burger and washed it down with beer as I watched their animated conversation. Holly pointed in our direction, and I raised a hand when the kid gave us a wave.

"Wonder what that's all about," I commented. They hugged, and Holly started walking our way as the kid headed to the stage.

"Wow, she's never hugged me like that," replied Tangles.

"And after your short people rant, she probably never will." In my mind though, I was thinking, *that was a pretty friendly hug.*

Holly came walking up with a big smile on her face. Apparently, Mr. Karaoke had lightened her mood. She ordered a margarita and sat down on the seat next to me, which had just become available. "How was the burger?"

I had been around the block enough times to know she was starting to play head games with me, and I wasn't about to go there. "The burger was fine. So, who's Huggy Bear?"

"Huggy Bear?"

"You know," I nodded toward the stage, "Mr. Karaoke."

"Oh, him?" she replied coyly. "That's just Jackson. We went horseback riding on the beach today. He's a real sweetheart."

I had to admit, I didn't see that one coming. "You did *what?* What the hell *else* did you do?"

"What do you mean? 'What *else* did I do?' Are you actually *jealous?*" She smiled.

"I don't know. Given your family history, maybe I should be."

Holly's smile suddenly evaporated quicker than an Obama-campaign promise. "What the hell do you mean by that?"

Tangles cut in. "What he means is—"

"Shut up, Tangles!" Holly stuck her hand out in front of his face and stopped him cold.

A voice came over the PA system. It was Jackson. "Get your singing voices warmed up, ladies and gentleman! We'll be starting our last set right after I make a quick call. I know you seen de flyers, so don't forget to come back for reggae night Saturday to see de Caribbean sensations... Doobius and de Orehos!"

Jackson ducked behind one of the large speakers and dialed a number on his cell phone. Forty-five miles away on St. Thomas, Remy VanderGrift's phone rang and he flipped it open.

"Did you find out anyting?"

"I know whose boat done blowed up."

"Who?"

"A couple guys staying at de Hibiscus. A Coast Guard chopper dropped dem on de beach."

"You pretty sure, huh?"

"Yeah, mon. I be positeev. I seen de chopper land and de girlfriend of one of dem just tole me."

"Tanks, I owe you one."

"Maybe you owe me two."

"Two? Why dat?"

Jackson craned his neck around the side of the speaker and took another look at the back of the T-shirts worn by the guys at the bar.

"Cuz dey be wit de DEA."

Chapter 23

The next morning I called my producer Jamie to tell him to cancel the trip down on account of the fact that the *Lucky Dog* was no more. He was understandably shocked and dismayed. After all, it was the boat that put our fishing show on the map. Condolences aside, he quickly wondered aloud how we would continue the show without a boat. I suggested the show buy a new one and was met with silence. For him, fishing was business; for me, it was a way of life. I could handle losing the show, but I couldn't handle losing my boat. I told him we'd talk when I got back and tried to put it out of my mind during breakfast with Holly and Tangles. Holly filled us in on the details of Joseph's non-death and the subsequent loss of his entire family in a plane crash. It was tragic on all kinds of levels, and I pointed out the obvious.

"This is unbelievable, and poor Millie....she never even knew he survived. How can that be?"

"I've thought about that too," said Holly. "If Millie had known he survived, there's no way she would have abandoned him *or* given up the baby. The only explanation is she *didn't* know."

"From how you described it in the letter, Millie was despondent," added Tangles. "*And* she was being medicated by some doctor under orders from…what was his name again?"

"Kilroy."

"Right, that snake Kilroy. Let's face it, he tried to kill Joseph, so it makes sense he would do everything he could to keep the guy's survival a secret from Millie. Once Joseph was taken to St. Thomas, it made it easier for Kilroy. That and the fact Joseph was in a coma."

Holly took a sip of coffee and slowly shook her head. "My God, do you suppose Joseph could still be alive?"

I had not only been thinking about *that* possibility, but the possibility that Kilroy might still be alive too, and put in my two-cent's worth. "Joseph was Millie's age, which would make him about eighty-two or three. Assuming he came out of the coma and didn't have any major health issues, sure, it's possible. But not only is *that* possible, it's also possible Kilroy could be alive, and maybe his fiancée too. After all, I think Millie said in her letter that Kilroy was about ten years older than her and…what was his fiancée's name again?"

"Genevieve," answered Holly.

"Right, and Genevieve was older than Millie but younger than Kilroy, which would put her in the mid-to late-eighties range."

Suddenly, Holly put her coffee down and pushed her chair back from the table.

"We have to go to the marina," she insisted. "Maybe Kilroy still owns it; maybe he's even there! C'mon, let's go!" She stood up, and I knew better than to ask if we could finish our coffee and muffins first. I looked at Tangles and shrugged while stuffing the rest of my muffin in my mouth, and he did the same. Holly was halfway to the parking lot while we were still gulping down the rest of the coffee. Tangles headed after her, and I tossed a fiver on the table before dashing out the door.

Tangles was in the backseat of the two-door jeep and Holly had the engine running by the time I hopped into the passenger's side. When we pulled out onto the main road, Holly started driving on the left-hand side.

"Whoa, whoa, what are you doing?" I asked.

"We're going to the marina."

"No, I mean, you're on the wrong side of the road." We came over a slight rise and a car zipped by my window, close enough to touch. I flinched and leaned toward Holly. "What the hell?"

She laughed and said, "Weird, isn't it? It takes a little getting used to....driving on the wrong side of the road."

"You gotta be kidding me."

"For once I don't mind riding in the back," said Tangles. "You know, just in case you forget which side you're on."

Holly adjusted the rearview mirror. "The lady at the rental car counter told me the trick is to remember to keep the driver's side along the shoulder of the road, where the bushes are. She said you know you're in the proper lane when you can reach out and touch the bushes." There was about five seconds of silence before Tangles snickered and said something along the lines of what I was thinking.

"You know, it's always nice to be able to reach out and—"

"Don't even say it, you little perv." Holly shook her head and gave him the evil eye as I chuckled and tried to sneak a fist bump. *Tried* being the operative word. Holly noticed me fist bump him and let out a deep breath. "You're no better; do you really have to encourage him?"

"It's good for his self-esteem."

"You two are lost causes."

"Speaking of lost," said Tangles. "You know where you're going?"

"I know where I'm going, but with that dirty little mind of yours, you should be worried you're going to an inferno with pitchforks and evil all around."

"I'm going to Oklahoma?"

"*What?* No…forget it. Why do I even bother? Wait, here's where we turn."

We turned off the main road and started winding through the jungle. After a couple of minutes with no cars passing from the other direction, I voiced my concern. "Are you—?"

"Yes, Kit, I know where I'm going! I got directions at the Hibiscus, alright? If you two would just relax, we should be there in a couple minutes."

"I was going to say, are you still glad you voted for Obama?"

"Oh, *please…*I know *damn well* what you were going to say. Besides, you know I keep my political opinions to myself. Look, ha! Here it is, just like I said it would be…*surprised?*"

"That you voted for Obama? Yes."

She gritted her teeth as we turned into the Salt River Marina. "Kit?"

"Yes?"

"Shut up."

Although the setting was gorgeous, the Salt River Marina was pretty close to being at the opposite end of the marina spectrum when compared to, say, Sailfish Marina back in Palm Beach. At least as far as the boats and the slips were concerned. Many looked to be as old as the marina itself and in dire need of repairs. There were a few nice sailboats and a handful of decent sport fisher's, but for the most part it was pretty clear this was not a high-end marina by any stretch of the imagination. Nonetheless, the surroundings were tropical and lush and the lagoon quite picturesque.

From the parking lot, I could see a couple old buildings leading to the docks. One of them had a sign that read 'Scallywags Bar & Grill,' and the other had a sign above the door that read 'Office.' As the three of us walked across the lot with Holly anxiously leading the way, I put my hand on her shoulder and stopped her. "Hang on a sec, Holl. In the unlikely event old Kilroy is sitting in the office, don't go throwing accusations around. Let's just—"

"Do you think I'm an idiot? Of course I'm not gonna do that."

"Good idea," said Tangles. "Why don't we poke around a little before we start asking questions?"

"That was my plan all along; I didn't think I needed to spell it out for you guys."

"Hey, c'mon now. We're all on the same side," I said. "Besides, I need to let them know we won't need the slip. Let's just play it by ear." I let go of Holly's shoulder and shrugged at Tangles as we followed her toward the office. As we got closer, I could see the restaurant had a menu posted outside and suggested we take a look. Tangles said, “I’m gonna take a stroll down the dock.”

Holly and I walked past the office door to the restaurant and pretended to look at the menu while simultaneously checking out the surroundings. Tangles had just started down the dock when the office door swung open. A lady stepped out, waved a hand in our direction, and then pointed at Tangles. “Excuse me? Could you please call your son back? No children are allowed on the dock without adult supervision.” Holly and I were laughing as we walked toward her, and Holly tried to explain things. “It’s okay. I know he may not look like it from a distance, but trust me, he’s an adult…and he’s *definitely* not our son… thank God.”

She looked skeptical and inquired as to our purpose. “Okay, if you say so. So, are you meeting someone for a charter, or is there anything I can help you with?” She was no spring chicken (maybe sixty-five), but she wasn’t old enough to be Kilroy’s fiancée either. Plus, she was white. Holly looked at me questioningly, and I whispered, “Go ahead. Ask her.”

“No, we’re not here for a charter, but there is something you might be able to help us with.”

“Well, come on in, honey. It’s a little hot out, and I have the AC running.” She held the door open, and I followed Holly inside. Introductions were made, and her name was Sally. She walked around the counter and turned the TV down. “So, what can I do you for?” Holly looked at me to go first, and I explained that we wouldn't need the slip we reserved due to the fact that we no longer had a boat. I gave her our cover story that the boat caught fire and blew up and that we were rescued by the Coast Guard. She seemed to genuinely care, as she should. "Oh, honey, you lost your boat?"

"Yeah, and everything on it."

"But none of you got hurt, right?"

"Pretty much."

"At least you have your health; that's the most important thing."

"Maybe so, but my health can't take us fishing."

"Alright, Kit, that's enough," said Holly. "Sally's right—you guys could have been killed."

"It's alright" responded Sally. "I know how hard it is to lose a boat. Don't worry about the deposit; I'll make sure it goes back on your credit card. Is there anything else you need?" I looked at Holly, and she took the cue. "Actually, we were, uh, wondering if you might know of someone named Kilroy…we don't know his last name."

"Kilroy? I don't think so. Does he keep a boat here?"

"Actually, I believe he owned this marina at one time. I guess he doesn't anymore, otherwise you'd probably know him. If he's still alive he'd be around ninety."

"He *owned* this marina?"

"Yes, back in like… 1948. I'm not sure how long he owned it for."

Sally's eyes suddenly grew a little wider as if something just dawned on her. "Oh, my gosh, you must be talking about Kilroy VanderGrift. I hadn't heard his name in so long I forgot. Of *course* I know who he is;

my father bought the marina from him back in '65. His son's a very powerful and famous senator from St. Thomas." Holly and I both asked at the same time.

"His son?"

"Yes, Lucky owns the Tiara Bay Marina, one of the most exclusive on St. Thomas. It's the one his dad bought after he sold this marina to my father."

At the mention of the name "Lucky," Holly and I looked at each other, slack-jawed. When Millie's baby was born, he had an unusual birthmark on his forearm that Millie thought looked like a four-leaf clover, and she named him Lucky. Holly pressed her for more information.

"I'm, I'm sorry; did you just say the senator's name was Lucky?"

"Yes, Lucky VanderGrift. Everybody knows Lucky; he's always in the news. You're obviously not islanders."

"No, no we're not," I interjected. "But, uh, his name is really Lucky?"

"His proper name is Chanceaux, but like I said, he goes by 'Lucky'. His mother was a French girl from St. Maarten, as I recall."

Holly grabbed my arm, "Oh my God, I can't believe it."

"Is everything alright?"

"Yes, yes everything's fine," I responded. "But what about Lucky's parents? Do you know if they're still alive?" Sally looked a little hesitant to respond, as if she had said something she wasn't supposed to. Holly sensed it.

"Please, Sally, it's important. Do you know anything about the parents?"

"Well, as far as I know, the mother lives, or lived, on St. Maarten."

"You wouldn't happen to know where, would you?"

"No, I wouldn't have the—wait a second, as a matter of fact I might. When my father bought the marina, Mr. VanderGrift held the mortgage, and he had to make payments to him. I know he used to send them to St. Thomas, but at some point, after the accident, he started sending them to Mrs. Vandergrift on St. Maarten. I don't have the information here in the office, but I'm sure I have it in storage. When I get a chance, I'll look for the last address we had and give you a call if you like."

"That would be great, Sally. Here, let me give you my cell number."

While Holly scribbled her number on a piece of paper, I looked at a map and an old picture of two men shaking hands hung on the wall. I pointed at the picture. "Would one of those men happen to be Kilroy VanderGrift?"

Sally looked up and slapped her forehead lightly. "Yes! That's him on the left. The other man is my father. That picture was taken on the day he bought the marina."

"You said your father started sending checks to Mrs. VanderGrift after the accident. What kind of accident?"

Sally frowned and shook her head. "It was a terrible, terrible tragedy. Kilroy VanderGrift was an avid scuba diver, and naturally, so was Lucky. According to the papers, they were diving somewhere off St. Johns and were separated in an unusually strong current. Lucky managed to make it back to the boat, but his father didn't, and was found on the ocean floor the next day by a search party. They speculated he had an equipment malfunction and drowned, most likely from being tumbled about in the current. It was only a couple years after he sold my father the marina—in 1967, I believe."

"Sounds sorta like what happened to Joseph at 'the wall,'" commented Tangles. Holly and I both shot him a shut-the-fuck-up look, so when Sally said, "sounds like what happened to *who?*" Tangles replied, "Nobody, it's nothing. I was just thinkin' out loud."

Maybe Tangles was thinking out loud, but I wasn't. I was pretty much brain-fried. Joseph ends up in a coma after diving with Kilroy—Kilroy basically steals Joseph's son and adopts him as his own—then Kilroy dies while diving with the son some twenty years later? *Coincidence?*

It took several moments for it to sink in with Holly, too, and when she finally spoke, her voice was unsteady. "You, you're saying, he...he died in a diving accident? With Lucky? Lucky was... he was the only one with him?"

"Yep, and he sure was lucky to survive. In more ways than one."

"How do you mean?" Knowingly or not, Holly was squeezing my arm tighter than Kelly Ripa's smile, and it was beginning to hurt.

"I believe he inherited the Tiara Bay Marina when his father died; in fact, the rumor was he inherited pretty much everything. With the financial success of the marina, he was able to bankroll his way into politics, and the rest, as they say, is history."

Chapter 24

Juan Carlos Cordero was a successful cattle rancher with a five-hundred-acre spread in the foothills of Pasto, Colombia. His ranch lay adjacent to the Putumayo River, on the east side of the Andes, near the base of the Galeros volcano, about one-hundred-and-fifteen miles from the Pacific, and not too far from the borders of Ecuador and Peru. He and his wife, Maria, wanted the best for their two sons, so when the eldest, Eduardo, came of schooling age, they sent him to the finest universities. Much to their delight, Eduardo excelled in academics and was accepted at the prestigious Wharton School of Business at the University of Pennsylvania, where he earned a BS in engineering and an MBA in finance.

Rico (eight years younger than Eduardo) was another story. Spoiled by his parents growing financial fortune and lacking guidance from Eduardo after he went away to school, Rico was a hot mess. His violent temper, indifference to academia, and utter disdain toward authority figures got him thrown out of one school after another. When his parents finally ceded the fact that thirteen-year-old Rico would never follow in his brother's footsteps, they gave him a job on the ranch; it was the summer of 1983.

Juan Carlos tried to teach Rico the workings of the ranch, but it was futile. Rico felt entitled and didn't want to work. Period. Much to his parents' horror, he became enthralled by stories of the notorious up-and-coming drug-kingpin, Pablo Escobar, who had taken over the Medellin cartel. Then, around Christmas, the movie *Scarface* came out, and young Rico was hooked. He was convinced that Pablo Escobar's real-life exploits and the aggrandizement of the lifestyle by Al Pacino were omens of sorts. He had been searching for his true calling and was certain he had found it.

Unable to contain his excitement and believing his destiny was to become a drug lord, Rico called his older brother at school to tell him the news. It was a phone call they would both recount and laugh at many times over the ensuing years.

"You're going to be *who?*" asked Eduardo.

"I'm going to be the next Tony Montana."

"Who is Tony Montana?"

"You don't know? You mean you haven't seen *Scarface* yet?"

"I just finished finals, Rico. No, I haven't seen it."

"It's *unbelievable*! The cars, the coke, the women, the machine guns, the blood—"

"Sounds like Sunday church service in Cartageña."

"Ha! Yes! Yes, that's exactly what it's like. This actor, Al Pacino, he plays a guy like Pablo Escobar—he's incredible! You know about Escobar, right?"

"Listen, little brother, I knew about Escobar when your cojones were keeping your pancreas company. I can tell from your voice they finally dropped; too bad I'm not there to teach you what to do with them."

Rico's voice took on a more serious tone. "Yes, Eduardo, I wanted to tell you about that too. I'm getting these feelings I am unfamiliar with, and my dick, well, my dick...sometimes it gets harder than Mama's frijoles when she forgets to turn the stove off."

"Ah, yes, the joys of puberty. Well, don't worry; it's only a short step to manhood."

"Please, tell me, Eduardo, how do I make that step? Every morning my balls are bluer than week-old goat cheese."

"I feel for you, little brother. You want to make that painful feeling go away, don't you?"

"Madre de Dios, yes."

"Okay, here's what you do. You know the casing that Mama uses to stuff the sausage with?"

"Of course."

"When she's not looking, grab a handful and go out to the llama pen. Once you make sure nobody's around—that's very important—put the casing over your dick. Then, and this is the tricky part, sneak up on one of the llamas and stick it in."

"Stick it in the llama?"

"Trust me, Rico; you'll have more relief than a Rolaids factory."

"Rolaids? What is—?"

"That's not important, just stick it in and the pain will go vamoose!"

"It does hurt...a lot. But I was hoping someone like *Elvira* would make the pain go away. That's who I want...*Elvira.*"

"Who the hell's, Elvira?"

"Tony Montana's girlfriend. She's a beautiful blond with skinny little legs. You gotta see the movie; I've seen it three times already."

"Listen, Rico, you want the pain to go away? Then pick out the llama with the skinniest legs and do her. Just close your eyes and pretend it's Elvira. Trust me, it'll feel about the same."

"Well, there is one that got sick and lost a lot of weight..."

"*Perfecto,* pound it like you're putting in fence posts."

"Fence posts? I hate pounding fence posts. That's hard work."

"You don't have to dig a hole in the ground, Rico. It's just 'bam, bam, bam,' and you're done. For a first timer like you, it'll probably be 'bam' and done."

"If you say so, but when I'm a drug lord, I'm gonna have a girl like Elvira, maybe even two or three. And I want a zoo, too, just like Pablo Escobar."

"You've heard about his zoo?"

"Yes, I want tigers and lions and snakes and—"

"You're really serious, aren't you?"

"You bet. Why shouldn't I be a drug lord? You too, Eduardo. We live in the perfect spot to grow coca instead of cattle, and we have plenty of room for the zoo."

"What about our parents?"

"What about them? Nobody lives forever, and the way they've been bossing me around, forever might be tomorrow."

"Listen to me, Rico. Don't do anything stupid. I've been studying finance, and I don't intend to waste it on cattle ranching. The biggest problem drug traffickers have is laundering money. The key is to take the illegal proceeds and roll them into legitimate businesses. If you spread it around properly, it's very hard to track when you take it out. Once I get my degree, I plan on getting a job with *el Banco de Bogota.* If I can establish enough trustworthy contacts on the inside of the Latin and American banking industries, well, maybe your dream of becoming a drug lord isn't so far-fetched."

"So, what should I do?"

"You need to make some contacts on the street. Start finding out what you can about who is doing what."

"Contacts within the Medellin cartel?"

"You know, Escobar is getting more famous by the day. He's becoming one of the prime targets for Reagan and his war on drugs. There is another group I have been hearing about that might be more prudent to get friendly with."

"Who?"

"The Cali Cartel. They are small right now, but if Escobar gets caught or killed, they will be there to pick up the pieces. See if you can establish a relationship with them, but for God's sake, keep a low profile and don't let our parents know."

"Okay, but I can't get started for a couple weeks—I'm grounded right now."

"*Grounded?* What did you do now?"

"You know Fredy, Papa's favorite ranch hand?"

"Of course, Papa always said he did the work of ten men."

"Well, maybe he only does the work of five now."

"What do you mean?"

"I chopped off one of his hands."

"You *what?* Rico, why would you do such a thing?"

"We were on lunch break, and he was looking at my tortilla funny. I thought he was going to take a bite."

"You *thought* he was going to take a bite?"

"Well, not any more. Turns out there was a worm on it, and he was going to warn me. Like I told papa, it was all just a misunderstanding. I feel horrible; I will never be able to eat another tortilla as long as I live."

"Jesus, Rico, you really need to watch that temper of yours. One day it's going to get the better of you."

"It already has. Mama found my bootleg copy of *Scarface* and threw it in the fire. She says it made me chop off Fredy's hand. I tell you, she is out of control. When you see the movie, you will understand what she has done."

"Well, like I said, don't do anything stupid. If you want to become a drug lord, you need to play your cards right. Do what I say, and maybe you'll have that zoo someday."

"No, Eduardo, *we* will have a zoo, and the Cordero brothers will be the most feared and respected drug lords in the world!"

***

Eduardo Cordero laughed after recounting their long ago conversation. "You remember that, Rico? You remember how full of bravado you were?"

The white Bengal tiger that sat at Rico's feet purred as he stroked the underside of her chin. Rico smiled at his brother and cocked his head slightly. "*Were?*"

This time they both laughed.

"My apologies, you still have the biggest cojones in the Atriz Valley."

"Just the valley?"

"Okay, okay, in all of Colombia!"

"That's better, but my cojones would be of little use if not for your brains, dear brother. Building a submarine that can dive to thirty feet and hold over seven tons of product was pure genius."

"Not really, it was just the natural evolution of our distribution methods. We have to stay one step ahead of the DEA."

"Don't be so modest; it was an incredible feat! By the time those stupid Americans figure out what we're doing, you will have one that can drive on the ocean floor!"

When the tiger sensed the excitement in Rico's voice and let out a growl, Rico moved to calm her. He stroked her head and behind her ears, all the while cooing; "Easy, Elvira, easy girl. It's okay now, everything's okay." Elvira stopped growling and curled up at her master's feet. "That's better. *That's* my girl."

Eduardo watched his little brother continue to pet and stroke the large white tiger while whispering sweet nothings in her ear. He knew that his affection for her was outside the norm— *way* outside the norm.Early one morning, their zookeeper woke to screams coming from the tiger enclosure and found Rico on top of four-month old Elvira, and Elvira's mother on top of Rico, mauling him. The zookeeper was forced to shoot the mother, but not before she tore Rico's scalp off and inflicted horrific wounds to his face and back. He lost one eye and one ear and gained a pair of deep gouge wounds on both sides of his face. Although

Eduardo was repulsed and disturbed at his brother's penchant for bestiality, he felt guilty for encouraging him to have sex with a llama when he was thirteen. He had meant it only as a joke, never dreaming Rico would take him seriously.

Developing a not-so-secret taste for llamas, and then cutting a man's hand off over a tortilla, had earned him the nickname "Rico Loco." But after Elvira's mother tried to turn him into paella and rumors of his sexuality surfaced, people started calling him "Rico the Freako," and the press picked up on it. Either way, everybody knew he was bat-shit crazy, and Eduardo felt partially to blame.

When Rico recovered, he ordered Elvira de-clawed and de-fanged (as a precaution) and continued to satisfy his unholy desires with her. Eduardo tried to convince him to stop and instead use prostitutes like he did, but Rico's argument was sound. Aside from the fact that his disfigurement made him undesirable, even to prostitutes, he preferred Elvira because she would never betray him. He even went so far as to suggest that Eduardo himself give up prostitutes for one of their exotic animals. After all, he argued, history was littered with the crushed lives of great men betrayed by scheming women, like Jose Canseco. In the end, Eduardo decided to look the other way and to try to help keep his brother's sexual deviance as quiet as he could. It was in this vein that he ordered Rico to chop up the zookeeper and toss him in the Putumayo River, just like he had done to their parents.

Chapter 25

Eduardo clicked on the computer screen in front of him to track the progress of the sub that had just made their biggest delivery to date. He left nothing to chance and had tracking devices on every sub in their fleet. With the big cat peacefully asleep on the floor, Rico asked, "You still haven't heard from McGirt?"

"No, that's why I'm looking to see where the sub is."

Eduardo noted the timeline, which showed it stopped for nearly three hours the previous day some forty miles south of St. Thomas before continuing on a westerly track.

"So, how does it look? Everything okay?"

"Yes, yes, it looks like the transfer took place a little farther south than planned, and took a little longer than usual, but the sub has skirted the Dominican Republic and is headed toward our Cuban friends."

"So, why do you think McGirt hasn't called?"

"He must have a problem with the satellite phone. We'll know when he makes it to Cuba and picks up the arms shipment. They're rolling the red carpet out for him; the transfer is taking place in port. He'll be able to contact us then for sure."

Suddenly, one of Eduardo's cell phones started ringing, and he answered it. "Hello?"

"We have a problem."

"Who is this?"

"Chanceaux."

Alarmed, Eduardo looked at his brother. It was never a good thing when someone broke protocol and made contact directly. "You shouldn't be calling—it's dangerous."

"I know, but in light of the magnitude of the problem, I thought contact was necessary. I'm speaking on a throwaway cell, to be safe."

"So, what is it?"

"We never received delivery."

"*What?*"

"There was an explosion and contact was never made."

"What do you mean— *explosion?* What are you talking about? When did this happen?"

"Just before sunset yesterday a boat blew up… some forty miles offshore. The Coast Guard won't let anybody near the wreckage."

"So, what does that have to do with us?"

"That was my initial reaction too, but clearly something's wrong. My son heard from one of his contacts on St. Croix. He told him that a couple DEA agents were dropped off by a Coast Guard chopper at a resort on the east end last night. He said it was *their* boat that blew up. Have you been in contact with the sub?"

"No, but we've had problems with the satellite phone before."

"I hope that's all it is, but I don't have a good feeling about this."

Eduardo heard what he said, but it wasn't computing. He knew from the tracking device on the sub that it had stopped like it was supposed to and was currently heading to its next destination as planned. Something didn't add up. He thought about telling the senator that he knew the sub had stopped, delivered, and appeared to be on schedule, but he decided to keep it to himself.

"Hello? Are you still there?" asked the senator.

"Yes, I'm here. I was just thinking. Why didn't you call me last night?"

"I didn't think the explosion had anything to do with the shipment either. I thought you were just running late. Considering the risk in calling, I thought waiting was prudent given your impeccable delivery record. So, what are you going to do? There's a lot of money at stake. My associates are going to want answers."

"Be careful what you ask for, my friend. Once I sort things out, I'll be in touch."

"Okay, let me give you a number to—"

"Don't worry; I know how to find you." Click.

The look of alarm on his brother's face had Rico pacing back and forth. Elvira was awake now and mimicking his every move. As soon as his brother hung up the phone, Rico asked, "What is it? What happened?"

Eduardo stared at the computer screen in front of him, watching as the sub kept up its west to northwest track. *What the hell was going on?* "It was the senator; he claims they never took delivery."

"*What?*"

"That's what he said...but I think he's lying." He pointed at the computer screen. "Look for yourself. The sub's right where it's supposed to be."

“If he’s lying, then McGirt must be in on it. Maybe that’s why he hasn’t called.”

“You think he’d cross us? All this time he worked for us, he never let us down—not once. Plus, he stands to make a million dollars. Something’s not right. The senator claims a boat blew up and a couple DEA agents got dropped off by a Coast Guard chopper last night… on St. Croix.”

“St. Croix? The DEA *and* the Coast Guard? What the…what the *fuck’s* going on?”

“I don’t know, but if the senator thinks he’s gonna fuck us out of six tons of blow, he’s got even bigger balls than you, Rico.”

“Not possible.”

“I know. How else could you make a tiger smile?”

“So, what do you want me to do?”

“Tell Mateo to provision the jet and to make sure both tanks are filled to capacity. He needs to be ready to go at a moment’s notice. ”

“Is that it?”

“No, call Andres and tell him to stop feeding Emilio.”

Rico smiled knowingly as he entered Andre’s number into his cell phone. Although they were sometimes referred to as Beauty and the Beast by the locals, Eduardo had a mean streak longer than an NBC Olympic special featuring Mary Carillo. Rico thought of all the fun he would have with Emilio, and his smile grew wider. “Good idea, my brother, nobody can squeeze the truth from someone like Emilio…*nobody.*”

Chapter 26

I talked Holly into letting me drive when we left the Salt River Marina, and I thought out loud while getting used to driving on the wrong side of the road. "This story about Kilroy dying in a scuba diving accident sounds fishier than a Jon Corzine alibi."

"Jon Corzine?" asked Tangles. Before I could answer, Holly beat me to the punch and turned to face him in the backseat of the jeep.

"You know who Jon Corzine is. He was the Wall street banker who became governor of New Jersey."

"He was also Obama's biggest campaign fundraiser," I added.

"Now I remember. The guy who looks like a wolf spider, right?"

"Good call," I confirmed. "He looks *and* acts like one, only his bite is more toxic, at least when it comes to investor's money. The firm he ran, MF Global, basically stole 1.2 billion dollars from the pension funds of Midwestern farmers."

"So he's in jail now?"

"You would think so, but apparently the explanation he gave to his Senate buddies that he just didn't know what happened to the money was good enough for the US attorney's office, which is, coincidentally, led by an Obama appointee."

"If that's a coincidence," said Holly, "then Kilroy dying in a scuba diving accident with Lucky is the *mother* of all coincidences."

I was thinking the same thing and expounded on it in a moment of Dali Lama-esque clarity. "You're exactly right. And if fate is the mother of coincidence, then chance is the umbilical cord, or in this case, Chanceaux." Proud of my twisted analogy, I smiled at Holly before raising an eyebrow and glancing in the rearview at Tangles. He was wearing a bewildered look, as if somebody forgot to put okra in his gumbo. "Fate is the mother of chance's umbilical...what the hell did you just say?"

Holly started laughing. "He's right, Kit, that was a doozy. Did you just come up with it or have you been sand-bagging us, just *waiting* to spring that beauty?"

"Great minds are faster than a pine-tarred rabbit in a forest fire."

"So you *have* been working on it."

"Very funny. I can tell it's killing you to think I might be capable of a spontaneous moment of profound insight."

"I don't know about her," Tangles snickered, "but it's killing me. That was like Kungfucious meets the Pink Panther."

"Kungfucious?"

"You know what I mean. Where do you come up with this shit? I mean, I know the fishing was slow, and you had a lot of time to think before old Tangles saved the day, but—"

"*You* saved the day? *I* saved *you*, you little—"

"Look out!" screamed Holly. Since leaving the marina, we had been driving along the north side of the island heading west, which put the ocean on our right, and it had just turned into the sheer side of a cliff. Lack of a guardrail made for a great view of the hundred-and-fifty-foot drop to the crystal-blue water below. Until the drop-off appeared, I had been overly-conscious about not driving too close to the cliff face. Since the traffic was light, I drove closer to the middle of the road. As we rounded a bend, there was a speeding pickup coming straight at us. I swerved to the left and nearly clipped the face of the cliff, then cut the wheel a little too hard to the right as we came within inches of the passing truck. Tangles and Holly screamed at the top of their lungs as the jeep fishtailed and the rear end swung out over the precipice. For a few ass-puckering moments, we slid sideways along the edge of the cliff before I managed to steer the jeep back to the center of the road.

"Holy crap! You almost killed us!" cried Tangles.

"He's right, Kit! For the love of God, slow down and keep your eyes on the road! You know how much I hate heights! Geez... I'm nervous enough already." Holly let out a deep breath and released her death grip on the dashboard.

"Alright, alright... sorry 'bout that. You'd think if they want you to drive on the right side of the road they would put the steering wheel on the right side of the car."

"Just slow down and pay attention, okay? Where the heck are we going, anyways?"

"West." I looked at her and smiled.

Holly rolled her eyes, and I glanced in the rearview at Tangles, who pointed a little finger at me and snarled, "Quit looking in the mirror and watch the fucking road!"

Holly said, "I *know* we are going *west,* smartass. The question is, where to? Don't look at me either; keep your eyes on the road, and your hands upon the wheel. And if you come up with some cute Doors reference, I swear, we are *so* over."

"Wow, you two would be no fun at all at Six Flags. Remind me to—"

"WHERE ARE WE GOING!"

"Okay, okay, everybody just calm down. When we were in the marina office I noticed a map that showed where the diving and fishing spot called 'The Wall' is located. That's the place where Kilroy and Joseph went diving when Joseph had his supposed accident. I thought we should check it out while we're here. Maybe we can learn something. I don't think it's too much farther."

Holly sighed and rubbed her temples. "You see, that wasn't so hard, *was it?*"

"Hey, Shag, bet you hear that a lot," quipped Tangles.

"I can see the world's shortest comedian has gotten over his erroneously-perceived brush with death."

"Erroneous my ass."

"Your ass *is* erroneous; it looks like your face."

"What? That doesn't even make sense. If my ass looked like my face, then I would have a great looking ass...which, by the way, the ladies *do* seem to appreciate."

"Whatever... ass-face."

"Can you two knock it off for a minute? You sound like Beavis and Butthead after lobotomies. Let's focus on the scuba accident with Lucky and Kilroy for a minute. If it wasn't a coincidence that Kilroy died while diving with Lucky, meaning it wasn't an accident, what does that say? Did Lucky kill him out of greed, or was revenge the motive?"

"That's the sixty-four-thousand-dollar question," I answered. "First, you'd need to know if Lucky even *knew* he was adopted. If he did, and if he also found out that Kilroy tried to kill his dad, then yeah, revenge might be the motive."

"Or it could be both," added Tangles. "Maybe he found out that he was adopted *and* that Kilroy tried to kill his dad *and* that exacting revenge would financially set him for life. Problem is, Lucky's the only one who knows, and seeing as how he's a big-shot, money-bags senator, I don't see him telling us the real story—even *if* we get a chance to ask."

"That's not entirely correct," replied Holly. "If Kilroy's wife Genevieve is still alive, she would know if they told him he was adopted, or she might have an idea whether or not he ever found out."

"That's a good point," I conceded. "Maybe the lady from the marina will find an address for Genevieve and give you a call. If she's alive, and we can get her to talk, who knows what we might find out."

Since our near-collision with the pickup, we had been gradually descending toward the shoreline, and finally the road left the coast and jogged inland a little. It was a semi-rural area with a few horses and roosters scattered about. The farmland was lush up to the tree line, which appeared to be rainforest. It was quite serene, and not what I expected to find on the island.

"Either way," Holly continued. "I need to see Lucky and let him know he's Millie's son, and that we're cousins. I just can't believe he would kill the man he thought was his father for money. I mean, maybe if he found out what Kilroy did to his *real* father, but not otherwise. I sure don't like the notion of being related to a killer, though, whether Kilroy deserved it or not. I'm hoping you're wrong about the coincidence thing and it was just an accident."

"Accidents happen in pants, and that's no coincidence," piped in Tangles. I started chuckling, and Holly turned to look at him. "What the hell does that mean?"

"Uh, it means it was no accident. It's just a saying, that's all."

"No, no, it's not a saying. Just because you said it doesn't make it a saying. In fact, I bet nobody in the history of the *world* has ever said that before."

"Why are you picking on me?" In my peripheral vision, I saw his finger point at me. "You don't pick on Mr. Death Cab for Cutie when he comes up with a saying."

"He *hasn't* come up with a saying!" Holly shook her head, and I felt her eyes burning holes in the side of my face. "You see what you started with your stupid, 'fate is the umbilical cord of chance' routine?"

"I'd look but that would require taking my eyes off the road."

"Seriously."

"Well, if we're being serious, the saying goes, 'If fate is the mother of coincidence, then chance is the umbilical cord.' Not 'Fate is the umbilical cord of chance,' that doesn't make sense. Maybe, 'Chance is the umbilical cord of coincidence.' Yeah...I like that. That works. That's my new saying; 'Chance is the umbilical cord of coincidence."

"For the last time, Kit, it's not a saying; nobody's ever said it."

"They have now."

"You have! Nobody else! Nobody in this universe or any other....EVER!" Tangles popped his head between the seats. "Damn, Shag. You're right."

"Nobody asked you!" Holly shot back.

"No, I mean, he's right about when you get mad—it's really hot. When you get hot, it's hot."

"Shut up."

I glanced at him in the rearview mirror. "Yeah, dude, that wasn't exactly for public consumption, you know? I must have let that slip during a bro-ment." I felt Holly's stare and waited for it. "Oh, *really?*" she said, "What *else* have you let slip during a *broment?*"

"Nothing. Shaggy don't play that game."

"That should be a saying," mused Tangles.

"What? Shaggy don't play that game?"

"No, 'When you're hot, it's really hot.'"

"It *is* a saying, you little moron. 'When you're hot, you're hot, and when you're not, you're not...and clearly, you're not."

"That's what that means? Damn, I always thought it referred to a hot streak."

"That's what I'm here for, bro, to educate and stimulate the mind."

Holly couldn't take anymore. "*Really?* Do you ever listen to the words coming out of your mouth? The only mind you've ever stimulated had a gaff sticking out of it. Unless, of course, you missed sticking it, which I've seen you do more than once."

"Oh, snap! No she didn't!" incited Tangles from the cheap seats.

"I'm gonna take the high road and let that slide, because it looks like we're here."

The road had meandered back to the coast, and I pulled in front of an open-air, roadside bar that literally sat on the water. It had a sign in front that read, "Hole-in-the-Wall Bar." Anchored about three hundred yards offshore was a big power catamaran. It was maybe sixty-feet long, and there were divers on board and in the water.

"You think it's open?" asked Holly as we piled out of the jeep. "It's only ten-thirty; I don't see anyone." Suddenly a head popped up from behind the bar, and a hand waved at us.

"Looks like we're in luck."

"Good, after listening to you two for the past hour, I've never wanted a Bloody Mary more than I do right now."

As we stepped across the parking lot toward the bar, Tangles rubbed his stomach. "I'm kinda hungry… hope the kitchen's open."

"The kitchen?" Holly looked at him sideways in disbelief. "How can you be hungry? We just had breakfast a little while ago."

"You know the saying about being in the Caribbean."

Tangles held open a little half-gate that led to the steps down to the bar and gestured for Holly to pass first.

"No, no I don't."

"You know," he grinned. "When in Rome…."

Chapter 27

Remy's cell rang as he poured himself a coffee in the Tiara Bay Marina office. Not recognizing the number, he answered with a hint of uncertainty in his voice. "Hello?"

"Remy? It's me, Shortshank."

Remy recognized the voice of the commercial fisherman known as Shortshank, who ran an old rig out of Red Hook Harbor on the island's east end. Instinctively he shifted to his hybrid-island dialect. "Shank, how you be, mon? What's kickin'?"

"I ran into one of your guys last night, and he say you be paying for word about de explosion on de water."

"Dat's right. If you know someting, I'll make it wert your while."

"How wert my while?"

"Depends what you have."

Shortshank looked down at the water-logged man lying on the floor of his cockpit in a semi-conscious state. "I tink I found someone from de explosion."

"What you mean?"

"I be pulling up nets when I seen someting in de distance. I look and dis guy's clinging to a cooler in de middle of de ocean. He burned, but nuttin' too bad."

"He's alive?"

"Yeah, but maybe not for long. I tink he's overdosing."

"*Overdosing?*"

"Big time. His face be whiter den Pat Sajak. He had a big sack of coke wit him, and it look like he stuck his face in it. He startin' to shake pretty bad. I taught about calling de Coast Guard, but I don' wan' no trouble, you know? Dat's why I called."

"You did a smart ting, Shortshank—what he look like?"

"Cold and wet."

"No, I mean, does he look, like… Latino?"

"*Latino?*"

"Yeah, you know, like a Colombian?"

Shortshank looked down at the man and shook his head. "No, but he got a wet back."

"He's a wetback?"

"No, no, he white, like I said—maybe American."

"*American?*"

"Like de cheese."

"I'm de first person you called, right? Nobody else know?"

"Nobody."

"Good, if you keep it dat way and bring him to de marina, I'll gas up your tank." After his offer was met with silence, Remy asked, "You still dere, Shortshank?"

"I dunno, Remy. Dere a lot of Coast Guard around—too risky. Maybe I just dump him over de side, keep de coke, and forget about it. Dere's a weed line out here like I never seen. I should be fishing."

"No! Listen! I need him. Bring him here, and I'll give you a credit in de ship's store for a tousand dollars...plus de gas."

"I don't need no vouchers. Make it five tousand and you got a deal."

"*Five tousand?*"

"Cash."

"How 'bout two tousand, and I fill you're tank?"

"I got two tanks."

"Okay, I fill 'em up."

"*And* I keep de coke?"

"Finders keepers, mon, it's all yours."

"You got a deal. See you in an hour."

"One more ting."

"What be dat?"

"I only fish wit live bait. If he DOA, de deal off."

"Okay, den. I see you in forty-five." Click.

Shortshank put the cell in his pocket and grew concerned as the man started bouncing on the cockpit floor from convulsions. He grabbed the freshwater wash-down hose, unscrewed the spray nozzle, and turned it on. Then he pinned the man to the deck and shoved the hose in his mouth, yelling, "Drink up, Whitey!" Immediately, the man's eyes shot open, and he began gagging. After a few seconds, Shortshank pulled the hose out and sprayed the encrusted cocaine off the man's face. Figuring he might be suffering from hypothermia too, he dragged him inside the small cabin and draped a blanket over him. Satisfied he'd done all he was going to do, Shortshank fired up the engines and headed full throttle toward the Tiara Bay Marina.

Chapter 28

Holly got her desired Bloody Mary, and the bartender talked me and Tangles into his latest rum-based creation of frozen slushiness. Frozen concoctions weren't normally my thing, but I hoisted it anyways, and the three of us fake-clinked our plastic cups together.

"When in Rome…" I said.

"To Rome…" responded Tangles.

"At least that's a real saying," added Holly.

"Sorta like 'well, well, jack crevalle.'"

Holly shot Tangles a look that was equal parts bewilderment and annoyance. No way was she gonna tell him about the bartender at the Hibiscus who loved it. "No, it's not *sorta* like that at all. You know why? 'Cause it's not a saying. Nobody ever said it but you and Mr. 'Fate is the umbilical cord of coincidence.'" She stuck her thumb out sideways at me, and I corrected her. "Actually…its 'coincidence is the umbilical cord of chance.'"

She turned and gave *me* the look. "Seriously, Kit, do you not get it, or are you just trying to get me going?"

Tangles saw an opportunity to make matters worse… and he did. "I think he's trying to get you going. You know why? 'Cause when you're hot, you're hot." Then he had to wink at her and add, "Seriously, I'm talking en fuego. If you could patent that look, you'd be a—"

Holly stuck her hand out in front of his face. "Will you *shut up* for once?"

I tried to diffuse the situation but somehow managed to do the opposite. "She's right, Tangles. It's time for a truce. No more sayings." I leaned over and gave Holly a kiss on the cheek that was received about as well as terpin hydrate to a toddler. "Besides," I added. "She's hot even when she's not…at least to me she is."

I was expecting her to maybe blush and say, 'Oh, that's sweet,' or something. Instead, she took a big gulp of Bloody Mary and gave me a steely stare. "So now I'm not hot? Anything else you wanna add, Romeo?"

"No, I mean, yes. What I meant was…even though you're dead sexy when your blood gets boiling; you're sexy *all* the time…for real."

She declined another Bloody from the bartender in lieu of a bottle of water and gave me a weird look. "Did you just say, 'dead sexy?' What's that?"

"It's just a saying."

Holly clenched her fists and looked at the thatch-covered ceiling while letting out some sort of primal grunt. Then she abruptly got off her barstool. Realizing I had inadvertently violated the 'no sayings' truce in record time, I tried to explain myself while Tangles stifled a laugh.

"I didn't mean it like that, but, seriously, it, uh, it really *is* a saying; it means 'way hot.' I was just saying you're—"

"Stop, just stop...please. Just stop talking. I'm going to take a little walk to clear my head. I can only take you two in small doses...*very* small doses at this rate. But don't get too comfortable, we need to head back to town and find a flight to St. Thomas."

"Sure, Holl, whatever you say. We'll be ready when you are. I didn't mean to—"

She put her hand up. "Just be ready to go in fifteen minutes...please?"

"Sure, no problem."

Holly walked out of the bar, and the bartender approached gingerly. "Everything alright?"

I was watching Holly walk down the shoreline and turned to face him. "Huh? Yeah, everything's fine. Couldn't be...couldn't be better. How 'bout another one of these, uh, what'd you call them?" I held up my near-empty drink.

"Ramblers—one more rambler coming up."

"Better make that two." Tangles pushed his empty cup over to him. "These things are good. What's in it?"

As the bartender whipped us up a couple more, he explained his formula. "Rum, vodka, coconut milk, a splash of soda water, blend it with ice and top it off with a dark rum floater."

"I like it," I commented, "it's not too sweet. So, what's with the name? Why do you call it a Rambler?"

"'Cause if you have more than two, you'll be rambling...guaranteed. Sure as your lady's ramblin' down the road."

I sat stone faced, not sure if I liked the friendly bartender, no matter how good his little foo-foo drink was. Tangles let out a belly laugh and fist bumped him. Ever the inciter, he lived to twist the knife. "Ouch.

That had to sting a little. You just gonna just sit there and take it, Shag?"

Realizing he probably shouldn't have zinged me, and that Tangles was stirring things up, the bartender apologized. "Hey man, I was just kidding. That was out of line. This drink's on me. We're good...right?"

He had no way of knowing that for free drinks I was pretty much willing to be a human punching bag, so I shook his hand, and he set a couple Rambler's down. "Yeah, we're good. I probably deserve it. I guess I pushed her a little too much. No biggie."

"I bet that's what all the girls say," cracked Tangles. He wasn't buying drinks though, so he got both barrels after I downed some more Rambler.

"Listen up, half-pipe. I'm a little out of my league with Holly, and it's hard enough not to fuck things up without having a Gong Show freak egging me on."

'Gong Show freak? What the fuck. I don't even know what that is."

"Too bad. It's exactly what you're like. You're like Chuck Barris on his knees, going blah, blah, blah, and every time I try to smooth things out with Holly, you bang the goddamn gong, and I get the hook! Now that I think of it, you even look like him!" I swirled my Rambler around in its plastic cup and knocked back some more.

"Dude, c'mon! It's all in fun, remember? That's what this trip is supposed to be about. I mean, besides helping Holly find out about Joseph and Lucky. Personally, I think she's acting a little touchy, don't you?"

"*Touchy*? What do you mean, *touchy?*"

"You know, she seems to have a shorter fuse than normal."

"You think?"

"Definitely. It's probably nothing, but then again..." Tangles cocked his head to the side and shrugged.

"Then again what? What are you saying?"

"Oh, I don't know. Maybe she's, you know... pregnant."

"*What?* What the *fuck* are you talking about— pregnant? Jesus H. Christ, don't even say that!"

"You gotta admit, it would explain a lot."

Momentary panic set in as I started to think the unthinkable, and I downed the rest of my drink. "Oh fuck, I think I need another rambler."

"You sure?" asked the Bartender.

"What are you, my mother?"

"One rambler... coming up!" As my life flashed before me, I saw a small zodiac making its way toward the bar from the big catamaran that was anchored offshore.

"Look at the bright side," said Tangles. "There are some choice country song lyrics in there."

"In where?"

"You know, 'my girl got pregnant and my boat blew up.' Could be a classic."

"You know what else could be a classic?"

"What?"

"Taking you to Papua New Guinea and shrinking your already tiny head down to key-chain size so when I tool around Palm Beach in the Beemer, I can use your face to scratch my balls."

"That's not funny, that's sick…*you're* sick."

"Sick of *you,* maybe."

"Wow! Did I hear you say your boat blew up too?" The bartender set my drink down in front of me, and I watched as Holly approached the small dinghy which had just reached shore. "Man that sucks. Losing your boat and gaining a kid…unless, you know, you were trying to."

I took a big gulp and eyed the young bartender who looked to be maybe twenty-five and fresh from the mainland. Clearly, he didn't know fuck-all. "Kid, let me tell you something. Nobody's *ever* tried to do that anywhere at anytime. Besides, my girlfriend's not pregnant, or she wouldn't be drinking." I watched Holly point at the boat and then at us in the bar.

"Maybe she doesn't know yet," chirped Tangles.

"You see what I'm talking about, kid? The little bastard just banged the gong again. He's like a wind-up monkey that never stops slammin' the cymbals together."

"I'm just saying, you know, maybe she doesn't realize—"

"Shut up. No more…no more prego talk. Three ramblers to two says the next wisecrack sends you over that railing there." I pointed to the railing that kept bar patrons from falling into the water.

"Whatever bro— fact is, the truth hurts…at least that's how the saying goes."

Despite my being miffed at him, I had to admit it was funny, especially on my third rambler. We were still laughing when a smiling Holly walked in with the guy on the zodiac.

"What's so funny?" She sat down next to me, and the guy from the zodiac sat on the other side of her.

"Nothing, Tangles' just being stupid."

"So... same old same old? Isn't that how the saying goes?" She smiled to let me know she wasn't mad anymore. It was a good sign, unless of course, her mood change was brought on by a hormonal imbalance due to pregnancy. *Gulp.*

"No, the saying goes, 'let's hit the road,' I'm ready." I pointed at Tangles and spoke for him (which I was prone to do). "He's ready too." I downed the rest of my rambler and signaled to the bartender for the check. "Set up Captain Zodiac before you close out the tab, he's probably parched."

Captain Zodiac nodded at me as the bartender reached in a cooler and placed an ice cold can of Budweiser in front of him. "Thanks," was all he said.

Holly placed her hand on my forearm. "Kit?"

"What? We're ready to go. Let's roll, baby."

"We're not rolling anywhere." She was pointing at the big catamaran anchored offshore. "Captain Mike's got a boat full of divers that he's taking back to St. Thomas after he eats, and we're going with him. How many of those rum drinks have you had?"

"What? Wait a sec, *where* we going?"

"I believe that was his third," interjected Tangles. "I switched to water after two—stay hydrated, that's my motto."

"You see, there goes little Chuck Berry, bangin' the gong again, throwin' ol' Shagball under the bus." I pointed a finger at him and added, "I shoulda left you on that pallet, thirty miles off." It finally dawned on me that I was feeling it. 'It' referring to the feeling of being a little hammered. Then it occurred to me that being a little hammered was like being a little pregnant. *Fuck.* The last thirty-six hours was catching up with me. Hell, it was leaving me in the dirt.

"What the heck are you talking about, Kit? You know Chuck Berry didn't play the gong, he played the guitar. Even *I* know that. Are you…are you *drunk?*"

"Me? Nah, maybe a little…maybe a little tired. Yesterday was a *bitch.* Did I tell you I lost my…I lost my boat?"

"Please, tell me you're kidding."

When the bartender placed the check in front of me, Holly picked it up and nodded in my general direction. "We're not going anywhere until he gets some food in him…and water…in fact, why don't you give us *all* a bottle of water?"

The bartender did as instructed, and as he handed out menus, Holly inquired, "What's in those drinks anyways?"

"Oh, just a little one-fifty-one, a little vodka, and a little more rum."

"*One-fifty-one?* Holy cow. Don't you think they should come with a warning?"

"They did. I told them more than two and they'd be rambling. It's not *my* fault only the little guy listened."

"Hey, now," said Tangles. "I'm right here; quit talking like I'm not, got it?"

"Sorry 'bout that."

I raised my hand and dismissed the notion altogether. "No apologies necessary, my man. It's not your fault you invented one of the greatest drinks of all time. I say Ramblers for everybody!" Holly punched me squarely in the shoulder, and I almost fell off the barstool.

"Ow! Whadja...whadja do that for?"

"You know damn well why. You're not drinking anything else but water. And the same goes for you, Tangles. We have a lot to do when we get to St. Thomas. Captain Mike says it's a solid two-and-a-half-hour ride, so hopefully you can take a nap and sober up by the time we get there."

"I like naps. Naps are good. So is pizza." I pointed to the menu which had a picture of a pizza on it. "You up for pie, Tangles?"

He answered, "Sure," and then mouthed the word, 'touchy,' to me. *Shit,* she *was* kinda touchy.

"Holly?"

"I might have a slice, that's it."

"Captain, uhhhh...?"

"Mike. No thanks, I got a burger coming."

After I ordered us a large pepperoni, I reached over and put my hand on her non-existent belly. "Maybe you should have two, you know, just in case."

"In case *what*? In case I wanna get fat? The continental breakfast at the resort was plenty for me. Of course, I haven't been drinking flammable slushies like they're going out of style. Seriously, Kit, drink more water. Your breath smells like a gas station. You're liable to spontaneously combust."

"Do you really have to talk about things exploding? If you haven't noticed, I'm mourning the demise of the *Lucky Dog*. She was a helluva boat. Caught a lot of fish on her, that's for sure. Good times... *lots* of good times...and then Tangles."

"Very funny, ramblin' man. Don't forget, I saved the show, among other things."

"How can I forget when you're always reminding me?"

Holly made one of those fake coughing sounds to get my attention.

"What?"

"Did you forget *we* first met on the *Lucky Dog?* As I recall, you thought I was a detective."

"That's right. And as *I* recall, I was hoping you were going to frisk me."

"And you got your wish…eventually. Proof that sometimes wishes do come true, however unlikely they may seem…especially now."

"You got that right," quipped Tangles.

"Can it, Gong-boy." I raised my bottle of water to put the matter to rest. "Anyways, here's to the *Lucky Dog*. The best boat I ever had. May her splintered remains find solace in the ever-changing currents of the sea."

"To the *Lucky Dog*," chimed in Tangles and Holly before we touched bottles and took a swig. Even the bartender and Captain Zodiac got in on it. "To the *Lucky Dog*," they echoed.

A little bit later, the bartender set a burger down for the captain and a pizza for us. "Man, that was a touching eulogy," he commented.

"You liked that?" I asked.

"It was poetic. You should be a writer."

"You think?"

Holly put her hand to her forehead. "Please, don't encourage him; he's hard enough to take as it is."

"If you liked that, how about this one: Chance is the umbilical cord of coincidence."

"Whoa! Duuuude, that is *mad* heavy. You *definitely* should be a writer."

"Wait a second," said Holly. "I thought it was, 'coincidence is the umbilical cord of chance'?"

"That's what I said."

"No, no its not. You said it the other way around."

"Same difference."

"Oh, really? How come when *I* said it that way, *you* said it was stupid and it didn't make sense?"

"'Cause *you* said, '*Fate* is the umbilical cord of chance.' That's...that's practically retarded... if you think about it."

"You're retarded! You can't even remember your own stupid sayings. You know why? 'Cause they're not sayings! So do us all a favor; drink more water, and eat your pizza. Think you can do that, Bacardi-brain? Geez Louise!"

Sensing tension at the bar, the bartender sought to calm things down a little. "Hey everybody...look, I can see how traumatic it was for you to lose your boat. How about a round of drinks on the house?"

"Are you crazy? Those Ramblers have done enough damage," complained Holly.

"With all due respect ma'am, don't hate the player, hate the game."

"What? What the heck does *that* mean?"

"Oh, you know, it's just a saying."

Chapter 29

Shortshank steered his old commercial fishing vessel around Banana Point and then crossed the busy West Gregerie Channel before slipping into the Tiara Bay Marina. Remy stood on the dock and watched as the boat idled past the glistening hulls of a pair of multi-million-dollar sport-fishing yachts that had just arrived. It was a week before Thanksgiving, and the marina was filling up with boats and crew who awaited their owner's arrival by prepping for the winter fishing season. There was a lot to do to get your typical sixty-eight-foot sport-fisher ready, and no one paid attention to the old boat as it putt-putted toward the large boathouse adjacent to the marina office. Remy signaled for Shortshank to proceed inside the structure that was made for dry-storing smaller boats on racks, and then threw him a dock line to tie off with. A marina employee approached and asked Remy if he needed any help. "No," he replied. "Why don't you go check on those new arrivals. We have some business to discuss."

"Yes, sir."

As soon as the young man was out of earshot, Shortshank waved Remy aboard as his eyes darted about. "He's in de cabin. Less make dis quick."

Remy jumped onboard and followed Shortshank into the small cabin. Lying on the floor and clutching a dirty blanket was one very wet and disheveled man whose pupils looked like little black BB's. He was shaking uncontrollably and appeared to be catatonic.

"He don't look too good," commented Remy.

"He doan smell too good needer, but he be alive... dat was de deal."

"Where's de coke?"

"You said I could keep it."

"You can, I just need to see de package. Where is it?"

Shortshank opened a cabinet and pulled out a tattered blue package. He handed it to Remy who nodded when he saw the blue plastic wrap with the familiar white stallion raised up on its hind legs. Although the package was torn, it still had a couple pounds of wet blow in it, and there was no mistaking it was part of the missing shipment. He stuck his finger inside and rubbed the white pasty powder across his gums. Suddenly his cell phone rang, and he glanced at the display before answering. "We're in the boathouse. Come quick." Click.

"Who be dat?" asked an alarmed Shortshank.

"No worries, mon. It's just a doctor. He gonna fix up our friend here so he can talk. He got some explaining to do." Remy noted his gums and teeth were already completely numb from the coke, conformation of its purity.

"Whatever he do, he better do quick. I doan—"

"Doan worry, here he is now."

Remy pointed at a man with a black bag hurrying toward them, and he opened the cabin door to wave him inside. The doctor shared a knowing nod with Remy before kneeling down by the man on the floor. As he took his pulse, he looked up at Remy. "You said it's a cocaine overdose?"

"Maybe hypothermia, too."

"His pulse is arrhythmic, and oh... this is not good...nearly two hundred beats per minute. He needs to go to the hospital."

"Not until after he talks, dat's why I called." Remy pulled out a wad of cash and started fingering it.

The doctor shook his head, already knowing the outcome of the game they were playing. Wad of cash—one. Hippocratic oath—zero. Another shutout. "Okay, I'll give him something, but I can't guarantee he's going to live. What then?"

"Den Shortshank be burying *two* people at sea, so you better get it right."

"I'm serious Remy, he's in bad—"

Remy pulled a small revolver from his waistband and pointed it at the doctor's head. "I'm serious too. Do what you gotta do—now!"

The doctor gulped and reached for his black bag, cursing himself for not being strong enough to refuse the lure of easy money. Hurriedly, he grabbed an elastic tourniquet out of the bag and cinched it around one of the prone man's arms. Then he inspected a couple vials of sedatives before settling on one and pulling out a large syringe. After filling the syringe, he tapped the tip of the hypodermic needle and squirted a little fluid out. "Okay, help me hold him down while

I administer the sedative; he's liable to react unpredictably."

Not wanting to get anywhere near the needle, Remy looked at Shortshank. "You heard him. Hold de guy down."

Reluctantly, Shortshank kneeled on the man's chest and pinned both arms to the floor. The doctor quickly jabbed the needle in, and the man struggled briefly before going limp and unconscious on the floor. As his head flopped from one side to the other, Remy did a double take. It had been a few years since he had personally taken delivery of an offshore shipment, but he thought he recognized the face from a prior deal.

The doctor quickly put the syringe and vial back in the bag and checked the man's pulse before he stood up. "It looks like he's stabilized. The sedative should keep him knocked out for a couple hours. I'm leaving you another syringe-full in case you need it. When he comes to, he'll be groggy for a while, but he should be able to talk after that." Remy put the gun back in his waistband and peeled off a number of hundred-dollar bills before handing them to him. "Tanks, doc, I was just kidding about de burial at sea ting. We good, right?"

The doctor turned as he exited the cabin and patted the five-hundred dollars in his pocket. "Fortunately, you have a way of *making* things right. You might want to throw another blanket on him—it'll help his circulation. Let me know if you need anything else."

As the doctor walked across the floor of the boat-storage building, Shortshank said, "I need to go, too. What you wanna do wit him?"

"Dere's an apartment up dere," Remy pointed at a door at the top of some stairs. "After I check in wit de office, you can help drag him up."

Remy hustled across the floor and entered the office. The girl that handled the phones was busy chatting with someone on the line, and he quickly crossed the floor to her desk. She caught him approaching out of the corner of her eye and turned as she smoothly transferred the caller to hold.

"Sir?" she asked.

"My father and I will be using the apartment for some meetings this afternoon. Under no circumstances are we to be bothered. That

means—"

"No calls and no visitors? Please, sir, I've been working here for a year now. Consider it done."

Remy eyed the young girl and nodded approvingly. "You're sharp. I like dat. Please, call me Remy from now on." He winked at her, slapped his hand on her desk, and left the way he came—purposefully.

It took some doing, but they dragged and carried the unconscious man up the stairs and into the apartment. Once they had him in a chair and thoroughly duct taped to it, Remy turned to Shortshank.

"You can go now, tanks." He peeled off a couple hundreds and handed them to Shortshank, who held his hand out for more.

"You said two tousand."

"Dat was before I realized dere's probably two pounds of coke still left in de sack. You can get twenty tousand for it back in Red Hook, no problem."

"Dat's if I make it back witout de Coast Guard boarding me."

"Or if I decide to fill you up wit bullets instead of gas."

Shortshank saw the look in Remy's eye and decided it was time to go. "Like I always say, 'Doan look a giff horse in de mout.' I be goin' now."

"Good idea."

When he reached the apartment door, Remy added, "Dere's anudder ting you better remember."

Shortshank looked back. "What be dat?"

"'Loose lips sink ships.' Doan forget it."

Chapter 30

Holly stood on the deck of the catamaran and breathed in the sweet ocean air as it zipped along at twenty knots toward St. Thomas. She had no game plan for meeting the senator *or* finding out what happened to Joseph all those years ago. She just knew that the answers were likely to be found in St. Thomas. Meeting up with the captain of the catamaran as he came ashore for lunch was a stroke of luck, even if she thought his hundred-dollar-a-head fee to take them seemed a bit spendy. *It would be worth it,* she thought, *if I could corner the captain and work him for some information.* Unfortunately, one particular diver was chatting his ear off up on the bridge, and she wondered if she would have a chance to talk to him at all.

As the island of St. Thomas loomed larger by the minute, she peeked belowdecks to see if there were any signs of life. As soon as they had been ferried to the boat by the captain, both Kit and Tangles found a spot in the cabin and curled up in power-nap mode. A quick look confirmed they were still out, as were many of the divers. Under normal circumstances, she might wake them as punishment for getting looped so early, but since Kit's beloved boat had been blown up, and they had nearly been killed, she just sighed. When she looked away, the guy chatting up the captain was stepping down from the bridge. *Yes, finally!*

Quickly, she bounded up the steps, and the captain smiled at her. “Sure, now you come up, after making me suffer through an hour and a half of listening to an accountant from Peoria who thinks he’s the next Jacques Cousteau.”

“I’m sure it’s due to your excellent dive instructors and captaining abilities.”

The skeptical captain eyed the attractive blond inquisitively. “You already paid for the trip, yet you insist on slathering me with unwarranted praise. Coming from such a beautiful woman that can only mean one thing.”

“What’s that?”

“You want me.”

“*What?*”

The captain laughed so hard he started to cough, and the ash from the cigarette dangling on his lower lip fell to the deck. After he regained his breath, he kicked the ash over the side and down to the main deck below. “I sure got you there, didn’t I, blondie?”

Holly shook her head and chuckled. The captain was small and wiry, with a sun-beaten face she pegged at somewhere between sixty and eighty years old.

“Yeah, that was…that was a good one.” Holly let out a deep breath, thankful that he wasn’t really making a pass at her.

“So, what’s on your mind? Why the spur of the moment trip to St. Thomas?”

“I’m trying to find out what happened to…to a relative of mine. He was seriously injured in a diving accident on St. Croix and taken here to St. Thomas for treatment… in a coma."

"Are you sure?"

"Yes."

"Then how come I don't know about it? I've been running dive trips in these waters four to five days a week for nearly twenty years."

"Probably because it happened in 1948; Thanksgiving Day, to be exact."

"*Nineteen forty-eight?*" The Captain let out a low whistle that could be heard just above the hum of the engines. "I'd say you're getting' a bit of a late start, honey, wouldn't you?"

"Not on my end. I just recently found out about it…and my name's Holly, remember?"

"Holly, that's right. Sorry if I—"

"No apologies necessary, captain. You already helped by giving us a ride."

"At a hundred bucks a head, *you're* the good Samaritan, not me. If I know anything that might help, it's on the house. So, tell me about the diving accident."

"Well, my aunt's fiancé and his friend were on a small skiff, diving for lobsters in the same area you were anchored in St. Croix."

"On The Wall?"

"Yes, that's where they were diving."

"For lobsters?"

"They were hoping to catch some for Thanksgiving dinner."

"Hope is the right word."

"What do you mean?"

"The Wall isn't where you would go to catch lobsters. Not back then. If you wanted lobster back then, you'd catch them right off the beach. All you needed was a mask and a tickler. The Wall is inherently more dangerous due to the currents and severe drop-off. Even if you did manage to tickle a bug out from its hidey hole, if you didn't snare it fast you'd find yourself chasing it down into the abyss. It's a good way to get in trouble quick."

"Really? What about now?"

"Now it's a protected area, you can't take anything from the water. It's for pleasure diving and snorkeling only. If you haven't been, you should try it sometime. Under conditions like we had this morning, it's spectacular."

The captain's words sunk in, and Holly's mind was racing. *If The Wall wasn't a good spot for catching lobsters, what were Joseph and Kilroy doing there?*

The captain noticed the look on Holly's face. "Did I say something wrong?"

"Huh? No, no it, uh, something doesn't make sense. They were definitely going out for lobster, and that's where they ended up."

"So what happened?"

"My aunt's fiancé didn't surface after a dive, and his friend called for help. The marine patrol found his body washed up against some rocks on shore. He had a gash on his head and never regained consciousness. His family flew him to St. Thomas for specialized treatment to try to bring him out of the coma."

"Where to?'

"I don't know. That's what I'm trying to find out…a hospital, presumably."

"Well, the main hospital on St. Thomas is Schneider Regional, right in downtown Charlotte Amalie. Even though it was built in the early eighties, my guess is a lot of medical records from private practices and smaller clinics might have ended up there. It's a good place to start, seeing as how it's a short cab ride from the harbor."

"Thanks, you've been very helpful."

The boat traffic picked up as they rounded Water Island and entered the harbor. Cruise ships and boats of all shapes and sizes went about their business (if you considered cruising in the Caribbean business). The captain stole another glance at Holly's ample cleavage, nestled in its Old Key Lime House tank top. Not wanting her to leave the bridge just yet, he asked, "Is that all? Anything, uh…anything else I can help you with?"

Holly was distracted by the hustle and bustle of harbor activity, admiring the view of the lush, green, hillsides, dotted with houses. Realizing the captain had asked her something, her attention snapped-to. "I'm sorry, what's that?"

"Anything else you want to know?"

"Um, yeah. This may sound a little weird, but…do you have any idea how I would go about meeting Senator VanderGrift?"

"Senator *who?*"

"I guess everybody knows him as 'Lucky.'"

The captain did a double take. "*Lucky?* Why would you want to meet him? He's a crook."

"He is?"

"Sure he is, just like most politicians. You shake his hand, you better count your fingers after. From what I hear, he's into all kinds of stuff, none of it good. So, why do you want to meet him?"

"It's uh, it's a long story, but…I'm pretty sure he's my cousin."

"*What?* You're *serious?*"

"Yep."

"My condolences, I'd rather be related to Bernie Madoff."

"Oh, c'mon!"

"You think I'm kidding? For him, having a cash cow like the Tiara Bay Marina just wasn't enough. He had to go into politics so he could stick his greedy fingers into everybody else's pie. If that's not bad enough, I heard a rumor that…nah, I better keep my mouth shut."

"Keep your mouth shut about what?"

"Nothin', it's just a rumor. Besides, I said enough bad things about your family."

"Oh, c'mon, it's just me. I'm not even positive I'm related yet."

"Still… I don't think so."

Undeterred, Holly clasped her hands in prayer fashion and semi-inadvertently squeezed her breasts together, much to the captain's delight. "Please, captain? I need to know all I can. I'd really appreciate it."

The captain pulled a small handkerchief out of his back pocket and stole a quick glance before wiping his brow. "Alright, but you best keep this to yourself."

"I promise."

"Okay, then. It's rumored the senator's son is involved in drug trafficking."

"*What?*"

"That's what I heard. The chip-off-the-old-block does more than run the marina. And if it's true, you can bet old Lucky's in on it too. Hell, he's probably running the show."

"Get out!"

"Like I said, it's just a rumor."

"Well, I don't believe it. He's a wealthy senator for crying out loud! Why take the risk?"

"He might not be as wealthy as he's portrayed. Everybody thinks he inherited his father's estate, but I heard his mother was the real winner. Maybe he needs drug money to help support his lavish lifestyle. Same goes for the son."

"Even if you're right, he'd have to be *crazy*. I mean...how could he think he'd get away with it?"

"This is the Virgin Islands, sweetheart. Things work different down here. When you've been in power as long as Lucky has, you're tentacles seem to have infinite reach. Trust me, everybody's on the take, and nobody sees nothing but dollar signs. Speaking of dollar signs, there's the Tiara Bay Marina up ahead."

"Where?"

The captain pointed it out. "You see that big boathouse with all those finger docks and those two, big, sport-fishing yachts docked on the end? That's it."

"You said his son runs the marina?"

"That's right."

"Then he should know where his dad is. Can you... uh, drop us off there?"

"Are you nuts? It's a private marina. I might get in trouble and you could get arrested for trespassing."

Holly reached into her purse and pulled out another hundred-dollar bill. Pinching it between her index finger and thumb with both hands, she stretched it taut and snapped it, directly in front of her lady humps. She let the captain stare for a couple seconds before placing one hand on his shoulder and gently squeezing it.

Using the same impossible-to-resist expression that was known to render most heterosexual men helpless, she conjured up her best puppy-dog eyes and scrunched them together. "Please, captain? *Please?*"

The captain shook his head and chuckled before taking the bill out of her hand. "Aw, shit. Better wake your friends; we'll be there in a couple minutes."

Chapter 31

McGirt slowly came to with blurred vision, a splitting headache, and a powerful thirst. He tried to rub his temples, but his arm wouldn't move. As his eyes regained focus, he realized he was strapped to a chair. *What the—?* Instinctively, he struggled to free himself, but only succeeded in bouncing the chair a few inches across the floor.

"Relax," came a voice from the corner of the room. "You're not going anywhere until we get some answers." McGirt shifted his focus to the distinguished-looking brown-skinned man in the white-linen suit. He was standing next to a younger man in shorts and a polo shirt who bore a striking resemblance to him. He wanted to say, 'What happened?' but his throat was so parched he could only muster a raspy, "Wa-wa water…need, need wa-water."

The senator forced a smile and nodded at his son. "Go ahead, he's all yours." Remy pulled a bottle of water out of the mini-fridge in the small apartment and unscrewed the cap. Then in one fluid motion he yanked McGirt's head back by his hair and shoved the bottle in his mouth. McGirt managed a couple gulps before he started gagging and water spewed all over. Remy pulled the bottle out and slapped him hard across the face. "Don't mess up the apartment," he admonished him. As the events of the past twenty-four hours came filtering back to his addled memory, a confused McGirt looked around. "Am I…am I under arrest?"

The guy who slapped him laughed. "Yeah, house arrest, and if you don't start giving us some answers… cardiac arrest. First question. How did you come into possession of a package with this emblem on it?" Remy pulled a scrap of plastic out of his pocket and held it in front of his face. It was blue and had a picture of a white stallion reared up on its hind legs.

"I, uh, where did—?"

SMACK! Remy pivoted and back-handed him hard across the other side of his face. "I ask the questions! Got it?"

McGirt shook his head, trying to shake away the sting, and tried to quickly process what was going on? *If they weren't the police, who were they?*

"Yeah, sure, I got it."

"So, how did you come to have this package in your possession?"

"There was an explosion and I ended up in the water. I found the package floating by and—"

"Wait a second, tell us about the explosion. What were you doing? What exploded?"

McGirt looked at the man in the white suit who stepped out from the corner of the room, his interest clearly piqued.

"Um, it was, uh, it was, it was the boat. The boat blew up. I was the only survivor. I'm lucky to be alive."

"You really tink so?" asked Remy as he pulled the revolver from his waistband and stuck the barrel in McGirt's ear. "'Cause I don't tink so. You know why? 'Cause I tink you tried to steal a shipment we were expecting and someting went wrong."

"*What?* No! Wait a second, just wait a second here. *You* were expecting a shipment?" McGirt rattled off some coordinates. "Does that ring a bell?"

Remy tucked the gun back in his waistband, quickly pulled out his cell-phone, and punched some keys. "Give me those coordinates again."

After McGirt repeated himself, Remy looked at his dad. "I thought he looked familiar; he knows the coordinates."

"Of course I do. *I* was making the delivery."

"*You?*" asked the senator. "You mean, you work for—"

"The Cordero brothers? Yes, and I need to call them— el pronto, so can you untie me and give me a phone? What a fucking disaster this is. This is bad. This is really fucking bad."

"Not until you tell us exactly what happened out there."

"No, not until you give me some water… and don't shove it down my fucking throat."

The senator nodded at Remy. "Go ahead, untie one of his arms and give him some water."

After McGirt chugged a bottle of water down, he rubbed his temple vigorously. "*Fuck,* does my head hurt. Where are we anyways?""

"St. Thomas, so quit complaining," said Remy. "If it weren't for a doctor friend of mine, you woulda OD'd from all the blow in your system."

"Hey, I'm no junkie, but if it weren't for the blow, I never woulda had the energy to swim as far as I did. By the way, who found me?"

"Don't worry about that, worry about telling us what happened."

"Sure, okay. Well, I was running us at depth, along the edge of this big weed—"

"Whoa, whoa, whoa...you said you were on the boat that blew up. What do you mean, you were running at depth?"

"I *was* on the boat...later on...but before that I was running the sub in about fifteen—"

"*You* were running the submarine? *You're* the captain?"

"Actually, we're called commanders, but you can call me captain if you want. Captain McGirt, given the circumstances."

"Given the circumstances, you better start making some sense...fast."

"Right. Well, I know this might sound a little hard to believe, but it's the truth...."

For a solid ten minutes, McGirt recounted the story in detail. The crux of it being the sub got sunk and the boat with the coke on it had blown up, killing everybody but him. When he finished, Remy looked at the senator, who shrugged, unsure what to believe. "I don't know, Remy. What about those DEA agents you told me about? You know, the ones from last night? Where do they fit in? I thought the boat was theirs."

Remy eyed McGirt even more suspiciously than usual. *What the hell was going on?* McGirt felt the tension and grew uneasy about the look he was getting from Remy. "What, uh.... what DEA agents? What are you talking about?"

Remy grabbed a roll of duct tape that was sitting on a table behind McGirt, and quickly re-taped his free arm back to the chair. "Whatta you, whatta you doing, man? I'm telling the truth, I swear!"

Remy shook his head. "I don't tink so. You said three fishermen overpowered your guy on the sub, and when they tried to pull the boat over on its side, it didn't work, and they sunk."

"That's right, we managed to cut the lines tethered to the boat and the sub went down with a busted-out viewport. It was leaking like a sieve. Just in case, I bounced a few grenades off the hull to make sure they had a one-way ticket to flounderville. When they didn't resurface, like I knew they wouldn't, we took off. I was about to make contact for the rendezvous when the boat caught fire and blew up, just like I said."

"You also said one of the fishermen was a midget."

"That's right; there was a midget, a normal looking guy, and a big black dude... so what?"

"So what is that I got a call from a contact on St. Croix. He said a Coast Guard chopper dropped two guys off at a resort on the beach last night."

"So?"

"So, one of them was a midget. They said their boat blew up, and they were rescued at sea. There was no mention of a submarine."

"What?" McGirt's mind was racing. *Had they somehow survived? How could they?*

"But that's not all. There's one other minor detail."

"What's that?"

"They're DEA agents, but you already knew that."

"WHAT?! They're…no, no way. I don't know *who* those fucking guys were…or are... I never seen them in my life!"

"You know what I tink? I tink you buddied up with some crooked DEA agents and tried to steal our shipment. I tink maybe they pulled a double-cross, blew up the boat with you and your crew on it, then left some coke behind to make it look like it went down with the boat, when it's really on the sub. So, where the *fuck* is it?"

"WHAT? Now *you're* talking crazy! I been working for the Cordero's for eight years. I *know* what they do to turncoats. No fucking way I would ever cross them… no way!"

"Not even for a sub-load of Colombia's finest? You lie." Remy drew his gun and pointed it between McGirt's eyes. "Where is it?!"

"I don't know, I swear! The last time I saw it, the sub was sinking with those guys on it!"

"You sure?"

"Yes, positive!"

Remy looked at his father, who shrugged again, then he looked at McGirt, who let out a small sigh of relief when he lowered the gun and smiled. "You still want someting for your headache?" Asked Remy.

"Huh? Oh, yeah, some aspir—" Crack! Remy smashed the butt of the gun into McGirt's forehead and knocked him out cold. As blood oozed from the gash, he turned to his father, who was rubbing his chin in thought.

"So, what do you tink?"

"I tink I'm sick of you talking like you don't know how to talk. Tell me, Remy, do you do it just to piss me off?"

"No, if I wanted to do that, I'd tell you what I spent to have this guy delivered and tended to by the good doctor." The truth was, he found it nearly impossible not to talk with a hybrid island-lingo. Plus, he thought it gave him street cred with the locals, and made him seem less like the silver spoon-fed punk that he was. Of course, he was wrong.

The senator vigorously rubbed his temple as he stepped to the window. "I don't know, Remy; I think he might be telling the truth."

Remy wiped the butt of the gun on McGirt's shirt and tucked it back in his waistband. "Fuck, me too."

Chapter 32

Once Captain Zodiac maneuvered the catamaran alongside the outermost dock of the Tiara Bay Marina, the three of us quickly climbed a barnacle encrusted ladder and waved him away.

"Thanks, captain!" yelled Holly. She held up the business card the captain gave her and added, "I'll call about the ride back!" The captain pointed behind us and yelled, "Good luck!"

As I turned to look, Tangles said, "Here we go… this should be fun."

A security guard was already halfway down the dock and closing in fast.

"He doesn't look like he's part of the red-carpet team," I commented as we walked toward him.

"Relax," said Holly. "Just let me do the talking for once, okay?"

"Be my guest."

"Tangles?"

"As you wish, madam. Thoust lips shall not flap unless—"

"Just shut up, okay? I'll handle this."

"Got it."

A second later, the guard was within perceived earshot, and Holly started her spiel. "Hi there! Maybe you can—"

The guard held his hand out and took command of the situation. "Just stop right there, ma'am." The three of us stopped in our tracks, and as he closed the last few feet, I noticed he was armed. *Hmmm.* "This is a private marina; who are you, and what are you doing here?"

"Oh, um, we didn't realize that, sorry, maybe you could just—"

"What do you mean you didn't realize it? There's a big sign posted on the end of the dock, you climbed right past it. You got eye problems or something?"

"Uh, no, no, I uh, don't."

"And that was a local boat that just dropped you off. Don't tell me you weren't warned you'd be arrested for trespassing."

"Oh, crap… yes, yes we were warned. I didn't think it was such a big deal. I was just hoping to talk to the owner of the marina, Senator VanderGrift."

"I take it you don't have an appointment or you wouldn't be trying to sneak in the back door, so to speak."

"No, I don't. But my names Holly Lutes and I—"

The guard held his hand up for her to stop talking as he answered his walkie-talkie, which suddenly crackled to life. The voice was a woman's, and she asked what was going on. He held the device up to his mouth and pressed a button to transmit.

"I got three people who just got off a dive boat and came strolling down the dock. One of 'em's a lady.

She wants to talk to the senator, but she doesn't have an appointment."

The guard was big, white, American, and overweight, but not fat. He had thick arms and one of those torso's that appeared solid as a rock as it stretched his shirt taut. The name tag embroidered on his shirt read, 'Norbert,' and he had an accent I couldn't quite place. *Philly maybe?*

"They're not marina guests?"

"No."

"You know what to do. Escort them off the property, and if they cause any trouble, call the police."

"Wait!" cried Holly. "I'm the senator's cousin, and I really need to talk to him."

The guard gave Holly an incredulous look, and then glanced at me. I shrugged, and he shifted his gaze to Tangles, who said, "True story." The guard pressed the transmit button again. "Hang on a second, the lady's talking in my ear." He looked at Holly again suspiciously. "You trying to tell me you're the senator's cousin?"

"Yeah, I'm pretty sure. That's what I need to talk to him about; he doesn't know it yet."

The guard smiled and shook his head. "And I'm pretty sure I'm gonna hit the Powerball this week, but as you can see, I didn't quit my job yet."

"I'm serious!"

"So am I. Nice try. Let's go... *this* way." He pulled a military-style baton from his hip and pointed for us to walk ahead of him. As we started walking, Holly kept pleading her case. "Please, I'm not kidding. I flew all the way from Florida, and we just spent nearly three hours on a boat ride over from St. Croix. All I need is a few minutes with the senator…it's important."

"You know what else is important? Me keeping my job, just in case the old lotto plan doesn't work out. Keep it moving."

The walkie-talkie crackled again. "Everything alright, Norbert?"

"No problem. I'm taking them to the gate."

"Okay, just checking."

True to his word, he escorted us straight to the exit, despite Holly's pleadings. After just a few steps, he lightly touched the back of my T-shirt with his baton. "Cute shirt…'Drink Every Afternoon.' You have an FBI shirt that says 'Feed Beer Interveneously?'"

"No, and it's in*tra*venously, not in*ter*veneously. That's not even a word. Intervening is what you did when—" He poked me in the back and said, "Can it, smartass, unless you want this *baton* to intervene with your *face*. Hey, there's another good one for FBI; Face Batonned Indiscriminately."

"Really, Norbert? *Batonned?* That's not a word either."

"You get the idea."

Tangles put his hand up to the side of his mouth to shield his words.

"More like 'Fatso Be Idiot.'"

"What was that? You got something to say, Pippy Shortstocking?"

"Knock it off, guys," cut in Holly. "For once, *just once*, try not to make things worse than they already are… okay?"

"You heard the lady. Put a lid on it before I put a lid on you."

As we walked in silence, we passed a guy at a cleaning table, working on a fifty-pound wahoo. There were two more in the forty-pound class lying at his feet on the dock. Tangles and I slowed down to check them out, but the guard prodded us on.

"Damn!" I commented as Tangles let out an appreciative whistle.

"What?" asked Holly.

"We should be fishing. You see those babies?"

"Is that all you think about?"

"What, babies? No, of course not." *Gulp.* " Why are...are you?"

"No, you know—agggh, why do I even ask? This is ridiculous! I just want to see the senator for crying out loud, not the pope."

"Pope-schmope, lady. You wanna see the senator? Make an appointment...and don't come back till you do."

Holly was visibly miffed as our escort signaled to someone in the guard booth to open the front gate. "Fine, give me the number, and I'll call right now."

The ten-foot-high, chain-link gate with barb-wire on top began rolling open. The guard reached in his shirt pocket and pulled out a business card. Holly reached for it, but the guard pulled his hand back. "Not so fast...you gotta call from off premises, please...." He waved the baton for us to leave, and as soon as we crossed the gate-track, the gate began rolling closed. "Here you go, ma'am." He held the card out, and Holly snatched it without a word of thanks. "Geez, I can't believe this. It's not like we're criminals!"

The gate rattled shut, and the guard, who had been walking away, turned and pointed at me and Tangles. He raised one hand to approximate my height, and he held the other down low at Tangles height. Then he closed one eye like he was trying to frame a photograph and laughed. "I'm not so sure about that, ma'am. Maybe you're with the Hi-Lo Gang, you know…hit 'em high and hit 'em low." He dropped his hands and walked away laughing. Tangles stepped forward and grabbed the chain-link gate with both hands. "You think you're funny, big guy?" He started shaking the gate, and I grabbed him by the shoulder. "Dude, chill out…he might call the police." He let go of the gate and jerked my hand off his shoulder with a final admonition. "That's right! You *better* keep walking!" The guard never broke stride, and we heard him laughing as he went. Holly, meanwhile, already had the marina office on her cell. "Yes, that's right," she explained. "It's personal…I'd like to meet with him as soon as possible….what? Yes, yes, that's my number; please make sure he gets it….it's very important. Thanks." Click. Holly put her phone in her purse and was still peeved as we started walking down the side of the busy road.

"I've never been thrown out of a marina in my life. This is absurd!"

"You know what else is absurd?" I queried.

"What."

"Walking aimlessly when we don't know where we're going."

"I know where one thing is—the hospital."

"What hospital?" asked Tangles and I at the same time.

"Schneider Regional. The captain told me about it while you two were in la-la land. He said it was close to the port, and it was a good place to start searching for old medical records. Maybe we can find out what happened to Joseph." She pointed at the busy harbor ahead and added, "There's the port, so we're headed in the right direction."

"And there's a cab." I pointed at a cab coming from the opposite direction and waved him down. The cabbie pulled a U-turn and stopped in front of us. The passenger window went down, and the cabbie leaned over. "Where you tree goin, mon?" I leaned in the window as Tangles and Holly piled into the back.

"The hospital—Schneider Regional."

"You wit de DEA? Somebody hurt?"

"What? Oh, the shirts...." He had undoubtedly seen the back of our shirts when he pulled the U-e. "No, they're not real. I mean, the shirts are real, but they're not real DEA shirts. It's just a goof." I turned around so he could read the small writing below the big letters. "See, it says 'Drink Every Afternoon.' We're not with the DEA, trust me."

"You better get in den; walkin' tru town wit doze shirt's a bad idea."

"You got it."

I jumped in back, and Holly asked, "How far is it?"

"Ten minutes. You said nobody hurt, right?"

"Other than my little buddy's ego," I answered, "and my girlfriend's pride, we're fine. No need to go all Steve McQueen on us. Thanks for asking, though."

As we drove off, Holly elbowed me in the side, and Tangles muttered, "Hi-Lo Gang...what an asshole."

Chapter 33

The senator continued rubbing his temple as he looked out the window of the apartment above the marina office. Whether the sub captain was lying or not, it seemed they were fucked. He was accustomed to being on the giving end, and didn't like the feeling one bit. Somebody either hijacked the shipment of coke, the Coast Guard had it, or it was in a can-opened sub on the bottom of the sea. He heard the sound of a carbonated beverage being opened and turned to see Remy close the refrigerator door and take a swig of a Heineken. "So, what should we do with him?" asked Remy, seemingly nonplussed about the situation.

"I don't know. I should probably call the Colombians again, but once I do, they're liable to go crazy. This could get bad, Remy, really bad."

"It's already bad."

"No, I mean, *really* bad. You won't believe what I heard about these guys....what they've done. They're flat-out nuts."

"Yeah, well, at least it's not *our* fault."

"I hope I can convince them of that, otherwise.... damn, you better get me one of those beers. I need to think this over."

As Remy turned to open the fridge, Lucky looked out the window again. His attention was immediately drawn to the front gate, which was opening. A guard was escorting three people off the property; an attractive-looking woman and two DEA agents. *Well, make that one and a half. Wait a second… WHAT?*

"*Remy*! Come here! Look at this!"

Remy slammed the fridge door shut and hurried to join his dad at the window. "What! What is it?"

Lucky pointed at the front gate. "Look at those DEA guys! One of them's a midget!"

"Holy shit! Is that them? What's that little fucker shaking the gate for? I'm telling you, we need to electrify it."

"I don't care about *that.* What are they doing here?"

Remy looked at McGirt. "They must have followed Shortshank."

"*Shortshank?* Who the hell is Shortshank?"

"He's a commercial fisherman, the one that found him." Remy nodded at the unconscious McGirt.

"What the hell's going on?"

"I don't know. Look, they're leaving on foot. Where did they come from?"

"Get that guard on the phone!"

Remy pulled out his cell and called the guard shack, asking to speak with the guard who escorted the bunch off the property. They both watched as the guard-shack door opened, and the guard inside waved over the guard in question. A few seconds later, Remy heard, "Hello?"

"This is Remy—what were those DEA agents doing here?"

"DEA agents? What are you...oh, those schmo's with the funny T-shirts? They're not DEA, they're just a couple smart-asses. The T-shirt's a gag. It says 'Drink Every Afternoon,' in real small letters below the DEA part."

"What? Are you positive?"

"One-hundred-and-ten percent, or as my granddaughter likes to say, '*totally*.' Besides, you ever hear of a midget working for the DEA?"

"No... but who knows? They probably got good noses from being so close to the ground. So, if they're not DEA, who are they?"

"I didn't get the bozo's names, but I think the lady said her name was Holly something or other."

"I don't care about her; what did the guys want? Where did they come from?"

"A dive boat dropped them off on the dock; they came from St. Croix."

"Son-of-a-bitch. It's *gotta* be them!"

"Gotta be *who?*"

"Hang on a second!" Remy covered the mic slot on his cell and relayed the info as fast as he could. "They're not DEA agents, but it's gotta be the same guys. They came over from St. Croix."

"*What?* What did they want?"

Remy lifted his hand off the mic slot. "What did they want?"

"The lady wanted—"

"I don't care *what* the bitch wanted. What did the guys in the fake DEA shirts want?"

"They didn't say a whole lot, except for wisecracks. I think they said they wanted to go fishing."

"*What?*"

"Who can blame them? You should see the wahoo that are being caught. Fishing's good right now. I hear there's a hellacious weed line out there."

"That's it? They just wanna go fishing?"

"No, like I was trying to say, the lady wanted to see your dad."

"She wanted to see...*what?* Why does she want to see *him?*"

"She thinks he's her cousin or something. Personally, I think it's a stretch, but if she is, she'd make a helluva kissin' cousin, know what I mean?"

Remy looked at his dad and repeated the information. "She thinks he's her *cousin?* What the fucks going on here?"

"Hell-if-I-know, you're the one who asked."

Lucky saw the look of disbelief on his son's face and grabbed the phone out of his hand. "This is Senator VanderGrift. Who am I speaking with?"

"Norbert Schnell, at your service, sir."

"Very good, Norbert. So, tell me, exactly what did the lady say?"

"She said she thought you were her cousin, and she wanted to meet you. The office told her to make an appointment. I gave her the number once the Hi-Lo Gang got outside the gate."

"The Hi-Lo Gang?"

"That's what they look like, you know, with the midget and all."

"I see...so, I noticed they left on foot, any idea where they were headed?"

"No, sir, other than they were headed downtown."

"They can't be far. Find them and bring them back."

"Excuse me?"

"You heard me. The lady wanted to see me, right?"

"Uh, yeah… that's what she said."

"Well, my schedule just opened up. So go find them… *now.*"

"You want me to bring *all* of them back, or just the lady?"

"*All* of them."

"Understood. I'm on it." Click.

Chapter 34

DICK agent Raphael Angel-Herrera, aka Rafe, looked at his watch for the umpteenth time and shook his head. His room at the resort had a direct line of sight to the two rooms rented by Holly Lutes on behalf of Kit Jansen and company, but so far they were nowhere to be seen. After checking in, he conducted a sweep of the resort premises and surrounding shoreline, but the Jansen crew had apparently gone on an excursion. Tired of waiting for them to return, he made his way to the bar to see if he could dig up any information on their whereabouts. He had been asked by his boss (the mysterious head of DICK) to keep an eye on them, and wanted to know where they were before calling in an update. As the bartender approached, he noticed the name tag that identified him as Bradshaw. "Can I get you something to drink?" the young man asked. Rafe pulled out one of the free drink coupons he got when he checked in and placed it on the bar. "May as well use this."

"Good call. I just made up a fresh batch of rum punch."

"Sounds good. What's in it?"

"Rum and punch."

Rafe smiled at the young man and laughed. It was just the sort of answer he would have given had *he* been behind the bar. "Guess I had that coming."

"You're not the first, but it happens to be true." As he poured him a tall glass full, he explained. "It's got three different kinds of rum and some fruit juices. It's all good... enjoy."

Rafe took a big sip and nodded in agreement. "It *is* good, so... Bradshaw...you wouldn't happen to be from Pittsburgh, would you?"

"Sure am, and thanks to my mother, everybody knows it. It's great being from a town that won a bunch of Super Bowls, but it kills my rap every time I meet a hot chick from Cleveland or Cincy."

"Mom must have been quite a Steeler's fan."

"Not so much the Steeler's as hillbilly quarterbacks.... What can I say, she's from Oklahoma."

"So, she was into Billy Joe Tolliver and Brett Farve?"

"Like a gay John Madden."

"Wow, that's really saying something."

"Tell me about it. It's totally out of hand. She even made a copy of the picture that Farve texted to that girl who worked in the Jets front office. You know the one I'm talking about, the picture of his pecker? Anyways, she uses it as a screen saver on her computer and as wallpaper on her iPhone. I tell ya, she's twisted. Friggin' pic looks like a couple SOS pads sprouted a wet kielbasa."

Suddenly, Rafe's punch didn't taste so good, and he winced. "You, uh, you paint quite a picture."

Bradshaw glanced around to make sure no other customers needed attention and shrugged. "Yeah, well, they say they're worth a thousand words, but who needs a thousand when just one describes it—*sick.* Anyhoo, it's one of the reasons I ended up fleeing Pittsburgh and my perved-out mother. So, what brings *you* to St. Croix?"

Like all DICK agents, Rafe was adept at shifting seamlessly from one false persona to another and didn't miss a beat. "I'm a writer for *Billfish Magazine.* I'm here to interview—"

"Shagball and Tangles? Dude, their boat blew up!"

"What?" Rafe pretended like he had no idea.

"It's all anyone's talking about. I'm so pissed I wasn't here. A Coast Guard chopper rescued them and dropped them on the beach last night. Right here on the beach, can you believe it? At least I met Shagball's girlfriend. She came in for happy hour—what a hottie!"

"You don't say... any idea where they might be?"

"No, and I can' *wait* to meet them. Their fishing show is legend...wait-for-it... dary. I'll bet they're not at the library, though."

"The *library?* Why would you say that?"

"'Cause that's where the girlfriend went yesterday. Just don't ask me where it is or why she went there. That's all Zelda."

"Zelda?"

"She works the front desk, and everybody goes to her for directions. If anybody knows where they are, it would be her. Excuse me for a second." While Bradshaw went to take care of some customers, Rafe downed the rest of his punch and threw a few bucks on the bar. Two minutes later, he was at the front desk, and the same woman who checked him in earlier asked how she could help. "What can I do for you, honey?"

"I'm looking for some resort guests I'm supposed to interview for an article. There's three of them, and ones a midget."

"I haven't seen them since they asked directions to the Salt River Marina this morning. They've been gone all day. I hope everything's alright, that sho is bad luck what happened to their boat."

"Yeah, it sure is. Would you mind giving me those same directions?"

As Rafe sped down the road, he hoped for their sake, and his job's, that they were alright or...*shit.* A few minutes later, he turned into the Salt River Marina, and the feeling in his gut told him he was about to find out. As he walked from the parking lot toward the marina office, he noticed a lady exit the office and turn to lock the door behind her. A quick glance at his watch told him it was five o'clock, and he jogged the last twenty yards to try to catch her. He yelled, "Excuse me!" She looked up startled, and fumbled with the keys. "Yes? What can I do for you? I'm just closing up."

"I'm looking for three people who might have come by here this morning. One of them's a midget."

"Sure, I talked to them earlier; what's going on?"

"Do you know where they went?"

"Sorry, no. If you have more questions, I'll be back tomorrow between nine and five. I really need to be going." When she turned to finish locking the door, Rafe realized the casual approach wasn't going to work. He quickly glanced around to confirm nobody was paying any attention and whipped a badge out.

Like all DICK agents, he had an arsenal of badges at his disposal. "This is an FBI matter, ma'am. It won't take but a few minutes. Can we go inside?"

Nervous now, she let him into the office and asked, "I'm not in trouble…am I? I don't know where they went, I swear. I don't know anything."

"Calm down, alright? You're not in any trouble as long as you answer a few questions, okay?"

She nodded and quietly responded, "Okay."

"Good, so what's your name?"

"Sally."

He pulled a photograph out of his shirt pocket and asked, "Okay, Sally. Tell me, are these the three who came here this morning?"

She looked at the photo and nodded. "Yes, that's them. They're not in trouble, are they? They seemed like such nice people."

"They *are* nice people, and no, they're not in trouble—at least not yet."

"So why are you here then?"

"I ask the questions, Sally, you answer them. Not the other way around, remember?"

"Yes, of course, sorry 'bout that."

"Alright, like I said, I'm just trying to locate them. They didn't say or do anything that might suggest where they were headed?"

"No—wait a second! I almost forgot! The girl, Holly, left me her phone number in case I found the address where my father sent his loan payments. I found it and left it for her on her voicemail when she didn't answer. Maybe that's where they're headed?"

"Do you still have it?"

"Yes, it's right here." She reached for a small notepad on her desk and tore the top sheet off. "Here you go."

Rafe looked at the address and read the last part of it out loud. "St. Maarten?"

"That's where she lives...or lived."

"Who does?"

"The wife of the late Kilroy Vandergrift. He used to own this marina until he sold it to my father back in '65. Their son is a famous senator from St. Thomas."

"You said it was the girl, Holly, who was asking the questions?"

"Yes, and when I mentioned the accident, it seemed to throw her for a loop."

"What accident?"

Sally quickly gave Rafe the details of the diving accident that left Kilroy Vandergrift dead and his son Lucky the apparent heir to his considerable fortune. Suddenly, a new thought occurred to her. "You know, now that I think of it, the little guy, I think his name was Tangles, said something about the accident being 'just like the wall.' The other two gave him a look like he said something he shouldn't have, but I didn't give it much thought till now. 'The Wall' is a famous diving spot just up the shore from here. Maybe *that's* where they went when they left."

The sense of urgency Rafe was feeling needed something to feed on, and his gut told him she might be on to something. "That's good thinking, Sally. How do I get there from here?"

Sally grabbed the notepad and was about to start drawing a map when she had a V8 moment and slapped her head. "What am I doing? There's a map right here on the wall." She stepped over to a framed map hanging on the wall next to the picture of her father and Kilroy VanderGrift shaking hands. She pointed her finger to show Rafe where they were (the Salt River Marina) and traced it along the shore to a point marked 'The Wall.' "When you leave the parking lot, take a right and keep the ocean on your right. In about fifteen minutes, you'll see a little roadside bar on the water called, 'The Hole-in-the-Wall.' The dive boats park just offshore."

"That sounds like a great place to start. Let me give you my number in case you happen to see Mr. Jansen and company again." Rafe scribbled a number on the notepad, then tore the sheet off and handed it to her. "Thanks for your help, Sally. C'mon, let me walk you to your car."

As Rafe sped along the shoreline, he eyed every passing vehicle. The boss had told him Holly rented a silver Jeep, and he had the license plate number in his DICK phone. The sun seemed to gather speed as it set on the horizon,, and so did Rafe's anxiety level. He had been under the impression that this would be a cushy assignment, just keeping an eye on some guys filming a fishing show. He thought he might even get a chance to do some fishing himself. But so far, things were not panning out as planned.

The ocean road meandered inland and then back out along the coast. He came over a small rise and could see cars parked on the side of the road next to a road-side shanty draped in Christmas lights. It was the Hole-in-the-Wall Sally had described. As he pulled into a parking spot, he noticed a silver jeep, three cars down. Excited, he backed up so he had an unimpeded view of the license plate. Then he pulled out his DICK-issued smart-phone and snapped a picture. Instantly, the screen lit up green, and the word 'MATCH' started flashing on the screen. *Bingo! It was them!*

Rafe strode down to the bar, hearing the waves lap against the nearby rocks. A quick scan of the patrons left him scratching his head. Jansen and company weren't there. *Damn!* He spotted an empty barstool and pulled it away from the bar, preferring to stand instead. The bartender wiped the bar top and asked what he wanted to drink. Deciding to take a different approach, he asked for a beer. The bartender got him to narrow it down to a Heineken, and when he set it on the bar asked, "You want a menu too?"

"If my friends show up for dinner, yes. I'm wondering if you've seen them." He pointed at the parking lot. "That's their jeep there—the silver one."

"Shagball and Tangles? Hell yeah, I seen 'em. They were the first customers of the day. Those guys like their rum, that's for sure. Who knows? Maybe they'll be the last customers too… if they ever get back from St. Thomas."

"*St. Thomas?* What do you mean, *St. Thomas?*"

"They didn't tell you?"

"Didn't tell me *what?*"

"They hitched a ride to St. Thomas on one of the dive boats. Shagball's girlfriend arranged it. I think she slipped the captain a few Benjamins."

"Shit."

"It's not a problem; we serve food till midnight."

"I don't care about the food. They didn't say when they'd return, did they?"

"Hey, they're your friends, not mine, but I *did* tell them not to worry about the jeep if they didn't make it back tonight. It's fine parked where it is. By the way, the burgers are really good… so is the pizza."

"Great, that's …that's just great. Do you happen to know the name of the boat they went on?

"Sure, Captain Mike's a regular. He's the skipper of the *Diver Down*. They come over from St. Thomas three or four times a week; weather permitting, of course."

"The *Diver Down*, huh?"

"Yep, I gotta take care of some other customers; let me know if you want to order anything." Rafe finished off the Heineken and tucked a ten-dollar bill under the bottle as the well-meaning bartender went about his business. As he walked to his rental car, he looked out at the ocean. Back at the resort, it looked crystal blue and inviting. Now, as he contemplated the name of the boat called *Diver Down*, it appeared dark and ominous in the fading light. Having a law enforcement background, the name reminded him of 'man down' or 'officer down,' and the connotation wasn't a pleasant one. He hoped it wasn't a sign of things to come as he pulled out his DICK phone and speed-dialed the boss.

Chapter 35

When we got to the hospital, Holly figured she might have better luck digging for information on Joseph without me and Tangles tagging along. We decided to check out the waterfront scene along the harbor and agreed to meet in front of the hospital an hour later.

At the front desk, Holly was directed to the records department on the lower level of the building. She followed the arrows on the wall to a windowless room with an open counter in front, much like a pharmacy. Sitting behind the counter was an older man placing documents into what appeared to be a scanner. Sensing Holly's presence, he looked up and greeted her with a smile. "Well hello there, young lady. What can I do for you?" Holly guestimated him to be in his mid-sixties and liked the fact that he considered her to be young even though she was thirty-two.

"Well, I know this is a long-shot, but I'm trying to find some information on a young man who was brought to St. Thomas for specialized treatment quite a while ago. Unfortunately, I don't know who his doctor was, I only know his name."

"How long ago you talking about?"

"Would you believe, late 1948 or early '49?"

The man stopped what he was doing and did a double-take. "Nineteen forty-eight? This hospital wasn't even built until the early '80s. "

"So I heard. Like I said, it's a long shot."

"Ma'am, that's more like a full court shot."

"Sorry, I know… I just thought, oh, I don't know *what* I thought."

The records clerk could sense Holly's exasperation and tried to lift her mood. "Now, hold on a second. At least you came to the right place. Most of the practicing doctors on the island have, or had, some affiliation with the hospital, and many transferred their records here for safekeeping on account of the hurricanes. As a matter of fact, one of my responsibilities is to scan old medical records and enter them into the hospital database when I get a chance. I'm working on some records from the '60s right now and the older the file, the less there are of them. So let's give it a try. What was this young man receiving treatment for? Maybe we can narrow down the type of doctor he was seeing."

"He was in a coma."

"Maybe a neurologist then?"

"I don't know, maybe."

He shook his head. "No, that probably won't help. We better stick to the tried and true. What was his name?"

"Joseph Brodie."

"He a relative of yours?"

"He was my aunt's fiancé—the love of her life. She thought he died."

"What a shame. I hate hearing stories like this." He pushed his chair back and exhaled deeply. "Alright, then. I'll go dig up some files, and we'll see what we can see. This is liable to take a while."

"I really appreciate it. Thank you *so much*."

Holly watched as he shuffled down an aisle full of cabinets and then disappeared around the corner. The sounds of cabinet drawers being opened and closed was soon followed by minor panting as he reappeared holding a large stack of files. After he dropped them on the counter, he laid down the ground rules. "I can't allow you to look in the files, but as you can see, most of them have the patient's name on the exposed tab. If you do happen to find the file we're looking for, I have to be the one who examines it; fair enough?"

"Yes, absolutely."

"Okay, then. You can start looking while I bring the rest out."

"There's more?"

"Plenty more, we have records all the way back to 1945."

Holly started leafing through the first batch while he brought out stack after stack until the entire counter and desk below was full. For half an hour, Holly stood at the counter thumbing through files as the records clerk sat at his desk and did the same with his reading glasses perched on the tip of his nose. They were getting near the end when the clerk asked, "You said his name was Brodie, right?"

"Yes, Joseph Brodie. Did you find something?"

Holly glanced down at the desk and the files he was sorting through, suddenly hopeful as he looked up at her. "Didn't mean to get your hopes up. I just wanted to double-check the name. No luck on your end either?"

"No," she shrugged. "I knew this was going to be a stab in the dark… darn! Oh, well, nothing ventured, nothing— wait a second." Holly glanced at the stack the records clerk made from files he already went through when something caught her eye. She pointed at one particular file sticking out of the stack that had the name "Grift" exposed on the tab. "That folder right there; the one that says 'Grift' on the tab. Can you pull that out for a closer look?"

"I thought you said the name was Brodie?"

"It is, but it looks like there's more writing under the tab."

"Well, let's just have ourselves a little look-see." The clerk opened the folder, and his eyes got wide. "You sure have good eyes. Looks like your stab in the dark hit pay-dirt. The full name's VanderGrift. Brodie-LeRoux-VanderGrift. You didn't tell me he had three names. Wait a second, *VanderGrift*? He's not related to *Senator* VanderGrift, is he? You know who I'm talking about? Lucky VanderGrift?"

Holly's pulse started racing, and it was all she could do not to reach down and snatch the folder from his hands. "Yes, I know who you're talking about, but I'm not sure what it means. What does the file say?"

"Let me see here…hmmm. You said his name was Joseph, right?"

"Yes, Joseph Brodie."

"Well, this has got to be him. How do you like that? He was treated by a Dr. Scanlon, who first saw him on…let me see… December 12, 1948. You were right; he was in a coma, in fact…" He shuffled through a couple pages, "It doesn't appear that he ever came out of it, how sad."

"Does it say what happened to him? Why are those other names in the file?" Holly was excited and dying to take a look.

"Hmmm...this is a little strange."

"What? What is?"

"He was released from the doctor's care in the spring of 1949."

"But I thought you said he never came out of the coma."

"He didn't, but it says he was released to his family."

"But his family was killed in a plane crash on the way home to St. Croix. He didn't *have* any family."

The clerk shuffled through some more papers and was silent for a little while as he read some documents and then began nodding. "Ah, I see what happened here. Now it makes sense."

"What makes sense? What happened?" The anticipation was killing her, and she leaned over the counter to try to read the documents herself.

"Young Joseph was released to the care of his cousin and her husband."

"*What* cousin?"

The clerk peered intently at the document and then removed his reading glasses, setting them on the desk. "That would be his cousin, who's listed as Genevieve LeRoux, and her husband, Kilroy VanderGrift. They became Joseph's legal guardians. They adopted him."

Chapter 36

It was approaching cocktail hour for Franklin Post as he leaned back in his command-center recliner and gazed at his cosmic ceiling. He was contemplating whether to make a martini when the rings around the planet Saturn started flashing, the signal that one of his DICK agents was calling. He pressed a button on the arm of the recliner, and a helmet-like apparatus with a microphone swung out and positioned itself perfectly over his head. As he switched on the Oralator, he saw that it was Rafe calling. Although he had threatened at the end of their last conversation to continue using the voice of Adam West, he decided to go with the voice of Tom Selleck of Magnum P.I. fame. "Rafe, how is it in sunny St. Croix?"

"Not so sunny right now; it just got dark."

"You don't sound like your normal cheerful self. You sound like TC when the price of aviation fuel spikes. What gives?"

"I just found out Jansen and company left the island and went to St. Thomas."

"*St. Thomas?* Why St. Thomas?"

"I guess it has to do with that personal business you said the girl was here on."

"How so?"

"They left the resort this morning and went to a place called the Salt River Marina. The girl, Holly, was asking about the guy who used to own the marina. His son is a senator on St. Thomas. I don't know if it's him they went to see, but they hitched a ride over on a dive boat named the *Diver Down.*"

"What's the senator's name?"

"VanderGrift. Lucky VanderGrift."

"Hmmm."

The line went silent long enough for Rafe to think the call might have been dropped. "You still there Thom—I mean, boss?"

"Yes, I was just thinking that name sounds familiar. I need to look into it."

"Sir, you know I'm not a big fan of this Oralator thing. Couldn't you just use a computer-generated voice to hide your identity? I almost called you Thomas."

"Sure I could, but what would be the fun in that? It would be like Magnum without Rick and TC, not to mention Higgins."

"No, not Higgins again, please?"

"Request denied. It'll help me to think if I switch over to his voice."

Franklin Post quickly scrolled through the menu on the Oralator and switched to the voice of Higgins as Rafe pleaded fruitlessly. "C'mon sir, he's the most annoying—"

"Too late, Rafe," he answered in the voice of Higgins. "You see, what may appear vague to one man, may appear crystal clear to another of higher intellect and insight."

"Ooookay…so, insighten me."

"Very clever play on words, young man, but this is no time for gamesmanship."

"My bad." Rafe shook his head, half-amazed at the dead-on voice replication the Oralator produced, and half-amazed the man using it was its inventor.

"Yes, as I was saying, one man's mud is another man's mirror."

"What?"

"Quit asking questions or this will take all day."

"Sorry."

"I want you to get to St. Thomas A-SAP, by whatever means possible. The Cordero brothers are undoubtedly aware their sub is missing and doing everything they can to find it and the persons responsible. Jansen and company hop-scotching around the Caribbean are sure to attract unwanted attention. Ironically, you can't keep a low profile with a midget in tow."

"Understood. Can you run a check on the *Diver Down* and let me know where it's docked?"

"I will, but that may not be necessary."

"Why's that?"

"When we became involved with Mr. Jansen during the Donny Nutz case last summer, I had listening devices placed on his phone, as well as his girlfriend's. They were eventually removed, but the proprietary adhesive membrane I developed to affix the listening device remains in place. Within the membrane is a nano-antenna made of a synthetic polymer that transmits an ultra-low frequency signal, utilizing the heat from the phone's operating system."

"What if it's turned off?"

"Please, Rafe, did you *really* think I didn't contemplate such a scenario? Naturally, the polymer is coated with a solar resin that stores power from virtually any light source. If the phone is off, the antenna will still transmit when it detects a radio frequency calibrated to its receptor."

Despite degrees in both hydrodynamic propulsion and marine engineering, Rafe was impressed. "Sooo, how do I generate this particular radio frequency?"

"With your DICK phone."

"You're kidding me, it can do that?"

"No, not at the moment, but there's an app for that."

"Let me guess, you developed that too."

"I hardly feel the inclination to respond when the answer is so blatantly obvious. When we're done talking, turn your phone off for five minutes. The app will be on your home page when you turn it back on. I'll send you a separate file with the operating instructions, but the key is this: when the phone you're trying to locate is turned on, the range is about two miles. If it's off, you'll need to be within a quarter mile to detect the signal. Once the signal is secured, the location will be brought up on the phone display via Google Maps."

"How do I know which phone I'm tracking?"

"That's easy. Both Jansen and his sidekick lost their phones when their boat blew up. The only phone we'll be able to track is Jansen's girlfriend's. If she's half as striking as I've heard, I don't imagine Mr. Jansen will be too far away."

"That reminds me; the lady at the marina left a message for Jansen's girlfriend with the St. Maarten address of Senator Vandergrift's mother. Maybe that's the next stop on their impromptu Caribbean tour. I'll text you the address."

"I strongly suggest you make haste; the hands of time don't play paddy cakes."

"Roger that, Higgins."

"I do exude a rather convincing portrayal of his overly-condescending air, wouldn't you agree?"

"No doubt about it. You nailed it, sir."

"Very well, then. Good luck and Godspeed." Click.

Rafe shook his head in wonder and softly chuckled as he turned off his phone. Within moments he was speeding toward Christiansted harbor, hoping to catch a late flight to St. Thomas.

Chapter 37

Eduardo Cordero stared at the blinking image on his computer screen in disbelief. The tracking device showed the sub was bypassing Cuba and headed toward the territorial waters of the United States. *What the fuck was going on?* Rico noticed the disconcerted look on his brother's face and inquired as to its origin. "What's the matter?"

"The fucking sub isn't going to Cuba; it's going toward Florida." He felt the blood rushing through his veins and pounded his fist on his desk.

"It must be as I feared. McGirt is stealing the shipment."

Eduardo looked at his brother as he calmly stroked Elvira's chin and reluctantly came to the same conclusion. "When we find him, and we *will* find him, we will do things to him that will make the Marquis de Sade seem like a *fucking* boy scout."

"He is obviously crazier than we thought."

"And suicidal. One thing troubles me though; if he was going to steal the shipment, why did he deliver a thousand kilos to the Jamaicans?"

"Perhaps he wanted to put as much distance between us as possible before raising our suspicions. He knows we won't chase him into American waters."

"You make a good point, Rico. I have taught you well. I thought I taught McGirt well, too, but it seems I was wrong." Suddenly one of Eduardo's phones started ringing, and he answered it. "Yes?"

"It's me again, Lucky."

"I told you *I* would be the one to make contact, yet—"

"I have the captain of your missing sub. He's sitting right here in front of me."

"You—*what?* You have *McGirt?*"

"Yes, and he told us quite a tale."

Eduardo looked at his computer screen which showed the sub tracking past Cuba. "How can this be?"

"A local fisherman found him clinging to a cooler with his face buried in a package of product. He knew of our interest in the offshore explosion and brought him to us. McGirt claims the sub got disabled by an American fishing boat and—"

"Give him the phone."

"I would, but he is incapacitated at the moment. He claimed to have hijacked the fishing boat and forced the crew to transfer the product off the sub. He said before the transfer was complete, the fishing crew overpowered one of his men and tried to capsize the boat by submerging the sub, which was tethered to it."

"I don't understand. You're saying the Americans made off with my submarine?"

"No, according to McGirt, he managed to sink the sub with the Americans on it, but I know he's lying."

"How?"

"The American fishermen in question have been spotted on St. Thomas. I saw them myself; they were here at my marina."

Totally confused, Eduardo closed his eyes and pinched the bridge of his nose as he tried to process the information. When he opened them, he noticed Rico had lifted Elvira's tail and was sniffing her nether region. *Madre de Mio.*

"You still there?" inquired Lucky.

"Yes, hang on a second." He put his hand over the speaker slot and admonished Rico. "Jesus Christ, quit sniffing that tiger pussy in front of me; you're making me sick." Rico dropped the tail and shrugged.

Eduardo lifted his hand as he shook his head. "Okay—go on."

"The Americans showed up at my marina, but they're not with the DEA, like we thought."

"How do you know?"

"It was a case of mistaken identity. They're wearing these T-shirts that have DEA in big letters across the back, but it's not real. Below the letters, in real small type, it says, 'Drink Every Afternoon.'"

"Cute shirts. They wear them down here, and they'd be *dead* every afternoon."

"It's not too smart to wear them around here either."

"So, they're not DEA…that's good, but what are they doing at your marina? Are you positive it's the same guys?"

"I don't know why they're here, but it's definitely them. The description McGirt gave matches the description we got from our source on St. Croix. Not only does the clothing match, but one of them's a fucking midget."

"A fucking midget? When I get through with him the only thing he'll be fucking is out of luck. So, how did McGirt end up in the water? I thought he hijacked their boat?"

"He claims the boat blew up, and he was the only survivor. Since he was plucked out of the water with some minor burns, I tend to believe that part of his story. The problem is, when the Americans got dropped off by the Coast Guard on St. Croix, they claimed *they* were on the boat when it caught fire and abandoned ship before it blew up. If that's a lie, then they must know where the sub is. I have one of my security personnel looking for them right now, and when he brings them back, I'll get to the bottom of it."

"No, listen to me! It's best to leave the interrogation to a professional, like my brother. He will squeeze the truth out of McGirt and the Americans worse than Obama squeezes the working man."

"How do you propose to do that?"

"He can be there in three or four hours; the jet is ready."

"You're going to fly him *here*? To *St. Thomas?*"

"Of course not. It's an American territory; he could be shot down or arrested upon landing. How far are you from St. Maarten?"

"About a hundred and thirty miles...why?"

"Because, the Directeur of the Grand Case airport is on my payroll. We can fly in and out of the French side with no problem. If you can get them there and secure a place for Rico to conduct a proper interrogation, I'll credit your deposit toward the next shipment, whenever that is."

"The whole twenty million?"

"Every penny if you can get them to St. Maarten. Of course, if we manage to get the sub back, any product recovered will be yours— with improved credit terms."

"What if the Coast Guard has it?"

"If they did it would have hit the news wires by now. Either McGirt's double-crossing us, or the Americans hijacked it, or both. Somebody's going to pay, and my brother Rico will set the price."

The senator thought about it for only a moment; taking a twenty million-dollar hit was unfathomable, he would be ruined. "It's about a four- or five-hour boat ride to St. Maarten. They can be there around midnight."

"What about a place to hold the interrogation?"

"My ailing mother lives in a villa overlooking Tucker Bay. I'll arrange it so you can use the guesthouse."

"Perfect."

"Not exactly. How am I going to get the Americans on board?"

"I don't care and neither should you. Do whatever it takes."

"When they see McGirt, they'll know something's up."

"They'll know something's up if you have to force them on board anyways, but if not, keep McGirt hidden. Lock him in a cabin and keep him gagged or unconscious or both. Just keep him alive."

"You make it sound easy."

"Practice makes perfect."

Just then the door to the upstairs apartment opened, and Remy blurted out, "We found the Americans; they're on their way here."

"Did you hear that?" He asked.

"No, what is it?"

"We found the Americans. They'll be here shortly."

"Excellent, I'll tell Rico to start packing. Give me the address of the villa."

He reluctantly gave him the address, wondering if he was making a huge mistake. When he hung up the phone, he looked at his hot-headed son. In the back of his mind, he questioned whether he was the right man for the job, but knew he couldn't afford to involve anyone else. Remy noticed the pensive look he was getting and inquired as to its source.

"What's going on?"

"Call the fuel dock and tell them to gas up the Hatteras."

"The fitty-four?"

"*No,* the fifty-four. Did you hear how I pronounced that? Fifty, with two fucking *F*s."

"Why are you so pissed? I thought you *wanted* to see the Americans? You should be happy."

"Really? Well, I'm not. We need to deliver them to St. Maarten, along with McGirt."

"Why?"

"The Colombians are flying in to interrogate them; I told them they could use the guest house at the villa. It's up to you to get them there…alive."

"So, how are we going to get them to cooperate? With this?" Remy pulled the handgun out and aimed at an imaginary target. The senator reached out and pushed the gun down. "No, I'm not sure how we're going to get them on board, but using force is the last resort. It might get messy and I don't want any evidence left behind. The woman claimed to be a cousin of mine, so maybe I'll play along. Just follow my lead and don't go all gangster on them unless I say so. In fact, I'm going to talk to her alone. Why don't you disappear on the dock."

As Remy tucked the gun away, he said, "Okay, but I can't wait to hear this bitch's story about her being a cousin; it should be good."

"Well, we're about to find out. You better shut off the security cameras too. We have the Americans on tape being escorted off the premises and we need to keep it that way. Knowing the Colombian's, this is a one-way trip you're taking them on. Once they disappear, someone's bound to come looking for them. Make sure the guard who brings them back understands."

"Got it."

Suddenly, McGirt started coming to, and Remy pointed at him. "What do you want me to do with him?"

"Keep him doped up. The Colombians don't want him to see the Americans and vice-versa."

Remy walked over to the table and picked up the syringe the doctor left him earlier. He kneeled down and stabbed it in McGirt's arm before plunging the clear fluid into it. Less than five seconds later, McGirt's head rolled to the side, and he was out cold again. "That's the end of the sedative the doc left; should I get more?"

"Yes, order enough to knock out three-and-a-half people for the next twelve hours, just in case, but drag McGirt into the closet first."

Remy tilted McGirt's chair back and started dragging him across the floor. "Three and a half?" He questioned.

"The midget."

"I forgot about him. It's gonna be like a circus around here."

"There's nothing funny about our situation, Remy. So far, everything's gone wrong on this deal. We can't afford a twenty million-dollar set-back, even for a few months."

Remy shut the closet door and nonchalantly dismissed his father's concern. "Don't worry about it—midgets are good luck."

Lucky had been looking out at the harbor as the sun descended on the postcard-like view, and turned to give his son a funny look. "They are? I never heard that."

"That's what I heard, that they're good luck... in Haiti."

"But we're not *in* Haiti."

"You see, it's already working. How lucky is that?"

Chapter 38

Tangles and I hadn't gone far before we got sucked into a local dive bar with a sign boasting 'De best conch chowder in de world.' While enjoying a bowl, the lone TV perched high in the corner had on The Weather Channel. Carl "The Nose" Parker, had been promoted to 'hurricane specialist' and was talking about a new low-pressure system that formed a hundred miles east of the lower Antilles. He reminded the viewing audience that even though it was mid-November, we were still in hurricane season until December 1. The Nose warned that, "Although development appears unlikely, I'll still be keeping an eye on it." Personally, I would've felt better if he kept his perfect nose on it, which was surely capable of detecting a drop in barometric pressure. By the time we finished our over-hyped conch chowders, it was time to head back to the hospital. When we got there, Holly was standing in front of it, talking on her phone. She raised her index finger to signal she would be done soon. Moments later, she ended the call and started filling us in on what was up. "Sally from the Salt River

Marina left me a message. I have the address for Genevieve in St. Maarten."

"Great. I wonder if she's still alive," I commented.

"The senator will certainly know…if we can ever get to see him."

"Have any luck finding out about Joseph?" Tangles nodded at the hospital.

"Well, the records clerk was a sweetheart and dug out stacks and stacks of files to look through. Unfortunately, we couldn't find one under the name Joseph Brodie."

"That's too bad; you knew it was a long shot, though."

"Yeah, Holl, don't let it get you down," I consoled her. "At least you got Genevieve's address." As we started walking down the side of the road, Holly gave me a funny smile, and I called her on it. "What are you smiling about?"

"I wasn't finished. The reason we didn't find a file under the name, Joseph Brodie, is because it was under the name Vandergrift. Joseph Brodie-LeRoux-VanderGrift to be exact."

Upon hearing the name VanderGrift, Tangles and I stopped dead in our tracks and stared at her. He echoed my sentiment with a single word. "*What?*"

"Oh, look at this. I got your undivided attention. You'd think I just shouted, 'free cheeseburgers and beer, here!'"

"C'mon, what are you talking about? What are you saying?"

"Joseph never regained consciousness, but he was released from the doctor's care in the spring of 1949... *to his family.*"

"His *family*? What family? You said his family died in a plane crash."

"Yeah," agreed Tangles. "You said his entire family died when they crashed on the way back to St. Croix after visiting him."

"They did, but apparently he had a cousin named….wait for it…Genevieve LeRoux."

"No way." Tangles was shaking his head.

"Way," Holly nodded. "And it gets better; she and her husband, Kilroy VanderGrift… drum roll please… *adopted* him."

"Ho-lee-crap! Are you *shitting me?!*" I was dumbstruck.

"I didn't say that to the helpful clerk, but that's pretty much what I was thinking too. You ever hear anything so crazy? Kilroy tries to kill him, but only succeeds in putting him in a coma. Then, when Joseph's family dies, he steps in with his new bride and adopts him. Why?"

"She was his cousin?" asked Tangles.

"Not according to Millie's letter she wasn't, and I'm pretty darn sure she would have mentioned it if she was. So I ask you, what in the heck's going on here?"

"Maybe Genevieve just *posed* as his cousin, so as not to raise any eyebrows concerning the adoption," I answered.

"But why? Why would they adopt him?"

"There's only one reason I can think of—Kilroy was worried that Joseph would come out of the coma and finger him for attempted murder."

"Do you think Genevieve knew?"

"Maybe she did, maybe she didn't," cut in Tangles. "If she didn't, maybe adopting him was Kilroy's idea.

Maybe he conned her into thinking he was doing it out of the goodness of his heart, when in reality he was just trying to erase any suspicions she had concerning his involvement in the accident. Who knows? Maybe that's why she finally agreed to marry him."

"You really think so?"

"Could be."

"Even worse," I added, "if it was Kilroy's scheme to adopt him, he'd never let him come out of the coma. He probably intended to finish him off. Maybe he did…eventually."

"Please! That's too horrible to even think of!"

"Sorry, you're right, maybe…maybe Kilroy, you know, had nothing to do with the accident… and the adoption was…just a sincere gesture on his part."

Tangles rolled his eyes, and Holly gave me a skeptical look. "But you don't believe that, do you?"

I shrugged and answered her question with my own. "*Do you?*"

Before Holly could answer, a Range Rover with a Tiara Bay Security logo pulled off the road next to us. I saw it was the same security guard that escorted us off the property earlier. I noticed his lips were moving, but his hand wasn't pressing the walkie-talkie transmit button on his collar, it was pressed to his ear. *Bluetooth?* As the window rolled down, he stopped talking and lowered his hand from his ear as he leaned over from the driver's side. "I've been looking for you for the last hour. Holly Lutes, may I have a word?"

Holly bent over by the window. "Yes, that's me."

"Would you still like to speak with Senator VanderGrift?"

"Are you kidding? Now more than ever."

"Well, today's your lucky day—no pun intended. The senator asked me to come find you. He has some time if you'd like to see him. Just hop in, and I'll take you back to the marina."

Holly got in the front and after Tangles and I piled in the back, Norbert put his thick arm along the top of the seat as he turned back to face us.

"Even though it's a short ride, I don't wanna hear a peep outta you clowns, got it?" Before we could respond, Holly put her hand on his arm and assured him we would be cooperative.

"They won't make a sound. Right, guys?" She stabbed me with her dagger eyes, and I responded, "Sure, no problem, no sound from me."

She shifted her sights to Tangles. "*Tangles?* Let me hear you say it."

"I got it already, okay? No sound from the back seat…fine."

"Good. Thank you."

As soon as Holly turned around and we started going down the road, Tangles added, "Unless 'de best conch chowder in de world' gives me gas; then there might be a few sounds."

Holly shook her head in disgust and spoke to Norbert, who was squinting at Tangles in the rearview mirror. "He starts farting and you have my permission to dump him on the side of the road. He wants to walk, let him walk."

"Gladly." He smiled.

Less than ten, fart-free minutes later, we were back at the marina and led into the main office. Waiting for us was a distinguished-looking, brown-skinned man in a white suit. He locked eyes on Holly and extended a hand, the way most politicians do. "So, you're the young lady who believes we have some common ancestry?"

She shook his hand and replied, "Yes, I believe so; it's a pleasure to meet you, Senator."

"Please, everybody calls me Lucky, and if such a beautiful young woman as you is, indeed, related to me, never has my namesake been more appropriate."

Holly blushed a little and I gagged a little. I was used to her getting attention from both men *and* women, but there was something smarmy and rehearsed in his delivery.

After Holly introduced me and Tangles, the senator pointed toward a door in the rear of the office. "I have an apartment in back where we can have some privacy. Shall we?"

Holly gently put her hand on my arm. "I think it's best I speak with the senator alone."

"Sure, no problem."

I asked the senator if it was okay for me and Tangles to walk around and check out some of the boats in the marina.

"Feel free to." He smiled. "As I'm sure you've noticed, there are some beautiful yachts here. Maybe you'll find a model that would be a suitable replacement for you."

"That's exactly what I was—wait a second. How do you know I'm looking for a new boat?"

"Excuse me?"

I shot a quick look at Tangles, and Holly looked at me questioningly.

"I'm just wondering how you know I'm looking for a new boat."

"Oh, yes, of course. That *was* your boat that had the unfortunate accident on the water yesterday, was it not?"

"Yes, yes it was, and it was *very* unfortunate. How did you know it was mine?"

Red flags were flapping in my mind with gale-force tenacity.

"Your shirts, and the fact that your companion here carries a rather, shall we say, *low profile?*"

"Huh?"

"I'm right here, Mr. Senator" said Tangles. "You don't have to talk like I'm not."

Holly nudged Tangles and whispered, "Let it go."

"Please, I meant no offense."

"Don't worry about it," replied Tangles.

"Yeah, don't worry about him, worry about me."

"Kit, c'mon! Let the senator finish, please?" Holly was clearly getting embarrassed, but I didn't care. I only cared about how he knew I was minus one boat. One, *very special* boat.

"Again, please, call me Lucky. As I was going to say, my son, Remy, runs the marina. He heard about the explosion from a local fisherman who went to the scene but was waved off by the Coast Guard. Since we're in the marine business, he was concerned on a number of levels and did some inquiring as to what happened. A friend of his from St. Croix called to say two men got dropped off at a resort last night by a Coast Guard helicopter. They were both wearing what appeared to be DEA T-shirts, like the ones you have on, and one of them fit Mr. Tangles' description. I'm not mistaken, am I?"

"No, but I don't recall mentioning anything about what happened." I looked at Tangles. "Did you tell anybody our boat blew up?"

"I...don't think so, but I'm not—"

"I did." We both looked at Holly. "What's the big deal? I told the deejay about it; the one who took me horseback riding on the beach."

"Oh, I didn't know, that's all. Like you said, 'no big deal.'"

"Well, now that we got *that* cleared up, perhaps you'll excuse us for a little while?"

"Sure, let's go, Tangles."

"If you don't mind me asking," queried the senator, "how *did* your boat blow up?"

"With a big bang, that's my theory."

"*What?*"

Holly gave me another one of her death laser stares, and I quickly tried to recover. "Just kidding, we, uh, we had an engine fire and couldn't get it under control. We abandoned ship just before it blew."

"Looks like you were fortunate in that regard. There doesn't appear to be a scratch on either of you."

Tangles turned his head to the side so he could see the lump by his ear. "Nothing but a little bump when I was scrambling to get off the boat."

"You know the saying, timing is everything." I added. "If we had waited much longer before jumping in the dinghy, we'd be crab food right now."

"So, why didn't you radio for help?"

"Huh?"

"You didn't mention radioing for help before abandoning ship."

"Oh, yeah… I tried, but, uh, it, it was, uh, shorted out. Probably by the fire, or, you know, now that I think of it, maybe the radio shorted out and somehow caused the fire. Who knows? Shit happens."

"Indeed it does… I guess your cell phones didn't work, either."

"Actually," said Tangles, "we were in such a hurry to get off the boat, we forgot to grab them."

"Yeah, that's right. As you can imagine, it was a bit hectic."

"Sounds like you were lucky the Coast Guard even found you."

"Lucky we got found, but not so lucky to lose the boat and everything on it."

"Well, like I said, I'm sure you'll find something in the marina that'll suit your fancy."

"My fancy doesn't suit, as you can see. It wears cargo shorts. But you're right, I'm sure there are plenty of boats out there I'd love to own. Probably none that I can afford, but plenty I'd love to own."

"You never know what the future has in store, Mr. Jansen."

"You can call me Shagball, and as far as what the future has in store, I just hope it has some boats on clearance."

Holly grimaced, but the senator smiled and laughed. "I'm afraid you'll have no such luck in the Tiara Bay Marina, but I wish you well in your search. Now, if you'll excuse me and your lovely girlfriend, I can't *wait* to hear her story."

The senator offered Holly the crook of his arm, and she waved at me as he escorted her toward the door in back. Once Tangles and I got outside the office and were headed down the dock, I voiced my concern. "Old Lucky seems pretty interested in how we lost the boat, don't you think?"

"I wouldn't read too much into it, like he said, he's in the marine business. Boats blowing up aren't something that happens every day."

"Maybe you're right; he threw me for a loop, though."

"Yeah, that line about the radio shorting out was a stretch."

"At least I came up with *something*. And what's with that Panama Jack outfit? The only thing he was missing was a monocle and hat."

"Hey, he's a senator, who knows? Maybe they wear uniforms down here."

"Really? That's the best you can come up with?"

"If a short in the radio can cause an engine fire, anything's possible."

"Good point." I looked down at him, and we both started laughing.

Chapter 39

For a solid twenty minutes, Holly recounted Millie's letter, being sure not to insinuate that she suspected Kilroy had tried to kill Joseph in an elaborate scheme to steal Millie's baby. Then she got to the part where Millie gave birth. "When my aunt finally gave birth, on President's day, 1949, the doctor Kilroy had hired let her hold the baby for just a minute or two before sedating her. Millie counted his fingers and toes, like all mothers do, and discovered the baby had an unusual birthmark on his forearm. It was a dark red stain in the shape of a four-leaf clover, and she named him, 'Lucky.' When she woke up the next day, the baby was gone and so was Genevieve. She was told that her baby had been adopted by a couple who lived off island, and was reminded she had signed an agreement to keep their identity secret. Millie never saw her baby again. Naturally, she was devastated and left St. Croix, never to return."

The incredible story had the senator on the edge of his seat and left him stunned. The implications seemed obvious; his father had killed a man in order to steal a baby. He rose from his chair and walked over to the window. He could see Shagball and Tangles gawking over the new Cabo 44 HTX that one of his customers had recently purchased. He knew their story about how their boat blew up was bullshit. Radios didn't cause boats to blow up unless they were made of plastic explosive. He needed to get them to St. Maarten and saw his opportunity. Holly watched him with his back to her as he gazed out the window and spoke. "You clearly know my father is the late Kilroy VanderGrift, and my mother is Genevieve LeRoux."

"Yes, I do. Your mother's still alive?"

"Yes, but I was born in September, 1949, not February; at least, I think I was."

"There's only one way to know; the birthmark. Do you have it?"

"My God, I can't believe this."

"So, *you do?*"

The senator turned from the window and walked over to Holly as he removed his jacket. He was wearing a short sleeve shirt and rolled his right forearm over to expose a small scar, halfway between his wrist and elbow.

"What's that? What happened there?"

"I've had it as long as I can remember. My mother told me I got it as a small child when I climbed on a stove and put my arm on the burner."

"You don't remember having a birthmark?"

"No, I don't even remember burning myself. Like I said, I never thought twice about it until now. Good Lord, this is unbelievable. Do you suppose my parents had the birthmark removed?"

"It's certainly possible. Especially knowing it was the surest way to identify you at the time."

The senator sat down across from Holly and put his head in his hands. Holly put her hand on his shoulder, feeling guilty about turning his life upside down. "I'm sorry, it's a lot to take in. I felt similar when I read my aunt's letter. We've got to talk to your mother; she's the only one who can fill in the blanks. She's the only one who may know the truth."

"If your story is true, it seems to imply my father killed this man, Joseph. Do you think my mother was in on it? It's a little hard to believe."

"She'd know about the birthmark, that much is certain, but Joseph didn't die—at least not immediately."

"What? I thought you said when he was pulled from the water his rescuers said he was dead."

"They did, but he was revived at the hospital. He never regained consciousness, though, and his family took him here, to St. Thomas, for treatment."

"So, what happened? Did he ever wake up?"

"No, and it gets even *more* bizarre. His entire family was killed in a plane crash on the way back to St. Croix after visiting him."

"He was in a coma with no family? How terrible."

"Yes, but not for long."

"What? What do you mean?"

"I was just at Schneider Regional, and the records clerk helped me pull some old files transferred there for safekeeping. In the spring of 1949, Joseph was released to the care of his new family, despite being comatose."

"His *new* family? What are you talking about?"

"This is the bizarre part. He was adopted by a woman purporting to be his cousin, one Genevieve LeRoux, and her new husband, Kilroy VanderGrift."

Although the senator had been holding back a critical piece of information, most everything he was told came as a bombshell, and this little shard of information was no different. "My God, Uncle Joe."

"*Uncle Joe?* Who's Uncle Joe?"

"When I was growing up, there was a man who lived with my mother's family on St. Maarten. He was bedridden the entire time. I was told he suffered a massive stroke. Everybody called him Uncle Joe."

"He's not still alive, is he?"

"No, he..." The senator rose again and walked to the window. He looked out at the glistening harbor and the beautiful boats heading back to port as night fell. It was a stark contrast to the ugliness unfolding around him, like a rotten onion whose stench grew worse as each layer sloughed off from decay.

"He... what? What happened to him?"

"I must have been nine or ten year's old, working with my father at the Salt River Marina on St. Croix. My mother got a call from her family that Uncle Joe seemed to be waking up. His eyes opened, and he kept muttering my father's name. They took it to mean he wanted to see him, and my father caught the next flight over. I... can't remember *all* the details, but the bottom line is that my father was the last person to see him alive."

"WHAT?"

"My mother told me the doctors said he must have suffered some type of cerebral hemorrhage—that the stress of waking after so many years probably triggered a dormant blood clot that broke free and traveled to his brain. Or maybe it was the excitement of seeing my father, someone he recognized. I think that's what she said, but it was a long time ago."

Holly's mind was racing, trying to process the new information. "We need to talk to your mother as soon as possible. She wouldn't happen to be here on St. Thomas, would she?"

"No, she's still on St. Maarten. She has a villa where she lives with a full-time nurse."

"She's sick?"

"She's got a laundry list of ailments, but nothing terminal at this point."

"I'd like to go see her and talk to her, if it's alright with you."

The senator squashed a smile and turned to face her. *Trap set, trap sprung.*

"Are you kidding? I want answers too. My son, Remy, is taking a boat to St. Maarten tonight for a customer, I'm sure you can catch a ride with him if you want. I'd accompany you myself if I didn't have a senate meeting tomorrow morning. I'll catch a flight as soon as it's over."

"That would be great, how long of a ride is it?"

"I think it's about four or five hours. Don't worry though; it's a fifty-four-foot Hatteras with plenty of room."

"A big Hatteras? The guys are gonna love it. When's Remy leaving?"

"I'm not sure. Let's go find him; he's out on the dock somewhere."

The senator's eyes were glued to Holly's exquisite derriere and tantalizing legs as she walked down the apartment steps ahead of him. Cousin or not, he licked his lecherous lips and reached in the breast pocket of his suit to remove a handkerchief to dab his brow. It was a shame she would end up as collateral damage once the Colombians finished with her boyfriend and the midget, but that was their fault. Somehow, they had something to do with derailing one of the largest drug deals in history. Heads were gonna roll like the *Andrea Gail*, and the outcome would likely be the same; they would never be seen again.

Chapter 40

Tangles and I were standing on the dock, drooling over the new Cabo 44 HTX, when I thought out loud, "*This* would be a suitable replacement for the *Lucky Dog,* don't you think?"

"Sure it would. Let me guess, the only thing standing in your way is about a million bucks?"

"Who knows? Probably more."

"Hey, maybe Holly will buy it for you as a wedding gift."

"Yeah, right. Besides, who's getting married?"

"Don't tell me you haven't thought about it...especially if she's prego."

"For the last time, she's not pregnant! Why do you keep saying that? You trying to give me high blood pressure?"

"Dude, relax, will you? Even if she's not, why *wouldn't* you marry her? She's smart, beautiful, rich, *and* she loves to fish... almost as much as we do."

"Look, I'm not ruling *anything* out, but first things first, we need a new boat."

"That's for sure; too bad you didn't have some insurance on the *LD.*"

"Even if I did, it was a thirty-year-old boat. Whatever I got would amount to a drop in the bucket toward what I'd *really* like. There is a glimmer of hope though."

"What's that?"

"Remember that call the Coast Guard pilot patched through to me?"

"Oh, yeah. I forgot to ask. Who was it?"

"I have no clue, but he sounded like Dan Tanna."

"Who the hell is Dan Tanna?"

"I guess he was a little before your time. He was a detective on a show in the late seventies called *Vegas.* After that he was Spenser in *Spenser for Hire.* I think he was banging Wonder Woman in real life."

"Lucky him, but I don't follow."

"That's the idea. The guy who called used some type of voice-altering device to protect his identity. Apparently, he's the one in charge of whatever agency it is that gave us the get-out-of-jail-free card I used last night. You know, the one that the guy we thought was an FBI agent gave to us last summer?"

"How could I forget, who the hell are they then, the CIA?"

"I suppose it could be, but I don't know why they wouldn't tell us. I can safely say they're not with the DEA, though. The agents who questioned me seemed to think I was an agent with Homeland Security because they're in charge of the Coast Guard and the commander let me make the call. I played along, 'cause it seemed like the thing to do, but again, why all the secrecy? If it *is* Homeland Security, why wouldn't they tell us? It's not like we're terrorists."

"I dunno, Shag, but it's gotta be an agency with some serious clout. One minute we're getting the third degree from some pissed off DEA agents, and the next minute we're drinking long-neck Bud's and doing tequila shots with the commander."

"Exactly. That was my idea, by the way...so were the sandwiches."

"I figured."

"Anyways, back to the phone call. The guy who sounded like Dan Tanna implied I would receive some assistance in getting a replacement boat. Since we're in agreement that whatever agency he heads has some serious clout, I'm angling for a *serious upgrade*, so to speak."

"Seriousness aside, I say, why not? *Especially* with Obama in office. The guy never met a bailout he didn't like. Forget about the billions he gave the banks and the auto industry, how about the tens of millions of people he's giving free housing, free food, free healthcare, plus a check every week, *not* to work. Then he gives them an Obamaphone so they can call each other and conspire how to game the system even more. The least he could do is buy you a new boat."

"You know? It worries me when a guy with an abnormally small brain thinks like I do."

Tangles swiveled with amazing speed and drilled me in the gut with an overhand right. I doubled over and complained once I caught my breath. "That was... uncalled for...damn."

"Too bad. Seeing as how we think so much alike, you shoulda seen it coming.

I was still bent over and rubbing my stomach when I heard an approaching voice ask, "Everyting alright?"

As I slowly stood up, I saw that it came from a guy wearing pressed shorts and a polo shirt with the marina logo on it. He had the same coloring as the senator, and the resemblance didn't end there. Before I could answer, Tangles replied, "Yeah, we're good. It's probably just his Transvaginal Mesh acting up—must be that time of the month."

"Sure it is... probably happens every time you punch him."

"It's okay," I assured him. "I guess I had it coming, everything's cool...right, Tangles?"

"Yeah, we're good. I didn't mean to hit you so hard... sorry, bro."

"Good," smiled the guy in the polo shirt. "I'd hate to be the one to escort you off the premises for the *second* time today." He extended his hand toward me. "My name's Remy, I run the marina, and you are?"

I shook his hand and replied, "Shagball, that's what most people call me, and this is my...well, he's *normally* my friend, Tangles. My girlfriend's inside talking to Senator VanderGrift. He wouldn't happen to be your—"

"Father? Yes, he is. In fact, here he comes right now." He pointed and I turned to see the senator coming down the dock with Holly next to him. Now he was wearing a panama hat that matched his elegant white suit. Moments later, the senator introduced Holly to Remy and asked if he was still planning on going to St. Maarten.

"Yes, I just finished gassing up the Hatteras. I'll be leaving after I go to the grocery and get some tings."

The senator narrowed his eyes and pursed his lips a little. "Some *what?*"

"Some, uh, some provisions…is what I meant to say."

"Yes, I thought so. Be sure to get enough supplies to keep our guests comfortable. Miss Lutes and her friends here will be joining you."

"Sure ting—I mean, *thing*."

"We are?" I asked, looking at Holly.

"Yes," she replied. "Since Remy's taking a boat over for a client anyways, Lucky was kind enough to offer us a ride. He's as anxious to speak with his mother as I am."

I nodded and looked at Remy. "How far is it?"

"About a hundred and thirty miles."

"We're going in a Hatt?"

He pointed his finger over the top of Tangles' head. "That one there…the fifty-four. It's about a five-hour trip running at twenty-five knots. She'll run forty-plus if I need her to, but I don't like to run top speed in the dark."

Everybody turned to look at the brand new GT 54 Convertible with the Palm Beach Yellow hull. Tangles commented, "Sweet," and Holly said, "I told Lucky you guys would love it."

I had to admit, it was a beautiful boat, and I especially liked all the big cabin windows that made for exceptional views. But despite its desirable aesthetics, I commented on its integrity. "That is one fine boat… and seaworthy, too."

"Yes, she is," responded Remy. "It should make for a smooth trip over. The winds are reasonably light."

"Let's hope they stay that way."

"Why wouldn't they?"

"Well, I just happened to see the Weather Channel and—"

"That low pressure system to the east of the Antilles? Don't worry about it. Even if it does form, this time of year they always go north. Those Weather Channel people over-hype everything."

"You mean… like *Super Storm Sandy?*"

Suddenly, Remy's big smile evaporated into thin air. "What I'm saying is, you shouldn't believe everything you see on TV."

Tangles gently elbowed me in the hip and whispered "Or from overconfident captains."

Holly heard it and tried to diffuse the situation. "Will you guys knock it off?"

Remy was not amused and stared at Tangles. "What did you say?"

"Oh, I said, uh, I'm, uh…confident… in you… captain."

"Good, you should be." Remy looked back and forth between me and Tangles, and added, "If it would make you two feel even *more* confident, you can wear life preservers for the ride. I'll double check to make sure I have a child-sized one on board."

"Now, wait a second!" Tangles started to move toward Remy, and I restrained him long enough for Holly to step in the middle. "That's enough! No more screwing around you two. Kit, really? See what you started again?"

"Me? I just commented on the weather; I'm sure everything will be fine. No more screwing around. Right, Tangles?"

"Yeah, everything's fine." He jerked his shoulder away from me and extended his own hand to Remy. "I was just kidding around. Sorry about that."

"No worries," replied Remy as he shook his hand. "Like I said, it should be a smooth ride."

"They won't be a problem, I promise," said Holly.

"I'll take your word for it. So, tell me, is it true? Are we really cousins?"

"I..." Holly appeared uncertain how to answer and silently appealed to the quietly observing senator, who took her cue. "Miss Lutes has come to me with an incredible story and has uncovered information that leads us both to believe that, yes, we *are* cousins. The only one that can confirm it, however, is your grandmother. When you get to St. Maarten, you are to take them to the villa and introduce her to Holly. I'll be flying over first thing in the morning. I would be joining you tonight, but I have a dinner engagement I must attend." As if on cue, he looked at his watch. "In fact, I need to excuse myself right now." He removed his hat and raised Holly's hand to his lips before placing a tender kiss on it. "It has been a pleasure meeting you, my dear, despite the rather startling news you had to impart. I look forward to seeing you at the villa tomorrow and can only imagine how our lives may change until then."

Holly blushed again. "Yes, it was a pleasure meeting you too. See you tomorrow."

"Thank you. Have a safe trip." The senator placed his hat on his head and looked at his son. "Give me a call once you've squared things away with our friends here. We still have some business to discuss."

"Will do."

As the senator strode down the dock, I asked, "Can we get something to eat before we go?"

"Yeah, I'm hungry, too," agreed Tangles.

"I swear you two have black holes where your stomachs should be." Holly shook her head in frustration, and Remy made a suggestion. "I know a place nearby you can grab a quick bite while I provision the boat. When I'm finished, I'll pick you up and we'll be off."

"Would you mind?" asked Holly. "That would really be great."

Remy flashed a toothy smile, but it was too much like his dad's for me…too practiced, too political. "Not at all," he grinned. "That's what family's for."

As soon as the senator was out of earshot he pulled out his cell and called one of his assistants. While waiting for the call to be answered, he glanced back and waved to the Hi-Lo gang. The assistant picked up the call and familiarly asked, "Did you forget what time your dinner reservation was, sir?"

"Not in the least. Cancel my dinner plans and get me on the next flight to St. Maarten."

Chapter 41

After missing the last seaplane flight of the day from Christiansted Harbor to St. Thomas, Rafe sped toward the airport and called DICK headquarters for assistance in finding a flight. His DICK phone rang just as he pulled into the airport parking lot, and he answered, "I just got here; what flight am I on?"

"We'll get to that in a minute. There's been a development." Rafe had expected to hear the voice of the emergency travel coordinator he spoke with earlier, but instead it was the voice of Jim Phelps, of Mission Impossible fame. It was a favorite Oralator selection of Franklin Post when he needed to convey seriousness.

"What's going on, boss? It must be serious if you're using Jim Phelps.""It is. I just found out the dive boat dropped off Jansen and company at the Tiara Bay Marina."

"Tiara Bay? Why does that sound familiar?"

"Because I mentioned it in the last quarterly briefing. A couple years ago, the DEA suspected large quantities of cocaine were moving in and out of the marina, and they opened an investigation. Less than a month later, the investigation was closed and no charges were filed. The marina is operated by the son of a powerful senator who has everybody in his pocket, including, it seems, someone in the DEA."

"Let me guess. The senator's name is VanderGrift."

"You got it. Chanceaux VanderGrift, to be sure, but he goes by Lucky."

"Yeah? Well, we'll see about that."

"That we shall. Now, the FBI is investigating the DEA, and whether the persistent rumors linking Tiara Bay to cocaine trafficking are true. They have a security guard at the marina who's an informant. He confirmed our friends were dropped off there."

"Something doesn't add up. Of all the places to get dropped off, they pick *there?* Are you sure they're not dirty?"

"During the Donny Nutz saga, we ran thorough background checks on Jansen, his girlfriend, and the midget. They're clean as a whistle."

"No drug charges at all?"

"No, well...just one, but I found it more amusing than disconcerting. Some years ago, Jansen and a young woman were arrested on New Year's Eve. They were found naked and smoking a joint in a Palm Beach lifeguard stand. The woman wasn't charged, but Jansen got cited for public indecency and the joint. Both were first degree misdemeanors. He pleaded 'no contest' and paid a small fine."

"How come the girl didn't get charged?"

"That's the amusing part. She was the nineteen-year-old daughter of the Chief of Police."

They both shared a laugh before Rafe asked, "That's it? That's the extent of his criminal record?"

"That's it."

"I don't know; something still doesn't smell right. Maybe Jansen flip-flopped the story on us. Maybe the Colombians *didn't* hijack his boat, maybe it was the other way around. Maybe *he* tried to hijack the sub."

"Maybe not, Rafe. His story checks out. The sub had fishing wire wrapped around the prop and a dead Colombian inside, not to mention more than a thousand kilos of the white stuff."

"Then why did they get dropped off at Tiara Bay?"

"According to the informant, Jansen's girlfriend thinks she's related to the senator and managed a private chat with him."

"*What?* Are you kidding me? You're kidding me... right?"

"Jim Phelps never kids. I suggested Jansen return to Florida last night, but he said he needed to help his girlfriend with some personal business first. Finding lost relatives would qualify as personal business, would it not?"

"Yes, but *him?*"

"The informant reported a couple other items as well. The senator's son is taking a brand new fifty-four-foot Hatteras named *Lady G* to St. Maarten this evening, and Jansen and company plan to go with him."

"St. Maarten? That's where the address I texted you is. Maybe that's where they're going."

"That's my guess too, which is why I'm sending you there. I'm concerned what might happen to them once they arrive... *if* they arrive. I ran the address earlier, and it leads to a villa overlooking the Caribbean. In the villa lives an elderly woman named Genevieve LeRoux, who receives round-the-clock nursing care."

"*That's* a new name. What's the tie-in?"

"Genevieve LeRoux is the senator's mother, and she owns the Tiara Bay Marina."

"This is getting complicated. I think I need a chart to keep track."

"She owns the *Lady G* too, although I doubt she knows it. It seems the senator and his son have racked up quite a bit of debt on behalf of their ailing mother."

"How nice of them to name the boat in her honor. You said *if* they arrive. What do you mean?"

"Jansen and company were initially escorted off the marina property by a security guard. When the senator found out Holly was claiming to be his cousin, he asked the guard to find them and bring them back. The aforementioned guard *is* the FBI informant, and he *did* find them and bring them back. Just before his shift ended, he also found out the senator's son ordered all the security camera's turned off…*before* his return with the Hi-Lo Gang."

"The Hi-Lo Gang?"

"That's what the informant calls them."

"Oh, shit. That means—"

"Yes, that means they don't want the Hi-Lo Gang to be seen on tape re-entering the property."

"Which means they think something bad's going to happen to them."

"Yes, very bad. At my request, the FBI instructed the informant to let Jansen know they're in danger—as quickly and quietly as possible. The problem is, he's at home more than a half hour away. Even if he gets there in time, alerting Jansen without blowing his cover may be impossible. That's the one thing the Feds instructed him not to let happen. The informant is too crucial to their DEA investigation to be compromised. I left a message on Holly's phone for Jansen to abort the boat trip to St. Maarten, but I don't know if he got it."

"Did you text her too?"

"No, but I will as soon as I get off the phone. Good call."

"You sure you don't want me going to St. Thomas first?"

"Quite. If we aren't able to warn the Hi-Lo Gang off the *Lady G*, you'll be needed in St. Maarten. If we *do* manage to warn them off, they may fly over in the morning anyways, in which case you'll already be staking out the villa, waiting for them."

"I notice these guys have a knack for going from one sticky situation to the next."

"You noticed right, and this one's stickier than a glue factory in August."

"So, St. Maarten it is. When do I leave?"

"In five minutes." "*Five?* Shit, what airline?"

"Yes, about that. There aren't any direct flights this evening. You would have to stop at another island first, but that takes too long."

"So, what's the plan?"

"I managed to secure you a seat on a NOAA flight. I told them you were a scientist with Woods Hole."

"NOAA? As in The National Oceanic and Atmospheric Administration? *That* NOAA?"

"Unless there's another NOAA I don't know of—yes. They'll drop you off on St. Maarten after conducting some atmospheric tests for the National Weather service."

"What kind of tests?"

"Don't worry about that; it's the fastest way to get to St. Maarten. Get moving."

"I'm in the terminal. What ticket counter?"

"Any counter, just tell them you're with the hurricane hunters and—"

"*HURRICANE HUNTERS!?* Are you—"

"Jealous? No. Have a safe flight." Click.

Chapter 42

We were a half hour out to sea and enjoying the nicely appointed accommodations in the salon, when Holly's phone chirped. I knew from experience it meant she had received a text message. She pulled the phone out of her purse and cursed as she read the message. "Damn it, Kit! My batteries almost dead and you have to have one of your friends send prank messages? As if the voicemail wasn't enough."

"What the hell are you talking about? What voice-mail? What did the text say?"

"Oh, c'mon! Don't tell me you don't know."

I looked at Tangles suspiciously, per usual. "Are you pulling some kind of prank I'm not in on?"

"Why do you always point the finger at me? What did I ever do?"

"You really wanna go there?"

"Alright, so maybe I've been known to pull a thing or two, but seriously, I didn't do anything, I swear. I don't even have a phone, remember? Neither do you. How could we arrange a prank?"

I looked back at Holly. "He's right. We couldn't pull your leg if we wanted to, so, what's got you in such a tizzy? What's the message say?"

Holly hated it when I accused her of being 'in a tizzy,' and the expression on her face let me know it even before the words spilled out.

"I'm *not* in a tizzy, at least not yet. But if my phone goes dead because of one of your stupid jokes, I will be."

"Nobody's joking here, Holl. What's it say?"

She looked down at her phone and started reading. "The message says; DO NOT take boat to St. Maarten, you are in danger…Dan Tanna."

"*Dan Tanna*? Are you sure?"

"Sure, I'm sure. You think I can't read? I told you, it was a *joke.* Isn't Dan Tanna the guy on that old detective show you like who chain smokes and never met a face he didn't wanna punch?"

"No, that's Mannix. I love that guy. Dan Tanna aired a few years later. His show was called *Vegas.*"

"Huh? *That's* him? The bald guy with the lollipop?" Asked Tangles. "*He* was banging Wonder Woman? No way."

"Not him, you idiot, that's Kojak. Although his show also happened to be based in Vegas, that's where the similarities end. Dan Tanna was more of a goody-two-shoes kind of detective. He even did one of those 'Got Milk?' ads, wearing the milk mustache. That's probably what got Wonder Woman so hot for him, but that's beside the point. I'm afraid the message isn't a joke. Shit, this isn't good." I looked at Holly, who was eyeing me skeptically. "You said there was a voicemail. Can you put your cell on speaker phone and play it?"

"I don't know if it'll play with the batteries so low, but here it goes." Holly pressed the touch screen a few times and then set her phone on the coffee table in front of the couch we were sitting on. Suddenly, the voice of Dan Tanna started speaking.

"Please tell Mr. Jansen that Dan Tanna says *not* to take the boat ride to St. Maarten. I repeat, do not get on the boat. I have information that your party is in danger. The senator and his son are suspected..." That was all that played before the message abruptly ended. Holly picked up the phone and shook her head. "That's it. The battery's dead."

"So, what did it say? What are they suspected of?" I asked.

"I...dunno. I didn't listen to the whole message; I thought it was a joke—still do."

"What? Why didn't you tell me?"

"I'm not buying it, Kit. You heard the message. 'Tell Mr. Jansen that Dan Tanna says not to take the boat ride.' Of course it's a joke. The jigs up. Who hired the impersonator for you? You're buddy, Layne, from the Old Key Lime House?

"No, I –"

"Was it the Admiral then? Maybe Tooda? How 'bout Hambone? Was he in on it?"

"No! None of the above, I swear. Listen to me. During a break in my DEA interrogation on the Coast Guard cutter, the commander recognized me from the show. I convinced him to let me make a call and less than five minutes later we were getting the red carpet treatment. On the chopper ride to the resort, the pilot patched a call through to me. After a while, I recognized the caller's voice as being Dan Tanna. The caller said he was using a voice-altering device to disguise his identity. He was with the group who helped bail us out of the Donny Nutz mess. Remember the fake FBI guy in the Porsche who gave us the get-out-of-jail-free card?"

"You better believe it. He was a *hottie-tottie.*"

"Whatever."

"Shit," said Tangles.

"Yeah, shit is right. If Dan Tanna says were in danger, I'm inclined to believe him."

"If this is some kind of joke," said Holly. "I swear I'm—"

"It's no joke. This is for real."

"You're really serious." She glanced at Tangles to make sure he wasn't wearing some goofy grin that would belie my story, but he was stone faced.

"Unfortunately, yes. Dammit! I wish I could hear the rest of the message. I don't suppose you have a charger in your purse."

"No," she shook her head. "It's back at the Hibiscus. So, if this isn't one of your elaborate jokes, what is it? Who are we in danger from, *Remy?* He's the only other person onboard. Why would *he* want to harm us?"

"Dan Tanna said the senator and his son were suspected of something," commented Tangles. "Whatever it is, that's probably why."

Holly shook her head and let out an exasperated breath. "Thanks, Captain Obvious."

"I'm just saying...you know, we figure that out and boom! Pop goes the weasel."

Holly remembered what the dive boat captain told her; that there were rumors Remy and the senator were involved in the drug trade. "I just can't believe it...I *don't* believe it."

I noticed the expression on Holly's face had changed, and I called her on it. "Don't believe what?"

"Oh, shoot. The dive-boat captain said he had heard rumors that Remy was involved in the drug trade, and that if it was true, the senator was in on it too."

"*What*?! I never heard him say that."

"You and Tangles were too busy sleeping off your Ramblers."

"And just *now* you're telling us?"

"It, uh, seemed like the right thing to do, even if I don't believe it."

"Well, well, jack crevalle," said Tangles. "How quickly things can change."

I raised my eyebrow and glared at Holly. "Anything *else* you haven't told us about?"

"You mean besides how I manage to put up with you two? No."

I had been thinking about a few things that didn't add up and voiced my concerns. "Drugs would make sense. Don't you think it's a little strange that Remy's delivering a boat for a client and we're the only crew? Doesn't that seem odd?"

"Maybe the crew and owner are in St. Maarten already," answered Tangles.

"I suppose, but why wouldn't the crew bring the boat over? Isn't that normally the way these things work?"

"There's nothing normal about people who own two-million-dollar boats."

"He's right, Kit. That doesn't mean anything," interjected Holly.

"Or it could mean we have some contraband on board. But why bring it over in the middle of the night?"

"'Cause it's not as hot?" quipped Tangles.

"Watch it, smartass, or I'll pop *your* weasel."

"C'mon Kit," pleaded Holly.

"Okay, fine, if it's not drugs, what about this? What about the name of the boat? The senator said Remy was taking the boat over for a client, but the name of the boat is the *Lady G.*"

"So?"

"So, maybe the G stands for Genevieve. Maybe the senator owns the boat and it's named after his mom. Maybe we're in danger because of something you uncovered that has to do with his family. Maybe it has to do with Joseph or the shady adoptions."

"*Or,*" said Tangles. "Maybe it has nothing to do with any of that and the owner is just a huge Lady Gaga fan. Hell, maybe the owner *is* Lady Gaga. After all, I heard she likes to bottom fish for young street dancers."

"You know? Thanks again for reminding me that the tiniest people can be the biggest assholes."

After stifling a laugh, Holly backed him up. "I don't know, Kit. I wouldn't read too much into the *Lady G* thing. I would say it's just a coincidence, but I don't want to hear your stupid saying again."

"You see, I told you it was a saying; you just acknowledged it."

"That's not what I meant. Lucky is as anxious as I am to hear what Genevieve has to say. If he was concerned she might reveal something he didn't want me to hear, why would he grant me permission to talk to her? Why would he offer us a ride and tell Remy to take us to her?"

"Maybe it's a ruse. Maybe that's why Dan Tanna called to warn us."

"Lucky's a senator, for Pete's sake, and we're both 99 percent sure we're cousins. You really think he intends to harm us?"

"I...don't know, but how come you're only 99 percent sure? Didn't you check for his birthmark?"

"Of course I did. There's a nasty scar where the birthmark should be. Lucky said his mother told him he climbed on a hot stove when he was a toddler, but he has no memory of it. We're thinking maybe she had the birthmark removed and concocted the stove story to protect his true identity. That's just one of the things I intend to get to the bottom of when I talk to Genevieve."

"She's right, Shag," added Tangles. "It doesn't make any sense he would find out Holly is his cousin and then want to harm her, or us, for that matter. What for? Why? And even if he did plan to harm us, how would Dan Tanna know? Speaking of Dan Tanna, who the hell does *he* work for? Who *are* these guys?"

"Quit asking me questions that *you* know that *I* don't know. If I knew who the fuck Dan Tanna was, I'd tell you."

"C'mon, Kit, that's uncalled for." Holly nudged me in the shoulder and I apologized as I stood and walked to the cockpit door.

"Sorry about that. You're right. We're missing something here, and it's bugging me."

"Well, don't take it out on Tangles... or me either."

"Apology accepted, bro. Don't worry about it. I figured out what we're missing."

"Really, what's that?" asked Holly.

"A cold beer—we missed happy hour. I'll check the fridge."

As Tangles rummaged around the fridge for beverages, I looked out at the big wake, which was illuminated by the transom lights. It seemed the two-to-four-foot waves were getting bigger, although the Hatteras was having no trouble skimming through them at twenty-five knots. Running twenty-five knots in the dark, in the open sea, wasn't the brightest idea in the world, even *with* radar. If we were to hit a log, or some other solid object, we would be in even more trouble than we already were. I felt Holly's arm slip around my waist, and I noticed Tangles gulping down what appeared to be some sort of punch.

"What are you thinking?" she asked.

I put my arm around her and gave her a gentle squeeze. "I'm thinking how much I don't like running in the dark. I can't believe the owner would want the *Lady G* brought over at night. I mean, why risk hitting something?"

"It is a little odd, I suppose. But who knows? Maybe the owner is so rich he doesn't care."

"Speaking of caring," announced Tangles. "Would you care for a Heineken, Miss Lutes? Or maybe some of this rum punch?"

"I'm gonna pass. My stomach feels a little funny."

"Oh, *really?*" Tangles raised an eyebrow and eyed me like a suspicious teacher.

"What, uh, what kind of, uh, funny are you...are you talking about?" I inquired, as I swept her bangs away from her forehead to make sure she saw my Shatner. My 'Shatner,' referring to an expression of overwhelming concern like the one Captain Kirk gets when he finds out the transporter's broke and he can't beam up Lieutenant Uhura for a quickie in the communications closet. In my case, however, no acting was necessary.

"I don't know...I hope it's not something I ate at the restaurant. Maybe I'll lie down for a bit." As I watched her walk over and lie down on the couch, worry seized my brain like a drunken pirate. With one hand Tangles handed me a beer, and with the other he discreetly rubbed his stomach while simultaneously mouthing the word 'prego.' I could only think one thing: *Please let it be a mild case of salmonella...for the love of all things holy, please, dear God, let it—*

"So, what's the plan, Shag?" asked Tangles, after taking another swig of punch.

"Huh? What?"

"Nice Shatner. What's the matter? Distracted? The plan, we gotta have a plan." Tangles was grinning from ear to ear, the little bastard.

"Yes, the plan...right. Well, for one thing, we sleep in shifts. We have to assume Remy is up to something. Whether it happens on the boat or when we get to St. Maarten, I don't know. But if Dan Tanna says we're in the shit, we better believe it. He saved us from Nutz, and he saved us last night on the cutter. He tried to save us from getting on the boat too but since we didn't get the message, it looks like we better plan on saving ourselves this time. Why don't you scour the boat for weapons?" My trusty Surefire flashlight was hanging from my neck on its lanyard, and I gave it to Tangles after he asked to borrow it while he searched.

I turned to Holly and suggested she get some shut-eye in one of the staterooms.

"Gladly, but what are *you* going to do?" She asked.

I took a couple slugs of beer and then wiped my mouth with the corner of my fake DEA T-shirt. "I'm gonna pay Remy a visit up on the bridge. See what I can find out without letting him know we're on to him."

When I opened the cockpit door, a rush of air blew the visor off my head. As I picked it up, I was reminded we were likely in for quite a ride…on a number of levels.

"Be careful, Kit," warned Holly.

"Careful's my middle name." I blew her a kiss and stepped out into the night.

With a raised voice she called out, "Famous last words!"

"Nah," I poked my head back in the cabin and smiled, "that's just a saying."

Chapter 43

An hour after taking off in the specially-outfitted Lockheed Martin P-3 twin turboprop, Rafe noticed the aircraft was dropping in altitude rather quickly. Along with the usual staff of hurricane hunter's, there were a couple other legitimate scientists as well as a member of the press tagging along for the ride. Rafe turned to the press guy to find out what was going on.

"Hey bud, what are we descending for?"

The guy gave him a funny look. "The storm, that's what. What is this, your first time?"

"Yeah, it is. Why are we descending into the storm? I thought they took their measurements from high altitudes."

"Some of their measurements, sure, like to get the surrounding atmospheric conditions, but they do that in the Gulfstream IV. These P-3's do the dirty work down low...*in* the actual storm. It's the only way to get accurate data."

"Really? How low?"

"It's up to the pilot, but usually they like to make a few passes in the fifteen-hundred- to two-thousand-foot range."

"*What?* That's, uh, that's low… isn't it? I mean, that's pretty low, right? You get much lower than that and you better have on a bathing suit."

"Relax, this isn't even a named storm yet." The press guy eyed him skeptically. "What kind of scientist are you, anyway?"

"One with advanced degrees in marine engineering and hydrodynamic propulsion, neither of which I planned on using on this flight." Suddenly, the plane dropped fifty feet in what seemed like a split second. Anything loose went flying, and everyone on board was jarred from the turbulence. The captain's voice came over the intercom as the plane leveled off. "Everybody, strap yourself in good; it looks like we got a feisty one on our hands. In about two minutes we'll be passing through the western edge of the system at an altitude of two-thousand feet. Based on the turbulence we just encountered, I think we might have ourselves a named storm by the time we come out the other side." Click.

Rafe looked at the press guy to see his reaction but there was none. "That's what he calls *feisty?* I gotta tell you, I don't like this at all."

"Then why'd you get on?"

"Good question. What's *with* this weather anyways? It's almost Thanksgiving."

"Global warming."

"Yeah? Well, we hit another air pocket like that last one and there might be some global warming in my pants." Just then a flash of lightning lit up the plane, and it shuddered before dropping another seventy-five feet. Not as much stuff flew around the cabin the second time because it had been secured, but the jarring effect was even worse. "Jesus Christ!" cried Rafe. "They do this intentionally?"

The captain's voice came over the intercom once again. "She's a feisty one alright. Hang on folks, we're going in!"

Rafe squeezed the arms of his seat so tightly he started cramping. "Who's flying this thing, Yukon Cornelius?" He shot a quick glance at the press guy, who was smiling at him. He looked oddly relaxed as they descended into the brewing storm. "What are you smiling about?" he asked. "This doesn't bother you?"

"Not anymore." The press guy reached his thumb inside his pants and started exposing his underwear.

Rafe instinctively leaned away from him, confused. "What, uh, what are you doing there? What's that?"

He looked around like he didn't want anybody to hear and lowered his voice a little. "My secret weapon."

"Huh?"

The press guy leaned toward him and conspiratorially put his hand up to his mouth to relay his secret. "A fresh pair of Depends."

Seeing that he was serious, Rafe's jaw dropped. "Ohhh, shhhhit."

"Exactly, that's why I like 'em," he winked. "Anytime, anywhere."

Chapter 44

I spent about ten minutes with Remy before heading back down to the salon. There was nothing he seemed intent on doing other than getting us to St. Maarten. I casually asked him about the name of the boat, but talking was difficult due to the sound of the engines and the wind whipping through the bridge. Remy shrugged at the question like he didn't know what the "*G*" in *Lady G* meant, and I let it go for the time being. As I left the bridge, I noticed the large illuminated chart plotter showed we had about a hundred and ten miles to go, and the radar looked clear. The wind was blowing ten to twelve knots out of the northwest, and we had a trailing sea with very manageable waves in the three- to four-foot range. Remy noticed me looking at the instrument panel and gave me a thumbs-up as I headed down the ladder to the cockpit. I responded with a thumbs-up of my own and smiled like I almost believed it. Kind of like the way you smile when a supposed "mechanical problem" strands you on the tarmac for two hours and the flight attendant announces for the seventh time, "It'll be just a *few* more minutes."

In the cabin below, Tangles managed to produce a fish tamer (billy club), and a nice-sized butcher knife. He informed me that Holly was napping in the forward VIP berth, and I complained about our meager weapons.

"That's it? That's all you could find?"

"Dude, there was nothing at all in the forward cabin *or* the crew cabin that would be useful. I found the fish tamer in a storage drawer and the knife in the galley."

"What about the master stateroom, nothing there?"

"I couldn't get in—it's locked. There's a sign on the door that says, 'Owner's Quarters/ Private.'"

"Well, at least we got *something*. We better stash them somewhere handy."

I shoved the billy club between the cushions of the couch and Tangles stashed the knife by the cockpit door under some magazines on a shelf. I told Tangles that Remy didn't appear to be doing anything suspicious, but we still needed to be on guard. Tangles said he was tired all of a sudden so I volunteered to take the first watch. He downed the rest of his punch and then shuffled down the hall to the crew quarters. I figured staying alert would be no problem for me as I was concerned about Holly's stomach nausea as well as the dire warnings from Dan Tanna.

At some point, though, I apparently succumbed to the rhythmic motion of the boat and the soft drone of the engines. Startled, my head snapped up from my chest and I realized I had fallen asleep. I also realized the boat was now going into a head sea, which probably was what woke me up. My watch said it was fifteen to eleven, which meant I had been out for over two hours. *Shit.* I quickly exited the cabin to check on Remy and realized it was raining. As I reached the top of the ladder, I noticed Remy had zippered the Eisenglass enclosure to protect him from the elements.

"What's going on?" I yelled.

He looked down at me and answered, "The weather turned; there's a small craft advisory out." He pointed his finger down with a request. "Turn on the satellite TV and see what they're saying." I nodded okay and asked how far we were from St. Maarten. He briefly looked at the instrument panel. "Sixty miles—go!" He waved me off, and I hustled down the ladder to the salon. When I got there, Holly was sitting on the couch.

"What's going on?" She asked. "I thought the weather was supposed to be good."

"Yeah, me too. How's your stomach?"

"It's been better. But being in that forward cabin is no picnic in this head sea. Where's Tangles?"

I found the TV remote and powered it up as I answered. "He's in the crew quarters trying to get some shut-eye, but I can't imagine he's having much success. Remy asked me to check out the weather on the TV; he said a small craft advisory went out."

"A small craft advisory? Oh, *great.*"

"At least we're not *in* a small craft; this baby's fifty-four plus."

Just then the bow of the Hatteras raised up as we powered over a wave and then smacked down with significant ferocity. Holly braced herself, and I reached for a well-positioned grab bar.

"That wasn't a four-footer, Kit…that was like six to eight."

I started scrolling through the channels, and I thought, *more like eight to ten.* I didn't want to alarm her any more than necessary though, especially when I had the Weather Channel to do that for me, so I kept my mouth shut. I stopped scrolling just as Carl "The Nose" Parker, began his Tropical Update spiel.

"This just in from the National Weather Service. It looks like megastorm Sandy won't be the last storm of the 2012 season after all. That low pressure system we've been monitoring east of the lower Antilles has unfortunately gotten its act together and is now tropical storm Tony. Hurricane hunters are reporting sustained winds of fifty miles an hour and the latest computer models have shifted the track to the west, which would take it over St. Maarten within the next two hours. Tropical Storm warnings are now in effect for the lower Antilles and island residents are urged to stay tuned to the Weather Channel for the latest updates. Although the storm is relatively small in size, with tropical storm winds extending out only sixty miles from center, it has proved to be hard to gauge in intensity and track. Just three hours ago, it was a disorganized low drifting to the north and expected to fizzle out as it reached the colder waters of the Atlantic."

A satellite image of the storm appeared on a monitor next to the Nose, and he pointed out the obvious.

"The latest satellite images show a tight band of violent thunderstorms have popped up around the center, and you can almost see an eye trying to form. There's a lot of concern that the storm may continue to strengthen as it approaches St. Maarten. If it passes over the southern end of the island, as projected, and avoids the more mountainous areas to the north, there will be little to impede further development as it

re-enters the Caribbean and churns toward the US Virgin Islands of St. Thomas and St. John. The next update from the National Weather Service won't be until two a.m., but as always, we here at the Weather Channel will do our best to keep you informed up to the minute." I muted the sound and looked at Holly who had her hand covering her mouth. As usual, I did my best to downplay our situation.

"This could be a bumpy ride."

She dropped her hand and looked legitimately scared. "*A bumpy ride?* BS! We're headed right at it and it's only gonna get worse!"

"Maybe we'll change course. I need to let Remy know what's going on. I'll be right back."

I rushed up to the bridge, and Remy had a rain jacket on, despite being protected by the Eisenglass enclosure. It was a smart move, because it was chilly and when I opened the flap at the top of the ladder, rain blew in from the stern. I didn't waste any time explaining our sorry situation. "That low that was supposed to go north didn't—"

"I know, I just heard on the radio. I planned on taking us to Tucker Bay because the villa is just a short walk up the hill from there, but there's a marina farther north that's more protected and easier to navigate. I already programmed the coordinates in the chart plotter. If I push us up to thirty-five knots, we'll make it before the storm does."

"You're gonna go *faster*? Are you, uh, are you sure that's a good idea? How can you see anything?"

"I can't without the radar, but it's the best idea I got. We can hammer our way in to port and probably beat the storm, *or* we can go slower and ride it out. I don't know about you, but I'd rather stay ahead of the storm than ride it out. Tell your friends to hang on. I'm throttling up."

"My friends are sleeping. I think they'll get the message soon enough."

"Did they have some punch?"

"What?"

"The punch in the fridge. I made my special rum punch. It's good, it helps you relax."

"Yeah, as a matter of fact…" I thought of Tangles slurping down the punch and then suddenly getting tired. *Oh shit.*

"They did? How about you? You look like you could use a drink."

It was true; I could almost always use a drink, but when someone pushes something on me, it makes me think twice. It rarely stops me, but it does make me think. Had he spiked the punch? Was that part of the plan? *Had to be.* I decided to play along. "Good idea, you want me to bring you one too?"

Remy smiled. "Not while I'm captaining. Besides, it's getting' too rough. I'd spill it all over. Go help yourself and then get some rest. We'll be in port before you know it."

"Sounds good," I lied. "I'll check back later."

I hurried back down and warned Holly not to drink the punch as I proceeded across the salon and down the stairs to the cabins.

"*Huh?* What's going on?" Holly called after me. "Why not?"

"Just don't drink it." I slid open the door to the crew quarters and found Tangles face down on a bunk, snoring. I flipped him over and slapped him across the face.

"Tangles! Wake up!" He was passed out cold, even more so than usual.

"Kit, what are you doing?" Holly stood in the doorway looking perplexed.

"I'm trying to wake him; I think Remy spiked the punch in the fridge. Get me a bottle of water and, uh… something I can stick down his throat."

As she turned to go back up the hall, the boat suddenly accelerated. I heard her cry out, "What the heck!?"

"Hang on!" I warned her. "Remy's trying to outrun the storm."

I flipped Tangles over, grabbed him under the armpits, and dragged him into the bathroom. It was no small feat given the pitching of the boat as we plowed through the waves. I pulled his shirt off over his head and stuck his hairy torso inside the shower. Holly tapped me on the shoulder and handed me a plastic stirring spoon. "Here, this should work, what do you want me to do with the water?"

"Just hang onto it for a second, here goes nothing." I took the slender spoon and stuck it down his unsuspecting throat. His eyes flicked open and he gagged as some vomit shot out his mouth and onto my hand. I turned the shower on and stepped back as water cascaded down onto his head. He started flopping about and continued to gag as I held my hand up for Holly to see.

"Worked like a charm."

"A disgusting charm," she commented. "That's gross. Wash it off already."

As I rinsed my hand in the sink, Tangles started to come to. "What the…what the *fuck?*"

Holly reached into the shower and shut it off as he tried to get to his feet. I helped him up and he stooped over the toilet, still gagging and spitting stuff out. "My fucking *head.* Oh, does my fucking head hurt. What… what happened?"

"Remy spiked the punch. Did you get it all out of your system?" I asked.

He had his hands on his knees and was still hunched over the toilet. We hit another wave, and he fell backward against the sink. I stumbled into the hall next to Holly and dropped the spoon in the process. It clattered on the floor at Tangles feet and as I kneeled down to get it, he rubbed his stomach. "My stomach feels like shit, almost as bad as my…as my head." When he raised his little hands to his head and started rubbing his temples, I took it as a sign. I *knew* what I had to do. I swiveled on my knees and gave him a hard uppercut to his simian-like stomach. A large stream of vomit shot out his mouth and nailed the upraised toilet seat and tank behind it. He collapsed forward on his knees and kept heaving up tainted rum mixed with undigested matter.

"Jesus, Kit, did you really have to do that? You probably hurt him." Holly pushed past me and grabbed the hair on the back of his head to keep his face out of the toilet.

"That hurt me more than it hurt him. Seriously, his torso's like a washboard wrapped in hyena hide." I shook my hand and held it out for her to see. "Look, I think I broke skin."

Tangles gave a few last heaves and started muttering, "You fuck...you fuckin' ass..." Holly held the bottle of water in front of him, and he eagerly chugged half of it down before spitting out leftovers.

"Feeling better, little buddy?" I asked.

He slowly cocked his head up and gave me a nasty look. It was made all the more convincing by the chunk of conch and mystery vegetable clinging to the scraggly new soul patch on his chin. "Fuck you, man; I think you broke my spleen."

I shrugged and looked at Holly. "He's definitely feeling better. Looks like we got it all. C'mon, let's get him up to the salon."

"*I'll* help him up to the salon. *You* can clean up the mess in here."

"*Me?* I was only—"

"Making things worse, as usual. I'm sure there's some extra towels in one of the hall cabinets—have fun." Holly led Tangles by the arm, and they pushed past me into the hall. Tangles said, "Yeah, have fun assho—" suddenly the bottom fell out of a wave, and we felt like we were flying. We were (for about a half second) until the boat crashed into the next wave. I stumbled forward and fell against the starboard side with Holly and Tangles right behind me. Then there was a loud thud and something banged against the door of the master stateroom.

"What the hell was *that?*"

'I don't know, and I don't care," answered Holly. "I'm going up to the salon before I get beat to death down here."

"Go ahead." I pointed toward the salon, and Holly steadied herself against the wall before leading the way. Suddenly, Tangles stopped and pressed his ear against the master stateroom door. "Did you hear that? I thought I heard something."

I pressed my ear to the door above him but didn't hear a thing. "I don't hear anything. I think you got punch on the ear."

"No, I'm telling you, I heard—" Then I heard it, an audible groan coming from the other side of the door. "There! Did you hear that?" Tangles looked up at me, and I nodded in semi-disbelief. Holly stood at the top of the stairs leading to the salon and looked back, holding on to a grab-bar for dear life. "What is it? What did you hear?"

"Somebody groaning… and not in a good way," answered Tangles.

"Sounds like there's somebody on board who your cousin Remy neglected to tell us about."

"*What?* Who could it…who could it be?"

I looked at the door, and as I unsuccessfully tried to visualize who was on the other side, came to the realization that I would have sucked on *Let's Make a Deal.* Fortunately for me though, Monty Hall wasn't running the show— I was, and one way or another, the fuckin' curtain was coming down.

Chapter 45

After touching down at the L'Esperance Airport (also known as the Grand Case Airport) on the northern, French side of St. Maarten, the private jet taxied down the runway and was directed into a hangar on the edge of the airport grounds. Inside the hangar, the *directeur* of the airport stood next to a white cargo van. The jet door swung open and out stepped one of the most feared drug lords of the twenty-first century; Rico "The Freako" Cordero.

"Monsieur Cordero, so good to see you again," greeted the directeur. "There is a storm coming. You have arrived just in time."

Stepping off the plane behind Rico were his bodyguard and pilot. As the directeur shook Rico's hand, he was careful not to look directly at his disfigured face. It wasn't easy to do, but being a Frenchman, he had long mastered the art of not looking somebody in the eye. Instead, his beady little eyes were trained on the small duffel bag in Rico's other hand. Rico ignored him and instead focused on the van. "I see you have the vehicle I asked for. Were you successful with my other request as well?"

"Yes, I think you will be pleased. In the back of the van there is a small garbage can full of rats, *and,* as a bonus, you will also find a cage... with a raccoon in it."

"A raccoon? Excellent. Here, this is for you." Rico handed him the small duffel bag containing five pounds of coke and ten thousand dollars in hundred-dollar bills. As he unzipped the bag and checked its contents, Rico instructed his men to transfer a crate from the jet into the van. Nervously licking his lips, the directeur shot a glance at the hangar door. He hesitated a moment before zipping up the duffel, half-fearing tonight was the night the authorities might come bursting in. Inevitably though, his greed and addiction had the last word. "There is a car outside that will lead you to the address you gave me. I suggest you leave as soon as possible. You will want to be at your destination before the storm hits. The latest update has it strengthening and turning this way; in fact, the hurricane hunters were just here and they advised us to button things down. "

They both watched as the crate was loaded into the back of the van, and when the doors shut, Rico responded, "I'll be leaving after I get a couple more things off the jet. My pilot will be staying behind to tend to some maintenance and the refueling."

"And you'll be departing tomorrow?"

Rico grew up idolizing Al Pacino in *Scarface* and loved issuing gangster-style threats; he considered them an integral part of his duty as a drug kingpin. Despite being a physically-deformed sexual deviant with a temper like a twelfth-century Mongolian warrior, he smiled at the little Frenchman. "Yes, many people will be departing tomorrow."

Against every instinct in his five-foot-four, hundred-and-forty-pound body, the directeur searched Rico's face for the meaning behind his ominous words. Unfortunately, he couldn't stomach the facial claw-marks and puncture wounds compounded with the single lazy, bulging eye. The fact that he was completely bald only drew more attention to his missing ear and the bite marks on top of his head. He looked a little bit like Mr. Clean if his head got stuck in a garbage disposal. The Directeur quickly looked away, deciding to try another angle of inquiry.

"Monsieur, if I may be so bold as to ask, what are the animals for?"

"Treats…for my lie detector."

"*Treats?* I don't understand. This lie detector, this is what is in the crate… *oui?*"

"*Oui…* and he has a voracious appetite, just like me."

The directeur rubbed his chin, leery now. "I must admit, I am still somewhat… confused."

"You better thank your lucky quiche, my friend, because if I ever thought you lied to me, I can assure you, you would never be confused again."

Chapter 46

As we tried to keep our balance in the hallway, Tangles and I both heard another groan coming from just beyond the master stateroom door. Private owner's quarters or not, I was determined to have a look at who or what Remy had stashed inside. I looked at Tangles and told him to step back as I coiled my body against the opposite wall and prepared to launch myself into the door.

"You're gonna try to break the door down?" He asked.

"No, I'm scared of it, that's why I'm up against the wall. *Of course* I'm gonna break it down. Let me show you how you do it *old-school* style."

"I don't know, Shag. I heard Hatteras builds a pretty—"

With every ounce of energy I could muster, I sprung into the door shoulder first, fully expecting my six-foot-two, two-hundred-and-twenty-five-pound frame to turn it to kindling. It turned out to be a slight miscalculation as I bounced off the door and crumbled to the floor. As I rose to my feet, I raised my arm up over my shoulder to make sure everything was still working. Tangles was leaning against the wall and commented on my technique.

"I thought you said you played football."

"Shut up."

"You went in too high. You can't bring down Tim Tebow with an arm tackle, dude… You need to hit him low."

"I suppose I can't argue with the world's foremost expert on all things low."

Holly looked on from the top of the stairs leading up to the salon. "Are you alright, Kit? You hit that pretty hard."

The only thing that was bruised more than my rotator cuff was my ego, and I shrugged it off as I sized up the door again. "I'm fine, don't worry about it. I think maybe I can kick it in." I pressed up against the opposite wall again and visualized springing at the door like Chuck Norris and karate-kicking it down. Subconsciously, I stroked my imaginary Chuck Norris beard and glared at the door handle. Tangles started laughing.

"Don't even tell me you're gonna try to *kick* it in. Who do you think you are, Chuck Norris or something?"

"You're breaking my concentration."

"Kit, I don't know," warned Holly. "You might hurt your—" Visualization complete, the only thing left was execution. I pushed off the wall with my right foot and hand while simultaneously kicking out my left foot at a spot next to the door handle. I let out a guttural, "Hiiiiyaaaaaaa!!!" and slammed my foot into the door. It felt like I had kicked a train as the door held firm and a jolt of pain shot up my leg. I fell backward against the wall and slid to the floor as the boat continued to plow through waves at thirty knots. I looked sideways at Tangles, who was shaking his head. "Not a fucking word," I threatened. "Not even a peep."

He turned to Holly and asked her to hand him the fire extinguisher under the galley sink. Moments later she handed it to him, and he positioned himself in front of the door. Standing sideways to the door, he swung the extinguisher back and forth a few times, gaining momentum and zeroing in on his target. "This is how we do it in Biloxi." Tangles slammed the extinguisher up and into the door handle, which broke off and fell to the floor. He set the extinguisher down and reached his little hand into the hole where the locking mechanism was. There was a click, and he pushed the door inward about eighteen inches before it bumped up against something. I craned my head around the door and looked down as I flicked on the light. There was a guy on the floor, face down, with both his hands and feet duct-taped together. Tangles squeezed past the door and tugged him backward so I could push the door open.

"Oh my God," said Holly, standing in the doorway. "Who is that? What's going on here?"

I reached down and grabbed the guy by the armpits. "Let's see if we can find out." I hoisted him to his feet and slung him on to the bed. As he rolled over on his back, Tangles said, "Holy crap." It was none other than the captain of the submarine. "You have got to be shitting me," I added.

"You guys *know* him?" asked an incredulous Holly.

"He's the one who hijacked the *Lucky Dog*; he was captain of the sub," answered Tangles. "The fucker tried to blow us up like he blew up the boat."

I couldn't believe what I was seeing. "What is *he* doing here? What the *hell* is going on?" He groaned again and Tangles suggested he may be coming to. Holly stepped past me and lifted one of his eyelids. His eye was completely rolled back into his head. "I don't think he's coming to anytime soon; he's out cold." Holly opened up a small bag on the nightstand and extracted a syringe filled with clear fluid. "This looks like the culprit. My God, you think Remy did this?"

"He's the only other person on board. He had to… this is bad. We are in some serious shit here."

"Are you sure? Maybe he…maybe he doesn't know he was on board either."

"Not a chance," I responded. "He's the one who provisioned the boat; he must know he's on board. He probably spiked the punch with whatever's in the syringe."

"Crap."

"I remember," said Tangles as he rubbed his temple. "Tasted like a dream, worked like a nightmare."

Holly sat on the edge of the bed and shook her head. "I don't get it, if this guy was on the boat when it blew up, how did he end up here? Why is he tied up and drugged? What does Remy have to—?"

"Just wait a sec, okay? Let's look at the facts and figure this out."

She shot me one of her looks. "That's what I was *trying* to do."

"Don't feel bad," added Tangles. "He interrupts me all the time, too."

"Your right, I tend to forgo conversational etiquette when our lives are in imminent danger, my bad."

"Fine," said Holly. "What do you thinks going on here?"

"We were warned not to get on the boat and that Remy and the senator were suspected of *something*. We *know* that Captain Cocaine here is part of a big-time drug-smuggling operation. The only plausible reason he's locked up in this cabin and not in custody is that your cousins are involved somehow. Just like the captain on the dive boat suggested."

"You're saying they're cocaine traffickers? Are you *crazy?* Lucky's a senator, for Pete's sake!"

I poked Captain Cocaine in the chest. "You got a better explanation for him being here? I'm all Obama's."

"You shouldn't poke him."

"*What?* He blew up my boat!"

"It's still not right."

"You know what else isn't right? What your cousin did to *him* and what he's trying to do to *us*!"

"Which is nothing, so far, except giving us a ride to St. Maarten. Besides, we didn't do anything!"

I studied the dirty, stubbled face of the captain. He had a knot on the side of his forehead with dried blood on it and some minor burns. The knot was recent but clearly hadn't just happened from falling off the bed. Had it happened when the *Lucky Dog* exploded? Maybe, maybe not. Maybe it came from whoever tied him up. Maybe before he was drugged, he was encouraged to talk. I thought about the senator's probing questions about how the *Lucky Dog* blew up. Suddenly, *I knew,* that *he knew,* what really happened. *Oh, shit.*

Holly saw my expression and asked, "Why the face?" I looked at her and then at Tangles, who was trying to put the broken door handle back in place.

"Tangles, what did this asshole say his name was?"

"McGurdy? McGirt? Yeah, McGirt. I think he said his name was McGirt."

"That's right, McGirt. Well, my money says good ol' McGirt here spilled the beans to Remy and the senator about what happened. They know we're the ones responsible for disabling the sub."

"So what," replied Holly. "It was a freak thing, an accident, you're not smugglers. Assuming you're right, what good are you to them?"

"The DEA didn't believe our story at first; they thought we were involved and tried to steal the shipment. Maybe the senator does too."

"But if McGirt told them what happened, then they know you didn't. They know the boat blew up with the coke on it."

"Yes, but not all of it. There was still a lot left on the sub, when…that's it! They don't know where the sub is! The last time McGirt saw us we were submerging in a leaky sub and he was bouncing grenades off the hull. He must have thought we sank! Since the senator knows we didn't, *he* knows, that *we* know where the sub is… *and* the rest of the coke!"

"But the Coast Guard has it."

"Yes, but nobody knows that. They said they wouldn't issue a statement to the press until they had the sub back in Miami."

"Oh...shoot."

"That's one way to put it."

"There!" said Tangles. He had taken some duct tape from the nightstand bag and taped the door handle in place from the inside. "It looks alright from the hall but as soon as Remy tries the handle, the jigs up."

"Did you not hear what I just said?"

"Yeah, I heard. We're on Fuck Street again, what else is new?"

"You ever hear of the Cordero Brothers?"

"In what context?"

"In what *context?* This isn't a spelling bee for Christ's sake, have you heard of them or not?"

"No, not in *that* context...asshole."

"I think I have," said Holly. "I think I saw something about them on *Sixty Minutes.* Aren't they like the Mexican mafia or something?"

"Close, they're notorious Colombian drug lords, but they do share the Mexican's passion for dismemberment."

"So, what about them?"

"It was their sub."

"Oh, well, thank God we're a long way from Colombia."

"There's always that. Oh, joy."

"Quit making fun of me, I'm just trying to look at the bright side."

"Sorry, you're right, the bright side is Remy doesn't know what's coming." I reached into the nightstand bag and pulled out the syringe full of fluid.

Holly looked at me funny. "What, uh, what exactly *is* coming?"

"Yeah, bro," added Tangles. "What's the plan?"

"I think it's time to relieve Remy from the helm, you know, let him rest a while." I squirted some fluid from the syringe and smiled. "What's good for the goose is good for the gander. Isn't that the saying?"

Chapter 47

After experiencing the most stressful and stomach-churning flight of his life, Rafe made the sign of the cross and kissed the tarmac upon landing at the Grand Case airport. A taxi took him to the Mont Choisy address he provided, which was a villa just down the road from his real destination. Along the way, the boss called to tell him that the Hi-Lo Gang didn't get the message and were headed his way. It was almost eleven o'clock when the taxi stopped in front of the gate, and the driver was surprised when Rafe paid the fare and exited the cab. He walked up to a security keypad next to the gate and acted like he was entering a code as the taxi turned around and headed down the road. As soon as it disappeared from sight, he jogged up the incline toward the next villa. It started raining again, so he removed the backpack he was carrying and pulled out a black GORE-TEX poncho. The poncho made him all but invisible along the side of the jungle road in the dark and rain.

As he approached the entrance gate to the villa, he saw an inscription on one of its pillars that was dimly lit by a solar landscape light. It read, "Villa Destin," a name chosen in honor of Genevieve LeRoux's

French heritage. The front gate was only meant to stop vehicles, so Rafe simply stepped around the pillar and jumped a small culvert to enter the property. He quickly knelt in the thick vegetation by the driveway and donned a pair of night-vision goggles equipped with a thermal-imaging sensor. Ever the professional, he was extremely wary of alarms and guard dogs. After scanning the premises for threats, he ran in a crouched position along the side of the drive for about fifty yards, stopping at the turnaround circle. About thirty yards to the west of the villa was a small guesthouse with an attached garage. Sitting next to the garage was a shed, less than twenty feet from the tree-line. He quickly crossed the drive and worked his way toward the shed.

Out of view from the villa, he emerged from the jungle and sidled his way around the side of the shed to the garage. He pressed his ear against the side door and, after hearing nothing, tried the doorknob. As the door swung open his heart rate picked up, and he swept the night vision goggles back and forth. *Empty.* He scanned the garage again and noted that there were no windows. He looked for an entrance into the guest house, but like many older Caribbean homes, there was none from inside the garage. He ruled it out as a vantage point for spying and closed the door behind him. He crept around to the front of the shed and quickly slipped inside. It was about twelve-feet long, six-feet high and maybe seven-feet wide. It held a couple gas cans and a lawnmower, but it wasn't too cluttered, and it was dry. Most importantly though, by pushing open the swing-out double doors just a little, he had a near perfect view of the entrance to both the villa and guesthouse. *Bingo!*

Rafe removed the poncho and shook it a few times before draping it over the lawnmower handle. He then slung the backpack off his shoulder and removed his DICK phone from its waterproof compartment. He was about to call the boss when the beams from a pair of headlights started dancing across the front circle. As the vehicle came down the drive, he pulled a hanky out of his pocket and wiped the lenses of his night vision goggles. A limousine with airport markings rounded the circle and stopped at the front door to the villa. Rafe pressed a button on the side of the goggles and the lenses extended out eight inches, zooming in on the passenger's side. When a man in a white suit stepped out and hurried inside, he pressed another button which activated a high-speed camera. As the limo exited the grounds, Rafe pressed another button, which beamed the high-res pictures up to a satellite and then down to DICK headquarters on the Puget Sound. He was checking out some of the images on the viewfinder when he heard the sound of the garage door next to the villa being opened. He looked up to see a woman in a nurse uniform go inside and drive out in a subcompact. As the woman got out to close the overhead door, he noticed another vehicle parked inside.

The wind and rain picked up in intensity, and he pulled the shed doors closed as the subcompact headed out the driveway. He knew the boss would call him as soon as the photos were analyzed, so he pulled a bottle of water out of his backpack and sat down on a rubber storage container. As he chugged down the water, he wondered how the Hi-Lo Gang was doing. They were in some deep shit between tropical storm Tony and whatever the senator and his son were up to. He leaned his head against a shelf and closed his eyes for a moment. He had been trained in the art of napping and was looking to recharge his batteries a little bit, wanting to be ready for whatever the night might bring.

Ten minutes later, his eyes popped open as he heard the sound of tires crunching on gravel. He quickly put on the goggles and pushed the shed doors open a fraction. A white van was backing up to the garage next to him! The garage door opened and the van disappeared inside. Standing in the driveway, the man in the white suit stood holding an umbrella with his back to the wind. Rafe snapped a couple more pics, and a few seconds later one of the occupants of the van emerged. He was bald and stood with his back to Rafe as he conversed with the man in the white suit. A minute or two later the other occupant of the van, a much larger man, emerged. As the three hurried to the guesthouse, he snapped dozens of photos and beamed them back to headquarters. Once the garage door closed and the only sound was wind and rain, he thought about the van. A little voice in his head said, *check it out, Rafe.*

After waiting five minutes, he slipped out of the shed and in the side door of the garage. As his night-vision goggles adjusted to the change in darkness, he heard some strange sounds coming from the van. *What is that?* He peered through the driver's side window but saw nothing. There was an empty bench seat behind it with a partition separating off the rear cargo area. Then he heard it again—a scratching noise and some faint squeaking. He walked to the back of the van and opened the doors. Incredibly, there was a cage with a raccoon in it that was scratching at the floor. He tilted a plastic garbage bin toward him and the sound of the squeaking became obvious; there were about two dozen rats climbing over and biting each other. *What the hell?* Next to the rats and the raccoon was a much bigger crate with small air holes all over it. He tried to look inside but the holes were too small. He pressed his ear against one of the holes but couldn't hear a thing. *What the fuck's in there?* Seeing that the latch on the crate wasn't locked, curiosity got the better of him and he slowly opened the lid.

Chapter 48

I held the hypodermic in front of me as I led the way up to the salon and over to the cockpit door. I opened it just enough to see that it was still raining, but at least it wasn't as rough as it had been earlier.

"What's the plan?" asked Tangles.

I shut the door and held out the needle as Holly sat down on the couch. "The plan is we stick him in the ass with this thing. I always wanted to run a big Hatt."

"Are you crazy?" cried Holly. "*Now,* you wanna run one? At night, with a tropical storm bearing down on us, in waters you've never navigated?"

"Columbus did it and he didn't have a GPS chart plotter."

"But you're not Columbus!"

"And I'm not a GPS chart plotter either, but I know how to use one...for the most part."

"Have you ever even *run a boat* this size before?"

"In, uh, in what context?"

"In the context of yes or no!"

Tangles reached his hand out. "Gimme that thing."

"Why?"

"I have a better angle of attack from the top of the ladder. You distract him and I'll stick him."

"He thinks you're knocked out from the punch."

"Exactly," he smiled. "A little surprise for Captain Overconfident."

As I handed him the syringe, Holly voiced her concern. "This is a bad idea. A *really* bad idea."

"No," I assured her. "The Flobee was a bad idea. New Coke? Now that was a *really bad* idea. This is just a marginally bad idea, like The Noid."

"The *what?*"

"The old Domino's Pizza mascot," answered Tangles. "You know, the one that looked like Underdog's retarded brother and jumped around like his Alpo was laced with crystal meth."

"Oh, yeah... he *was* annoying."

"He was a scapegoat," I argued. "It was the shitty pizza that doomed The Noid. Now that they're making a decent pie, they oughta bring him back. He just needs a makeover. They could hire Usher to be his mentor. I mean, look what he did for Justin Beiber. If it weren't for Usher, the Beebs would be singing in a food court in Saskatchewan right now."

"Oh-my-God." Holly looked genuinely concerned. "If that was supposed to inspire some sort of confidence in me, it's not working."

Suddenly, the boat decelerated and Tangles and I stumbled toward the bow. After regaining our balance, I put my hand on his shoulder, making sure to steer clear of the syringe. "I'll go first, just give me a minute and then creep up and stick him. It's go time, little buddy. Let's do this." As we fist bumped, Holly shook her head and commented, "Oh, crap, what do you want me to do?"

"Make sure McGirt doesn't wake up."

"How am I supposed to do that?"

I opened the cockpit door and looked back. "Turn on the satellite receiver in his room and see if you can find some HGTV. That oughta do it."

When I got up to the bridge, Remy had his rain jacket half unzipped and was talking on his cell phone. He held up a finger like he was just ending the call. As I waited for him to hang up, I looked at the chart plotter which showed we were forty-one miles from some place called 'Anse Marcel.' When he finally did end the call, I asked what was going on.

"Since we changed our arrival point, we need transportation to the villa. It's a good fifteen-minute ride. It's all taken care of; they'll be meeting us in an hour."

"They?"

"Our ride."

"I see..." I glanced down at the top of the ladder, wondering when Tangles was gonna appear. Remy looked at the ladder too, and I quickly tried to distract him. I pointed to his cell phone which he had placed next to the chart plotter. "I'm surprised you get a signal this far out."

"We had a signal booster installed in the radar arch; it's good for about sixty miles."

"We?" I said, as Tangles' head popped up through the flap at the top of the ladder.

"Yeah, me and, uh, I mean, the client. The client had it installed; we did the job."

Tangles held the hypodermic out and was taking aim as I took a deep breath and made sure I had Remy's full attention.

"Client my ass. How fuckin' stupid do you think I am? The jig's up, fucknuts."

Gone was his easy smile and laid back island demeanor. "What did you—?"

Tangles slammed the syringe into his backside but it all went wrong. Instead of the needle burying into Remy's gluteus, it dislodged a concealed gun that clattered to the deck. Tangles momentum carried him forward and he fell on the deck too, still holding the syringe. Before I even realized what it was, Remy was picking the gun off the deck. I'm nothing if not a quick study though and grabbed his gun hand as I jumped on his back and wrestled for control of the weapon. Tangles recovered and was about to stab him again with the needle when Remy kicked his foot out and sent the syringe flying. He was stronger than I anticipated and managed to stand me up, but I held onto him in a reverse bear hug, He tried to aim the gun at Tangles as he scrambled for the syringe and fired a shot that tore through the Eisenglass enclosure. Remy tried to kick at Tangles again as he picked up the syringe, and I jerked him backward against the helm, inadvertently pushing the throttles forward. With the sudden acceleration, Remy's phone slid off the dash, bounced on the deck twice, and then went over the edge to the cockpit floor below. I had both my arms under his armpits and desperately tried to gain control of the gun as we stumbled against the railing. "Stick him!" I urged Tangles.

"You're in the way!" He yelled.

With adrenaline pumping, I swung Remy around to face the helm and he fired another shot that blasted into the dash and sent sparks flying. Tangles had one hand on a grab-bar and the other was pointing the needle at Remy's midsection.

"Now!" I yelled and pushed Remy toward Tangles. I figured he would try to kick the syringe again so I hooked my foot around his leg. Nobody was steering the boat, and a wave threw us off balance. We lost our footing and fell forward just as Tangles swung the needle up and stepped to the side. Remy gasped as he collapsed with me on his back, and I immediately felt the tension release from his body. Tangles pulled the gun out of his hand and warily aimed it at Remy's head. "The fucker tried to shoot me! Did you see that? He tried to fucking shoot me!"

I stood up and took the helm, pulling the throttles back as I nudged Remy to the side with my foot. "I'd shoot you too if you came at me with a hypodermic. He's not moving, I think you can relax a little. Did you inject the whole thing?"

"*Inject?* Hell no I didn't *inject.* I was just trying to stick him without getting shot!"

"Really? I think he's out cold. Gimme the gun, and roll him over."

"You roll him over; I think he's playing possum."

"I'm running the boat."

"We're idling!"

"Alright, alright." I knelt down and flipped Remy over. Beneath his open rain jacket, he was wearing one of those polo shirts with an alligator logo on the left breast. Directly beneath the logo the hypodermic needle was buried in his chest and the plunger was fully plunged, presumably from him falling on the deck. A small blood stain was spreading beneath the alligator's tail, like it had hemorrhoids. *Oh, shit.*

I stuck my finger under his nose. It was hard to tell under the conditions, but I was pretty sure he wasn't breathing.

"Jesus," said Tangles. "That doesn't look good."

I cocked my head. "I take it you mean the large needle you just buried in his heart?" I stood up and surveyed the electronics as I grabbed the wheel. The ship to shore radio had been pulverized by a bullet and was smoking.

"Oh, *fuck*, is he dead?"

"That would be my guess, just like the radio." I checked the chart plotter and discovered we lost ground during the struggle with Remy. We were now forty-two-point-five miles from port. The waves were a steady four- to-six feet, and I knew it would only get worse. We needed to get a move on. Fast.

Tangles tugged my arm. "C'mon man!" he pleaded. "Help me throw him over before Holly sees him."

"*What?*"

"She's gonna freak; it's her cousin. Let's say he slipped and fell overboard."

"We can't just *throw him over*, shit; let me think."

Suddenly, I heard Holly's voice yelling from the cockpit below. "KIT!? TANGLES!?"

I looked at Remy with the needle sticking out of his chest and the blood stain slowly spreading from the alligator's ass. It looked bad, and I whispered to Tangles to pull out the needle and zip up the jacket. I made hand motions to show him what I meant and then reached down and pulled back the flap at the top of the ladder. "It's alright, everything's okay."

Holly looked up at me, unconvinced. "*Alright?* Are you kidding me? Were those gunshots I heard?" Before I could talk her out of it, she came up the ladder. I stepped back and noticed Tangles had propped Remy up against the console. For a dead guy, he looked much better. Tangles gave me a quick thumbs up and tilted his head to the side, placing both hands together against his cheek; the universal symbol for sleeping. He was going for the *Weekend at Bernie's* ploy. *Oh, Christ.*

Holly popped her head through the flap and came face-to-face with Remy, whose eyes were thankfully shut. She looked at him a moment and then at Tangles. "It *worked?* You actually managed to sedate him?" After she secured the flap open, she stepped onto the bridge and gave me a hug.

"Yeah, it, uh, worked like a charm," lied Tangles.

"What about the gunshots? What happened to the radio?"

"When Tangles went to stick him, he dislodged a gun that Remy was concealing in the small of his back. During the struggle, Remy managed to squeeze off a couple shots. Fortunately, neither of us got hit, but one of the bullets destroyed the ship-to-shore radio."

"And I suppose this is his cell phone?" She pulled out the shattered remains of Remy's phone from her pocket. "The rest of it is scattered around the cockpit."

"Shit! I was hoping for a soft landing."

"What are we gonna do?"

"Remy re-programmed the chart plotter to take us to a marina farther north than originally planned, because he said it was easier to navigate and more protected. The thing is, there's gonna be some people waiting for us, and I'm pretty sure the only red-carpet treatment they're planning involves us being rolled up into one. I say we go back to our original course, which puts us in a place called Tucker Bay. Remy said the villa overlooks the bay, and we can walk there from the dock."

"And then we can call the authorities...right?"

"We definitely need to call *somebody*; this is *way* out of hand."

"Okay, so how do we get to Tucker Bay?" asked Tangles.

I pointed at the chart plotter. "We just enter it in; I saw it on the screen earlier. It's in there *somewhere.*"

"So, go ahead, enter it in. Let's get going," pressed Holly. I fidgeted and pushed a couple buttons on the plotter, but I was stalling for time; I had no idea how to use it. *Shit.*

Holly gave me a funny look. "What are you *doing?*"

"What do you mean what am I doing? I'm trying to find Tucker Bay."

"You're not even in the right mode."

"I'm, uh, I'm not totally familiar with this model."

"You have no idea what you're doing, do you?"

"Uh, no, not exactly."

Holly pushed my hand off the plotter as she shook her head in feigned disgust. "Unbelievable," she muttered, as her fingers started pressing buttons and moving around the screen with authority. Less than thirty seconds later, Tucker Bay popped up and the chart showed we were forty-six miles to the northwest. Holly pressed another button, and our course was plotted. "There you go, Mr. Columbus, now you can take us to the new world."

"Very funny. I'm more of an old-school sea-dog. You know, dead reckoning and such."

"If I had any vomit left in me, you'd be wearing it right now," said Tangles.

"And if we had a beer right now, you wouldn't have to go down and get some, would you?"

"You have a point there…that sounds good. I'll be right back."

As he headed down the ladder, I pushed the throttles forward a touch. I was only moments away from pushing the big CAT turbo diesels to their limits and nervously licked my lips.

Holly put her hand on my shoulder. "Are you sure that's a good idea, Kit?"

I kissed her forehead and gave her a squeeze. "You're right; I shouldn't drink on an empty stomach." I turned toward the stairs and hollered, "BRING SOME FOOD TOO!"

Chapter 49

Back in the early nineties, when the Cordero brothers were establishing their zoo, one of their first purchases was a juvenile African Rock python. When it reached maturity, it mated with a Green Anaconda captured from the nearby Putumayo River. The result was a new hybrid they dubbed a Rockaconda. It had the surly temperament of the African python combined with the incredible size and strength of its Amazonian cousin. Rico released all of the offspring back into the Putumayo except for the meanest, most aggressive snake of the lot. He named him "Emilio" in honor of the late, Pablo Emilio Escobar— his boyhood idol.

When Emilio reached fifteen feet in length and weighed two-hundred pounds, Rico started using him to interrogate suspected spies and informants. He found that anybody strapped to a chair with Emilio slithering toward them was capable of imparting great volumes of information. He also discovered that once Emilio latched his powerful jaws onto a victim and got his coils around them, there was no getting him off. It was his older brother Eduardo who came up with the idea of implanting an electric-shock generating device that would cause the snake to release its prey when triggered. At the expense of a few like-sized snakes, they finally got the intensity of the shock figured out.

As Emilio grew to his current length, they had to tweak the voltage to keep his twenty-two-foot-long, three-hundred-and-fifty-pound body in check. Rico and Eduardo each had a small device that looked like an ordinary remote used for cars with power locks. The main difference being that theirs unlocked the jaws of death. Emilio became a far more effective interrogation tool than either had first imagined. Before the electric implant, everyone who was interrogated died, whether they were guilty of something or not. Afterward, the terrifying tales told by survivors sent shock-waves of fear through the streets of Colombia and neighboring South American countries. Between stories of traitors being mauled to death by tigers and having the truth squeezed out of you by a giant Anaconda hybrid, the Cordero organization had an extremely low turnover rate.

Of course, the key to controlling the reptilian monster was keeping it safely contained; something Rico's bodyguard had failed to do. After parking the van in the garage, Rico asked him to feed Emilio a couple of rats. He did so, but forgot to re-lock the crate. Big mistake.

Rafe had the crate lid a half-inch open, and his night vision goggles had just detected movement, when the rats started going crazy. The squealing was unnerving, and as he turned to see what was causing them so much distress, his goggles pushed the lid up another quarter inch. The strike was so fast and powerful he had no time to react. Emilio's gaping mouth forced the lid up and slammed into his goggles; it felt as if he had been hit in the face with a baseball bat. Rafe yelled in fear and surprise as he fell backward onto the garage floor. He scrambled to his feet and adjusted the goggles just in time to see the snake's head dip into the can full of squealing rats and tip it over. Rats started jumping from the back of the van and scurrying out the side door. It was one big-ass snake, but exactly *how big* was unclear. His eyes focused on its girth as it continued to slither out of the crate, and he was shocked. It had to be over two feet in circumference, and the belly of the snake wasn't even exposed yet. Suddenly, the snake lifted his head out of the garbage can and used the roof of the van for leverage in downing a particularly large rat head first. He couldn't believe it, but the snakes head looked as big as the terrified raccoon which was on the verge of having a coronary. As soon as the rat's tail disappeared down its throat, the snake looked directly at Rafe and flicked its tongue out. *Oh shit!*

Emilio lunged at him again, but Rafe's black belt in Jujitsu paid a life-saving dividend as he kicked one of the van doors closed into Emilio's head. It slowed him enough for Rafe to spin one-hundred-and-eighty degrees and kick the other door shut. As Rafe leaned against the doors and tried to catch his breath, he heard and felt the giant snake slamming against them. Then he heard the raccoon cage being tossed about and suddenly the raccoon stopped screeching. *What kind of godforsaken snake was it?*

Wanting to compose himself and figure out what to do next, he staggered out the side door and slipped into the shed. He sat down on a storage bin and removed the face-and life-saving goggles. When he leaned forward to grab another bottle of water out of his backpack, he felt something funny. He had been impressed with himself for surviving the hurricane hunter flight without soiling his pants, something he proudly pointed out to the press guy upon landing, but he could no longer claim such pride. His run in with the giant snake left his underwear more soiled than a Beverly Hills housewife. The first feeder band from tropical storm Tony struck, and the wind and rain both picked up in intensity. As he undid his belt, he heard a squeal and something brushed against his foot. *Rats.* He kicked his foot out instinctively and sent one crashing into some paint cans. He tossed his underwear to the back of the shed, and when he put his pants back on, he let out a nervous chuckle. The rest of the operation he was going balls in the breeze, commando style, and he prayed for the sake of his Hagar's he'd seen the last of the giant snake.

Chapter 50

It was the proverbial calm before the storm; it had to be. For over an hour, I hammered the throttles and we sliced through the modest waves doing forty knots. Then came the first line of thunderstorms. The chart plotter indicated we were only two miles from Tucker Bay when we were hit with strong winds, rain, and lightning. I slowed the boat down to twenty knots and let go of the wheel every time lightning flashed, thinking it would somehow protect me from being fried. Holly was belowdecks checking on McGirt. Remy was laid across the bench seat in front of the helm, and Tangles was next to me hanging on to the co-captain's chair for balance. After a few minutes, the squall line passed and the rain let up. Seconds later, a flash of lightning in the distance back lit the island ahead, and I nudged Tangles in the shoulder. "We're almost there; help me look for a channel marker or something."

Tangles climbed up on the chair but quickly got down. "I can't see shit up here; I'm going down to the cockpit. I'll let you know if I see anything."

Tangles disappeared down the ladder, and two minutes later I felt a hand grab my ankle. I turned to see Tangles at the top of the ladder and pointing at the starboard side.

"Starboard side, two o'clock, two-hundred yards!"

"Got it! Stay down there to keep a lookout."

Not surprisingly, the chart plotter had us heading just inside the first marker. I turned on the bow spotlight and managed to light it up as we passed by. I swept the light back to the port side, and moments later heard Tangles holler from the bottom of the stair.

"Port side! Eleven o'clock! A hundred yards out!"

I swept the light in that direction and caught a glimpse of green just as a bright flash and large boom of thunder rang out. *Was that white water I spotted just to the left of the marker?*

"There's a reef!" Tangles cried out. "Stay tight to the marker. Wait! There's another marker to starboard! Turn to starboard!"

I was down to ten knots and cut the wheel to the right. Even with the wind and rain, I could hear the sound of crashing waves close by. *Shit!*

"That's it!" he yelled again. "Stay inside the red marker! Keep out of the white water!"

"NO SHIT!" With one hand on the spotlight, the other on the wheel, and my balls somewhere between my spleen and lower intestine, I steered through the small gap in the reef.

"You got it! You got it!" Tangles assured me. A few seconds later the boat stopped rolling as we entered the bay, and I let out a big sigh of relief.

Tangles scampered up the stairs and congratulated me on my captaining. "Nice driving, Shag. That wasn't as bad as I thought."

"Are you kidding me? That was practically a miracle."

"Miracle or not, we made it. So, where do we dock this thing?"

"Good question."

"You don't know?"

"No, Remy didn't mention it, and our plotted course ended at that first channel marker."

"Shit, well, at least we beat the storm." No sooner had the words left his mouth when a torrent of rain hit, reducing visibility to near zero.

"You had to say it, didn't you? You couldn't wait until we were tied up."

"Hey, you should be—"

Suddenly, Holly's voice loudly interrupted from the top of the ladder. "Was that a *reef* we just went past?"

I reached my hand down and helped her up. "Thankfully, yes. We made it into the bay, but I don't have a clue where we're supposed to dock. We're running blind again. We can't see shit with this rain—thank God for the electronics."

I noted our depth was twenty-five feet, then twenty-four, then twenty.... The radar showed land directly ahead and to both sides.

"I was just watching the TV. We're in a feeder band; the storm will be on us in about thirty minutes. It's got winds of sixty miles an hour."

"What about McGirt?" I asked.

"He's still out cold. Where's Remy?"

Tangles pointed to the forward bench seat. "We laid him across the bench seat. He's out, too."

"So, what are we gonna do?"

"Well, we could drop anchor and take the dinghy—"

"KABOOM!" The deafening roar of thunder came simultaneously with a blinding flash of lightning. Everybody flinched and the boat went dark. All the instrumentation on the bridge, the spotlight, the deck lights, presumably everything except the engines, shut down. I reached an arm around Holly and pulled her close. "You alright?" I asked.

"Yeah, wow, did that hit the boat?"

"Sure seemed like it."

"We're lucky we didn't get zapped," commented Tangles.

"Dude, c'mon. Don't jinx us again."

Holly put her arm around my waist and gave me a squeeze. "Kit, what are we gonna do?"

The rain was coming down sideways and the wind was pushing us toward the north shore of the bay. I had no idea exactly how deep we were or how close we were to shore. Instinctively I turned the wheel into the wind and checked off my options. "Well, we can't get the dinghy off the bow without the winch. Not in this weather. It would be suicide."

"Should we just drop anchor and wait till the storm passes?"

"We could, but then we'd be sitting ducks, totally exposed. If the storm has sustained sixty-mile-an-hour winds, it could have gusts of seventy or eighty. If a tornado or waterspout forms in one of the bands, it could flip us."

"So, what do you wanna do?" inquired Tangles.

"Go down and see if you can give me a bearing."

"A *bearing?* A bearing on what?"

"You tell me. I can't see shit up here."

"Alright, maybe you should slow down a little."

Tangles went down to the cockpit, and I gave Holly a quick peck on the cheek.

"I hope the beaches on St. Maarten are as sandy as the pictures in the travel magazines."

Holly gave me a funny look. "*What?* Why?"

Just then, Tangles yelled, "We just passed a buoy on the port side!" Then he popped his head up from the stairs leading to the bridge. "Didn't you hear me?"

"Yeah, what kind of buoy?"

"The kind that lets you know it's getting shallow. Slow down!"

Instead, I unwrapped my arm from around Holly and said, "Hang on tight," as I bumped the throttles forward.

"*Kit?*" Holly sounded concerned.

"Dude! What are you *doing?*" Cried Tangles.

"Better hang on, little buddy!"

"Oh, no, you're not gonna—"

"Go to the beach? Great idea. We should be there any—"

The bow buried in the sand and everything went flying forward, including Remy, who hit the bridge deck with a thud. My gut buried into the wheel, and Holly lost her balance and grabbed onto me. I heard Tangles yell as he slipped off the ladder to the cockpit floor. I killed the engines and after confirming Holly was alright, guided her to the ladder. 'C'mon, let's go. We need to get off this boat."

"What about Remy?"

"What about him? He'll be fine."

"We're just gonna leave him?"

"We sure can't take him with us, same with McGirt."

"Okay, but we call the police as soon as we get to the villa…right?"

"Don't worry; somebody will probably beat us to it. Let's go!"

I followed Holly down the ladder and into the salon where she grabbed her purse and announced she was ready to go. I called out for Tangles and heard him yell something from one of the forward cabins. I told Holly to stay put and hurried down the hall. The door to the master stateroom was half open, and Tangles was feverishly cutting off the duct-tape restraints on McGirt, who was still knocked out.

"What the hell are you doing?" I asked. "We gotta get out of here!"

He ripped off the last piece of duct tape and then placed the hypodermic needle into one of McGirt's hands, squeezing his fingers around it. "There! How does that look?" He asked.

"Staged. Let's go!" I grabbed him by his soaking-wet T-shirt and pulled him into the hall, then led the three of us to the bow where we continued to get pelted by the rain. I jumped into the sand and then helped Holly down while Tangles leapt off. We ran up the beach toward a darkened building and huddled under an overhang.

"Gimme the Surefire." I instructed Tangles. It was dangling from his neck by its lanyard, and he lifted it over his head and handed it to me. "Here you go; I can't believe you carry a flashlight with you all the time."

I draped it over my neck and shined the light on my watch, illuminating the dials. It was almost one in the morning. "You're damn right I do; you never know when you might need one."

"Of *course* you know when you might need one; it's called nighttime. During the day? Not so much."

"Really? Then quit asking to borrow it all the time."

"I think you think it looks cool hanging down your neck. What gives? You trying to be the Flavor Flav of illumination or something?"

"Shut up, ass licker."

"Knock it off, guys! How are we gonna find the villa?" asked Holly.

"I don't know," I answered. "But Remy said you could walk there from here. What's the address?"

Holly opened her purse and I shined the light inside. I looked at Tangles and smirked. "See? It's handy again."

"Yeah, 'cause it's dark out…asshole."

Holly pulled out a slip of paper and read the address; "Twenty-two, Bayview Road, Villa Destin."

I stepped around the corner and looked at a sign on the front of the building that read, "Bayview Watersports Rentals." I hurried back under the protection of the overhang and relayed the information.

"The sign on the front says 'Bayview Watersports Rentals.' The road in front is probably Bayview Road, *right?*"

"Maybe, but even if it is, which way do we go?" asked Holly.

I looked up the hill to the north and pointed at a couple well-lit houses. "Remy said the villa overlooked the bay. Those places overlook the bay."

Tangles pointed in the other direction at some other lights. “What about those? They overlook the bay, too.”

“Those are too far; he said it was a short walk.”

“Okay, I’m game if you are. What about you, Miss Holly? You ready to hoof it up the hill?”

“Why not? My hair’s already a mess.”

Chapter 51

Lucky switched the bedside light on and said, "Hello, Mother."

Eighty-six-year-old Genevieve LeRoux's eyes fluttered open, and she was shocked to see her distinguished son standing at the foot of her bed. Instinctively, she pulled the covers up tight to her chin. "Where's Mattie?"

"The nurse? I sent her home. In case you didn't know, there's a storm passing through."

"What are you doing here?"

"Now, is that any way to greet your loving son?" Lucky stepped to the head of the bed and smiled. As he bent down to kiss her, she turned her head to the side.

"Just leave me alone."

Perturbed at the rebuke, Lucky grabbed her by the throat and twisted her head to face him. "Don't you turn away from me!"

"Let me go!" she pleaded. "You're hurting me!"

He released his grip and flashed his famous pearly whites, which glistened in the flickering bedside light. "No, I haven't hurt you...*yet.* But if you don't do as I say, I'll kill you just like you and father killed Uncle Joe."

Genevieve gasped and her eyes went wide.

"Did you really think you could keep a secret like that from me forever? You tricked a young woman and your husband killed a man, all so you could steal a baby?"

Genevieve's mouth was opening and closing, but no words came out.

"What's the matter? Cat got your lying tongue?"

"No, it wasn't like that. I didn't know *what* your father was up to. He tricked me, too. Who told you this?"

"That doesn't matter. What matters is that you've been keeping secrets from me. *Big* secrets. So it got me thinking, what *else* are you keeping from me?"

Although it was widely believed he was the owner of the Tiara Bay Marina, the big estate on St. Thomas, and even the villa his mother lived in, the fact was that all the properties were in Genevieve's name or a corporation controlled by her. As she grew old and frail, he tried to get her to transfer the titles to him, but she steadfastly refused. She knew her greedy son better than anybody and suspected that once her leverage was gone, she would be too. Indeed, Lucky would have dealt with her long ago had he suspected he and Remy were the only heirs, but his mother kept him guessing. She hinted some charities and non-family members might be beneficiaries of her estate. The last thing he wanted was to have her die and then watch her estate be carved up by charities and other undeserving souls, like her personal nurse. Especially while he and Remy were using the Tiara Bay Marina as their own personal piggy bank. To make matters worse, a young woman had suddenly appeared with an incredible, yet convincing story, that she was a cousin—*another* possible heir. She was doggedly pursuing the twisted truth of his family history, and it didn't sit well with him one bit, even if he was reasonably certain Holly would soon be killed by the Colombians. There was only one clear solution; He needed to see the will and force his mother to change it to his liking.

"What do want?" his mother asked.

"What do you think I want? I want to see the will—now."

"It's at the lawyers."

"I'm sure it is. I'm also sure you have a copy here somewhere. Where is it?"

"I don't have—"

"You *lie*!" He grabbed his mother by the shoulders and shook her violently. "Where is it? WHERE IS IT?"

"Let me go, you bastard!" she cried.

He lifted her ninety-five-pound body nearly out of the bed so her face was only inches from his own, and she cried out in pain.

"You think this hurts?" he snarled. "I haven't even—"

"Beep-beep-beep." The alarm on his wristwatch started beeping to let him know it was time to pick up Remy at the dock. He briefly glanced at it and cursed as he slammed his mother into the bed. She hit awkwardly and bounced off the bed and onto the floor with a thud. A sharp pain in her side took her breath away and tears welled in her eyes as she tried to push herself up off the floor, but it was useless. "I can't...I can't get up."

"You're a bedridden old bitch anyways; what difference does it make?" He walked away but turned back to face her in the doorway as she pleaded to him one more time.

"Don't leave me here! I'm your mother!"

"Are you? Are you really? Or is that another secret you've been keeping from me?"

"No! I swear!"

A sudden flash of lightning and simultaneous clap of thunder rattled the house, and the power went out. A battery-powered backup light in the hall kicked on and back lit Lucky as he stood in the doorway, casting his elongated shadow over his injured mother. "We'll see about that, but guess what? I've got a little secret of my own. Maybe it was no diving accident that killed Father."

She had long suspected as much, but to hear her son admit it made her sick to her stomach. "But why? Why did you do it? He loved you. He doted on you."

"He loved money, just like I do, and he promised me everything would be mine when he was gone. He was a liar, just like you."

"You disgust me."

"I disgust *you?* You're a baby thief and accomplice to murder!"

"I am not! I would have never condoned it!" She grimaced as another jolt of pain surged through her body.

"Does it hurt? Good. If you don't tell me where the will is when I return, I swear I'll make you wish you were dead. I have some acquaintances in the guest house that specialize in dealing with two-faced liars like you." As he headed out the front door he heard his mother sobbing in pain and despair, and smiled.

Less than five minutes later, Rico "The Freako" Cordero and his driver/bodyguard were in the cargo van, following the senator out the front gate. Lucky was driving his mother's fifteen-year-old Isuzu Rodeo, and the plan was for the Hi-Lo Gang to ride in the van and Remy and McGirt in the Isuzu. Lucky left the front gate open, just like the garage door, so he wouldn't get soaked having to manually open and close it again upon his return. As he led them north toward Anse Marcel, Lucky thought about what the Colombians would do to his mother when he wasn't focused on the winding mountain road. Under normal conditions it was no picnic, but with driving wind and rain, it was treacherous at best. He glanced in the rear-view to make sure the van was behind him but wasn't too concerned about their ability to follow as they were the only ones on the road.

Meanwhile, in the van, the driver complained about the horrible conditions. "This rain is crazy; we should have waited until the storm passed."

Rico, however, was unfazed. "Quit complaining. This is like a spring shower in the Atriz valley. Keep your eye on the senator's car; he said it's not that far."

"That's what I'm doing. I can't believe they came by boat in this weather. Do you think they made it?"

"The senator's son called an hour ago and said they'd be here. I can't wait to see the look on McGirt's face when he sees us. Between him and the Americans, Emilio is going to be a busy boy." At the mention of Emilio's name, it suddenly occurred to him that he hadn't heard the rats squealing. In fact, there was no sound at all coming from the back of the van.

"Roberto?"

"Yes, boss?"

"Did you notice the rats aren't making any noise? Neither is the raccoon."

"What?"

"On the way from the airport it sounded like an animal orchestra in back. Now it's quiet."

"I didn't notice; I'm trying to keep us on the road. Maybe they're sleeping. It's late."

Rico glanced over his shoulder and noticed that the plastic partition behind the bench seat on the driver's side was pushed out from the wall. "Did you remember to lock the crate after you fed Emilio?"

"Of course I… uh… I'm *pretty* sure I did."

Rico suddenly detected movement out of the corner of his eye and ever so slowly turned his head toward the back seat. To his horror, Emilio's giant head slowly rose up between the two front seats. As Rico started fumbling for the remote in his pocket that would send an electric charge through Emilio, he muttered, "*Cogeme,*" which means "fuck me" in Spanish. Roberto was wracking his brain, trying to remember whether he had locked the crate or not, and stole a quick look at the wide-eyed Rico as he dug for something in his pocket. "What is it?" he asked nervously, but deep down he knew what it was. As they rounded a bend, he glanced in the rearview mirror a split second before Emilio sunk his gaping fangs into his neck, smashing his head into the driver's side window in the process. The van never made the turn and plunged off the road into the foreboding jungle below. Their screams, along with the sounds of metal ripping and trees snapping, were lost in the raging storm like a shadow in the night.

Chapter 52

After slogging our way up the hill we found the "Villa Destin" and jogged down the darkened driveway in the rain. Not a single light was on in the villa, or guest-house, or anywhere on the grounds. Strangely, the garage doors next to the guesthouse, and the one next to the villa, were both open. Anxious to get out of the wind and rain, we dashed into the garage by the villa. The three of us stood inside, shivering and soaked from head to toe like sewer rats. I wrapped my arms around Holly and hugged her tight in an attempt to warm her up. Aside from being wet and miserable, we were all tired from the trek up the hill.

"That was the longest 'short walk' I ever had in my life. I felt like a salmon swimming upstream," said Tangles.

"What are you talking about?" I responded. "All your walks are short, just like everything else about you."

"Really?" said Holly. "Now, of all times, you're going to start something?"

"Yeah, man. You can't ever let one go by, can you?"

"Nope, life's too short—no pun intended."

"That's enough, Kit. I'm freezing. What now?"

I had my trusty Surefire around my neck and shined it around the garage. There didn't appear to be anything useful, and I clicked it off.

"Wait," said Tangles. "Shine it on that shelf over there." I did as he asked, and he walked over and grabbed what appeared to be a rolled up cushion or something. He untied a string and unfurled it in front of us. "Look, it's a sleeping bag."

"Dude, this is no time to take a nap."

"No kidding. I was thinking maybe you could check out the house while Holly and I climb inside and keep each other warm."

"In your dreams. I'll never be *that* cold."

"Gimme that thing!" I snatched it out of his little hands, unzipped it, and draped it over Holly's shoulders. She thanked me, and Tangles said, "What about me? I found it!" Holly reached down and ruffled his wet mop of hair. "Thanks, Tangles. I mean it."

"You're welcome. That wasn't so hard, was it?"

"I bet you say that to all the girls."

Despite the predicament we were in, the three of us started laughing in earnest. When the laughter died down, I re-assessed the situation. "Okay, here's what we know. Remy arranged for us to be picked up at a marina some ways north of here. Since both garages are open and empty, I'm guessing our welcoming committee went to get us. I can't imagine anybody going out in this storm, at this time of night, for any other reason. I'm also thinking the front door to the villa might be unlocked too."

"You think Genevieve's inside?" asked Holly.

"There's only one way to find out. Let's go."

We draped the sleeping bag over our heads and ran side by side up to the front stoop. I slowly turned the knob, and it clicked as the latching mechanism released. I signaled to keep quiet by putting my index finger up to my mouth and gently pushed the door open.

***

After watching the van follow the Isuzu out of the driveway, Rafe spent several minutes trying to contact headquarters. Unfortunately, the storm was disrupting the satellite service for his DICK phone. He was hoping the boss could identify the men in the van from the photos he uploaded as well as the man in the white suit. He knew that the Hi-Lo Gang was supposed to be arriving by boat and surmised that the vehicles had gone to pick them up.

He briefly considered his harrowing flight with the hurricane hunters and shook his head when he thought about trying to come ashore in a boat. Contemplating his next move, he donned the night vision goggles and peered at the villa from the small opening between the shed doors. The power had been knocked out and everything was completely dark. He swept the goggles right and then left and then—*what?*

To his astonishment, he saw three hunched figures running from the garage to the front door, holding a blanket or something over their heads. As they stood on the front stoop, he zoomed in, and his jaw dropped. He didn't need the new locator app on his DICK phone to confirm it was the Hi-Lo Gang. *Where in the hell did they come from? Where was the senator's son?* A few moments later, he watched in disbelief as they slipped into the villa. Rafe lowered the goggles and said, "You have got to be kidding me." A few minutes later, he slinked out of the shed and crept around to the back of the villa.

Chapter 53

We stood in the dark foyer for a few moments and just listened. Hearing nothing, we crept a few steps until reaching a hallway. There was a doorway to our right, and Holly tugged my sleeve. "That must be the kitchen; the lights on the stove are flashing," she whispered.

"The powers gotta be out," I whispered back.

"I bet there's a phone in there."

I flicked my Surefire on just long enough to spot it for her, and she quietly picked it up. It was a cordless, and I could see the keypad was dark. Holly shook her head and confirmed that the line was dead.

Tangles crept further down the hall and wanted us to follow. "I heard something. C'mon!" he quietly urged. Holly and I gingerly trod on the tile floor behind him, and then we heard it too—moaning coming from around the corner. As we got closer, a faint light appeared. A battery-powered light was mounted on the hall wall. There was a bathroom on one side and some closets on the other. At the end of the hall was an open door. As we inched toward it, there was a loud crash like something big falling over, and then a woman cried out in pain.

"Somebody's hurt!" whispered Holly. "C'mon!" Holly rushed into the room before I could stop her. *Shit.* Tangles and I hurried in and found Holly on her knees next to an elderly lady lying on the floor next to a bed. A nightstand was lying on its side in the corner.

""Don't hurt me! Please, don't hurt me!" She pleaded.

"We're not going to hurt you. What happened?" Responded Holly. Even in the dim light, it was easy to see the look of confusion on the old woman's face. "Who are you? What are you doing here?"

"We came here to talk to you…I think. Is your name Genevieve LeRoux?"

"Well, yes. Yes it is."

"My name's Holly Lutes."

"How did you—what did you say your name was?"

"Lutes, Holly Lutes. My aunt was Milfred Lutes."

"Oh my God, somehow I knew this day would come. You must be the one who talked to Lucky. We have to get out of here. He's coming back, and he's gonna hurt me again. If you're still here, he'll probably hurt you and your friends too. He has some people with him."

"Wait a second," I cut in. "Lucky's *here*?"

"Yes, he left a while ago, but he's coming back. He went to get my grandson, Remy—another bad apple. You have to help me; I think he broke my hip." At the mention of Remy's name, I looked at Tangles who put his finger up to his lips.

"*Lucky* did this to you?" asked Holly. "Why?"

"He's demanding to see my will because the marina and the properties are in my name. He suspects he's not the primary beneficiary and he's right. I have little doubt he plans to try and force me into changing it for his benefit. Please, we need to hurry. We can talk later. There's a lot you don't know."

"We can't go anywhere without a vehicle," I informed her. "And if anybody tries to hurt you or anybody else, they're gonna get a belly full of bullets. So let's talk now." I pulled Remy's 38 Special out of my pocket and held it up for all to see.

"Put that away, Kit," said Holly. "Let's lift her onto the bed."

I slipped the gun back in my pocket, and Holly stepped aside so Tangles and I could lift Genevieve up on the bed. She yelped in pain, and Holly admonished us for not being gentle enough as she pushed me aside and draped the bed sheet over her frail figure.

"Do you have any pain medications?" inquired Holly.

"Yes, in the bathroom...please...I'll need some water from the fridge too; I knocked mine over with the nightstand when I tried to get up off the floor."

I gave Tangles my Surefire and sent him off for the meds and water. Genevieve was holding Holly's hand and forced a weak smile. "You're a beautiful young woman, just like Millie was...is she...? How is she?"

"She, um... passed away earlier this year."

Genevieve closed her eyes, and when she opened them a tear dripped down her cheek. "I'm so sorry. I'm so sorry for how I acted, too. It's shameful. Millie told you?"

"Sort of. She left me a letter with a picture of her and Joseph to be opened after her death. I know all about her whirlwind romance, the pregnancy, Joseph's apparent death, and the shady adoption. It wasn't really an adoption though, was it?"

"No, Kilroy insisted we pass the baby off as our own. It was important to him that people believed he was our biological child, even though I was the one who was infertile. I was desperate for a baby, and Kilroy played on my insecurities. I was young and naïve and thought I was in love. I never suspected Joseph's diving accident was anything but what he said it was…nobody did. They were great friends; we were *all* great friends. I mean, who would do such a thing?"

"You never had any suspicions at all?"

"At the time? No. If I had, I would have never taken Millie's baby."

"Whose idea was it to adopt Joseph after his family was killed in the plane crash?"

"It was—how did you know about that?"

"It's a long story. Who was it?"

"It was Kilroy's. I was here on St. Maarten and didn't even *know* about the plane crash. He showed up at my parent's house and told me. He said Millie decided to give the baby up since Joseph was gone, and he asked me to marry him and raise the baby as our own. I said yes, and we got married on Valentine's Day just a week or so before Millie gave birth. Soon after, he suggested we adopt Joseph. He said he felt responsible for losing track of him on the dive and thought it his duty to look after him. At that point, any remote suspicion I may have had concerning the accident went right out the window."

"Hold on. In Millie's letter she mentioned driving by the funeral service but being too distraught to attend. How can that be?"

"Kilroy told her it was a funeral service, but it was actually a prayer service. He even drove her past the church. It was all part of his ploy to get her to give up the baby."

"How incredibly heartless."

"Kilroy didn't tell me about it until I returned to St. Croix a couple weeks before she gave birth. I knew I should have told Millie, but I was too blinded by the prospect of having a child of my own. I pray some day you can forgive me for deceiving her; I know it's asking a lot."

Holly ignored her and kept drilling for answers. "And he convinced you to pose as his cousin for the adoption?"

"Yes, how did—"

I held my hand up and cut her off. "Please, we need to wrap this up and figure a way out of here."

"Don't you dare cut her off!" said Holly. "We came a long way to get here, and I have a few more questions."

"He's right," said Genevieve. "We don't want to be here when Lucky gets back."

Tangles returned and handed Genevieve the pain pills, then gave everybody a bottle of water. While Genevieve took the pills, I instructed Tangles to watch the driveway and holler if anybody pulled in. I noticed the storm had eased up as the thunder rumbled in the distance.

"So, what changed?" continued Holly. "What happened to make you think the accident wasn't an accident?"

"Well, for one, it didn't take long to see the real reason he wanted to adopt Joseph."

"Which was?"

"Money."

"Huh?"

"Joseph's family was fairly well to do to begin with, and there was also a large settlement with the airline over the crash. By adopting Joseph, Kilroy took control of his estate and used much of the money for his own purposes. When I realized what his true motive was, I began to wonder about the accident. He was my husband though. It was one thing to look at him as greedy and opportunistic, but quite another to look at him as a possible killer. But that all changed when Joseph came out of the coma."

"What happened?"

"He wasn't altogether coherent of course, but he kept saying Kilroy's name. Kilroy was working at the marina on St. Croix, and when I called to tell him the news, he caught the next flight over. It was late when he got here, and he asked to have some time alone with Joseph. He visited for a few minutes, and when he came out he said that Joseph was too tired to talk and that he would see him in the morning. The next morning, he was dead."

"Nobody checked on Joseph after Kilroy left his room?"

"No, like I said it was late, just like it is now. The coroner's office wrote it off as a massive stroke or aneurysm, but back in those days it was a guessing game. He could have just as easily been suffocated—nobody would have been the wiser."

"That makes it twice that Kilroy was the last person to see Joseph before he had something catastrophic happen to him."

"I realized it too and confronted him on it that night. He had been drinking all day, and I threatened to take the kids and leave him if he didn't come clean. He adamantly denied having anything to do with Joseph dying that day but admitted the diving accident years before had been no accident. He hit Joseph over the head with a dive weight and then took the skiff over to 'The Wall' to dump him overboard. He figured Joseph's weight-belt and gear would cause him to sink to the abyss and he would never be found. After he radioed for help, Joseph must have regained consciousness long enough to drop his weight belt and float to the surface. I was horrified, naturally, and things were never the same between us."

"My God, he wanted a baby bad enough to kill for one?"

"There's more to the story. A few days before the accident, Millie told us she changed her mind. She and Joseph decided to keep the baby, and they were going to tell his family at Thanksgiving dinner. I was devastated after thinking the baby would be mine. Kilroy and I had a horrible fight, and I flew back to St. Maarten to be with my family. He told me he thought I had left him for good, and to be truthful, I intended to. I was sick of lying to Millie and Joseph, and I wanted a fresh start. That's when Kilroy hatched the plot to kill Joseph. He figured that with him out of the way, he could convince Millie to give up the baby again, which she reluctantly did. He thought if he could get me the baby I'd stay with him, and I'm ashamed to say he was right."

"Do you have any idea what that did to her? She was destroyed! She lost her baby and the love of her life! If that wasn't bad enough, by the time she returned to Florida, she had developed a pelvic infection that left her unable to have any more children! She thought it was God's way of punishing her for giving up her baby. How could you do that to her? She wrote so fondly of you. She looked up to you, for crying out loud!"

Genevieve began sobbing, and I put my hand on Holly's shoulder as she sat on the bed next to her. I knew that no matter how mad she was, she didn't intend to make an old lady cry, and she immediately tried to get her to stop. "Please, Genevieve, stop, just... stop crying, okay?"

"You need to understand," she sniffled. "Kilroy was ten years older than me. I was only twenty-two and easily manipulated because of my own perceived inability to have children. I'm so sorry for what I've done. Please, *please,* believe me."

Holly stroked her cheek. "I do believe you. We all make decisions we wish we could take back, some are just more life-altering than others."

"If anybody deserves punishment from God, it's me, and judgment day could be any time now. He let me know I made the wrong decision sixty-four years ago. Fate can be crueler than you know."

"What do you mean? What are you saying?"

"As soon as I had Millie's baby in my hands, Kilroy put me on the next flight home. No sooner had I unpacked my bags when I fell ill. I went to the doctor and he ran a few tests. He paid me a visit the next day and told me I was two-months pregnant."

Chapter 54

Preoccupied with navigating his way down the mountain road in the torrential rain, the senator failed to notice that the van was no longer behind him. It wasn't until he pulled into the marina that he looked into his rearview and noticed that the headlights were absent. He stopped just inside the gate, which had been left open by the marina operator so mariners would have unimpeded access to their vessels. Since the storm wasn't anticipated to strike the island, many owners were caught off guard and found themselves tying off their boats in the middle of the night. After waiting five minutes and still not seeing the van, he slowly drove through the marina, looking for the *Lady G.* Realizing it wasn't there, he pulled out his cell and tried to call Remy, but cell service was down along with the power. For twenty minutes he sat wondering where in the hell the van and his very expensive yacht were. When the storm eased as it moved off island and into the Caribbean, he saw that he had a signal and dialed Remy again, only to get kicked to voicemail. "Dammit!" he cursed. "Where the hell is everybody?"

Unable to sit idle any longer, he turned the small SUV around and followed the road back to the villa.

Every time he came around a bend, he expected to see the van pulled over with a flat or some mechanical issue, but there was nothing except scattered debris in the road. Fifty yards before the driveway to the villa, a large tree blocked the road and he muttered, "Shit." He pulled to the side and killed the engine, then grabbed his umbrella and headed out on foot. He worked his way up the long dark driveway and noted that the van wasn't back in the guest house garage like he thought it might be. *Where the hell are they?* As he walked around the circle, a small light suddenly bounced around the kitchen in the front of the house. *What?* He knew it wasn't his mother, who he had left lying on the bedroom floor, and nobody else should be there. He dashed into the open garage next to the villa and fumbled around in the dark until he found an old tackle box and extracted an eight-inch filet knife.

Knife in hand, he quietly entered the villa and stood in the darkened foyer to listen. Very faintly he heard voices coming from the back bedroom and inched his way down the hall to the opening that led to the kitchen. With his back pressed up against the wall, he heard a kitchen cupboard creak open and peeked around the corner. The midget was standing on a chair shining a flashlight in a cupboard, apparently looking for food. He ducked back into the hall, his mind racing. *What the fuck? Where's Remy?* He slipped past the doorway, quietly stepping into the open bathroom down the hall.

Around the corner, the emergency back-up light faintly lit the hall, and he was close enough to make out voices. His mother did most of the talking, but he also heard the girl Holly and her boyfriend, but no Remy. *Where the hell was he?*

Suddenly he heard footsteps coming from the kitchen. As soon as the midget passed by, he stepped behind him and clamped a hand over his mouth. With the other he put him in a headlock and pressed the knife against his throat. “Don’t make a fucking peep,” he whispered, before pushing him toward the bedroom.

Chapter 55

"*What?*" said Holly, echoing my thoughts. "I thought you said you couldn't have kids?"

"I did. The doctor told me when I was seventeen that I could never have children. Much to my delight, he was wrong. Seven months later I gave birth to Lucky."

Holly popped up from the bed like she had sat on a tack. "What do you—what do you mean, *you* gave birth to Lucky?"

"Just what I said."

"You're not making sense," I interjected. "Lucky was Millie's baby; you just got done telling us how you and Kilroy took him away from her."

"Not Lucky. He truly *is* my baby. I gave birth to him on September 14, 1949. Believe me, I'm not mistaken. It was one of the happiest days of my life— today being one of the worst. Just before you got here Lucky threatened me and implied the diving accident that claimed his father's life wasn't an accident. It's something I've had a nagging suspicion about for years; Lucky killed Kilroy. He told him his estate would pass onto him when he died, but Lucky didn't realize it would go to me first. My husband was a killer, and so is my son. I'm afraid God's just getting warmed up for what he has in store for me.'"

"What am I missing here? What kinda meds are you on, anyways?" I asked.

"Wait a second," questioned Holly. "What about his birthmark? Millie's letter said her baby was born with a birthmark on his right forearm in the shape of a four-leaf clover, and she called him 'Lucky.' When I met him yesterday and asked to see it, he showed me a scar in the same spot. He claimed to not know how it got there, and said you told him he put his arm on a stove burner as a child. We were thinking the birthmark was removed to hide his true identity."

Genevieve shook her head. "I had no idea she named him Lucky, but you should know better than to believe a politician. He knows damn well he never had a birthmark *and* how he got that scar. He tore his arm up on a reef while body-boarding when he was thirteen or fourteen years old."

"But... but his name's Lucky. You're saying it's just coincidence you named him Lucky, too?"

"No, I named him Chanceaux, which is the French word for luck. Lucky's just a nickname. I wasn't supposed to be able to have kids and considered him a miracle. I thought I was the luckiest girl in the world—that's how he got his name."

"Holy crap! Are you kidding me?" I didn't know what to think except that everything was all fucked up. I looked out the window at the back patio and lightning flashed in the distance. There was some sort of outdoor kitchen, and I thought I saw movement behind the built-in grill. I walked over to the window for a closer look, but when the lightning flashed again,

I saw nothing. Holly held her face in her hands and slowly shook her head in disbelief before asking the obvious. "My God! If Lucky's not Millie's baby, then who is? What's his name? Where is he?"

"I noticed the same birthmark Millie did and named him Patrick."

"*Patrick?* Why Patrick?"

"In honor of St. Patrick, you know, like Millie said, the birthmark looked like a four-leaf clover."

I turned toward Genevieve and said, "Wow." I wasn't normally one to get sucked into somebody else's family drama, but this was some crazy shit.

"You said 'looked' as in the past tense," queried Holly, as she squeezed my arm. "Are you telling me he's dead?"

"I wish I knew. I think about him every day."

"What do you mean? Where is he?"

"I have no idea. I haven't seen or heard from him in nearly fifty years."

"*What?* Why? What happened?"

Genevieve took a sip of water and closed her eyes. I thought she might fade off to sleep, but Holly wasn't about to let that happen. She sat down at the foot of the bed and gently shook her leg. "Genevieve, please, I'm trying to locate him. He's my only connection to Millie."

Her eyes slowly opened, and she put her hand on top of Holly's. "I'm sorry, dear. The medication's really kicking in, and I'm rarely up this late." She yawned and continued on. "When I discovered that I was pregnant, I wanted to give the baby back to Millie. But Kilroy dismissed the idea altogether. He was friends with Millie's father and also had a business relationship with him that he didn't want to jeopardize. It was all about money with Kilroy, just like it is with Lucky. They were like two peas in a pod of greed. Millie's pregnancy was unknown to her parents, and he said they would never forgive him if she came home with a baby, let alone a baby of mixed race. It was 1949 and the social stigma would have been horrendous. He said her father would black-ball him in the marina business just for starters. He said we simply couldn't afford to let it happen and convinced me to keep baby Patrick.

Everything was fine until Chanceaux was born, then it was like someone flipped a switch. Kilroy wanted nothing to do with Patrick and spent what little family time he had doting on Lucky. The older they got, the worse it became. Kilroy treated Patrick horribly, and I spent countless nights comforting him as he cried himself to sleep. When he was about ten years old, the abuse became physical, and I threatened more than once to leave Kilroy if it didn't stop. When Joseph died and Kilroy basically admitted to killing him, I realized Patrick's life may be in danger too. Patrick asked me time and again why his father treated him so badly and Lucky so well, and I never had a good answer for him."

"You didn't tell him he was adopted?"

"No, I thought about it, but knowing my husband was a killer, I feared what he might do if he found out. Despite my pleas and threats to leave, the physical abuse grew worse. When Patrick was fifteen, he told me he couldn't take it anymore, that he wanted to stow away on a ship. I couldn't argue with him; by this time not only was the abuse coming from Kilroy, but Lucky too. The tension between them was unbearable, but I knew that if he ran away, Kilroy would be furious. I think he enjoyed abusing him so much that he would stop at nothing to find him and bring him back. So Patrick and I concocted a plan that would free him forever."

Holly and I shared skeptical looks and peered down at Genevieve who had a faraway look in her eyes. "What, uh, what did you do?" asked Holly.

"Why, I helped him fake his death, of course. *Then* I put him on a boat. The year was 1964, and it breaks my heart to say I haven't seen or heard from him since."

Chapter 56

I was looking out the window again, unconvinced that I hadn't seen movement, when I noticed something stuck to the window. At first I thought it looked like a slug, and then I thought it looked like a miniature suction cup. *What the hell?* Genevieve's words were still sinking in when I heard a commotion behind me. I turned just in time to catch Tangles, who had been thrust across the room at me. Holly yelled as the senator snatched her and put a knife to her throat as he dragged her to the doorway.

"Nobody move or she dies!"

"Way to keep a look out," I chided Tangles.

"I don't know where he came from! He jumped me in the hall."

"You two shut up!"

"What are you doing? Let her go!" cried Genevieve.

"You!" He glared at her. "You *faked* Patrick's death? I should put this knife through your cold, conniving heart!"

"Go ahead, but just let Holly go first. She didn't do anything."

He was about ten feet away, and his head was to the side and maybe six-inches higher than Holly's. I was fingering the 38 Special in my pocket, trying to muster the nerve to try to put a bullet in his head. Then I remembered he was a murderous, coke-peddling politician and took a deep breath. “Hey, asshole, maybe you should listen to your mother once in a while.” Even in what little light there was, I could see Holly’s eyes go wide. He turned toward me, and Holly squirmed as he increased the pressure on her throat.

“Maybe you should shut up unless you want your girlfriend’s throat slit from ear to ear.”

“You really think it’s going down like that? Apparently you never saw *Raiders of the Lost Ark*.”

“*What?*”

I pulled the snub-nosed revolver from my pocket and fired at his face. Unfortunately, unlike in the movies, I missed my target badly. The bullet smashed into the top of the doorframe, sending splinters flying. Holly cried out as he dragged her back a couple steps and used her as a shield. “Drop the gun or she gets it!” He pressed the knife into Holly’s throat so hard she could barely breathe, and she struggled to speak. A weak, “Help,” was all she could manage.

I could tell she was near panic, and I folded like a thrift-store lawn chair. “Okay! Okay! I’m putting it down! Don’t hurt her!” I bent down and placed the gun on the tile floor. Tangles said, “Nice shot.”

“Shut up.”

“Kick it over here! Now!”

I did as I was told and slid it across the floor using my foot.

He told Holly to bend down with him, and he picked the gun up. After slipping the knife into his jacket, he did a double take as he held the gun to her head. "This is—this is Remy's gun! What are you doing with his gun?"

"Would you believe he gave it to me for safe keeping?"

He pointed the gun at me and said, "One more smart-ass comment and I'll shoot you!"

"If your aims anything like mine, I'm not too worried."

He put the gun back to Holly's head, and she closed her eyes as she rubbed her throat.

"You're right; I think I'll just blow her pretty brains out if you don't start giving me some answers. Where's Remy?"

I nudged Tangles in the shoulder. "Care to take this one?"

Tangles cleared his throat and said, "He's, uh, sleeping, just like your buddy McGirt."

"Only I don't think he's going to be too happy when he wakes up," I added. "Friends don't let friends get duct taped and drugged...not that he doesn't deserve it after hijacking and blowing up my boat."

"Nobody cares about *your* boat. Where's mine? Where's the *Lady G?*"

I pointed out the window. "Down there in the bay."

"Tucker Bay?"

"No, San Francisco."

"I warned you!" He pointed the gun at me again, and I crouched behind Tangles.

Tangles put his hands up and pleaded, "Don't shoot, man. I'll tell you whatever you want. He can't keep his mouth shut."

"So I noticed...you moored it?"

"Moored what?"

"The *boat,* you idiot!"

"Uh, not exactly."

"What do you mean, *not exactly?* There aren't any available docks for a boat the size of the *Lady G* in the bay."

"You don't say. Well, there was plenty of room on the beach."

"You *beached* my new Hatteras?! I oughta shoot you right now!"

"Not me!" Tangles stuck his thumb over his shoulder. "Him, he beached it!"

"Why does that not surprise me? I think I'll shoot you both. What happened to the sub?"

"What sub?"

"Don't play dumb with me! McGirt told us everything, but he said the sub sunk with you on it. So tell me where the sub is, or I start pulling the trigger." He pointed the gun back at Holly's head.

"Just tell him!" urged Holly.

"It's on its way to Miami," I answered as I slowly stepped out from behind Tangles. "The Coast Guard has it."

"My God, Lucky, what's all this about?" asked Genevieve. "What have you done?"

"Your son's a major cocaine trafficker," I replied.

"I told you to shut up!" Lucky pointed the gun at me again, and I raised my arms.

"So was your grandson," added Tangles.

Lucky swung the gun at Tangles and said, "What do you mean *was?* You said he was sedated."

"He is," I answered. "Permanently. He's dead, just like your political career."

"You *killed* my son?" He swung the gun back at me.

"Not intentionally," answered Tangles. "He tried to shoot us. It was an accident—I swear."

Sensing an opportunity, Holly stamped her foot down on top of Lucky's and broke free as he cried out in pain. She rushed toward me, and I yelled, "No!" as Lucky aimed the gun at her back. Simultaneously, the bay window behind us exploded, and Lucky flew against the wall. He slumped to the floor, and I could see in the minimal light that he had been shot in the shoulder. Although blood was spreading across his white suit, he still managed to loosely hang onto the gun. I was holding Holly, and we looked at the shattered window behind us. A gun with a silencer poked through the broken glass, and it was pointed at the senator. "Drop the gun!" the mystery shooter yelled. The senator's hand opened and the gun slipped out onto the floor. "You, Tangles! Grab the gun!" the voice instructed. Tangles was as stunned as Holly and I were, and it took a moment to register. "Get the gun, now!" Tangles snapped out of it and quickly snatched the gun off the floor. The gun pointing through the window started knocking out chunks of glass until there was a hole big enough to step through, and that's just what the Mystery Man did. He was wearing a black poncho and had these large goggles or binoculars dangling from his neck. He took the gun from Tangles and asked, "Is everybody okay?"

"I've… I've been *shot.*" The senator sounded weak and seemed to be surprised.

Mystery Man looked down at him and said, "No shit. I'm not talking about *you.* Is everybody *else* alright?"

"I think my hip's broken," said Genevieve. "Is it true? Is my son a drug dealer?"

"No, we believe him to be much worse; he *supplies* drug dealers, but not anymore."

"Who are you?" I asked. "Where the hell did you come from?"

Before answering, he reached under his poncho and pulled out an oversized cell phone. I could see that it was flashing, and he held his finger up to indicate it would be a minute. As soon as he answered and stepped into the hall, Holly hit me in the chest. "You almost shot me!"

I put my hands up in front of me as I plead my case. "No I didn't. I almost shot him!" I pointed to Lucky, who was moaning in pain.

"I was standing in front of him! You could have killed me!"

"Baby, he was standing to the side, and he's almost a head taller, or I never would have taken the shot."

"Don't you '*baby' me!*"

"Trust me, Holly, it wasn't even close," said Tangles. "I think he hit the ceiling."

"I hit the doorframe, asshole. I aimed a little high to be safe."

"Safe for *who?*" questioned Holly. "He had a filet knife to my throat. Jesus, Kit, what were you thinking?"

"I thought that even if I missed, the distraction would give you a chance to make a break for it."

"Well you thought wrong!"

Mystery Man stepped back into the room as he put his phone away and knelt down next to the senator. "Where's Cordero?"

"Who?"

"I got no time for games." He pointed his weapon at the senator's head. "The guys in the van, where are they?"

"I need a doctor!"

"You're gonna need a coroner if you don't answer me!"

"Okay, alright. I don't know *where* they are. They were supposed to follow me to Anse Marcel to meet the boat, but they never made it."

"You're lying."

"No, I swear! I waited at the marina for twenty minutes, but they never showed. Please, I need an ambulance."

"What are they doing here?"

"I want my lawyer."

"And I want world peace, but that ain't happening either." He chambered a round and put the silencer against Lucky's temple. I didn't know who the guy was, but I definitely liked his style.

"Don't kill me!"

"Then answer the question!"

"They flew in to interrogate the captain of the sub…and these clowns." He nodded at me and Tangles.

"Why?"

"They think one of them stole the submarine."

"How can Rico Cordero fly in to St. Maarten? He's an international fugitive."

The senator closed his eyes and faintly shook his head. "You don't know what he's capable of. The stories I've heard… I don't want to cross him."

Mystery Man stuck the silencer in Lucky's ear. "And you don't know what *I'm* capable of, so answer the question or this walls gonna have your brains splattered all over it."

"This is torture. I'm in pain! I need medical attention!"

"You want the pain to go away? Just say the word; you're only a finger twitch away."

"Who *is* this guy?" whispered Tangles. I shook my head, wondering the same thing. The senator opened his eyes, and they were teary. I wasn't sure if it was from fear of having his brains blown out or from talking about this Rico character, but he was a broken man.

"He's got the directeur of the airport on his payroll. His jet's parked there."

"Which airport?"

"Grand Case."

"Okay, now we're getting somewhere. Where's your car?"

"There's a tree blocking the entrance to the driveway. I had to leave it on the road."

"Where are the keys?" He started reaching for his pocket, but Mystery Man told him to stop and looked at me. "Shagball, reach in his pocket and get his keys. See what else he's got too." As I knelt down and pulled out the car keys and a phone, I said, "How do you know our names? Who *are* you?"

"We'll talk later. Right now we need to get out of here." I pulled the knife out and held it in the light to examine it.

"What are you doing?" he asked.

"Dude, it's a Forschner. Can I keep it?"

"Really, Kit?" said Holly.

"Knock yourself out," said Mystery Man as he began to zip-tie the senator's hands and feet. "Just try not to stab anybody; I saw how you shoot."

"C'mon, man. That was semi-intentional."

"What are you doing?" complained the senator. "I need an ambulance!"

"I'm gift wrapping you. Don't worry, I'm sure you'll get better treatment than you deserve." He reached under his poncho, pulled out something that looked like a thimble, and slipped it on his thumb. Then he delicately removed a thin protective cap.

"What's that?" asked the senator.

"A nightcap." He pressed the thimble behind the senator's ear, and his head immediately flopped to the side. With the senator secured and knocked out, Mystery Man rose to his feet and said, "Let's get out of here."

"What about Genevieve? We can't just *leave* her here too," said Holly.

"We can and we will. I'll make sure she's well-tended to." He pulled his phone out and stepped into the hall again.

"Don't worry about me," said Genevieve. "Listen to him and get out of here while you can. I just hope you can forgive me someday for what I've done."

Holly stepped to her bed and reached down for her hand. "Thank you for telling me what really happened."

"I owed you that much at the very least. Your aunt was a wonderful person and so was Joseph. They didn't deserve what happened. I pray every day that Patrick found all the happiness they were denied." A tear rolled down Genevieve's face, and Holly wiped it away.

"I don't know how, but I'm going to find him if it takes the rest of my life. It's a vow I made to Millie."

"When you do, tell him I love him and that I'm sorry for taking him away from his mother."

"I will. You can count on it."

"You're so much like your aunt, so beautiful and strong. Even though I'm ashamed for what I've done, I'm glad to have met you."

"Me too. Take care." Holly bent down and kissed her on the forehead.

Mystery Man stuck his head through the doorway. "We gotta move! I just got word the French authorities are climbing all over the *Lady G.* Let's go!"

We ran out of the villa, and Mystery Man said he needed to grab something out of the shed. As we started down the drive, Holly stopped. "Wait, I left my purse in the garage!"

"You go on. I'll get it," I said. I ran back into the garage and clicked on my Surefire, quickly spotting her purse on a shelf. As I grabbed it, I noticed an open tackle box with a knife sheath about the size of the one I was holding. I slipped the knife in it and stuck it through my belt. I ran down the drive and caught up to the others as they piled into the car. Mystery Man stood by the passenger door holding a small backpack and asked, "Can you drive? I need to make another call."

"No problem. Where are we going?"

"To the airport. There's a jet we need to steal."

Chapter 57

Because of the tree in the road, I turned the car around and headed down the mountain. The storm had passed, but it was still blowing about twenty knots and there was lots of debris to avoid. I mentioned to Mystery Man that I didn't know the way to the airport, and he said, "Just keep following the road until you see the sign."

He pulled out his fancy phone again and dialed. Nobody said spit as he conversed on the line. "I'm with the Hi-Lo Gang; we had a situation at the villa. You need to send an ambulance. The senator's been shot, and his mother may have a broken hip... No, it's not a fatal wound. I needed some information. Send the DEA too. I've got everything on tape, and he's in it up to his eyeballs... *What?* Hang on a second." He covered the speaker slot and looked back at Tangles. "I thought you said the sub captain was on the boat."

"He was.... You're saying he's not there?"

"No, they only found Remy's body. Shit." He took his hand off the slot and resumed the conversation. "They're saying he was on the boat when they left. He must have come to and slipped away. No, I don't know where Cordero is either, the senator claims he was following him to meet his son at the dock but never made it… I don't know, but there's no way he came this far and left before—stop the car!"

We were rounding a bend, and I stopped in the middle of the road. "What? What is it?" I asked.

"Hang on, sir, I just saw something." He left the phone on the seat, and we all piled out of the car after him. He carefully walked to the edge of the road and pointed over the side. "Look, there are some lights on the side of the hill; do you see them?" Sure enough, about a hundred feet down, I could see what appeared to be headlights shining at a weird angle.

"Yeah, I see 'em."

"Me too," said Holly. "Is that a car?"

"No," said Mystery Man. "I think it's a van. I think it's the van that was following the senator."

I shined my Surefire down the side of the hill, and I could see that some trees were broken off at the top. "Look, the treetops are broken; somebody definitely went over the side. What should we do?"

"We need to go; the boss can deal with it. C'mon!"

We got back in the car, and Mystery Man picked up the phone as we continued down the mountain. "You still there? Good. It looks like I found Cordero's van. He went off the road about two miles north of the villa. What? No, there's no way we can get to him. Right… agreed, if we don't get them off the island before the French get a hold of them, they may never get off… No, we can't wait that long. I'm hoping you can find me a pilot…yes, a pilot…I don't know what kind it is, the kind Colombian drug lords fly. Their jet's standing by at the Grand Case airport. The directeur is on their payroll…I'm not sure how, but if you find me a pilot, I'll find a way... I know it's ballsy, but I figured as long as we got their sub, we may as well snatch their jet too. Besides, it's the quickest way out of here...Okay, let me know...thanks boss." Click.

"Just to be clear, your boss is the guy I talked to from the Coast Guard chopper, right?" I asked. "The one who sounds like Dan Tanna?"

"I haven't heard him use that voice in a while, but yeah, that's him."

"You've been following us?"

"I've been trying to, but you haven't made it easy. I didn't catch up with you until tonight."

"You have a name?"

"You can call me Rafe."

"Well, Rafe, thanks for saving our asses back there."

"Duly noted, but I'm just doing my job... and it's not done yet."

"Right, we still need to steal Cordero's jet."

"That's the plan."

"That *is* ballsy," said Tangles. "Basket-sized-ballsy... I like it."

"You would," said Holly. "But I don't, I mean, we really didn't do anything ...right? I'm not sure about this."

"Maybe *you* didn't do anything;" replied Rafe, "but your friends here can't say the same. It's bad enough they incurred the wrath of the Cordero brothers, but they also left the *Lady G* on a French beach along with the senator's dead son. Try explaining that to the *Gendarmerie.*"

"The who?" Asked Tangles.

"The French police; it's a whole different ballgame here."

"He's right," I agreed. "The French played both sides in the war. I'd trust a wet fart over a Frenchman."

"Wait a second!" Said Holly. "Remy isn't *really* dead; they just knocked him out with a sedative. You were just bluffing the senator, right, Kit?"

We reached the bottom of the mountain, and I saw the picture of an airplane on a sign. It was a good opportunity to change the subject. "Look, here's the airport turnoff; we must be getting close."

"I'm ready to earn my wings," said Tangles. "Let's steal a jet and get the hell out of here. I don't need some Clouseau giving me the third degree. Fuck the French."

"Tangles? You said you just knocked him out. Were you *lying* to me?"

"In, uh, in what context?"

"Just answer the question!"

"Oh, shit, I thought he was your cousin. I didn't want to upset you. It was an accident, I swear."

"Oh my God! You killed him? I *said* it was a bad plan!"

"He tried to shoot me! It all happened so fast. He just kinda fell forward...onto the, uh, needle I was trying to stick him with, and it, uh, went in his heart."

"It's the truth, Holly," I added. "I know it sounds bad, but it really was an accident."

"*Sounds bad?*" said Rafe. "Good luck getting the police to believe you. That sounds worse than a Yoko Ono record."

Holly made a grunting sound and said, "I *hate it* when you guys lie to me."

"Actually," I answered, "it was Tangles who lied to you, not me, you know, I'm just saying..."

"And I'm just saying bullcrap! And you know I hate it when you say 'I'm just saying'… I *know* what you're saying, 'cause I heard you say it! You don't have to tell me you just said it!"

There was about five seconds of silence before Tangles had to push her over the edge. "Geez, Holly, he was just *saying…*"

"Ugggh! How do I put up with you two?!"

"I'm beginning to wonder that myself," said Rafe.

"Here we are," I announced as we pulled into the airport. "Where do you want me to go?"

"Pull into that parking area over there and back into a spot so we can see the terminal."

After I did as instructed, he told me to pull out the senator's phone and gave me a number to call. A few seconds later, his phone started flashing, and he said, "Good, now we have each other's numbers."

'What now?"

"Now we wait for—" His phone lit up again, and he said, "this." He answered, "Yes sir, we just got here… excellent…tell him I'm on my way in…right…the pilots' lounge…thank you sir…wait! There's one thing I forgot to mention. Whoever goes after Cordero needs to know there was a gigantic snake in the cargo area of the van…yes, a snake. It had to be over twenty feet long…some kind of anaconda, I think…right, me too. Okay, okay, I'll call when we're in the air." Click.

"Okay, we caught a break. Here's the deal. The last few flights out got scratched due to the storm and several flight crews are holed up in the pilots' lounge. One of the pilots is an ex-US Air Force colonel who does occasional off-the-grid work, and he's our flyboy. I'm going to pose as a DEA honcho, and we're gonna find Cordero's jet. Once we snatch it and get positioned for takeoff, I'll give you a call."

"How are you gonna pose as a DEA honcho?"

He took off his poncho and asked me to shine the light inside his backpack. He pulled out a DEA badge on a lanyard and said, "With this."

"What's with the snake?" I asked.

"Until now, it was just a rumor the Cordero's used a giant snake for interrogating suspected turncoats and informants. Not any more. It almost got me in the garage back at the villa. If they went to the trouble to bring it all the way here, they planned on using it." I glanced at Tangles and Holly in the back seat who both had their mouths hanging open at the thought of being interrogated by a giant anaconda.

"How, uh, how exactly do you, uh, suppose that would work?"

"Use your imagination, and be glad that you don't know the answer."

"Jesus."

After checking his weapon, he pulled out some ammo and re-loaded Remy's gun before handing it to Tangles and nodding at me. "I take it you're a better shot than the ceiling killer here."

"With my eyes closed," answered Tangles.

"For the last time," I protested. "It was the doorframe not the ceiling, alright? I didn't want to hit Holly."

"Whatever," said Tangles. "It looked like the ceiling to me."

"Everything looks like the ceiling to you."

"That was low."

"*You're* low."

"Guys? *Really?*" said Holly, who then turned to Rafe. "See what I put up with?"

"Yeah, you definitely got your hands full. Anyways, Tangles, you shouldn't need the gun, but you have it just in case." Rafe stuffed the poncho and his goggles in the backpack and draped the badge over his neck. "One of you needs to bring my backpack."

"Wait a second. How are we gonna get through security?" I asked. "You think they're really gonna let us through with all the stuff you got in your backpack?"

"Yeah, dude," added Tangles. "I got no ID and a loaded 38. Something tells me they're gonna frown on that."

"Who said anything about going through security?"

For once Holly, Tangles, and I were on the same page, and we answered in unison. "*What?*"

"This isn't JFK or O'Hare. The only thing between the parking lot and the runway is that chain-link fence over there." He pointed at the fence, about a hundred and fifty yards away. "When the jets ready for takeoff, I'll give you a call, and you just drive through it."

"WHAT?"

"Are you *serious?*" asked Holly. "You want us to crash through the fence and drive out on the runway?"

"Yes ma'am. As it's been pointed out, going through security isn't an option. The police are looking for us, and I promise you, they don't serve brie and chardonnay in French prisons."

"I don't even like chardonnay. I prefer Pinot Grigio."

"You get the idea. So, are you guys in or out?"

"I always wondered what it would be like to be in a *Die Hard* movie," I said. "I guess it's time to find out. I'm in."

"Tangles?" said Rafe.

"Forget what I said about being basket-sized-ballsy, this puts King Kong's nut sac to shame. *Hell yeah* I'm in, and if any of those...what'd you call them? Edamame's? Come chasing after us, I'll shoot out their fancy French tires!" Tangles held up the 38 and grinned.

"*Gendarmeries*...they're called *Gendarmeries.*"

"Whatever."

"Please, only shoot if it's absolutely necessary. Holly? What about you?"

"This is nuts, but I guess I don't have much choice. I'm in too."

"Excellent. Okay then, just wait for my call. Here we go." He opened the door to get out, and Holly said, "One more thing."

Rafe turned to look at her. "What's that?"

"If we pull this off and manage to get airborne, anybody who asks me to get them a drink better have a parachute."

Chapter 58

We sat in the car for about ten minutes discussing our plight before I couldn't take it any longer and unzipped Rafe's backpack.

"What are you doing?" asked Holly.

"Checking out what else he's got in here." I clicked on my Surefire and pushed the poncho to the side.

"You shouldn't be going through his stuff."

"I shouldn't be crashing through an airport fence in a stolen car either...relax—Holy crap!"

"What is it?" asked Tangles.

I started lifting out badges one after the other. "Look at this! He's got an FBI badge, CIA, Homeland Security...what is this? NSA? Jesus, who *is* this guy?"

"He's a bad wammajamma, that's who he is."

"How can he have that many ID's?" asked Holly. "He can't be with *all* those agencies... can he?"

"I don't think so, and let's not forget he's using a DEA badge right now."

"He's gotta be CIA," said Tangles. "Hey, can I see those goggles he was wearing?"

I handed him the goggles and said, "I don't know, the guy who smoothed things over with the cops when we had the showdown with Donny Nutz flatly denied being CIA. He insinuated he was with some *other* agency."

"Really, Kit?" said Holly as she rolled her eyes, "You think a real CIA agent would admit he was with the CIA just because you asked him?"

"Yeah, I know, but he seemed like he was telling the truth."

"CIA agents are professional liars—it's what they do."

"You have a point there… sorta like lawyers and politicians."

"Wow, are these things cool!" Tangles had the goggles on, and he was looking out the back window. "They're night vision goggles, dude. They sure would come in handy for late night fishing. I can see *everything.*"

"Can you see how stupid you look in them, too? You look like a baby ET after visiting a drunken optometrist."

"I'm going to ignore your lowly digs because these things are *so friggin' cool.* Look, they even have zoom lenses." Suddenly, the lenses extended out about eight inches.

"I bet you wish you had something else that extended out like that."

"Kit? My God, you're not in junior high anymore." Holly shook her head in semi-feigned disgust before adding, "Hey! I see a plane taxiing out on the runway; I hope that's Rafe."

I looked at my watch and threw in my two cents. "It's gotta be. It's almost three in the morning."

"Uh-oh," said Tangles.

"Was that an 'uh-oh, the boats sinking?' Or was that just an 'uh-oh, I think I crapped my pants?'"

"It was an uh-oh, the…what did he call them again? The Generalities are coming."

"They're Gendarmeries," corrected Holly.

"The cops?" I asked

"Yup," confirmed Tangles. "There's a car with flashers turning into the parking lot."

"Shit."

"What are we gonna do?" asked Holly.

I craned my neck to the side and saw a pair of small headlights enter the parking lot. "Can you tell what kind of car it is, Tangles?"

"It's, uh, something small. I dunno…. Shit! It's coming this way."

"Gimme those goggles," I ordered. "Everybody get down; maybe it's just a routine patrol." Tangles handed me the goggles, and I put them in the backpack and zipped it up. Then I shoved it on the floor and lay sideways across the passenger's seat with my fingers crossed. After about fifteen seconds, I asked Tangles to take a peek from the backseat. As soon as he looked out from under the driver's side headrest, he said, "Fuck! It stopped right in front of us. It's blocking us in!"

I sat up, turned on the headlights, and then handed the cell phone to Holly. "You better hold my calls."

"What are you? What are you doing?" She asked with apprehension.

The police car was a tiny, two-door, Renault, and the passenger's side was only two feet from our front bumper. I could see that the officer was by himself, and as he exited the driver's side, he had a hand up in front of his eyes to shield them from our headlights.

"I'm gonna try to buy us some time. Hang on, and stay down." I threw the senator's SUV into drive and floored it. We slammed into the passenger's side of the police car and the front end of the Renault clipped the officer's knee and sent him sprawling off to the side.

"You hit him!" cried Holly.

I kept the pedal to the metal and pushed the tiny Renault across the aisle and up against another vehicle. There was no way the driver's door could be opened, and as I reversed, I was confident that the crumpled passenger's side was inaccessible too. I considered driving around the downed officer but saw him reaching for his weapon and decided to keep going in reverse. As we accelerated backward, I yelled, "Stay down!" Shots rang out as we hit and went over the curb. The windshield shattered and the rearview mirror flew into the backseat.

Holly pointed out the obvious and shouted, "He's shooting at us!"

"What did you expect!?" We fishtailed backward for fifty yards down a small embankment and came to rest parallel to the airport access road. I shifted into drive and jumped another curb as I crossed over the access road toward the runway. Then the rear window shattered, and Tangles shouted, "Step on it, dude! Frenchy shoots better than you!"

"Everybody okay?" I asked.

"We are in so much trouble," bemoaned Holly.

"Hang on, we're about to get in more!" The SUV bounced again as we hit another curb, and I accelerated up the opposite embankment fast enough to get airborne when we hit the top. After landing with a jolt, Holly screamed, "Rafe hasn't even—wait! The phone's ringing!" She answered, "Okay...Okay, we're on our way!" Click.

"You're gonna kill us!" hollered Tangles.

"Better me than Frenchy. Here we go boys and girls, it's crunch time!" I floored it the last thirty yards, and we hit the fence going sixty. Just like Rafe predicted, we crashed through with ease. Unfortunately, a section of fence got tangled under the car, and the barbed-wire began slicing into the tires. "Where's the jet?" I asked, as we motored across the grassy area adjacent to the runway.

"Turn right!" answered Holly. She leaned over the front seat and pointed. "Over there! You can see the lights."

Naturally, it was at the other end of the runway, nearly a half mile away. I kept the pedal down, and as we barreled past the darkened tower, the front left tire disintegrated. "Oh, c'mon!" I said as the rim started grinding on the runway. I fought the wheel as it pulled hard to the left, and sparks started flying up on the windshield. "Is there anybody on our tail?!" I asked as I tried to keep our speed up.

"I can't see! Cover your ears!" said Tangles.

"How am I supposed to?—BOOM! BOOM!" I flinched as Tangles shot out the splintered rear window, and the smell of gunpowder filled the car. "What the fuck are you doing!?" I yelled.

"Just making a hole."

I glanced over my shoulder as he kicked out a chunk of the shattered window.

"You guys are crazy!' cried Holly.

"Coast is clear, dude! No Frenchy's in—oops, we got company."

"I *hate* company! What kind?"

"Looks like a police van; you better go faster!" The right rear tire was next to shred apart, and there were more fireworks on the runway. Thankfully, it wasn't the left rear tire, or I would have had little chance of driving in a straight line.

"Are you kidding? How close are they?!"

"You have a good lead, but you better step on it!"

I estimated that we were about three hundred yards from the jet and decided to put what was left of the hammer down. The sound of the rims grinding on the runway and the tangled fence scraping along the undercarriage was God-awful as I pushed the SUV up to fifty-five. A hundred yards from the jet, I could see the stairs were down, and I yelled, "Get ready to bail!" Fifty feet out, I slammed on the brakes, and we screeched to a stop only fifteen feet from the left wingtip.

I grabbed Rafe's backpack and rushed up the stairs behind Holly, with Tangles trailing. Rafe was in the doorway, urging us to hurry, and I could hear the engines whine as the pilot prepared for a high-performance takeoff. "Strap yourselves in! We gotta go!" Rafe yelled.

As soon as Holly disappeared into the cabin, I heard gunfire and looked over my shoulder. Tangles was kneeling at the bottom of the stairs, unloading the 38 at the oncoming van which was a good hundred and fifty yards away. "C'MON!" yelled, Rafe. Seconds later he shoved Tangles into the seat next to me and then jumped in the co-pilot's seat. He looked back momentarily to confirm that we were strapped in, and then nodded at the pilot. "Let 'er rip, Colonel!" The colonel released the brakes, and the tires smoked before we rocketed down the runway, pinned to the backs of our seats. Seconds later we were airborne, oblivious to the machine-gun fire strafing the night sky around us.

Chapter 59

In a matter of minutes, we reached a cruising altitude of forty-thousand feet, and the pilot looked back over his shoulder at us.

"You guys sure know how to show a retired Air Force colonel a good time! What the hell did you do to piss them off so much? Swipe some croissants or something?"

"Nah," I answered. "We just had a little fender bender in the parking lot that got out of hand."

Holly was sitting directly behind Tangles and said, "Don't believe a word he says. He rammed a police car and ran over an officer. He thought he was playing *Grand Theft Auto.*"

I turned to defend myself. "I didn't run over *any-body*. He twisted his knee after bumping into the front of his own car."

"Which you rammed."

"That was awesome!" added Tangles.

"Are you complaining, or would you rather be sitting in a French jail working on the screen play to *Papillon II?*"

"Hey now," said the pilot. "No more talk about French jails. St. Maarten is history thanks to this fine airplane we managed to acquire. Rafe has me taking you to Palm Beach International. Is that where you high rollers live?"

"Not hardly," I replied. "I'm from Lantana."

"I never heard of Lantana, but I've heard of Lake Worth."

"That's the next city north. A good friend of mine's the mayor there, her name's Pam Triolo. She's really helped them turn things around. Maybe someday it'll be as nice as Lantana. We have a solid Mayor too—Dave Stewart.

"This thing can make it all the way to Palm Beach?" asked Tangles.

"This *thing?*" The pilot shook his head and glanced at Rafe. "I can see your little friend knows as much about airplanes as he does about handguns."

"Hey, man, I'm right here. Don't talk like I'm not. What the hell do you mean, I don't know about handguns?"

"That reminds me," said Rafe. "Gimme the gun." Tangles reached in his pocket and reluctantly handed it to him. "What he means is, a weapon like this is good for shooting only at extremely close range. What were you thinking shooting at that police van from a hundred and fifty yards?"

"I was trying to shoot out their tires. Didn't you see them swerve? I think I got one."

"They were probably swerving to avoid all the shit falling off our car," I said.

"Bullshit, I *know* I got one."

"Anyways," said the pilot, "let me tell you what this 'thing' can do. This is an Eclipse 500; one of the finest jets in its class. It's got a range of roughly twelve-hundred miles, which is just about what we need to get to Palm Beach. But thanks to the extra fuel tank installed in the rear cargo area, we're good for at least sixteen-hundred miles."

"How fast can it go?" I asked.

"Right now we're cruising at Mach .64."

"Thanks, Chuck Yeager. In English, please?"

"Three-hundred-and-seventy knots."

"Which is...?"

"Four-hundred-and-twenty-five miles an hour; we'll be there in about three hours." I looked at my watch, and it was three o'clock in the morning. With the one hour time difference, the flight would put us into Palm Beach around five. Perfect, just when the breakfast joints start opening up.

"But that's not all this bird's got," he continued. "It also has a TCAF system, which makes it especially nice when you're flying blind or by instrumentation like we are now."

"TCAF?" asked, Holly.

"Yes, sorry, it means, Traffic Collision Avoidance System."

"I like avoiding collisions... unlike some people I know."

"Very funny," I commented.

"But one of the niftiest options this baby has is thrust reverse, which enables it to land on short runways."

"How short?"

The pilot nodded in Tangles' direction.

"You know," said Tangles. "I really liked you when we were screaming down the runway. Now? Not so much."

"I'm just kidding. What do you mean by short?"

"Well, believe it or not, we have an airport in Lantana. My buddy Layne flies out of it all the time. You think you could land us there instead of PBI?"

"Son, I could land a shooting star on a railroad car… a moving one if I had to. I'll have to check the runway stats to be sure, but it's fine with me if it's fine with Rafe."

Rafe said, "No problem here."

"Alright, then. Why don't you call whoever you need to call to let Miami control know who we are and that we'll be entering the ADIZ in about two and a half? Also ask them what the runway length at Lantana is."

"Will do."

"What's the ADIZ?" I inquired.

"The American Defense Identification Zone. All aircraft need to identify themselves when they get within twelve miles of the coast. Nothing can ruin you're day faster than being shot down."

"As long as you're making calls," said Holly, "can you arrange to have our rental car returned and our luggage sent back from the Hibiscus Resort? My aunt's remains are in an urn in my carry-on and if something were to happen to them I'd be devastated… Please?" She flashed her beautiful smile, and I knew what the answer would be. Rafe smiled back at her and replied, "It's already in the works. I'll send word to handle your carry-on with the utmost care."

"Thank you *so* much…for everything."

"No problem, ma'am. I'm just doing my job."

"Well, you do it very well."

Wanting the mutual-appreciation fest to end as quickly as possible, I said, "Okay, then, let's let Rafe do his job so we don't get shot down." Holly gave me a look, and Rafe chuckled as he pulled out his DICK phone.

The pilot said, "Everybody just sit back and relax, get some shut-eye if you want, we'll be in Lantana before you know it." A few minutes later, Rafe covered his phone with one hand and said to the pilot, "The runway in Lantana is thirty-five-hundred feet."

"Hell, we won't even need the thrust reverse," he replied.

Tangles was across the aisle from me, and when he reclined his seat, he glanced over and said, "How did I not notice this? There's a mini fridge behind you."

"What?" I craned my neck, and sure enough, the sixth seat had been removed and there was a compact refrigerator in its place. Tangles got up and opened the fridge. "Hot damn, there's beer! Who wants one besides me and Shag?"

Holly looked over at the open fridge and announced, "There's bottled water too. I guess it's for the non-alcoholics on the flight."

"I'll take a water," said the pilot. Rafe was on the phone but signaled he wanted a water too. Tangles said, "Suit yourself. Here you go," and handed waters to Rafe and the pilot after giving one to Holly. Then he handed me a bottle of a Colombian beer called Usaquen Stout and sat down with his own. We popped the tops and clinked bottles before taking a long pull. It was strong but surprisingly good.

"Wow, that's got a kick," commented Tangles.

"It's definitely hearty," I agreed, "I bet it goes good with alpaca."

Chapter 60

A couple hours later, I woke up to the voice of the pilot. "Miami, this is Eclipse three-five-two-bravo-bravo entering the ADIZ."

"Roger that, Eclipse. You are cleared to proceed to the Palm Beach County Park Airport in Lantana. PBI control will take it from here."

"Thanks, Miami." Click. The pilot looked over his shoulder at me and said, "I didn't know that was the name of the airport in Lantana. I'm pretty sure my old buddy Dave works there."

"I didn't know either."

Minutes later a similar exchange took place with the tower at PBI.

"Palm Beach, this is Eclipse three-five-two-bravo-bravo. I have Palm Beach County Park Airport in sight, requesting to cancel flight plan."

"Roger that, Eclipse. Flight plan canceled. Have a good day."

We touched down without incident and taxied over to a waiting cab. At the bottom of the stairs, we said our good-byes in the headlights of the cab. Holly gave Rafe and the pilot a big hug, and Tangles and I shook hands with them. As I was shaking the pilot's hand, he said, "You know, you look vaguely familiar."

"You like to fish?"

"Well, *hell yeah.*"

"You ever watch fishing shows?"

"Sure I do, in fact—" He did a double take and looked down at Tangles. "Wait a minute. You're not those guys that caught that big tuna a while back... are you?"

"Guilty as charged. That's us, *Fishing on the Edge with Shagball and Tangles.*"

"Well, I'll be damned. I'm retired Lieutenant Colonel Paul Strama, at your service. Wait till the boys back in Gainesville hear about this!" Then he turned to Rafe. "Why the heck didn't you tell me we had celebrities on board? Better yet, why were they getting shot at by the French police?"

"It's a long story, Colonel, and classified too, unfortunately."

"Of course. I know how it goes." He turned back to me and said, "Well, it was nice meeting you Shagball. Here's my card in case you ever need someone to fly you to the islands or something." He handed me a card and turned to Tangles. "Hey, I hope there's no hard feelings over anything I said. I was just kidding around."

"Don't worry about it. I'm use to abuse."

"Glad to hear it. Everybody take care now." He saluted and climbed up into the jet.

I turned to Rafe and said, "That's it?"

"Pretty much, but the boss wanted me to remind you that keeping quiet about everything could be very beneficial to you."

"Could be or will be?"

"I talked to him on the plane while you were sleeping. If you can keep your mouth shut, believe me, it will be *very* beneficial."

"Excellent, I like benefits. So, we're good to go?"

"At your leisure. Just try to stay out of trouble for a while, okay?"

"I'll try; it seems to be harder and harder to do, though."

"Give it your best shot."

"I'll pretend I'm dating Pat Benatar. Thanks again for stepping in and saving our ass."

"It was my pleasure; everyone should get to shoot a senator just once." We laughed and shook hands one more time before he saluted and climbed back in the jet. The three of us piled into the taxi, and as we were driving down Lantana road, we heard the roar of the jet as it streaked past, wings tipping in acknowledgement.

Chapter 61

After spending the previous day sleeping, eating, and sleeping some more, the three of us woke up ready to go fishing. Hambone picked us up at Holly's, and we jumped on board his old center-stack, diesel-spewing, charter boat, the *Ham it Up*. As soon as we got on board, I called Ferby at the hospital in Miami where he was recuperating and was glad to hear his scruffy voice tell me that the surgery had gone well. He said he was being transferred to Delray the next day, and I promised we would come see him. It was a couple days before Thanksgiving, and it was cool by south Florida standards, which meant it was about sixty-eight. A minor cold front passed through overnight, and a light wind was coming out of the north.

We chugged out the Boynton Inlet and stopped outside the south jetty to catch some pilchards and mullet for live baiting. We also caught a handful of blue runners and even managed a couple stray goggle-eyes. With a live well full of bait, we headed north, trolling some Clark spoons along the way. The Spanish mackerel were moving south, and we managed to pick up a dozen nice ones by the time we reached the Ritz Carlton in Manalapan. Hambone sent a couple of pilchards down in a hundred-and-twenty feet of water and put the goggle-eyes out on balloon rigs. Within an hour we released two sailfish and put a twenty-pound dolphin in the box. Fishing was good and everyone was enjoying themselves.

During a break in the action, Tangles told Holly he was moving out of the apartment she owned in the building that housed the C-Love office. He explained to her that he found an apartment next to the Old Key Lime House in Lantana so he could be nearer to his long-lost father, Rudy, who bartended there. He added that his mom was now living with Rudy in South Palm Beach, and he wanted to spend more time with the two of them.

While it's true that spending time with his parents was a factor, the other big reason was the pretty waitresses and barmaids at the OKLH. I had recently pointed out to him that he played all his cards at the Three Jacks and Habana Boat in Boynton, and it was high time to move on to greener pastures. When he mentioned that he was hoping to meet some more refined women, I told him about the great wine bar and restaurant, Tapas, which was up the street from the OKLH on Ocean Avenue. It had, in fact, been voted the most romantic restaurant in Palm Beach County the year prior. I convinced him that when the new Lantana Bridge opened up, Ocean Avenue would be hopping, and he would be right in the thick of it. Holly agreed that it was a good move, and when Hambone and Tangles went up on the bridge, she broached the subject of unfinished business.

"We never got to see Millie and Joseph's property."

"*Or* look for the gold." I added.

"I never got to spread the rest of her ashes either. I don't know, maybe it's a sign I should save them for Luck—I mean, Patrick. Kit, how am I ever going to find him?"

"We don't even know if he's alive, baby."

"Please don't say that. He is… I know he is. I can feel it."

I put my arm around her and gave her a kiss. "I know better than to question your intuition. Sorry about that."

"We don't even know what name he's using. It could be anything."

"We'll find him. One way or another, we'll find him." I tried to sound convincing, but in my mind I was thinking, *Shaggy, you are so full of shit.*

Suddenly her phone rang, and she pulled it out of her pocket. "You gotta be kidding me," she said as she looked at the display.

"Who is it?"

"It's Dan Tanna again."

"You better answer it."

She answered, "Hello? Yes, this is she…thank you…yes, it's good to be back, even if our trip was cut short. Yes, the fishing's good— wait, how did you know we were fishing?...uh-huh…of course… Kit? Yes, he's right here. Here you go…what?...it was nice talking to you too, here you go." She handed me the phone and winked. "I have to admit, he *does* have a nice voice."

I rolled my eyes and answered, "Yes?"

"Mr. Jansen, that was quite some departure you made from St. Maarten. The French police are none too happy about it."

"Hey, what can I say? When you gotta go, you gotta go."

"Well, you definitely went, I'll give you that. That maneuver you made ramming the police car up against another vehicle so the officer couldn't chase after you was pretty slick. It left quite an impression on some high-ranking people, me included."

"It seemed like a good idea at the time. I hope the officer didn't get hurt too bad."

"Fortunately, no, or things would be a little tougher. Taking control of the senator's boat, navigating it into Tucker Bay, and managing to beach it during a tropical storm was impressive too…even *if* his son ended up dead."

"Actually, Holly was the one who figured out the GPS. Without the coordinates plugged in, we would have been up shits creek. Remy taking a needle to the heart was accidental, although he *was* shooting at us."

"When you're a cocaine trafficker, accidents happen. You play with fire, and sometimes you get burned."

"That's the way the cookie crumbles. I'd throw in another cliché if I could think of one."

"How about loose lips sink ships?"

"I'm not a believer in that any more. *My* ship sank, and my lips are tighter than a clam's ass. To some people, losing a boat might not be a big deal, but to me, it's everything." I looked at Holly who was reeling up another dolphin and corrected myself. "Well, it's *almost* everything. I didn't have any insurance and lost all my fishing gear too. You have *no idea* what that stuff costs. Plus, like I told you before, I just invested a bunch of money into high-def cameras for my fishing show, which no longer exists without a boat."

"Are you through?"

"No, I had a Tupperware container on board with eight grand in cash."

"Easy come, easy go."

"Easy for you, not for me."

"I was kidding, Mr. Jansen. Your role in foiling one of the largest cocaine shipments in US history will not go unrewarded as long as you continue to remain silent about what transpired."

"Hey, like I said, you can call me Quahog 'cause my lips are watertight."

"The same goes for your girlfriend and sidekick; they have to keep quiet too."

"Holly's not a problem, and I'll kill Tangles if I have to…just kidding. They won't be a problem."

"I didn't think so."

"Okay then, what's the reward?"

"You'll be reimbursed for the loss of your boat and all the contents, including the cash."

Although it sounded fair, my boat was thirty years old, and its book value was negligible. What was it worth, twenty grand if I was lucky? Even if he gave me fifty grand for the contents, what would that leave me? Seventy grand? I couldn't find anything remotely comparable for seventy grand, and even if I did, I'd have no gear to fish with. I briefly thought of all my Black Bart lures now residing on the bottom of the Caribbean and almost cried.

"Mr. Jansen? Are you still there?"

"Yeah, I'm here."

"You don't sound too excited."

"Why would I be? My boat was thirty years old. It's not worth spit, but you already know that."

"Indeed I do, which is why I'm prepared to make you an offer you can't refuse."

"I'm glad we're back to clichés, but don't the guys that get that offer usually end up dead?"

"We all die one way or the other; it's how you live that matters, wouldn't you agree?"

"Wow, I never knew Dan Tanna was such a philosopher—must have been all that calcium. Okay, I'll bite, what's the offer?"

"How would you like full time use of any fishing boat of your choice, rigged to your specifications, with all maintenance and expenses paid by the US Government...including gas."

"Gimme a break, what do I have to give up, my first born son? Okay, it's a deal."

"This is no joke, Mr. Jansen."

"I'm not joking either; you can have my first girl, too. Weddings are expensive. C'mon, whats the catch?"

"It's simple; once or twice a year you may be asked to take the boat somewhere to do some intelligence gathering, that's it."

"Intelligence gathering? Now I *know* you're joking. Have you *seen* my show?"

"Yes, it's precisely why you're being made this offer. A fishing show offers the perfect cover for traveling just about anywhere without raising the suspicion of local authorities and government agencies. I run a number of highly-trained agents from all types of military and law enforcement backgrounds, but by their very nature, they tend to act and think the same. This is usually a good thing, but it can also leave them vulnerable to detection by the other side. More importantly, there are places you'll be able to get to under the guise of your fishing show that would be extremely difficult to get to otherwise. If you accept my offer, one or more of my agents will assist you during these assignments and possibly become part of your fishing crew. Someone like Rafe, for example."

"I don't believe it; you're fucking *serious*, aren't you?"

"Absolutely."

"But why me? There's a zillion guys with fishing shows out there."

"Well, for one thing, no one in their right mind would ever suspect you of being involved with an intelligence agency after seeing your show."

"I can't argue with that."

"But the clincher is we *know* you, Mr. Jansen. Twice in the last year you have more or less inadvertently stepped into the middle of incredibly dangerous situations involving hardened criminals and stepped back out relatively unscathed. The same can't be said for those who underestimated you and your pals."

"Luck is fickle and fleeting, like a woman's love. Here today, gone later today."

"*Now* who's the philosopher? If I believed you were just lucky, we wouldn't be having this conversation. You've demonstrated remarkable resourcefulness, intuition, and the ability to think—"

"Please don't say 'outside the box.' I hate that term."

"You're not the only one. I was about to say, 'the ability to think on your feet.'"

"That's an acceptable cliché, even if I do some of my best thinking in the horizontal with a cold beverage in hand."

"You can get an icemaker."

"A reverse osmosis one?"

"Mr. Jansen, I'm not sure you're fully grasping what I'm telling you. You can pick *whatever* fishing and comfort-related accessories you want, and I'll handle the rest."

"What do you mean, 'the rest?'"

"Naturally, it will be fitted with the most advanced communications and navigation equipment available, as well as anti-piracy and security features."

"You mean it'll have Q-like gadgets from a James Bond movie?"

"Gadgets are toys; I prefer to call them devices. Trust me, the devices I install to ensure the safety of those aboard will make Q look like l-m-n-o-p."

"Let me see if I got this straight. You're telling me I get the boat of my dreams, with all expenses and gas paid for by Uncle Sam?"

"Correct."

"And I get to use it year-round for my fishing show?"

"Yes."

"We can go wherever we want on your dime?"

"Dime is a mischaracterization, but yes."

"And all I have to do is take the boat somewhere you direct me, once or twice a year, to help your agents gather information?"

"You *are* a quick study."

"Funny guy— And I don't have to go to some kind of boot camp?"

"Well, based on what happened at the senator's villa, you'll require some basic firearms training."

"I was aiming high so as not to shoot my girlfriend. Maybe it got away from me a little, but c'mon!"

"A day's worth of training won't kill you, Mr. Jansen, but lack of it might."

"Okay, alright, it probably wouldn't hurt."

"So, you're on board?"

"I have a couple more questions."

Tangles appeared and whispered in my ear, "Hambone wants to make a move." Then Holly gave me a winding hand signal to indicate she wanted me off the phone. "Hang on a second," I told him, and put my hand over the mic slot. Tangles was reeling up the baits, and I waved to Hambone on the bridge. "Hey, Ham!"

He looked down and said, "We're making a move. There's some nice weed action at four-hundred feet. I heard they're slayin'em."

"Gimme a couple more minutes to wrap up this call before you fire up the engine."

"Okay, but make it quick. I heard they're thick!"

I shot him a thumbs-up and removed my hand from the mic slot. "Sorry about that. I have to go in a minute."

"No problem, I think I've covered the critical stuff. What else did you want to know?"

"I saw all the IDs Rafe was carrying in his duffel. Are you guys CIA?"

"No, everybody knows about them. Nobody knows about us."

"So who *are* you?"

"The reason nobody knows about us is because we don't go telling everybody."

"You expect me to sign on, not knowing who I'm working for?"

"At this point, yes. You're an experiment, Mr. Jansen—the first civilian we've asked to join our team, albeit part-time. If things go well, you'll be brought into the fold."

"What about Holly and Tangles? They know everything I do. Holly's a computer whiz, and Tangles is the best deckhand I've ever seen."

"I'm well aware of that and already know their backgrounds inside and out, which is why they're welcome to be part of your team. Keep in mind, you'll be responsible for their actions and their silence. So what do you think? Are you ready for some *real* adventure?" Holly had her hands on her shapely hips and was scowling at me, wanting me off the phone. I winked at her and held my index finger up to let her know I was almost through.

"This is a no-brainer; of course I'll do it."

"Great, I'll—"

"On one condition." I turned so my back was to Holly.

"What's that?"

I glanced over my shoulder to make sure Holly wasn't listening and lowered my voice a notch. "You help us find Holly's long-lost cousin."

"That shouldn't be a problem."

"It shouldn't be, but it is."

"How so?"

He faked his own death in 1964 in St. Maarten. The only thing we have to go on is the fact that his dad was black, his mom was white, and he has a birthmark in the shape of a four-leaf clover on his forearm."

"What's his name?"

"It *was* Patrick VanderGrift, or LeRoux, if he used his mother's maiden name. Assuming he's alive, *who knows* what it is now."

"VanderGrift? You mean... as in—"

"You got it; he was the senator's illegally adopted step-brother. Holly's aunt was his mother."

"*That's* what you were doing down there? Talk about a coincidence."

"I know, it's the umbilical cord of, uh... fate...I think."

"What?"

"I'm still working on that one. So, you'll help us find him?"

"Yes, it might take a while, but if he can be found, we'll find him."

"Then it's a deal." Hambone beeped the horn, signaling he was about to fire up the engine. "I have one last request," I added.

"What's that?"

"I'm not much of a Dan Tanna guy; he was too Goody-Two-Shoes for me. I'm more of an M&M man."

"M&M?"

"Yeah, Mannix and Magnum. If you have them in you repertoire, can you use one next time we talk? Especially Mannix... I loved that guy."

"You're a little young to be a Joe Mannix fan."

"I watched re-runs with my old man back in the day. Mannix kicks ass."

Hambone fired up the engine, and I stuck a finger in my ear long enough to hear him chuckle and reply, "Indeed he does, Mr. Jansen, indeed he does. Welcome aboard. You might want to head out to six-hundred feet, I'll be in touch." Click.

Chapter 62

When I handed the phone back to Holly, she said, "What was *that* all about? You missed some good fishing."

"Yeah," said Tangles, "What's up?"

"I think our ship just came in, literally."

As we chugged offshore, I told them about Dan Tanna's proposal, and their reaction was much like mine—incredulous.

Tangles said, "Dude! We really *are* gonna be the Tango and Cash of the high seas; this is epic!"

"More like Tango and Small Change."

"You never stop, do you? You're like the Energizer Bunny of put-downs."

"Everybody's good at something. Hang on a second." Hambone slowed the boat down and was meandering through some scattered weed. I looked back at shore and figured we must be at the four-hundred-foot mark. "Hey, Ham!" I yelled up at him. "This doesn't look too promising."

"I don't get it; Robo said he heard they were cleaning up in four-hundred feet. This sucks. It's just scattered weed everywhere."

"Why don't you run us out to six hundred? I got a tip!"

"I don't know," he shook his head. "I doubt its any better out there. Let's go back inside and do some bottom fishing."

"C'mon, man. I'll spring for gas!"

He looked down at me with a raised eyebrow. "You sure about that?"

I pointed offshore and nodded, "Full steam ahead!"

"This is gonna cost you," he grinned. "Everybody hang on! Here comes the Hambone Express!" He made a motion like a trucker tooting his horn and yelled, "WOOOOOOOO!WOOOOOO!"

Of course, full steam ahead for the Hambone Express meant a top speed of maybe fifteen knots, so I had no problem fielding a barrage of questions from Holly and Tangles. Finally, Holly asked, "So, you told him yes?"

"I did, on one condition."

"What was that?"

"That he help us find your cousin, Patrick…or whatever his name is now."

Her eyes lit up, and she beamed. "You did? *Really?* What did he say?"

"He said no problem," I lied. "He said he could find an ice cube in an iceberg."

"He *did?* Oh, that's great!" She threw her arms around me and started kissing my face all over. Tangles shook his head and rolled his eyes before dipping his hand in the cooler. "This calls for a beer," he announced. He pulled out two and then hesitated. "You, uh, want one too, Holly? I noticed you haven't had anything in a couple days." Holly had her back to him and her arms around me as she finished kissing my face. "Um, I don't think so," she answered, "Just grab me a water, please." Tangles rubbed his stomach and mouthed the word "prego" as he handed me a beer. I had totally forgotten about her stomach discomfort a day or two earlier. *Fuck.* I popped the top and took a couple swigs, nervously thinking about the possibilities, when she said, "Actually, that looks good. I think I will have one." I winked at Tangles and mouthed the word, "YES!" He put the water back in the cooler and as he fished for a cold one asked, "Are you *sure?*"

"Yeah, I think a half a beer would be perfect." He pulled one out and rocked it in his arms like it was a baby before she turned to take it from him. I watched her closely as she took a sip and asked, "Tastes good, doesn't it?" She gave me a funny look and said, "Yes, it does... why?"

"You can have half a beer, a whole beer, a six-pack, you know, whatever you feel like."

"A six-pack? When have you ever seen me drink a six-pack?"

"I'm just saying..."

A couple minutes later, Hambone slowed the boat down and yelled for Tangles to get the baits out. Then he yelled for me to come up on the bridge. I jumped on the gunnel, and as I climbed up, he said, "Who gave you that tip, bro? Wait till you see this!" I stood next to him and right in front of us was a big, juicy, weed line. There were birds diving and fish splashing, and it looked to be about the size of two or three football fields put end to end. *How in the hell did Dan Tanna know?*

"They're gonna be thick, Shag," Hambone predicted, "Just like the old days. Like fleas on a dog's back. I can feel it!" He turned around and yelled, "Get those runners out, Tangles!"

"They're out!" he yelled back.

"C'mon, let's get ready for some action!"

We climbed down to the cockpit, and Holly stood up on the gunnel. "Wow!" she said, "That's the nicest weed line I've seen in a while."

"This is what it's all about," mused Hambone in anticipation. "A good weed line is like a magic carpet; drop a bait down next to one and you never know *what* kind of ride you might take, know what I mean?"

I slapped him on the back and said, "You have no idea, buddy...*no idea.*"

Tangles had been watching the baits like a hawk but turned around and busted out laughing. When Holly joined in, Hambone asked, "What's so funny?"

I was thinking of what to say when both down lines bent over double and started burning drag. Then a dorsal fin appeared as a nice-sized dolphin shot out from the weed line and went airborne after attacking one of the blue runners on top. An instant later a bigger dolphin did a somersault after getting hooked on the other runner. Everybody grabbed a rod and jostled for position as Hambone screamed at the top of his lungs, "They're thick! They're THICK!"

It was good to be home.

THE END

To find out about the next Shagball and Tangles Adventure please visit **www.acbrooks.net**. Your comments and questions are greatly appreciated. At least most of them are.

Made in the USA
Charleston, SC
08 January 2014